The Lost Chronicles of Ara

THE

MiRKWOOD

CODEX

THE LOST CHRONICLES OF ARA: THE MIRKWOOD CODEX

Incorgnito Publishing Press
A division of Market Management Group, LLC
33 S. Wilson Avenue, Suite 113
Pasadena, California 91106

FIRST EDITION

Printed in the United States of America

ISBN: 978-1-944589-00-4

10 9 8 7 6 5 4 3 2 1

The Lost Chronicles of Ara

THE
MiRKWOOD
CODEX

STEPHEN HILLARD

JOEL EISENBERG

TB
TOPOS BOOKS

"O! for a Muse of Fire, that would ascend the brightest heaven of invention!"

~ William Shakespeare

DEDICATION

———

To my own grandfather, Jess, who while distinct from the Scissor Sharpener, shared with him a country man's eye and an authentic sense of adventure.

To my children, Jessica, Scott, and Stephanie, who sat abed as we read aloud the entire *Lord of the Rings*. It was they who asked the question: "So, where are the heroines?"

To my wife Sharmaine, who asked one of the best questions: "What are we waiting for?"

To Professor Bernard Rollin at Colorado State University, who opened my eyes to thinking outside the box.

To my best friend, Dennis, the original proprietor of The Mirkwood Forest.

To Veronica, who braved all the edits.

To Professor Tolkien, whose work still inspires generations to tempt a secret gate and travel *yon bonny road . . . to fair Elfland*.

Stephen Hillard

Family, as ever. First and foremost.

And then to those who dream. To those who strive.

To those who hope for and create worlds beyond the senses.

To my fellow artists, this book would not be possible without *your* inspiration.

Joel Eisenberg

ACKNOWLEDGMENTS

—

This novel, in addition to being a work of fiction, is also an exercise in literary criticism. It focuses in part on the role of heroines, echoing the sentiment captured by Marion Zimmer Bradley in her excellent review of Tolkien: "The books are, in fact, almost womanless." (*Men, Halflings, and Hero Worship*, 1961)

The internal artwork for this book was created by Mike May, www.mikespencil.com.

PREFACE

—

Scriptorium.

As *The Lost Chronicles of Ara* are collected and compiled, one scribe turns to another—

"Do you ever wonder? Are we but scribes of these myths, or do we create as well? All we have to work with are fragments."

"Ssshh! Blasphemer! Your pretty whispers are like shouts in these halls. The Provisioner will neglect us again!"

The questioning scribe's tone drops, even as it becomes an insistent hiss. "Answer me then, my short-quilled twin!"

"Very well. It is like life, Montefur, of which you, my limp-quilled brother, know little. All that we ever see is but a fragment of all that is. All tales are but one, and the one cannot be told without all the pieces. Anything less is a corruption."

"Then will these survive? Who will remember Ara as she once was?"

"Ara was once not corrupted," Plaxe responds, his palm face up and open toward his brother's work. "You see? It is the goddess' will that we do what we do. You are scribing what has been lost—the light of the goddess—"

"Let it be, I beg you. Please do not talk to me about the *dark* you record. I must not be distracted from my task—"

"Of a sudden your questions lost their vim? Be content. Tell me of your tale, of the light. Tell me about Ara in the beginning . . ."

INTRODUCTION

—

The Chronicles of Ara series is about man's path to the dark, as led by his art. Like most other similar literary pathways, however, there is a way out, a way back to the light.

Hence, *The Lost Chronicles of Ara*, the roadmap to that destination.

Steve and I began writing the Ara series in 2014. Our main series is eight volumes in length; this spin-off series is three. Our logline, as it is: "The end of the world begins when man is betrayed by his greatest creation: his art." We're looking at a *Frankenstein* meets *Fahrenheit 451* melange here, where our great entertainments are said to hold the key to our lives, and beyond.

We hope you enjoy *The Mirkwood Codex*, the first volume of *The Lost Chronicles of Ara*.

And we hope you find this roadmap useful . . .

Joel Eisenberg

DRAMATIS PERSONAE

—

J.R.R. Tolkien	Renowned author and professor.
Ara (Aragranessa)	The most famous heroine of Middle-earth, a female halfling whose tale has been hunted down and destroyed.
Yvonne Shelby	American liaison to Bletchley Park, daughter of U.S. Senator Crawford Shelby.
Alan Turing	Brilliant, reclusive, gay mathematician. Principally responsible for breaking the Enigma Code and later inventing the computer.
Kim Philby	Officer in His Majesty's Secret Service and liaison to Bletchley Park. He consorts with the Nazi regime and is later exposed as a traitorous triple agent.
Ian Fleming	Assistant Director of Naval Intelligence, occultist, and, later, author of the James Bond novels.
Winston Churchill	First Lord of the Admiralty. Soon to be Prime Minister of Britain.
Jodl Strieger	Oxford graduate.

Timothy Lessons	Graduate student at Oxford and assistant to Professor Tolkien.
Inklings	Informal, principally male, literary discussion group whose members include Tolkien, C.S. Lewis, Owen Barfield, and Charles Williams.
Jess Grande	Proprietor of The Mirkwood Forest.
Cadence Grande	Granddaughter of Jess.
Mel Chricter	Media agent.
Osley	No data found.
Bossier Thornton	Assistant detective.
Brian de Bois-Gilbert	French forensics expert.
Pazal	Wraith.
Barren	Assassin.
The Dark Lord	Just as you might imagine.

THE FACTS

August, 1939. Threatened by a dark power, the world teeters on the brink of total war. J.R.R. Tolkien's effort to write his greatest work, *The Lord of the Rings,* lies stalled and all but abandoned. He is unexpectedly recruited by His Majesty's Secret Service to serve as a codebreaker at the top-secret spy compound at Bletchley Park. Ian Fleming, Alan Turing, Kim Philby, and Winston Churchill all visit or work at Bletchley.

After two weeks, Tolkien's service is summarily terminated. All records of his activities are mysteriously lost.

He never speaks of his time at Bletchley. Thereafter, he enthusiastically resumes his writing. He completes the *Rings* trilogy. He becomes the Writer of the Century.

THE SOURCES

The curious history of the "Tolkien Documents," witnessed herein as fully as can be restored, is based on translations, journals, tapes, and interviews with those principally involved. How those sources have been placed in sequence—both amenable to the reader and probative of their authenticity—will be made clear in the reading. You may probe for the truth yourself, but take care. A tale can be a dangerous thing.

Since the publication of "Mirkwood" in 2011, and the international support it garnered over free speech rights, Dr. Timothy Lessons has kindly come forward with additional materials. As one of a long line of student assistants to Professor Tolkien, and a recorder of many sessions of the Inklings, he bore unique witness to the events chronicled herein. This material, plus interviews with individuals who have seen the still-secret MI6 files taken from Bletchley Park, form the backbone of this story.

BOOK I
SUDDEN EVENTS

———

If ever a name signified a realm of dangerous enchantment, it is "Mirkwood," the Great Forest of Doubt, whose pedigree of reference extends back eight hundred years in the known literature.

~ Franz J. Heibowitz,
The Mythical Forest

Through Mirkwood to fulfill their fates, the young fairy maidens flew.

~ Eddic Lays
(Icelandic, thirteenth century)

J.R.R. Tolkien, about age 40.

Chapter 1

A SECRET GATE

———

This modest story, a tendril from the Great Tree of Tales, spans but a few weeks. It begins with an early morning theft from a kitchen in late August, 1939.

It is two o'clock in the morning in the grey, rain-soaked, English city of Oxford. A becandled light gleams from a dappled window at the rear of a tidy brick house at 2020 Northmoor Lane. Inside, John Ronald Reuel Tolkien, still fully dressed, has just arrived home from an evening at the pub. He stands suspiciously before the open fridge.

His unnamed muse, ever active until of late, whispers into his guilty conscience. *Late is the hour of your return.*

A flickering candle on the kitchen table, favored in this time of blackout exercises, casts a haunting shadow on the wall. There a misshapen, hunched figure, a visitor perhaps from some mysterious otherworld, lurks and reaches out. The real Tolkien is oblivious. He is hungry and his nose is deep in the fridge. He is humming, preoccupied with the immediacy of this perilous business.

He holds in one hand a bowl and in the other is poised an over-size spoon. He hesitates and then does what he knows is absolutely forbidden. The spoon descends into the pristine surface of a sticky toffee pudding which his wife Edith has prepared for Thursday dinner. Tomorrow.

Midway through his forty-seventh year, Tolkien is far from the amiably paunched, genteel professor he would become. His posture is upright, his figure lean, his hair dark. His unmellowed moods can be intense: the melancholy of an orphan, the slicing intolerance of fools, the joyous exhilaration of experiencing his imagined world as, just possibly, real. The solemn pride in work that has achieved a modest measure of financial security for his family.

He fills the bowl. *Risky indulgence,* he reflects. He goes to the table, sits, and savors the pudding. The Devonshire cream, the dense cake, chocolate, with a promise of fig, all blended into a concoction whose intensity never fails to surprise the palate. Tolkien wears an indulgent smile on his face, an impish grin that might best adorn one of his *hobbits,* perhaps in the middle of a similar wee-hours meal. He leans back to aid his digestion, letting the contentment of food, family, and, in his literary circle, a measure of fame, sink in. He also knows that, at least for the stolen pudding, Edith will give him a royal pranging.

Within her realm, she too does not tolerate fools.

He steals a final lick at the spoon. *Well, to bed then.* Ambling toward the stairs, he comes to his study. It is a tiny room with an electric fireplace. It is strewn with books and papers. His desk is crowned with a Remington manual typewriter. Next to it is a stack of yellowed manuscript pages. They are cluttered, lined with scrawls.

He knows the words there. They are stale. Their story lifeless. Hovering outside the doorway, as if at a precipitous threshold, he peers in. The pages, now cold and barren, denounce him with their neglect. He last typed a month ago, and that was a banging, desultory effort that he crumpled angrily and chucked into the waste can.

He declines to enter the study, backing away and observing it as might a tourist peeking into a wrecked and ancient ruin.

He ponders his situation. *Overlong have I lingered at Balin's Tomb. This tale, forever unfinished, will accompany his long sleep.*

He knows that next to the manuscript is an equally dreadful document. It is a letter from his editor, Stanley Unwin, who, two years previously, had championed *The Hobbit* into a publishing success. The note is dated three months ago, a response now unforgivably late even for Tolkien's consistent but sometimes unpunctual habits of correspondence.

He knows that one line in the letter stings like a wasp. "John, we must move soon to completion of your great work, or the opportunity to capitalize on the popularity of 'The Hobbit', at best fleeting, will be lost."

Perhaps he should respond with the bloody truth. Something like, "the story has fallen to sleep, as if under some fell enchantment." No, it would be better to speak plainly. "I'm not sure I can go forward. I no longer believe in what I am creating." Then the judgment: "My muse has abandoned me."

He shrugs and starts to go upstairs, giving his back to his study. He is resigned to a cosmic writer's block that has grown into a dark, marauding monster in his mind.

He berates himself, the indulgent glow of the pudding now extinguished. He knows his precious, half-finished Tale of the Great Ring is in peril. Even when he can summon his muse, he dithers and squanders it in a poorly conceived story about, of all things, time travel. No wonder her inconstancy.

It is in this dispirited moment that the toffee confection, the late hour, and too many pints at the Eagle and Child pub, all conspire together. He knows from experience that soon, when he is asleep, the result will be as a dry log wedged into a seething fire. Flames will erupt, boiling the cauldron of his dreams. A strange, luminous light will beckon from its depths. His mind will quest, restless and eager, through old territories and lands as yet unmapped.

Step by labored step, he mounts the stairs. Edith's bedroom door is closed. He tiptoes into his separate bedroom. He dare not go directly to sleep. Taking a moment to turn on the reading light, he reclines on the bed, adjusts his glasses, and reads from one of his favorite authors, H.G. Wells' *The Time Machine*. He can't concentrate. *Time ... to think ... about time*, he ponders as the day's last waking thoughts float away and the uneasy drift toward dreams begins.

At first the images are singularly pleasant, like elusive fireflies flitting in a thick hedgerow, flashing now and then, always there and always a surprise. His dreamself follows a narrow road, beset with thorns and briars, choked with vines. At last he approaches an arched, vine-encrusted, rune-inscribed, and obviously secret gate. In his dreams and fantasies, he has found such gates scores of times, and yet each such moment is a discovery. One never knows what lies beyond. He always hesitates, and he never fails to test the gate.

He forces ancient hinges that squall and begrudge every inch. He squirms through the narrow opening. Immediately beyond is a place he knows well. It is Bloemfontein, South Africa. He is a young child, and he is exploring what to him is a dim, murky wood. It is a grove of trees planted by his father. He is speaking out loud to himself in a language of his own invention. He is looking for something. In the distance he can hear a woman's voice. It is his mother.

"John, come out of there! And quit speaking to yourself!"

He ignores her. He finds a stick, then stops and stoops down.

His eyes focus on a small but ominous hole in the ground. It is partially obscured by leaves and twigs. He continues to talk in the strange tongue, as if taunting whatever it is he seeks. The stick pokes cautiously into the hole. His face draws closer and the hole seems bigger.

Suddenly, from the mouth of the hole, erupts a huge, hairy, tarantula. The aggressive Baboon Spider. It has a horrid, other-worldly array of eyes. Cruelly hooked pincers twitch below its face.

It rustles with horrid progress up the stick and onto his arm. It bites him hard, injecting a toxic serum that drenches his veins with fire.

He screams.

His dream screams.

Until all sounds are erased by a great silence. He looks about, sees the signal corps insignia on the sleeve of his field jacket, and knows that, once, again, he is at the Battle of the Somme, it is 1916, and he is twenty-four years old. This will soon become an even more frightful nightmare.

But for now, the sky is blue and he is high up in it, looking over a gondola's edge, down three thousand feet, at a miniature world of opposing trenchworks and razor wire redoubts and muddied roads and plumes of gray smoke. He is in aerial balloon, a bloated and ungainly monstrosity. He is busily observing and then sending information with his arms, red flags in each hand, semaphore.

A pinpoint of silent light, a German "sausage" canister exploding in the British trenchworks. He watches the flash followed by the uncoiling cloud of smoke and debris, long before the tiny epic *crump* reaches his ears.

The disaster below is emotionally distant. The summer air flows and the sense of immense floating solitude, something he has never before experienced, settles over him. He feels for a moment like he is soaring on some winged beast, clinging perhaps to the back of a great eagle. His binoculars provide stunning acuity, for he can see lories running their errands. He sees horses assembled, and watches a forward group of

German observers in turn observing him through their own binoculars. Their hands are pointing at him, their silent mouths yelling. An ominous sign.

He continues his observations. Between the lines of trenches, a distance of a quarter mile or so, lies a vast, blackened wasteland. Every bit of life has been obliterated, leaving the skeletal trunks and odd, de-leafed limbs of a tree or two as bleak monuments to the ruin. Smoke, like steam from some demonic subterranean realm, rises in coils and mists from blasted pits.

In the gondola with him is his balloonist, a French chap named Étienne Renot. With a devil-may-care smile, Etienne displays an *elan* that only the pilots of the *Caquot*, in truth, high-flying, slow ducks, could understand.

The world is quiet and the vista spreads out for hundreds of miles. A distant river, the Ancre, meanders and twinkles in the hazy distance. Renot makes token adjustments at the controls. The balloon drifts lazily, as if disinclined. The quiet returns and the moment lingers as Tolkien scribbles information on a map.

He fingers a point in the lines of the British Expeditionary Force, Boggart Hole Clough and the opposing Lelpzig Salient. Here wait the rankers of his unit, the Lancashire Fusiliers, its officers sprinkled with his boyhood chums. His dearest friends, the TCBS. *Fellows*, as they call themselves.

His body shifts in sleep, anticipating the coming horror, even as Tolkien's dream becomes even more exquisitely detailed. Across the no-man's land from his friends, Tolkien sees a strange flag. It is waving like a slow metronome from a spot in the German lines. He focuses the binoculars and sees that it is the Turkish flag. The fiendish message is clear. The Hun already knows the storied British unit that is gathering across the battlefield. The flag lets the Lancashire Fusiliers know they are about to relive the slaughter inflicted on them by the Turks less than a year before, at the disaster at Gallipoli.

The balloon is far too high for insects, but a droning buzz can be heard. Renot looks about, nervous, and then points north. Flayed with sunlight and cloud-shadows, perhaps a mile away, a lone Fokker triplane is executing a turn and vectoring straight at them. Soon they can see its iron cross insignia, the red of its colors, and the silhouette of the pilot behind its Ruger propeller-synchronized machine gun.

Without speaking, Renot hurriedly unties a large canvas sack at his feet. He tosses a parachute to Tolkien, who, his hands occupied with binoculars and papers, catches it basket-like in his arms. Belts and buckles flop about in a confused tangle. His eyes and mouth are open, as if saying *now what?*

Renot nods gravely at the triplane, then at Tolkien's parachute. As Tolkien watches, still frozen, the Frenchman deftly dons and cinches and buckles his own parachute. He adjusts his goggles and yells, "*Apprêtez-vous?*" *Are you ready?* The plane's approach is louder, the pilot increasing its power to keep tight control and steady aim.

"*À antre envaye!*" *Let's jump!* With that, Renot clambers up the rigging of the gondola, raises his hands, and simply falls away. Tolkien fumbles and fusses. He finally finds the embroidered red "up" arrow, and gets the pack to his front. Leg and waist and shoulder buckles follow. His hand grasps and re-grasps the ripcord handle. *Enough practice! Enough dithering!* The sludgy pace of his action is a terror in itself.

The Fokker is coming dead on as Tolkien hesitates, his hands clutched tight on the rigging. He steps up and lets himself fall into the cold expanse as machine gun bullets shred the gondola into a confetti of cane.

In the strange metaphysics of dreams, some part of Tolkien's mind knows that he has never, ever, been in a balloon, and this is all jolly old make-believe. He feels comforted by that fact and knows that he must have survived, for now he is standing in the trenches with his schoolmates.

And here the dream reality becomes most intense. The true terror of this side of the secret gate settles on him like the clammy fog hiding his mud-encased boots. This moment is real, he has lived it, and the horrific things that are about to happen cannot be stopped.

In another universe, at a textile factory outside Oxford, the morning work whistle blasts, stirring Tolkien in his tormented slumber, and accelerating the events in his mind.

The whistle becomes a series of shrieks in the fantastic pre-dawn of the trenches. Cannon shells rocket overhead. Tolkien smells the stench of battlefield dead and the low stink of an entrenched army. He stares down the line. He sees the repetitive array of soup bowl-shaped Brodie helmets strapped on tight to clasp beardless chins of eighteen and nineteen year olds. Those chins are surprisingly resolute. They have not seen action, and the calm orders of their officer comfort them. "Check your loads, lads. Bayonets tight. You'll know what to do. After we go over the top, follow me, and don't stop! Don't stop until you see the ruin our cannons have made of their defenses. There are two thousand of us along this half-mile, and by God this morning we will overrun the Hun!"

The sky, seen from within the trenches as a mere gash of fitfully lit clouds, suddenly glitters with innumerable flares. *Fairy Lights* they are called in the black humor argot of the pitmen and colliers in this unit.

Between the thudding explosions, a senior officer yells, "Signal man to the front!" Tolkien rushes up to the officer, who yells into his ear, "Your batman?"

"Dead, sir."

The officer continues to scream, "Very well, take these yourself. To HQ at Glidden Point! You'll have to get out of the trenches up ahead. Get a horse. The lines are close there. Can't trust the wires. Now hear me, copy this into your secret language, in case you get . . . in case this falls into Bosche hands. Now go!"

Scribbling on his notepad as he navigates the muddy gutter full of jettisoned gear and ammo boxes and ration crates, Tolkien comes to the knot of his Fellows.

He stops. Their youthful faces, marked with splatters of mud, peer at him from beneath their tin pots. One of them nods. *We're okay.*

"I'll be back. I've got to courier a message through the break." He adds, "By horse," as if that is of critical significance.

"Miss all the fun," one of them says. "Color Sergeant Bourne says we're going over at 0700."

Tolkien checks his watch. Fifteen minutes. "I'll hurry."

They instinctively form a tight scrum, putting their hands on each other's shoulders. The words they speak are so deeply engraved in Tolkien's memory that they are uttered now as if all sound, all movement has drained out of the universe.

"Remember! We are the Tea Club, Barrovian Society—the Fellowship—and that," one grasps Tolkien's coat, "that will never die! Our singular deaths can never break this bond!" Another says, "Yes, we are the TCBS, and our stories have a destiny!"

Tolkien takes a deep breath, a sigh of resignation to this fated moment. He says, "Let each of us be remembered in our Fellows' stories."

The four of them then regard each other solemnly, so catastrophic and exhilarating is the moment. It sweeps upon them like a channel gale.

Tolkien recalls how they jostled and joked in line at the enlistment office a short six months ago.

Another hand reaches out, unbuttons the flap of Tolkien's breast pocket and stuffs a folded envelope in it. The hand re-buttons and pats the pocket. "I don't know who among us is going into more danger. This is just in case, now go!"

Tolkien scrambles and struggles through the packed trenches to a right hand intersection where the path leads to the rear and a waiting horse. At that corner, several steps rise to an observation bunker. He mounts two of the steps and looks back down the line. He sees them, diminished in a muddy trench in which flows a muddy river of men. They look back at him.

He waves and his waking mind, dimly conscious now, prays that he can grasp onto this moment with all his might. Let it last forever, forestall and perhaps change the fates under whose banner they stand. He knows that a daylight assault is the deadliest maneuver on a vast and deadly battlefield. His sleeping body tenses to somehow grip this fearsome NOW and never, ever let it go.

As always, it is futile. The whistles blow and his Fellows disappear in the cresting wave of men clambering from the still-shadowed trenches to a blood-red dawn and the open killing ground above.

He is also running now, his dream-thoughts passing through the unsettling soldiers' tales of troglodytes, crazed men, deserters from both sides, who live in a deeper hell of tunnels below the No-Man's Land. The tale tells that they gather the dead and, if necessary, the newly wounded, to eat.

He navigates a labyrinth of deep trenches, bermed and unpopulated. The sounds of battle seem distant, almost muted here. Still, the enemy lines are close. At places the trenchworks bleed together as the weekly fortunes of war shift conquered realms by a hundred yards or less. With each turn he feels more lost, more in danger. He imagines that around the next curve he will come upon a group of troglodytes huddled like trolls. Misshapen cannibals wearing tatters of all uniforms and eating tatters of all the dead.

He swings around just such a bend and confronts . . . the enemy. A *Meldengäeger*, a lone batman, lost and on errand much as Tolkien himself. The man carries a message rucksack. He is dark-haired, small, and wiry of build, wearing what Tolkien guesses is a kind of Austrian beret. With an odd flourish, the man removes it to wipe his face. He has a black mustache that dives down from his nostrils before flaring extravagantly to each side. A face that is oddly familiar. The man is surprised, but fearless. Tolkien pulls his side arm and aims at the man. The man does likewise. There is little room for either to maneuver.

The German clearly values his mission above all. He abruptly turns his back and rather than run, deliberately retraces his steps. Tolkien now has three choices: kill the enemy and draw attention to himself, declare himself lost and return to his Fellows, or find a way to complete his own mission.

He turns and retraces his own steps. Soon he finds his way, rounds another curve in the trenches and finds open ground and a string of tethered mounts. A bearded handler is yelling, his voice gliding, rich and sing-song, as is proper for a man from south Wales. "Up with you lad, no time to waste!"

He mounts a mottled grey horse, perfect color for such a time and place, adjusts the stirrups, and tests the bit and bridle. He is experienced and confident in his horsemanship.

The Welshman yanks on the saddle girth, tightening it for strenuous ride. "He's called Shadow! Knows this bloody battlefield better than any bloody officer, so trust him! A born jumper he is. First order at that, so hang on, laddie! Don't slow down. Follow the defile till you reconnect with the line."

He can hear the eruption of sound as thousands of rankers start their final sprint toward the waiting machine guns, their voices raised in involuntary, animal sounds. Sounds they don't themselves hear. The machine guns begin to chatter like an unseen horde of great, devouring insects.

A bitter reaping has started.

Tolkien spurs Shadow and races into the now ill-defined No-Man's Land. The horse deftly maneuvers around bomb pits in which soldiers float, eyes open and unseeing. Shadow skirts wrecked equipment, his hooves beating relentlessly. A tangle of razor-wire looms ahead where two separate kinds of hellish strands, one German and one French, have become an impenetrable snarl. It is the height of a man. Shadow accelerates and stretches and jumps, clearing the barbs by an easy foot.

The end of the defile, and the British line, a redoubt of sandbags and timber, are visible up ahead. He looks up to his left and, fifty yards away on a slight rise, stand three mounted riders. Imperial Dragoons. The dreaded, merciless *Uhlan*. Their steeds are shiny black and pluming smoke from their nostrils. The dragoons' dark weather capes flow in the morning breeze, and spiked black helmets adorn their finely mustachioed heads. They are armed, improbably even for this war, with great lances, each festooned with a heraldic flag near the glittering spear tip. They regard him with a haughty attitude, as stupid, blundering prey. Spurring into a sudden gallop, they close on a course to follow the defile.

Tolkien sees they have the killer's angle on him, and there is nothing he can do to escape their inexorable close. They gallop parallel and above him, their voices mocking him with fell Teutonic jests. Clods of dirt splatter on him.

Shadow, the old war horse, knows an enemy and a battlefield far better than his rider, and so bides his time until, seemingly already at a full gallop, his great laboring heart pumps forth even more blood flow. His speed redoubles. He flies to the end of the defile and vaults unto the open ground. The foremost dragoon, well in front of his comrades, pulls within a few feet. They are striding side-by-side, the Uhlan officer so confident he bestows a devilish grin upon Tolkien.

At that moment, Tolkien can feel a gathering and readiness ripple through Shadow's flanks. The mount breaks stride, almost stumbles, then cuts behind the black steed. The dragoon is confused but still very close. He swings his lance clumsily. Tolkien feels its point whisk by his face. In a moment, the black-robed rider and his black steed are confounded and left behind. But the other two riders have now caught up. They are so close—a thundering, wind-sucking, leather-creaking havoc of men and horse. Suddenly, the chasm of a large, abandoned trench opens just ahead. Shadow vaults it in stride. The black riders, daunted, pull their reins hard and pull up. They rise in their stirrups and salute their quarry with bitter oaths and upraised lances .

There is never a finer horse than one that saves your life.

As Tolkien's dream shreds apart, his hand goes to his breast. To the spot where once lay the pocket in which rested his Fellow's letter. The letter Tolkien duly delivered after the war and which he carries in his heart to this day.

A more restful sleep finally drapes across Tolkien.

He will need it sorely in the days to come.

Chapter 2

LÁRSPELL
(A Tale That Must Be Told)

———

Belief, the stuff of which each of us constructs a more or less coherent world, and our own place therein, is, for J.R.R. Tolkien, fitted and mortared in a Catholic faith as solid as the stones of the cathedral where he was baptized at the age of eight.

And yet, somewhere in that vaulting theological edifice, a few foundation stones rest uneasy. At some deep level within him there dwells a yearning, a wild, weightless, and pagan hunger. A lust for what he calls the realm of *faerie*, the place where fantastic beings and deeds actually exist independent of the conceiving mind. A place of exalted joy, not unlike, but very different from his Catholic faith. To, just once, see, touch, experience this "otherness" is a hunger that roams the unlit chambers of his cathedral of beliefs. A Quasimodo, a phantom, a wraith . . .

No, it is worse yet. It has become a Grendel of Doubt of his mind. As fearsome as the walker in darkness that stalked the great hall of Heorot in his beloved *Beowulf*. It will not be still. It slouches forth and will night-stalk until it scatters every muse his creative mind can summon.

It is this act of sub-creation, this summoning of the world of *faerie,* that Tolkien has embraced as his life's work. Beginning with the magical ring found at the conclusion of *The Hobbit*, he has embarked on the creation of a vast epic. He toils at a tale wrought from the linguistic artifacts of pre-Christian peoples in the land of *Mitgaard*, Middle-earth, the essentially northern realm of Saxons, Jutes, Geats, and Danes. Peoples, languages and tales of old Britain and Northern Realms, unfiltered by any Christian dawn, unconfused by the Romans, unslandered by the slippery tongue of uncouth Normans.

This Great Tale of the Ring, as yet untold, has become his mission, a quest in some way impelled by the loss of his Fellows. If their own creative lights should be cruelly extinguished, then, as cosmic recompense, so much brighter should be his own. And yet, these days there is no brightness. His creative self is alone in a dark, cheerless keep, unlit, undoored, and unroofed, sport to the seeping rains of fall.

Something mocks his desire for the genuine "other-worldliness" of his tale.

One thing is clear. He has indeed tarried overlong, paralyzed by uncertainty about the path forward. He *tells* himself that the causes are pedestrian and provincial: worry over the imminence of another great war, worry over his family's safety, worry, as always, about the unmet needs of a modest academic's income, sheer frustration with the ongoing tedium of endless duties at University. He *knows* in his heart something else, that the real cause is this Grendel of Disbelief.

Meanwhile the Great Tale lies fallow, growing colder. Soon its fire will extinguish completely, and with it will die unfulfilled his promise to his Fellows.

BEOWULF LIVES!

——

Mid-morning finds the night's stormy torment gone. The sun, like an autumn friend, strolls amiably among lagging shreds of cloud. Pools of water glisten as Tolkien, wearing his wellies, clomps through them. He is intent, needing to arrive with a few extra minutes to complete preparation for his most important and most public moment of the school year.

He passes the building that houses his academic office, just as two men slip from a side door. They are not students and, he senses, not faculty. Rather than the academic gowns favored by many students, they wear bulky overcoats and hats that suggest continental fashion. One man, the shorter, has a limp.

Hurry along, Tolkien thinks, looking at his watch.

He arrives at Bristlethorn Hall at ten thirty. Standing outside, holding open the door like a silent scolding, is Timothy Lessons. Tolkien sighs good-naturedly as he sees his irreverent, impertinent, perpetually exasperating, and ultimately invaluable student assistant. Lessons is perhaps the best of a line of assistants, all of whom, rather all save one, were exceptional. The memory of that one, a young man also born in Bloemfontein, is as disappointing as he was promising. The recollection flits as a brief shadow over a fulsome sunlit day.

Tolkien approaches and gives Lessons a dour nod, sufficient for the gravity of what is to transpire. He enters a large, closed anteroom connected by a single door to the lecture hall. There he immediately strips his coat and flings it onto a chair. Before him is a large table, which he silently studies.

It is laden with gear of war.

His assistant stands at the ready, his fingers casually entwined at his waist, a mischievous smile holding court on his youthful, freckled face. His countenance is partially obscured by a windblown hayrick of yellow hair.

"Ah, my Tim. Tim the ostler. You do look a bit peaked this morning."

"Yes, thane. Stay on task now. Only a few minutes to go." Lessons approaches the table with solemn purpose. "Cloak first?"

Like some squire of old, Lessons raises a huge, ungainly, densely furred cloak. "Bit of a smeller—eh, master? But then you always like stinky old bear skins." With a wrinkled nose, turned face, and extended arms, he hefts the heavy garment, finding a path for Tolkien's outstretched arm. The rest of the outfitting is an effort, accomplished with grunts and exertions, as if they—lord, squire, and skin of bear—are engaged in an intricate and unpracticed dance.

"Like to get all up, *ergh,* eh, professor? We'll, *hrff,* have you attired in a cinch!" Lessons pulls on the rope that serves as a belt. "Now you look like a perfect sword-steward, a strange visitor from the whale-road come to grace the hall of Heorot that lies just beyond that door. Let's see, ah, your helm, sire." Lessons places on Tolkien's head an iron helmet, ornamented with outlandish, upturned bullhorns on either side. "And now, my liege, your weapon?"

Hefting one in each hand, Lessons offers a great sword and a battle axe. "*Sweord* or *Gefeunt Aex?*" he asks. Tolkien selects the latter. "Aye, a wise choice, my lord. Better to behead those grim man-eating monsters. I say you're set, a bit cracked, but all the better. Nothing like a wild curtain-raiser to get their attention, I say, get the lectures off in a bit of eye-opening context."

Tolkien turns to the door, then stops and says softly, "Like us all, Tim, you must accept your station in life. Which at this moment is to be a proper squire. A lesser rung shall certainly be yours if you . . . don't . . . cinch this . . . blasted thing up!"

Lessons is already tugging the unruly waist-rope, as if it were a corset, until it tightens around Tolkien so that it vaguely resembles an article of clothing, rather than an animal skin that had swallowed a man whole.

"Quite right, sir, there you go!"

Tolkien steps forward, violently swings open the door, and enters the lecture hall.

Bristlethorn Hall, three hundred years old, had at one time served as a venue for human vivisection. It is, in effect, a pit, a descending, almost circular array of seats that bottoms at a small stage. The hall is packed, with an overflow of students standing at the top tier, and others crammed on the narrow aisles of steps.

They are all leaning forward and, as the door to the lecture platform is flung open, they utter a collective gasp.

Tolkien, no longer recognizable save as a bear-skinned ring-liege of a great and ancient Anglo-Saxon hall, bounds unto the tiny stage, raises his axe and buries it into the floor with a resounding *Thunk!*

"*Hwat!*" he cries. The astonished crowd is utterly silent. He proclaims loudly in perfect Old English: "*Hwæt wé Gár-Dena in geár-dagum péod-cyninga þrym gefrúnon, hú Óá æþelingas ellen fremedon.*"

(Listen! The Spear-Danes in days gone by and the kings who ruled them had courage and greatness. We have heard of those princes' heroic campaigns.)

No trace of his habitual mumbling stains these lines. They spin forth, as he might say, as priceless gold from men of old.

Undisputed master of this forum, he now lays his helmet on the floor in counterpoint to the embedded axe. Then he unties the cinch and lets the bear-skin cascade to the floor as if a shape-shifter had abruptly opted to return to the world of men. He steps to the small podium and speaks loudly, so that all can hear. "Now begins our exploration of the great epic poem, *Beowulf*. It is a window into an ancient, pre-Christian time. A time when fear and valor wrestled with the great questions of man's existence. The questions arrive cloaked as monsters. It is a time when a man's final stand, heroic to the end in a world of inevitable defeat, is the mark of a life well-lived."

Tolkien speaks for a further hour, relishing the gravity he has imposed on his students as they are introduced to this, his most cherished work, the very fulcrum of his chosen profession as a philologist and esteemed professor of Old English. He anticipates the details that will be found in his later lectures.

At last he arrives at a few remarks about the history of the great tale.

"The poem *Beowulf* was composed sometime between the middle of the seventh and the end of the tenth century. It is written in a language that we today call Anglo-Saxon or Old English. It takes place not in England, but in Scandinavia. It comes to us in tatters, singed, charred, incomplete, once utterly lost and then refound centuries later. The history of the manuscript, its provenance and narrow escapes, is a heroic journey itself. We shall visit what we know of the story in due course. For all that, it is a tale still able to sweep in off the moors, down through the mist-bands of time and open for us a secret gate into that old world of Mitgaard."

Tolkien pauses here. He is at the end of his lecture. He considers a few epilogue remarks, then settles on one. "We will explore also the significance of the very sounds, the alliterations, the purely auditory and sensuous evocation of feelings in this language. They are as important to understanding of this work as the semantics of the words. A quick example from our own time: an ordinary phrase, unassociated from its meaning, has often been called the most beautiful sound in English. It is 'cellar door.' The sonorous 'o', the most pronounceable consonant 'r'. Far better sounding than, say, 'sky,' or 'horse.' From such aesthetically pleasing sounds one can discern a bit of the deep feeling, the belief, of the scribes of this tale."

There. A nicely done bow to tie it up, he thinks.

Questions from students are not customary, but sometimes granted by a lecturing professor. Enjoying the rapt attention of his audience, and having completed his presentation with a few moments to spare, Tolkien decides to grant the indulgence.

"Questions?" he asks, and soon comes to regret it.

One student bounces upright, his hand raised. "Your new children's fairytale, professor, *The Hobbit*, inhabits much of this same world, does it not? Orcs and ents and dragons and rings? They are all mentioned in *Beowulf*. Are they the same?"

Having opened the window, Professor Tolkien cannot summarily close it. He speaks directly and without hint of apology. "Quite right, for some, but not all, of the world in my book, in tone as well as events, is inspired, and to some extent, borrowed, from *Beowulf*."

A young woman, odd in this hall filled almost exclusively with men, stands and raises her hand. Tolkien nods his assent.

"And why, Professor Tolkien, are there so few, perhaps no, heroines in those worlds, both the ancient one and that of your recent invention?"

Tolkien furrows his brow like an angry bear, and is momentarily speechless.

* * *

In the anteroom, after the lecture, Lessons is bustling about. "Don't let the lady's impertinent question bother you, professor. Now, to the rest of your day. A burdensome stack of exams to grade, I'm afraid. They await you in your office. Mr. Lewis has suggested a second convening of your Inklings friends. At six this evening. Something about bucking up your spirits. More rain expected, by the way. Now, here's your copy of *The Guardian*. Nasty headlines."

Tolkien takes the paper and scans the bold print:

Germany Threatens Poland!
Invasion Likely to Trigger War!

Chapter 4

THE EAGLE AND CHILD

———

That evening, the storms indeed return. Two trench coated men, their fedoras pulled low to shadow their faces, peer into the night through a rain swept windscreen. The wipers labor, overwhelmed by the lashing rain. The car's single hooded headlamp casts a tepid cone of light that barely seeps into the careening darkness. The men study the signs as they speed recklessly through empty urban streets. They pass brick buildings with red-lettered "Air Raid Shelter" signs hastily nailed up, sandbag walls, a few people, scattered and running.

The passenger, his unsmiling face lit by the dashboard, has a military bearing. He is used to carrying out missions of substance. He glances through his side window, and his eyes fasten on the unusual sight of a massive steel cable extending upward, diminishing into the rain-cast gloom. A flash of lightning reveals its ascent all the way to the underbelly of a massive barrage balloon.

An air raid siren wails nearby.

He turns to the driver. "Forget it. Only a drill."

The Alvis Saloon touring car, long and powerful, fights for traction as it boats through the narrow streets. The driver suddenly pumps the brakes and the passenger points.

"Damn blackout! Turn here!"

The auto executes a sliding, bouncing turn on the wet cobblestones.

"Here! Here it is!"

The Alvis slams to a stop. Its light settles across the front of a pub. A sign hanging over the door reads "The Eagle and Child." Warm, almost candled, light, seeps through the edges of the blackout curtains. From within, dim shadows move and cut the light. There is lively activity inside.

The two men check their weapons, then consult a file, preparing to enter. The driver turns and says, "The subject's name, *Tolkien*. Sounds Kraut to me."

"We'll see. Let's go!"

* * *

Within the "Bird and Baby" as it is known by its patrons, there is light, noise, smoke, yeasty alcohol, and the pungent mundungus of strong Moroccan tobacco. Many voices, many clanking mugs. Tolkien sits at a corner table with five other gentlemen. They are academics, tweed-suited, Edwardian-club types engaged in a comfortable and regular event: laughing, pipe-smoking, ale-drinking, story-swapping. They are the Inklings, and they are all looking at him.

C.S. Lewis, known as Jack, leans in and asks, "So, Tollers, what *was* your response to the lady's question about heroines?"

Tolkien sits back, puffs his pipe, and says, "I'm afraid I blathered a bit. Something about Anglo-Saxon authors, and my poor footsteps down their path, reflecting a world where adventures, heroic journeys, great feats of valor, are the province of men. She frowned when I said this, and remained standing. I suppose to soften it a bit, I added that there were undoubtedly such feats by women, and that the scribes of *Beowulf* perhaps had lost such, and I, in my own "discovered" tales, have yet to find the same, the true heroine's journey."

Another of the Inklings, Hugo Dyson Clive, closes in. "That's it? You let her put you back on your heels? Not your usual style, I'd say."

Another piles on. "A bit condescending, I'd say."

"Well, *Cherchez la femme!* as they say."

"Would you let *a man* get away with that?"

Tolkien, frustrated with the onslaught, sizes up which barb to deflect. They keep at it like taunting children.

"Feeling an *attacque en fer*, eh Professor?"

"Hardly, Clive. I do, however, detest certain kinds of men: petty book critics who dare not risk their own hand, industrialists who would ravage a forest or overturn the very hills, tax collectors—damn them! And, yes, to the point right now, those who insist on using French phrases in a proper English conversation. Of any or all of these, I've never been intimidated."

"Ah, a worthy *riposte!*"

"Why, Tollers, such animosity to the French?"

"They are—hah!—uncouth, and their Norman forbearers sullied the royal Saxon tongue! Much like you Owen, after a few pints!"

Jack turns to Charles Williams. "*Pas espirit de l' escalier n' est ce pas?*"

Tolkien answers quickly. "Yes, quite, Jack, I didn't think of a belated wit only on leaving by the stairs."

There follows among them an unusual moment of quiet, a regathering of serious thought.

Tolkien takes a deep breath and blows it out. "I dare say I can't satisfy any of you tonight. The plain truth, among us here, is that women, bless them, are by nature apt pupils, but not heroic leaders. They are attracted to and follow men for reasons having more to do with their bottom drawer, so to speak, then dreams of glory. So, the answer to both your questions is 'of course not.' I calmly closed my lecture with a few other questions, then left the stage to a resounding wave of applause. Went as well as I might imagine. I left the battle-axe imbedded in the floor for Lessons to explain to the building proctor."

Jack senses the topic is done. "Let's get back to this pickle of yours, Master Tolkien. Your writing is stumped?"

"You have that English talent for understatement, Jack. I'll be blunt: It's over. The story I've been reading in serial to all of you—now months ago—about the Great Ring? It is over. I'm afraid it will lie unfinished, like an unkept promise."

As if choreographed, the Inklings raise hands and objections.

"No!"

"Afraid we're not quite with you. Did you just say you were quitting?"

"A pity really, your fine young hobbit lads, their fellowship, frozen forever. Like trolls caught in daylight. Or stuck, forever underground in a dwarf-king's tomb. Nasty fate for your Fellows."

"Quite unacceptable, Tollers. We were rather looking forward to discovering, along with you, the fate of the Fellowship."

"You lost one such fellowship in the war, we all understand. Now you are losing the second. These hobbits. Lose them and know that three's come with a steep price. Likely you'll never find another such fellowship, even with us fair weather Inklings at your side!"

"Not to put too fine a point on it, Tollers, but why?"

Tolkien gathers himself like a sapling after a sudden windy onslaught. "That's a gale of questions, and the last is the real one. I suppose I don't *know* why. I think the feeling I used to muster when I was writing this story—a suspicion, a wish, a yearning, all rolled together—that somehow the tale exists independent of me, that I am only unearthing that world. All that—something close to belief—has fled into confusion and doubt. I can't write it if I don't believe it."

"Enough whining." Jack speaks with an unusual gravity, and they all fall silent. "Perhaps you need to step back, Tollers, decide just what it is you are writing. Do you know?"

"What do you mean? Of course, I know, or at least I *knew.* "

"Do you? Look, we are here, in part at least, to give each other unvarnished advice. So here it is. Fairytales are entertainment, with things resolved and tied up in a bow. *Once upon a time* and *ever after* and *happy endings* and all that. Their descendants are moving pictures: the Méliès films, *Snow White*, *The Wizard of Oz*. Myths, however, are less ordered, more arbitrary, the product of an unsettled world rather than some tale-teller for bed and board. They are the stuff that coils in the mind like dragon's smoke. They are for adults. Which will you tell?"

Tolkien is plainly affected. "Well, I aspire . . . to create a mythology for England."

"Not mere fan fiction for *Beowulf*? Bravo! Now do it!"

"I'm still lost . . ."

"Imagine then, the thoughts of a child hearing a story. The child asking with all the earnestness a human can muster, 'Is it true'? If you're telling the child a fairytale, you have to say 'I'm sorry, child, no it isn't.' But if you provide a myth, then your answer, for child and adult, is, 'well, maybe.' That's a big difference. Do you believe your story could be true? As true as your *Beowulf* bards believed as they evoked once-existing dragons?"

Tolkien is stirred, pondering. The others can almost see his fleeting vision of a great hall, rude but noble still, and the scop, animated and alive, telling his audience an ancient tale. And all, all save one, believing. The disbeliever is Tolkien himself.

"Perhaps you need something new, even a new pipe perhaps, to ponder things with, Tollers. Your old Dublin Briar is a bit long in the tooth, filling your head with stale thoughts. You need a change, and more than a new pipe. Perhaps an adventure."

Tolkien is indignant and avoids the last point. "It's a Dunhill, if you must, and it is straight and plain as I am and as I plan to remain. But . . ." he points his pipe like a weapon at Charles, "if so, then it is quite like you chaps, old and toothy already."

The humor falls flat as a flannel cake. They are all serious.

"No escaping now. Face your quandary."

Tolkien puts the pipe to rest on the table and looks about at his Inkling fellows. The moment is loud as a library.

Robert Havard, an infrequent Inklings member, breaks in, "So you remain lost."

"Lost in your own Forest of Doubt. Your own . . . what did you call it . . . *Mirkwood*?"

"Yes, not my term, but borrowed. Apt all the same."

"Well, we're back to the question, then. Fantasy and reality, forever separate, or sides of the same coin? What say you, Jack?"

"I side with the Tollers we used to know, Charles. He may be lost for the moment, but he has told us what is in our hearts." Jack holds up his hands, tents his fingers. "That there truly is a borderland where the imagined . . . and the real . . . flow together." His fingers slowly slide through each other. "You never know what may come through a doorway."

Across the pub, the door swings open. Two stern men, rain-drenched, in fedoras and trench coats, enter and look about. They are noticed by all save those at Tolkien's table.

"Well, for my money, we need to summon up one of your loyal dragons, a real one, that will put that German paper-hanger in his place!"

"Here, here!" Tolkien raises his mug and looks to Sarah at the bar. She holds up five fingers as a question. Tolkien nods in a thirsty affirmation. "Enough of this inquisition."

Suddenly one of the trench coats is looming over their table. "Which of you gentlemen is John," he glances at a card, "Ronald Reuel . . . Tolkien?"

Tolkien carefully puts down his pipe and regards the man closely. "I am, sir. Who might you be?"

The man does not respond. His eyes, like ball bearings, mean business. Never letting his gaze waiver from Tolkien, his right hand slowly moves to his coat pocket. The one with the bulge. He fishes for a moment, then settles in a grasp. All eyes at the table follow the hand as it slowly withdraws from the pocket. The other man draws closer, taking a backup position.

The hand that emerges holds only a small leather case. The man flips it open, brandishes it close to Tolkien's face for a fleeting second, then flips it close and returns it to the pocket.

From his brief view, Tolkien could see an identification card, a black-and-white photo that just might be the man before him, along with three lines of text:

> Clugdahl McCrory
> Services Bureau
> MI5. Box 500, London

The man pauses for a second, then decides to resolve any ambiguity about the moment. "Professor Tolkien, you are directed to come with us. Now!"

Chapter 5

BLETCHLEY PARK

——

Tolkien would later remember only bits of the trip that followed. A confusing maelstrom of images and thoughts cycled within his mind. The astonished look of his fellow Inklings, their mouths all identical "O"s. Jack standing up in a futile attempt to intervene—cut short by a blunt order from one of the strange men, as effective as a drawn weapon: "Step aside, sir! Speak no more of this!" Being sequestered in the deep well of the huge sedan's rear seat, all but drowned in droning darkness and the rich smell of luxurious English leather. A few passing road signs, Kidlington and Bicester, suggesting their direction of travel to be northeast.

Coming out of his swirl, he looks at his watch: 9:40.

His thoughts run to Edith, who would by now be fast asleep in her own bedroom, not to awaken for several hours. Surely he would be back home by then, this increasingly unpleasant experience all cleared up as a mistake, or, at worst, perhaps a frenzied inquiry about suspected communists and Nazi sympathizers at Oxford.

War hysteria is reaching a fevered pitch. The papers already speaking of mass evacuation of children from London, of possible internment of German citizens residing in Britain.

A lone motor car bearing one lidded headlamp, like a luminous cyclops, approaches. It careens perilously close, rocking the sedan and trading with it walls of spray.

Tolkien, frustrated with fidgeting in this upholstered cocoon, decides to try a bit of conversation, some banter to loosen things up, perhaps pry out a bit of useful information. If only he knew what to say. He gathers his thoughts, and then speaks in a too-loud voice. "I say, rather nasty storm to be out in, eh? Especially to drive so far. Where is it we're going again?"

Silence.

"Would've rather bought you chaps a round of pints back there. Properly introduce you all around. Bit of recognition for your good work in these difficult times."

Nothing. He lets a few minutes pass, allowing a fresh start to any unlikely conversation.

"You gentlemen like films? Just saw *Gone with the Wind*. Now that's a ripper! You get time off to relax, go to the theatre?"

The only answer is windshield wipers, wind, and engine drone.

He tries one more tack, "I daresay you've been decent and let my family know of this. Save their concerns?"

The front seat passenger speaks without looking back. "All is in order, sir. Not to worry."

Tolkien convinces himself that this thin gruel is mildly encouraging, just as they bounce around a corner to confront a gated guardhouse. A uniformed soldier, all buttons and polish, steps out and asks for their identification. After a phone call, the gate opens and he waves them through. They navigate a tree-lined campus and stop at the entrance to what is soon confirmed to be a rather distinguished manor house. The front entrance is open, and in the doorway stands a man in a tailored suit, silhouetted by a foyer light. He has his hands in his trouser pockets. It is a casual, almost jaunty, stance, as if patiently waiting.

Tolkien's impassive escorts stay behind at the autocar, one of them giving him a sweeping gesture of invitation to go forward.

Crazy thoughts play in Tolkien's mind as he approaches the door. The man in the suit stiffens, clicks his heels, and says "Sir!" in a way that resembles a dog's bark. The way is shown down several hallways. Tolkien studies the oaken doors and paneled walls in passing. *Solid English craft here, yes. Quite the place . . .*

A final door is opened, he is motioned to enter, and the door closes solemnly behind him. The room is large, stately, crowned by an ornate crystal chandelier that is conspicuously dark. A single, hooded lightbulb, insultingly utilitarian in this fine building, dangles by a long cord from the ceiling. It casts a downward cone of light. The room is otherwise stripped of all ornamentation. Jarring blackout curtains cut the richly brocaded wallpaper. The feeling is of haste and ill-preparation. A few sturdy chairs loiter about. Three men are standing there regarding him, their figures partially obscuring the only other furniture, a large library table that might well have served the Bodleian Library a million miles and a million years back at good old Oxford.

One of the men, tweaky and brisk, steps forward. His hand is extended in casual bonhomie, as if they are well known to each other.

"Ah, Professor Tolkien, good of you to . . . stop by . . . as they say. I trust your trip here was not too distressing. All to be explained in due course. I am Kim Philby. Lurking in the corner there is Ian Fleming of Naval Intelligence. Tolkien exchanges nods with the Naval officer as Philby continues. "And lurking there is Alan Turing." Among these proper dressers, Tolkien sees a young, dark-haired, distinctly disheveled man who couldn't care less about this meeting and even less about these boresome introductions.

Philby rattles on. "You were a crackerjack communications officer in the Fusiliers at the Somme. Bloody work there!" He pauses a moment, "Your service to crown and country is needed once more."

"Where . . . am I?" is all Tolkien can muster.

"Why, my man, you are in the Government Code and Cypher School at Bletchley Park! Top secret and all that. A quiet place the Jerries won't figure out. Now, no time to stand on protocol. Come forward, and we'll get to the crux of it."

Philby looks at the other men, both of whom bear lit cigarettes as if they are natural appendages, in the manner of heavy smokers.

"I'll go first. War is almost upon us. England is unprepared. Her fate lies as much in codes as bombs and planes. We have a meager staff of a few dozen people to master such things, when we should have four hundred! You are not the only person so summoned."

"But . . . what could I possibly do?"

"Glad you asked, old boy. Here's to the chase: There is afoot, even now, a desperate, worldwide race between the Allies and Hitler. The Third Reich is searching for the *ubersprache*, the unbreakable code language. Exotic tongues, Yupik, Vandalic, Sumerian, are being poured over." Philby turns. "Ian?"

The naval officer, dressed in full blues, steps forward into the light. "Philby is right. We are bloody short on experts, and you happen to be one of those 'University men' that can . . . just perhaps help us. To that in a second. Here's the whole cricket match: England lives by her sea lanes. Our real, practical abilities, including the mindset of many old dodgers here at GC & CS, haven't advanced since Lord Nelson's time. Dockside spies, surveillance, treachery, tide tables and outdated maps. Throw in numerology, and a few mediums! Our peril lies in our own damnable sloth! This war is mere days away and it's going to be real. The bloody bastards have the edge on us! We need a crystal ball to see into their thoughts."

Philby interrupts, "Which brings us to Alan. The Germans have a devilishly complex code, numbers and cyphers beyond imagining. It is run by an infernal machine called Enigma. Breaking that is Alan's all-but-impossible task. His team works in what we call Hut 8."

Turing nods, a desultory gesture, otherwise letting the description stand on its own.

"Now, to get to the matter. You, Professor Tolkien, are needed in Hut 11. We need to find this *ubersprache* before they do. We know Hitler wants it exclusively for his High Command, the *Torenkopf*." Philby's German is spoken with zest. "The death's head insignia buggers. Perhaps just his direct staff, answerable only to him. The bastard trusts no one." Philby pauses, his eyes checking with the other two men. "We have said too much, but the question is now to you, Professor, will you join us? Are you our man?"

Staring almost blankly at Philby, Tolkien appears impassive. That is hardly the case. There are a thousand reasons to say "no," from the sublime to the pedestrian and the just plain silly. They play a panicky cavalcade in his mind.

I am . . . incapable of doing this. My . . . my lectures. My family! Dear Edith's health, Michael's illness, the exam-grading I've taken on. The bills, yes, the bills! The water pipe repair! Has to be done soon. The damnable tax man! All too much! And . . . and my book!

Tolkien feels in his heart that the last reason is the weakest. His soul has already despaired of the project. Nonetheless the pressure of an immediate decision is clear. Like steam escaping through a valve, his voice hisses, "No. I just . . . I just can't . . ."

Philby is unprepared for this. "Stop man, get a hold of yourself! Let's not be hasty." His interruption is led by a stiffly extended arm and upraised palm, as if he were a talking tree. "Don't be hasty. Before you give your final answer, give us a further moment. Perhaps you would appreciate a bit more information. Arrangements have been made at the University. All is well there. As for your income, if that's a consideration, we are prepared to pay five hundred pounds, a nice stipend. And, most important, kindly take a look at what we have here and let that inform your decision." He pauses to underscore his next words. "Moments such as this, professor, come seldom, rarely once in a lifetime."

There is a pause, and the three men step aside. Pooled in the glaring, singular cone of light from the hanging lamp is a weathered, battered trunk. It is a solid, medium-sized "steamer trunk" once favored by those venturing abroad. Along one side it is severely charred, as if rescued from a rather nasty fire.

With small, hesitant steps, Tolkien approaches the table. The open trunk is full of antiquated documents, many of them water-stained and darkened by heat.

"These were taken from Nazi agents as they ransacked a warehouse that held an uncatalogued cache of surviving documents. From Ashburnham House. Ring a bell, yes? Where the thousand year old, sole surviving manuscript of *Beowulf* was re-discovered."

Tolkien's interest is not just ignited. It is now total.

Philby rambles on, "To be frank, these documents, have us stumped. Though apparently of the same provenance and the same age as the *Beowulf* manuscript, for the most part they correlate to no known language root. Based on a few random manuscripts in Old English that are also part of this cache, and notes by Sir Robert Cotton, the bloody bloke that owned Ashburnham House, we surmise they may be about a hero, someone named 'Ara.' Perhaps even a woman, though that would be odd."

Tolkien hears little of this. He fondles one of the scrolls and his eyes devour the inscription. Save for the *Beowulf* manuscript itself, only a handful of documents from this era have survived. And here lies an entire trunk, a priceless treasure. His mind can't help it, *worthy of a dragon's hoard!*

Fleming offers an observation. "You are a fan of Jules Verne, no doubt. You look like Professor Aranax, you remember? When Captain Nemo reveals to him that his entire life's work in oceanic zoology grasps but a superficial sliver of the truth."

Philby makes a final point. "Back to this hero, this *Ara*. I rather doubt that ancient scribes would spend so much vellum on the tale of a woman. Not to mention ink and scrivener's time."

From somewhere, a confident woman's voice arrests the manly dialogue. "Aren't you the one being a bit hasty now, Director Philby? I wouldn't be so fast in dismissing the tale of a heroine."

A young lady, mid-twenties, very, forward and very "American," steps out from the shadows. She is dressed smartly, in dark blue pants and khaki shirt with no-nonsense, rolled-up sleeves.

Philby, momentarily startled, overcomes his flustering. "Ah, yes, sorry, I should have introduced ... Yvonne Shelby. The Yanks have sent us a most . . . capable liaison. A paleographer—sort of close to your field, eh, Tolkien. She is also, I daresay, connected. Her father is Senator Shelby, Chairman of the Subcommittee on Naval Affairs. Keep us on our toes, no doubt."

The woman ignores Philby and comes up to Tolkien's side. Her gray eyes drill into his, then turn downward. His gaze follows hers. Together they look with fascination at the documents, which offer a yellowish glow under the stark overhead light.

Tolkien's eyes continue to feast on the documents, some scrolled, some bound by sinew, some loose pages. The loose pages are brittle and consistent with his one and only viewing of the original *Beowulf* manuscripts in the musty British Library years before. Many are fire-charred, and all are variously yellowed, water-stained, and mouse-tracked.

"Did my Ph.D. work on Celtic writings," she says. "Under Professor Rollin at Columbia. I'm the one that suggested we enlist your help."

Tolkien, absorbed, steals an estimating glance at her, then silently points to a particular sign, a large runic mark that looks like an elaborate 'A.' His eyebrows float upward and his shoulders rise in a questioning gesture. *What do you make of this?* An unspoken, collegial question among fellow experts.

Shelby talks in an undertone as she and Tolkien jointly hold the scroll. "I've been at this for a week, and it's tough to crack. No antecedents in anything I've ever seen, except perhaps the Welsh Kabindoos."

Tolkien nods sagely, his mind racing over the subtleties, the patterns. They seem remote . . . yet eerily familiar.

Shelby is watching his reaction. "What is it?"

"Well, you may think I'm cracked, but if I were to have to describe it in one word, I'd say: *Elvish.*"

After a moment, Yvonne says, "You're cracked."

"Gone daft, I'd say," chimes Fleming.

He ignores their comments because his mind is racing to weigh it all. He is teetering on the edge of an embarrassing flip-flop. How could he refuse such an offer, a once-in-a-lifetime opportunity to hold in his hands such . . . *precious* artifacts? On top of that, here he is, at least indirectly, at the bidding of King George VI. Seldom does an average Englishman—particularly a younger professor specializing in an obscure and largely ignored portion of the Oxford syllabus—have the privilege of such an overture. He can once again lend his hand to Crown and Country, perhaps put a spot of polish on the war effort, all by engaging in the very work to which he has dedicated his life.

In his mind, an archaic voice speaks to him from the vibrant realm of his own Middle-earth:

If your loyalties lie not here, then where could they?

Tolkien finally finds his voice. He speaks clearly, with the authority of a committed volunteer in a hazardous moment. A voice he hasn't used since the Somme. "I am judged an authority of certain ancient languages. My skill for this task, whatever it is, may prove poor. Nonetheless, I will do my utmost. If this is a threshold, I step across it."

He pauses, looking at them, before continuing, "*Now* what happens?"

Fleming speaks. "Ha! Now is indeed the question. Professor Tolkien. It is, however, late. Your two new friends out in the Alvis will drive you back to your home. As I said, arrangements have been made with the University and a temporary leave for government service has been granted. I believe your assistant, Mr. Lessons, will work with your syllabus and the other professors to complete your courses.

Tolkien frowns slightly at this, the bluntness of sudden dislocation of a patterned life.

Fleming continues, "Let's dive into this tomorrow. Get a good night's sleep. You will be picked up at 0800 sharp. Forms, paperwork, sign the Secrecy Act oath, all that tommyrot. Then down to business. Find out what these Huns are onto!"

A battered wall clock, haphazardly resting on the floor at the far side of the room, buzzes the hour. The men consult their watches. None of their timepieces agree, except to confirm that Bletchley time, like Bletchley, is woefully confused.

Chapter 6

THE WATCHER

—

A thousand kilometers and two time zones to the east, in a windowless anteroom similar in size to the one at Bristlethorn Hall, Truppenführer Jodl Strieger looks up and checks the Lenzkirch world clock on the wall. The clock is precisely calibrated with two hundred identical pieces spread throughout this massive building, the Reich Chancellery. Each clock displays every continent and every time zone on earth. He reviews his typed notes. Strieger is thirty years old, with brown hair, tepid blue eyes, and an intellect to embarrass a honed straight razor.

Five minutes until one in the morning. Exactly.

He will be meeting with his superior at this late hour.

Herr Strieger draws an arrow-straight red line through a sentence in his notes. *Imprecise and unnecessary*, he thinks. He extends his arm, mutters "*Schnell*," and his orderly, standing at attention, grabs the page for retyping.

His desk is organized with neatly stacked reports, each stack exactly aligned, each the same size, each identified with a tiny folded card, as might inform guests at a formal dinner party. The entire desktop is as ordered as a procession of Panzers rumbling in review down the Wilhelmsplatz, as they recently did to commemorate his superior's fiftieth birthday.

His two objectives are clear, and his updates must be also. Each is a message, weighed and calibrated, embodying Jodl's particular gifts: analytical depth and a surprising sense for the subtleties of things, the unspoken and unseen.

With Enigma, we have the edge, he muses in rehearsal for his upcoming audience. *If protected, it will deliver victory. If subjected to carelessness, to underestimating our enemy, then we stand exposed. It must be monitored. Its performance overseen from a high vantage point. It must be watched.*

He knows his second message will be . . . more difficult. The search for the *ubersprache,* the supreme, unbreakable, but spoken language for use by his superior's personal staff, has not gone well. Scouring every continent, every ancient civilization, using scores of linguistic experts, and nothing promising to show. This lack of progress on the personal idea of the man in the next room will not be taken well.

He turns from his desk, lets out a deep breath, and orients his thoughts. An ornate sideboard hugs the wall, its top arrayed with personal mementos. A picture of his wife and children, now secured away in a remote Bavarian village. A snapshot of him as a child, trout fishing with his father, the two of them tending their lines and smiling broadly. An unusual diploma. Exeter College, Oxford, 1933. Beside it is a trophy for being the lead bowler on the University's championship cricket team. All in all, impeccable English credentials.

He glances at the wall, a small frame holding a faded photograph. It is of poor quality, its gray-tones seeming to show a family, bags spilled on the ground, strands of barbed wire . . .

A low chime. The second hand of the clock has arrived at the hour. The door opens, a gray-uniformed orderly at the ready.

"The Führer will see you now."

Chapter 7

BLETCHLEY TIME

—

Turing shakes his head at the forlorn Bletchley clock, and Philby wipes his hands together in the manner of one done with one task and about to embark on another. "Very well, that accomplished in good form, how about a libation?"

There are no takers. Turing is walking away without any mannerly goodbyes whatsoever. Philby, hapless, looks around.

Fleming breaks in. "Splendid idea, Philby, but it is, of course, rather late. Let me rescue the professor, if I might. He may wish to return home and put some things in order. Talk to the missus, all that. Bit of sleep perhaps." He turns to Tolkien. "Can I offer you a ride? I'm a bit of a talker, but I also know the roads."

Tolkien looks at his watch. Eleven, more or less. Yes, Edith will be upset if he is out late for a second night this week. "If you get me home by midnight, that would be most appreciated."

Fleming and Philby huddle, and Tolkien feels a pull at his sleeve. It is Yvonne. Her eyes signal a segue to the side. "Just a quick moment, professor, if you please."

The glare from the spot-lit table ebbs almost immediately into comfortable shadows. She speaks quietly, almost in a whisper, "Thank you for accepting this ... calling. I need to tell you," almost involuntarily, she looks around, "I believe there are already spies here at Bletchley. You, I trust. Don't ask why, I just do. It's the career folks, the pros . . . I don't know. I suggest extreme caution about who you talk to. I recommend you follow my lead. After all, we will be working together."

Tolkien is feeling pulled in different directions, but one word of her advice is spot-on: *caution*. Beginnings are fragile things. He nods and does the cautious thing: he keeps his mouth shut. She continues. "Tomorrow I want us to spend a few moments with Alan. As you can see, he's not too social, but he's the oddball genius of the bunch. Problem is, he is cooped up with other eggheads. He needs someone . . . normal to talk to." There is an undercurrent of tenderness in her voice.

"As in, *like us?*" Tolkien is tired, putting an edge of doubt to his comment.

A voice cuts them short. Fleming is by the door, holding open Tolkien's coat. "Hurry along now, professor, time for all that tomorrow."

* * *

Fleming's auto is a plain little rolling box without the stuperific, almost nautical, drone of the Alvis. It has, however, some things that are much improved: front seat conversation, a decent view of the road, morsels of information, a bit of clarity about what he is getting into.

Fleming's driving is sure-handed, confident in direction, even as he talks, gestures, and talks some more.

"Read your book, Tolkien. I quite agree with the anonymous review by your friend Lewis. All that left-hand rubbish from other critics, about it being just a nice children's tale. Forget them. I'm an adult. I like it. There should be more. Sequel in the works perhaps?"

Tolkien is sheepish. "I've tried. It's just been . . . slow. Fatefully slow. I can't get it going again. Now, it's like an unwheeled wagon. My publisher is pulling his hair out."

"Not to worry. Whatever it is will work itself out. Rough business this writing—a game of frequent discouragement. Keep at it, old boy. Besides, I'm a bit of a linguist myself, and someday after this war has come and gone, I'm going to try my hand at writing."

This perks Tolkien's interest. "Really? What sort?"

"Well, I've got this character in mind—a spy type. Like us, I suppose. Ha! But, my man, he's tough, ruthless, a bit naughty. A globe-trotting rogue."

A comfortable silence intervenes, allowing each to ponder deeper reflections. Fleming says, "How about us, professor, do we learn from, even resemble, our fictional characters?"

"I devoutly hope so. I am one of my characters."

"Let me guess, your little guy . . . Bibbo?"

"B-I-L-B-O, just to get it right." Tolkien gathers himself, purposely allowing a dramatic beat to intervene, then continues in a lowered voice, "*Baggins* (pause) *Bilbo Baggins.*"

"Nice cadence, that. My alter ego is named James Bond, or, rather uh . . . *Bond,* (pause) *James Bond.* Borrowed it from an ornithologist chap. Solid name, can carry a lot of character."

The moment flows quietly, as if each man is considering the question of character—that of his creations and his own.

"So, what has Baggins, Bilbo Baggins taught you?"

"I think it's, to put it in a cup, the power of humility."

"Good God, old boy, a bit quaint, wouldn't you say? Humility won't take you far in this age of men—wouldn't fit much of a mover and shaker in our time. Now, I, he, rather, Bond, has embraced the trait of, well, polished and cynical hubris. Often necessary in this fallen world. Much like a friend of mine. At Bletchley."

"Yes?"

"Biffy, yes. Wilfred Deanderdale. Right character, wrong name. Definitely a *bon vivant.*"

Tolkien hrumphs. "You should know, Fleming, I passionately dislike French, as well as those who speak it voluntarily. So what else does he, this rogue, do?"

"Well, I think he smokes more that even you or I, or your Bilbo friend. Maybe sixty cigarettes per day. Morland, custom made. Three foil bands on the filters. Mirrors his rank as Royal Navy Commander."

"Sounds like, all in all, our alter egos couldn't be more different. Rather like you and I."

"Ah, but there is one trait they share, as do we, that is crucial."

Tolkien waits.

"Loyalty, dear chap. Unsurpassed loyalty." Fleming looks over at Tolkien. "Ah yes, you've already been thoroughly vetted. Thought you should know that."

"Well, in that case, how about the really fun spy stuff. After all, I'm also a cad—tough, ruthless, maybe even naughty. When do I get my issue of cyanide pellets?"

Fleming laughs. "Well, Tolkien, I'm afraid that's not your cut, so far as we can tell. Your dossier says you admire the German people, not surprising for someone with a Teutonic name that loves Germanic folklore. Anyway, it informs us that even as an Englishman, you view them as close kin from your Anglo-Saxon perspective. But you hate Hitler. You've remarked more than once that you wish he'd died as he ran courier across the lines from you at the Somme."

The curious moment in the trenches, facing the Bosch courier, comes back to Tolkien.

Fleming continues, "Instead of your chums, I believe."

"How do you know about that!"

"Easy, old boy. Many ways. No great trick to eavesdrop on a bunch of smoky old dodgers in their cups at the pub. Recall a long-legged, pipe-smoking gent sitting alone in the corner? Why, of course not!"

"You . . . sneaky . . . bastards?" Tolkien hisses.

"In any case, you'll be working with Yvonne, lucky bastard."

"You were looking at her work?"

"No, just looking."

"*You* are the cad, Fleming."

"On the contrary, I love women. I am fascinated by them. I like how they think. Don't you?"

"To tell the truth, I hold them a bit apart, even Edith. She is the better half of my world, but in some ways a separate half. I fell in love with her early, and I've never wavered."

"Face it, you're a clubby, old boy's school type, Tolkien. I hope you don't hold with that 'women in the kitchen and nursery' nonsense."

"Well . . ."

They are surprised as a blur of speed passes them. Oblivious to the wet roads, it growls like a night-hunting, road-prowling cat. It quickly vanishes into the darkness ahead of them. A bit of profile, captured by a flash of lightning, shows a sleek two-seater, its convertible top snugged down.

Fleming peers after it and exclaims "Aston-Martin! By Jove! World's best car. And we get issued this bugger buggy."

Tolkien looks over to see if Fleming is serious. He is. So much so that Tolkien sees a man who yearns for—perhaps lives in his head—a very different life. Fleming is certainly an accomplished gentleman, but inside there shows bits of a different man. Cosmopolitan, suave, independent, irresistible to women. For all that, supremely dangerous and a bit callous.

"You're unhappy with your service?"

Fleming seems to catch himself. "Hardly. Like any good soldier, I bitch. I see opportunities, calling for bold plans that could make a difference. Bloody shame."

"Denniston and Philby don't share your vision?"

"Hardly, Philby's a fake. How deep a fake I don't know. Denniston's just an administrator, but . . ."

"What?"

"The bastard's got money. Tailored suits. He owns a new Aston-Martin. Parks it behind the mansion. Clugdahl, one of your friendly escorts tonight, says he leaves the keys under the floor mat. Batty, I'd say."

Out of the blue, Tolkien can't resist asking, "You spies carry firearms?"

Fleming smiles. "Yes, but you wouldn't notice." He twists his torso and opens a flap of his coat to show a shoulder strap and holster. "That's a spring-loaded holster, holds a Beretta Model 1935. Small, easy to get your hand around, short-recoil." He pauses, adds, "accurate follow-on shots. Given to me by my counterpart in the Italian navy. In friendlier times, of course."

"When do I get mine?"

Fleming laughs. "'Fraid all that Denniston will issue you university men is paper and a pencil. Now, where were we? Ah yes, women. By your underestimation of women, old boy, you're missing out. Take Yvonne, she's terribly clever, terribly ambitious, terribly frustrated. Don't look at me that way! There's no double-entendre, excuse me, no double-meaning, here. She wants to have a real part in this war. What she doesn't know is what I'm now going to tell you. Her father, Senator Marcus Shelby, is departing from Canada in a secret convoy to England. The largest yet. Apparently the bloke hates to fly. They lost her mother only a year ago."

Tolkien feels the stab of the words . . . *lost . . . mother.*

"In any case, he insists we not tell her. Wants his arrival to be a bit of a surprise. Now, should the war start and the Jerries get at that convoy, if something should happen to Shelby, then the bottom might fall out."

"Fleming, I suggest you speak plainly."

"Very well. Shelby is key to our American support."

"I thought Roosevelt had the matter well in hand."

"Hardly. Messy, unpredictable American politics. Shelby is FDR's right hand. Roosevelt can't single-handedly steer America into war, much as he'd like to. There are too many voices for American neutrality. Sit this one out, not our fight, all that. That damn hero of theirs, Charles Lindbergh, telling the press that England will lose the war! Well, without the Yanks, we will." He lets the last sink in.

"So, if that convoy goes down, Shelby included, the U-boats will be seen as unbeatable, and Germany as invincible. The Lindberghs in the press will have a field day. It all hangs in the balance. Stray but a little, and all will be lost."

The empty road bleeds away from the lone headlamp as Fleming corrects back to the centerline.

Tolkien is doubtful. "Look, you obviously know who I am and am not. What can I possibly do?"

"Modesty? Come now, no time for that. We're in a crunch. We've got so little time, a pressing engagement if ever there was one. Bletchley, my friend, is a leaky ship on her own, and one right now given to the doldrums. She'll never make it to port. No one believes we can consistently pierce their codes. But if we could, Bletchley just might alter the balance, even for this hapless convoy. You can be a fresh wind, a new set of eyes, not glazed over with cynicism. Keep your instincts sharp, get to know the chaps in the other huts. Well, forget Hut 13, it's hopeless. Feel free to muck around. Just keep me informed."

"So I'm your own little spy?"

Fleming brushes past the remark. "Hardly, my good man. As for your main task, this wild goose chase about *ubersprache,* there just might be something to it. The documents you saw, they look to have an uneasy history. Know this: men died retrieving those scraps. No matter what, their meaning might be, there's still something important there."

"Such as?"

"The Nazis want them." Fleming holds back until it is clear that Tolkien is clueless. "Trade bait, Master Tolkien, and you are the proprietor of this particular bait shop. Even if we can't figure out the mysterious language, it doesn't matter. We need a distraction."

"A what?"

"Misinformation. Decoys. Inventory. Spying should always involve barter. Commerce if you will. Let's face it, they want this trove. They are watching us. We need something to feed back to them. Scramble their heads. We may be bloody slow in grinding down their damnable codes, but we can still play the old game of intrigue. We need a distraction. Preferably something with flair."

Without prompting, Fleming eases off the highway, cuts through a roundabout and enters Tolkien's neighborhood.

"I'll do what I can. But why are you telling me?"

"Ah, good question, Tolkien. One can't be too careful, can one?" Fleming looks jauntily over at him. "Perhaps I'm just feeding this to you as false information. Bit of a test. Wait a bit, let it leak out, then I know its source. Eh, Herr Tolkien?"

"You bastard, how dare you question . . ."

"Easy now, old boy. Just a bit of levity. Couldn't help it. I'm your ally. Anyway, so far we've got just enough code-breaking done to maybe protect Shelby's convoy, direct it away from the wolves. But, here it is, old chap: if the Germans detect we're reading them, they add a few rotors, change codes every hour, all that. We're blind again. Believe me, they are watching us. Some smart Kraut bastard is sitting in some immaculate office, scanning us like a bloody hawk. Hitler may be arrogant, but not this chap. I suspect he's patient, watchful."

Fleming brakes and turns right. "Ah, here's Northmoor, and here's your flat if I'm not mistaken."

The car stops and Tolkien, surprised, fumbles for the latch and opens the door. "Thank you for the lift. See you tomorrow?"

"'Fraid not. I'll be lurking around from time to time. You'll need to be back at Bletchley bright and early. Regretfully, you'll have to settle for a ride with your same old friends in the morning. And, two more things." Fleming leans over toward him.

"Yes?"

"Since you see yourself as one of your hobbits, remember this— you, like them, seem to have an unsuspected bit of pluck to call upon."

"And second?"

"Not a word to friends or family. Not Edith. Not your friend Jack. That's an unbreakable rule. For everyone's sake."

Tolkien assents with a nod.

Moments later, he stirs Edith, apologizes for the late hour, and lets her return to sleep. He volunteers nothing of what has happened. It is all too new, too unsettled. He won't lie, because he won't have to. She won't ask. His professional life is as distinctly walled-off as it is distinctly male. So, no worries there.

He retires to his room and falls in bed. His mind is flush with rapid-fire possibilities. Such a sudden change from the routine that he has embraced as his life. And the damnable Ring Story! Just a story, nothing real there. His heart chastises him. He knows the story is everything, a creation he has literally cried over in its writing. He knows it is dead.

At some level, he already mourns.

At breakfast, Edith pours his coffee and, just as he begins to foray into his Weetabix and broiled tomato, she asks straight out, "Now, sir, what is this business about being out so late, and leaving the Eagle and Child? And these men in a big black car idling at our curb this very instant?"

Good God, he thinks, *there ARE spies everywhere!*

In the brief time before he has to leave, and with the scant information he has, he obeys one of Fleming's cardinal rules of spying: If necessary or convenient, lie. It is uncharacteristic and awkward. He spins a story about an investigation at the University. *Hush-hush and all that. Not to worry.*

Moments later, as he bursts out the front door, it occurs to Tolkien that this road, this morning, this stepping forth, is every bit like his own Bilbo. *Know this as you step unto a road, it can lead anywhere. Even a garden pathway can be an unpredictable, dangerous thing.*

Edith calls and catches him on the sidewalk. She hands him a bulging paper sack, neatly folded at the top. "Lunch? They may be short of provisions there, wherever that is. A bit of toffee pudding in the jar, just in case. Now, off you go."

Cheery enough, but her look says it all. He knows, that she knows, that he is a flat-out horrible liar.

Nonetheless, bag in hand, Tolkien the unlikely adventurer clambers into the Alvis Salon car and settles comfortably into the rear seat. His two familiar companions are up front, still dour as prison doorknobs. Before they can get the advantage, he proclaims too loudly, "I dub you, driver, Mr. One, and you, passenger, Mr. Clugdahl McCrory, I give you the secret spy name 'Mr. Two.' Now, Jeeves, er, Mr. One, on to Bletchley Park. No more idle chatter and be smart about your driving!"

Chapter 8

HUTS

—

Yvonne is waiting when he arrives at the mansion. "Hang up your coat, Professor, the nickel tour starts now. What's in the sack?"

"Uh, lunch." He says it a bit defensively, like a new kid in school. A fleeting thought comforts him: Any good hobbit, would absolutely, always, on any outing, pack a knapsack of provisions.

Yvonne cuts his woolgathering. "Leave it. A bit of orientation and then we'll get to our business. Come along now." In a moment they exit the mansion with its pronounced green-roofed cupola on top, and follow a manicured gravel path along a row of bland, inconsequential wooden buildings bearing drab shades of what once might have passed for paint. Each is bleakly utilitarian, bespeaking temporary use, little better than a Quonset. She nods at several as they pass, "Hut 1, Japanese codes. Hut 6, German Army and Air Force codes. Hut 3, the grunts that decipher for Hut 6. I spared you from that hellish assignment. Same with Hut 4. They serve the famous Hut 8."

"Odd, what about the other numbers?"

"Don't ask . . . don't worry about those. The only other number you need to know about is Hut 13."

He stops and tilts his head, as in *Come on, really?*

She stops and smiles. "I'm serious. They're the *really* weird folks. Propeller heads. We can meet them later. But for now . . ."

Tolkien looks up and they are standing at the door of another derelict building. Its only distinction is that its number, "8," is tacked on so loosely that it rides at an odd angle.

"Seems to be listing to starboard."

"Apt, professor. This building houses the effort to break the German naval code." She puts a "hush" finger to her lips and whispers "U-boats" as they enter. The room is in the midst of an orientation lecture for a dozen new recruits. At the front is the same man that smartly acknowledged Tolkien at the foyer to the mansion last night. She nods toward him and whispers, "Alistair Denniston, Deputy Director."

The man, in another impeccable suit, is at a podium. A freshly erased chalkboard is to one side. On the other side, a small table bears a cloaked object.

Tolkien listens to Denniston as he and Yvonne sidle along the back wall.

". . . now to the heart of it. England is a maritime country. Unlike Germany, we live by sea. That advantage is now our Achilles' heel. The U-boat can lurk, loiter, hunt, and destroy our ships with impunity. And yet it is not the submarine that is the crucial invention. No, it is the blunt, damnable logic of their communications."

Denniston lets that settle in before continuing.

"As we all know, only wireless provides instantaneous long distance communications to a moving platform . . . such as a submarine. By its very nature, a wireless transmission is a voice to all who care to listen. Thus codes are the vital key to the security of wireless communications."

A hand goes up. A gray-haired, uniformed, and profusely decorated naval officer stands and interrupts Denniston. "Sir, these . . . ciphers are certainly not new. Why, Caesar used them to disguise his messages when fighting the Gauls. Used them myself in the Great War. Surely we can break through these . . . petty German contrivances!"

Denniston looks hard at the officer, and his face says it all: the moment to make a point. "I'm afraid, Admiral, that despite all the war stories at the Royal Academy and Aldershot, this is a different time. In fact," he looks around the room, "it is precisely the Edwardian prigs in our leadership that have thus far failed to comprehend the gravity of what we are up against. Imagine Caesar's simple code. In effect, a few transpositions of letters. Now think of each transposed letter having orders of magnitude of variables. A trillion? That's not an exaggeration, gentlemen."

He steps to the side table and, with a magician's flourish, sweeps away the cloak. On the table squats an apparatus that looks like an overgrown typewriter, with rotor wheels on the top, rows of small lamps, and a keyboard. He lets a dramatic moment pass. "*This* . . . is . . . Enigma. A primitive version of what the Germans have perfected. Every German military communication by wireless goes out through a vastly more complex version of this, and is decoded by an identical machine at the other end. Our Polish friends, for whose sake we are about to go to war, figured out this simple version. Unfortunately, it is but a toy compared to the complex immensity we face."

Yvonne signals to Tolkien that they should exit by a rear door, just as the Deputy Director makes his final point: "Right now, gentlemen, we are as blind as the Gauls against Caesar."

They enter the rear door, which leads to a small office. In it are jammed four desks. The room's lone window is covered by a metal blast shield. The room's lone occupant is slouched at a desk, twiddling a pencil with one hand and staring at the non-window. Yvonne, looking concerned, shuts the door. The closed room is filled with an understated, but relentless sound, as if hundreds of knitting needles were busily clacking away. Its source is not obvious.

"Alan , something wrong?"

Turing, unsmiling, looks around as if Yvonne is the only person in the world who might break his foul mood. *There it is again*, Tolkien thinks, *some chemistry between them.*

The man gives a dismissive look at Tolkien, then turns back to face the windowless wall. "It's unsolvable," is all he says, as if that encompasses the end, the beginning, everything in between.

She sits down at a desk chair across from him. "But you were breaking the code just last week."

"They changed something. We don't even know what. Another rotor added. A second plug board. Who knows? Seven weeks of mind-numbing work by us and they crash it with one little move. It's asymmetrical. We'll never catch up."

Tolkien, feeling like a third wheel in their midst, wants to be helpful. He intrudes, "Maybe the question isn't what they did, but why?"

Turing turns back to him, then to Yvonne, who nods an okay. "Well you're right. They know, somehow. A spy among us? Some metaphysical clue? Something we did with the intelligence? I just know they are organized, smart, and so damn far ahead of us. It's a will-crushing desolation here. A pathless, impenetrable forest of numbers. As soon as we think we see a path, establish or guess a crib of a few knowns, it changes."

He picks up and angrily scatters a sheaf of flimsy green papers. Tolkien guesses the stock is reserved for translations. Top secret. As if the gesture isn't enough, Turing petulantly snaps his pencil and throws the pieces, one at a time, at the wall. "We're going to lose this bloody war!"

He looks darkly at Yvonne, who is speechless, and continues. "And who do we get to help us? The tin pots in London recruit chess champions, Times cross-word puzzle winners, an occultist or two, and" he laughs with frank derision, "some bugger officers who don't know math from their asses." His caustic tone is now pointedly out of control, "Oh yes, a paleographer and a fairy-story writer." He signals he is finished by folding his arms tightly across his chest.

Tolkien, no stranger to dark moods and righteous anger, feels his blood come up. "You may have no use for our skills, sir, but you are a fool to hold them in contempt. I am a philologist, a student of the myths, and therefore the minds, of the Northern races. That includes the Germans. More important, unless you disdain American help, you would be wise to apologize to Miss Shelby immediately!"

Turing unfolds his arms and, more with his hangdog look than his words, mutters an apologetic "Sorry. I guess I'm starting to crack with this setback."

Yvonne nods to Tolkien.

"Apology accepted," he says. "Now, if I may, your comment reminded me of the ancient myth of Mirkwood, the Great Forest of Doubt. It too is pathless. It deceives. It misleads. It beguiles, and it never willingly gives up a true path."

Turing, passably indulgent, asks, "and was this . . . place ever bested?"

"Oh yes! Not often, but yes. The key, in the world of men, is one word you touched on: *will*. That, fueled by belief in the worth of your endeavor."

Turing purses his mouth. He is mildly challenged, and he leans back in his chair. "To be frank, professor, pretty language and high calling is futile in the face of this particular immensity."

"Well, there's always a way around it. I could talk all day about solving ancient riddles, but there is something closer to what you need."

"For God's sake, out with it!"

"A Palantir."

"A what?"

"An ancient artifact, a crystal ball if you will, that can see into the enemy's mind. It is not merely something spoken from the untrustworthy mouth of an oracle, or a god. It is a physical thing. Perhaps a tool. Or, in our fallen time, regretfully, a *machine*." Tolkien speaks the last word with a kind of resigned contempt.

The look on Turing's face is one of bemused surprise. "Well, in a way you've put your finger on something. I suppose there are no secrets here at good old spy school."

With this he gets out of his chair, eases around a desk, and walks toward the far end of the room. He stops at a pair of double doors. "I have been working on just such a machine, one of your palon ... palontics, whatever the devil you call it."

He swings wide the thickly padded doors to reveal a deep, closeted space. In it stands an open cabinet. In the cabinet is a monstrosity of wires and lights, but the dominant feature is four rows of rotating, cylindrical devices. The noise, previously a low distraction, is suddenly an ominous cacophony of click-clack-clunk, tick-tick, click-clack-clunk. The sounds repeating for each of sixteen devices that seem to be racing at full throttle. They sound desperate.

"We call each of these a 'Bombe.' Ticking and all. Just prototypes. We don't know yet if they will work. I keep trying to compress the logic down. I'm at a standstill. I'm lost in your . . . forest of doubt."

"But you're on the right track?" Yvonne asks.

"Well, if we have it right, and we get the money and machinists to build a few hundred of these . . ." He stops and considers the next statement. "I wrote a pretty damning letter to Churchill himself, just last week, but I'm sure he'll never see it personally. Bloody penny-pinching bureaucrats! *And even then* we need a lucky break with a few known letter pairs. With that we can winnow the possible combinations down. From a trillion to, oh, say maybe, oh, a million." He pauses, looking at them as if that is quite an accomplishment. "Unfortunately, even if it works, every code change by them means we have to start over. This is industrial warfare by numbers, and, for the first time in history, we're trying to invent a machine to do mass-production spying."

Yvonne looks down at Turing with a caring, almost maternal warmth. Her regard drifts behind him, to a wall, and the temperature of her gaze falls to zero. Covering the wall is something new, a huge map showing a blue expanse with quadrants and dotted lines and red and black push pins here and there. Fragments of earthly brown and green frame the expanse on either side.

Tolkien follows her eyes and studies the wall. It is a map of the Atlantic Ocean, from the equator north to the Arctic. The cold blue is exactly right, perfect to suggest endless, rolling swells and frigid depths. All soon to become a merciless battleground.

She looks once more at Turing, who has returned to his dark mood. Inert as a raw turnip. She turns to Tolkien, "Professor, time is moving on. Let's go see our own hut."

Chapter 9

HALIFAX

——

U.S. Senator Morris Shelby, riding in a non-descript Studebaker, arrives dockside at Pier 27 in Halifax, Nova Scotia, at one in the morning on August 30, 1939. He ascends the steps to the *Empress of Atlantis*, a Canadian merchant ship of six thousand tons bearing flour, canned goods, and munitions. He is her lone passenger, known only as "Mr. Hillside." Her cargo and her destination are not specified on the manifest. She will slip out of the port and into the dark sea with the huge Nova Scotian tides at ebb flow. Of course, everyone in town, friend and foe, and there are more than a few of the latter, knows that such a Canadian vessel, her unbarnacled keel first breaking open water barely a month earlier, is bound for a British port. Her passage would take seven days across a stormy Atlantic prowled by U-boats eager to engage their all-but-inevitable enemy.

Senator Shelby knows the danger far better than the captain or crew, most of whom will perish in the year ahead. The senator is privy to intelligence that Germany's invasion of Poland is both certain and imminent. That in turn will precipitate war with Britain, making the *Empress* a fair and legal prize for sinking by German submarines. Reason enough to get across the Pond as soon as possible. And, of course, there is his surprise appearance for his only daughter's birthday. Yvonne will be thrilled.

BOOK II
INTO MYRCWUDU

—

"O see ye not yon narrow road
So thick best wi' thorns and briers?"
~ Thomas the Rhymer,
anonymous seventeenth century poet
quoted by J.R.R. Tolkien in *On Fairy Stories*

It is not down in any map; true places never are.
~ Herman Melville

Chapter 10

HUT 11

—

When Tolkien and Yvonne arrive at their own Hut 11, its dismal appearance is beyond any expectation. It is a leaky-roofed, one-room wooden cabin set apart from the other buildings. Prior to its recent impressment into service for the crown, it might have served as an accommodation catering to mice, spiders, and the Estate's occasional transient help. A hasty broom sweeping has left cobwebs in the corners and a gritty texture on the scuffed and gouged linoleum floor.

Tolkien notices there are no blast shields on the windows. He can't help but think of foolish little pigs living in a house of straw, facing, not a wolf, but the likely onslaught of German bombs. Even the fate of working in a bull's eye pales, however, as he thinks of his lunch sitting back in the main house. No hobbit could have felt more famished.

For now, Hut 11 is all theirs. In its center stands a table. The table is flanked by poles bearing spot lamps. He clicks on the lights. In an instant they glare viciously on the same ancient trunk Tolkien saw the night before. The intense light reminds him of a third-degree scene in a Hollywood gangster movie. Yvonne, speaking low from the shadows, deadpans a noirish cop with an overdone Brooklyn accent, "C'mon Mr. Trunk, tell us whatcha got inside there. Don't try to be a wise guy, cause we're gonna find out anyways."

They look at each other and laugh. They know it's a bluff. Despite their CVs, they are amateurish strangers to the secrets hiding in that trunk.

Next to the trunk are various supplies: large plasticized envelopes, cleaning rags, pens, writing pads, an oversized magnifying glass worthy of Dr. Holmes, an odd pile of little cloth sacks. Tolkien hefts one and feels the metal shot inside.

"Pellet bags," says Yvonne. She wipes the table clean, opens the trunk lid, and pulls out several of the better-preserved scrolls. These, spared the worst of the scorching, are still pliable. Carefully, each corner and side secured by the ample weight of a bag, she unfurls the scrolls. Tolkien takes a chair at one end of the table as she looks up at him. "Hardly a proper curating process. But what's war but a process of destructive shortcuts. Let's get to it."

Then, as if thinking through a process, she stops. "Professor there's more to these documents than you might think. Before we begin, maybe I should tell you the rest of the story."

Tolkien plays the eager student. "I agree. How could we start without knowing *where* we're starting from? And, say, how about a spot of lunch?"

"Relax. It's only ten. You eat every hour? Never mind, now some of this you certainly know." She pauses, gathering herself as if to deliver a presentation to a VIP audience. "As you might guess, it starts with a fire."

"Ah yes, Cotton's estate."

"Precisely. The time is October 20, 1731. In my country, well, your colonies, we are still proud of being Tories—God, King, and Country and all that—basically monarchists like I fancy you are in your heart, professor."

Tolkien shrugs. She could be dead-on right.

She continues, "As a point of minor irony, at this not-so-distant time in human history, Benjamin Franklin is already putting together two milestones for America: the first public fire department and the first public library."

"Yvonne, if you don't pick up the pace, I'm going to *eat* this scroll!"

"Fine, fine! You have a blood sugar problem? Anyway, over here in Merry Old England, libraries have always been big. And one of them, assembled a century earlier by your eccentric antiquarian, Sir William Cotton, houses at this time the most extensive collection of Anglo-Saxon manuscripts in the world. The collection is fragile, irreplaceable, and slovenly curated with dust and location references to, of all things, the busts of Roman Emperors that presided over parts of the library.

One such emperor was Vitellius, paunchy, unlucky, and short-lived, who was publicly executed on the infamous Germanian Stairs in full view of the Forum. Nonetheless centuries later, beneath his bust in Cotton's library were piled vellum manuscripts that included an untitled and essentially unnoticed tract. One that you today pour over endlessly. It now goes by the title *Beowulf*."

"Yes, Vitellus A."

"Which brings us back to 1731. This entire collection has been moved to an estate called, ironically, Ashburnum House. We know that the collection had innumerable priceless treasures, such as original letters patent from King George recording the Magna Carta."

She stops. Tolkien is as rapt as his students were yesterday morning. His hands are on each knee and he is leaning forward as she continues.

"Now, in the space of an hour that very evening, a fire of unknown cause erupts in Ashburnham House, and the greatest bibliographical disaster in British history unfolds. Smoke boils from furious flames, followed by a belated deluge of water from firefighters. Fire bells clang as volunteers arrive, pails in hand. One Doctor Bentley, the then owner and custodian of Ashburnham, is seen in nightgown and wig, clutching the Magna Carta and fleeing the inferno.

"At dawn's light, the scene is even more dreadful. Ashburnum is a smoldering ruin. The surrounding yard is littered with fragments of burned manuscripts. Piles of documents, hurled from upper story windows, lay in heaps. The surviving documents, many scorched, are soaked with water. As we know, moisture is an agent that, given time, is as destructive as fire itself. In the ensuing half-century, sporadic and ill-informed attempts at conservation actually contributed to their further deterioration. Finally, the documents are left to rest once again, gather dust, and slide into further disarray in closeted rooms in the basement of the British Library.

"Hidden in this chaos is the single known copy of Beowulf. Untitled, it sits there until, say, 1815. Then it first draws spare attention. A few scholars of Germanic languages comment upon it."

Tolkien is nodding. He knows the story in general terms, but this is perfect. He could eat it with a spoon, if he wasn't so hungry for lunch.

Yvonne continues, "So, the poem's popularity, especially among scholars such as yourself, is a recent arrival, a late-bloomer as literary classics go, eh? From the surviving document, we believe it was hand-scribed by two monks in a scriptorium in 700 AD. It probably is a recording of a long, oral work from centuries earlier."

Tolkien raises his bushy eyebrows and tobacco-tinged hands to mark a question. "Or perhaps a retelling, a translation of some account . . . written in another language?"

"Possibly so. Now don't get too far ahead of me."

Tolkien foregoes thoughts about his lunch sack. His eyes remain wide open, he leans back in his chair, as Yvonne unfurls this tale of a tale.

She suddenly asks, "Do you still want me to continue? I'm sure you know much of this."

"Yes, yes," he gives a rolling gesture with his hand. "Never so well put. Keep going please."

"Very well. As you have made clear in your Beowulf lecture, professor, it is the content, the story itself that matters. The monsters—ravaging, misshapen Grendel, and his raging mother in her watery lair. Of course, surmising from your recent book, your favorite borrowed image is a dragon inflamed to fury by a mere cup stolen from his treasure hoard. These, and the small band of intrepid *men* who as always, leave the women behind and make heroic journeys to meet these monstrous foes. Man to monster, so to speak. Oh, I forgot, the only female of note in the whole Beowulf adventure is a villain*ess*. Grendel's mother?"

She is not really asking a question. She is making a rather cutting point about gender and heroic journeys. Tolkien fidgets, slightly annoyed, because it reminds him of the articulate young woman at his lecture just, my God, one day going on a thousand years ago.

She studies him for a further moment as her question lingers in the air. Resolved that her point is made, she moves on.

"This brings my long-winded story to the point where, I believe, knowledge stops. I say that because, despite your academic pedigree, what I'm about to tell you is known by few scholars, and its import to fewer still. What was once a bibliographical mystery—the tantalizing possibility of a lost book of *Beowulf*—is not only true, but a matter of national security."

Tolkien stiffens. His hands grip the table. When, as a dedicated academic, nay an *authority*, your whole intellectual structure shifts on its foundation, then all you can do is hang on. Try to see if the building is going to collapse.

His heart is literally pounding. He can't help himself. "Don't hold up, for God's sakes! I get the top secret part. What in blazes are you saying?"

"Good word, yes. In the desperate aftermath of the Ashburnum fire, stacks, piles really, of documents were taken to various homes, businesses, warehouses, to get them out of the mud and rain.

"A particular group of documents, identified as Vitellius BX, part of the same folios in which your meager version of *Beowulf* lay hidden, were apparently kept separately, in a locked trunk.

"Why, Miss Shelby? Why should they be sequestered away?"

"Ah, that's the question. Bear with me a moment longer. So, the trunk was duly tossed out the window. Like a fuming smoke bomb, it bounced and rolled and lay smoldering for the night."

She walks over and puts her hand on the trunk.

"As you will see, there is something in here that was deliberately hidden away. It was bound up in a locked trunk to protect it."

"Well," says Tolkien, "I'm not much on trunks, but I do know something of locked gates, especially secret ones. They can serve two purposes: to keep what's outside out, and also to keep what's inside in."

Yvonne deliberately, smoothly lifts her hand from the trunk, as if it contains a ticking bomb. "You put your finger on it, professor. Want to know more of the truth?"

"All right," Tolkien huffs, "so that we don't sit here all day, what exactly is the secret truth, Miss Shelby."

"I suspect it is more bizarre than even you could imagine . . ."

Chapter 11

PROGRESS AND NOT

—

His meeting with the Führer finished, Streiger is back at his desk. He is distraught. As always, the Führer has both given and taken. Streiger's suggestion, perhaps over-bold, that he should be authorized as a supreme "Watcher" over the integrity of Enigma, is quickly approved. Streiger will draft the order immediately.

Watcher! Ja!

The glow of this accomplishment was darkened almost immediately by the remaining sting of the Führer's tantrum. He was livid about the fruitless search for the *ubersprache.*

Streiger impatiently sorts through new intelligence reports. After a few moments, he stops. A thin smile plays on his face. In his hand is a single page, a decoded message from the German Naval Attaché in London. It has not been protected by Enigma, for the obvious reason that they would never allow the apparatus on English soil. Still in the text is a clever code that once unraveled, reveals a cryptic message: "Office of Pipe searched by Curly. Negative results. BP assets say lost Vitellius Trove exists. Proceeding to intercept Pipe directly."

Jodl looks up, indulges a broader smile. He is bemused and intrigued. "Curly" is code for Gauss. Bald as a cue-ball. A good agent. More interesting is "Pipe." That is Jodl's old professor. Putting aside the unpleasantness that ended their mentor-pupil relationship, Jodl thinks fondly of him. He would be a natural choice for "BP," Bletchley Park, to recruit. For the moment the English might have an advantage in developing the *ubersprache*, but soon the tables would turn. Our assets can disrupt things at BP, perhaps get the physical documents, a sample even. The Führer would then understand the situation. He will have progress, oh yes, and very soon.

And getting it will be fun. Jodl scribbles out a one-line message and thrusts it at his orderly with instructions to encode and send it immediately:

> Compromise but do not eliminate Pipe.
> Imperative to obtain sample of
> documents.

A STRANGER TRUTH

—

"Damn it! Out with it, young lady!"

"Very well ... *Dad*." The term is not meant as an endearment. Yvonne is intolerant of interruption. "The ages of these documents span roughly a thousand years. They begin with these confounded, what you call 'elvish,' tracts. Then there is a series of Anglo-Saxon translations, apparently by the same scriptorium, even the same scribes, that gave us the known Beowulf document. These are followed by a long, frequently interrupted course of notations and translations running up through a document dated 1847. It looks like some group, cult, fellowship, call it what you will, has dedicated itself to preservation and interpretation of the original documents. Many hands, many times, always secret, always working on this same trove."

"Mystery within a mystery. What do you make of it?"

"There is a common thread. I think it is all about a single story. An epic pre-dating the arena of your studies by centuries. From a northern world bounded by sea and mountains, described by its inhabitants as *mit-gard*, what you have rendered in your own writings as 'Middle-earth.' It is an ancient tale about a heroine. Perhaps the greatest heroine of all time! Greater certainly than your brave braggadocio, Beowulf. He slew three monsters, saved Heorot and his own kingdom, performed great athletic feats, and ruled long and wisely. He justly deserves to be remembered, even if he was in the end a local and minor figure."

She could see the reflexive frown on Tolkien's brows.

"Now, about this *heroine*. Her name was Aragranessa. She was known throughout the land, Middle-earth if you will, as simply 'Ara.' It appears she was a mortal from one of many races of diminutive beings. 'Halflings,' they were called.

"And what is *her* story?" His tone is reserved, a tad skeptical.

"Only that she saved the world. And, in cruelly ironic payment, was condemned as a traitor to the world. I guess the old saying, 'No good deed goes unpunished,' applied even back then. In time, however, the truth became well known. She was for a time renowned, her story told by bards even before that of mighty Beowulf. Then, after a brief time, perhaps no more than a few score years, her tale was persecuted and censored into virtual extinction. Save for this trove of documents, its survival no doubt purchased with blood and fear, she would be forever erased from the world. And even with the documents in hand, most of her tale is untranslatable, locked away in this strange language. Fortunately, I have what I believe is the key."

Tolkien's eyebrows lift.

She reaches into the trunk, pulls out a folio-sized piece of vellum and hands it to him. It is marked with a runic "A" in the center. That is circumscribed by an intricate circle with lines like rays, and exquisite markings in the strange language. Overlaid are notes in Old English, Middle English, and proper modern English scribbles. The document appears to have been intensively used, worked as if were a tool, over centuries.

"The 'A' stands, I believe, for Ara. That was her mark. There are other known cognates scribbled here. Just like Alan over in Hut 8, if we can get enough knowns, a crib, maybe even a codebook, if that is what this is, we can unravel all this. That's why you're here."

His response is immediate. "Okay. How do we start?"

"With this." She whips out a paper, yellowed, but of more modern vintage. "It was in the trunk, at the top, the most modern document in this trove." Then she adds, "It's from Baltimore, 1847."

"Now, you're the one that's cracked, young lady." Tolkien snatches the page and looks at the first word. He knows it well. "*Searucaeg,*" he says, "Old English. It means 'an insidious key'."

Yvonne is excited. "With this, and your ear for word-evolution, we can surely crack this code and learn her full story!" Should I read the page? It's better out loud."

Tolkien hands back the page. "By all means! You mind?" He leans back, takes out his pipe and, as Yvonne begins to read, commences the relaxed ritual of the pipe-smoker: cleaning, filling, tamping, lighting. Smoke curls into the air as her words fill the tiny room.

My name and humble literary efforts matter little, save as I am keeper of these documents. Entrusted I am, most unworthy of an otherwise noble and diverse line of patrons, to preserve this tale. A story so precious, yet so damned. Chased across the fathomless and unshored seas of time by those who would destroy it.

I have recorded elsewhere, without reference to names, how these pitiable documents came to me. As instructed, I have kept them hidden.

For the sake of veracity, I must confess certain feelings that have haunted my stewardship of this strange collection. As I first studied the papers before me—gazed upon their charred and crinkled vellum of obviously ancient origin, at their labyrinthic runes—upon their bleak loneliness—upon the vacant eye-like window into the past that these unreadable words might somehow render—I felt an utter depression of the soul which I can compare to no earthly sensation more properly than to the after-dream of the reveler upon opium.

This deep unease was soon swept away by a kind of revelation. As if of a hideous dropping of the veil to reveal a sense of doubt, of being lost in a vast and wild landscape. Perhaps a forest. Unmapped and unpathed.

In time, with the use of a remnant scrying-stone, a most distressing experience, I blundered into the most rudimentary level of translation. The feelings grew more intense, as if every word, once given over to meaning sensible to me, also stealthily placed another foot of some presence, cunning and lurking, into this world.

Nonetheless, I persevered. I came to realize that the words—as I was able to translate them through the use of a particular document dominated by a runic 'A' and displaying a complex circle or wheel—gave a message of hope that for some period dispelled my fears. The words seemed to tell of an heroic figure, of the gender we commonly regard as frail and delicate. She overcame immense perils and rescued the world from an enslaving force named "Bind."

My feeling of exalted joy was momentary. It was replaced as I struggled to unearth, and then involuntarily shuddered, at a bit of verse imbedded in the runes:

Hrac-nor
Darkness for Elves
Darkness for all

While I cannot fathom the full meaning, the sound of that first word, the rhythm, echoes endlessly in my beleaguered mind. I think of an opposite, the inherently beautiful English phrase "cellar door," and similar evocative words such as "Celador."

I doubt if I shall ever find respite from the tempo of this harsh word.

Elinore
Nevermore.

What was it—I pause even now to think—what was it that so unnerved me in the contemplation of these slyly designed documents? They remain a trove with no name, save as some refer to them as the "Ara Lays," others as the "Mirkwood Codex." They are encompassed by the single word whispered to me by my predecessor:

Myrcwudu

I entrust these now to their fire-scarred trunk, locked and hidden for safekeeping, the key in my pocket. Should I not return, I trust my successors, more worthy than I, will intercept and protect all that has preceded me, and add to this meager contribution.

E.A. Poe
Baltimore, Maryland
July 17, 1847

Tolkien sits wordless.

Yvonne asks him, "The letter is authentic. I had it checked. The handwriting matches his known samples. Now, the date underneath his name, ring a bell?"

"No, not really."

"Poe died, mysteriously, the next day. Any other bells?"

"Yes, of course. I have long admired Mr. Poe. I spoke just recently at my lecture and again to my friends at the pub about the American observation, at about his time, that 'cellar-door' was considered the single most beautiful sound in our entire King's English."

"And the others, *Hrac-nor* and *Myrcwudu*, what of them?" The words came harshly off her tongue, evoking something brutal and pitiless.

"I know, of course, of the second word, rendered in later times as 'Mirkwood.' It has anecdotes, though its derivation becomes clouded in the early Germanic texts. Of the other word, I have no knowledge, and no inclination to learn more of it."

Yvonne arches an eyebrow to show her skepticism at that remark, then continues, "A baggage tag says this trunk was shipped on July 21, 1847, three days after Poe's mysterious death, by the Baltimore Factor and Transit Company, to an address in London. From there, its history is lost, save as it was recovered in 1924 from certain unsavory characters by Scotland Yard. Thereafter, it languished, unclaimed, in a government warehouse. They wouldn't tell me more. So, here we are."

It is already noon.

"And the scrying stone? What do you make of that?"

"Odd, but then Poe was odd, wasn't he? You've not seen it in your look through these?" He gestures at the trunk, the documents.

"No. In any case, are you fresh enough to dive in, give all this a shot?"

"I'm eager to get going, I assure you. Nonetheless, I must first insist on a good meal."

Without saying a word, Yvonne snaps her fingers, gets up and goes out the door. In ten minutes, she returns, his lunch sack in hand. Tolkien offers to share, and she obliges by accepting a taste of the toffee pudding.

"Incredible!" she says. "The 'cellar-door' of desserts!"

"Yes, my Edith, bless her, toils to make this for me exactly twice a year."

The pudding consumed, and the rest of his lunch arrayed before him, Tolkien is more relaxed. He munches a gammon sandwich, then a cake. He burps modestly and looks up at her. "We have hours of my best focus time ahead of us. Now to this document. He holds up the key. It must be the same one mentioned by Master Poe. Let's dance with the devil. I'll sit here with this pile, and you work over there with your documents. We can do this!"

"I agree. Brilliant plan," she says as she organizes her end of the table.

In the air is an atmosphere, the chipper smell of impending achievement, of fruitful work about to be well done. Reading, even translating, a tale untold for centuries, after all, cannot be *that hard*. Words are but words, especially for experts.

They hone in on the runic tomes before them. Their efforts are soundless, save for occasional shuffling and scrapings, and deep sighs of exasperation and struggle.

From the outside, Hut 11 stands mute, another isolated island of hope battling frustration in Bletchley Park.

Chapter 13

CABLES

—

Strieger stares at the cable from the London attaché's office. Von Ribbentrop himself has sent this, wanting to insure that he receives full credit.

The Führer will be pleased, but, as always, therein is the danger. Every good thing raises the bar, increases the tasks, risks his displeasure. The hunger, the drive of the man is insatiable.

Nonetheless, this information has the potential to sweep past any fickleness. It could easily turn the war before it has started. He knows the die is cast, that the border with Poland will be obliterated. That war with Britain will swiftly follow.

Only American intervention can save England, and now the key to locking that gate is in Streiger's hands. Admiral Donitz will be pleased. The deed will be done. The Führer will be effusive in his praise.

An hour later, the Enigma Machine at Kreigermarine headquarters at Wilhelmshaven, home of the U-boats, is readied. A change of rotors is set and a new codebook section is entered on the keys. The wireless signal flows into the ether. U-99 and U-417 receive it and prepare to take action even as Bletchley Park listens in helpless anguish to another endless, unintelligible string of letters. The transmission is entered into Turing's hapless little assembly of Bombes. Let them cluck and calculate and grind away.

* * *

The *Empress of Atlantis*, late to her rendezvous point, plows through heavy seas. She is slowing dangerously, her crew anxiously scanning the horizon. A lost child in a perilous realm.

From a mile to starboard, the lost child is pinged with a single, brief radio signal, then hailed in Morse code through the flicking shutters of an Ablis long distance signal lamp: "E-M-P-R-E-S-S G-O T-O 1-7-4-J."

The *Empress* corrects her course as her wiser sister, a six-thousand-ton Liberty Ship, vectors toward the rendezvous.

To the stern of both sisters, two different siblings, U-99 and U-417, creep forward. Their periscopes cut the gray seas like the tips of unpraised wolf-tails in a fog-bottomed forest.

* * *

Like many recruited to Bletchley Park in those frantic days, whom legal restraint and history have rendered anonymous, the name of the man newly assigned to Hut 2 and scurrying home this night with a laden briefcase, is remembered in no tale. Whether motivated by greed or grudge, whether he was noble or base, is unknown. He is a cipher. He is also every bit flesh and blood.

He had been to a meeting in London, well across town from the German Embassy, from whence his instructions came. Nothing was written down, nor need it be. He knows exactly where Huts 8, 11, and 13 are.

Chapter 14

DEAD END

—

Uncounted hours later, Tolkien looks up from his work. Yvonne is staring at him from across the length of the table. No words are necessary. Their eyes and dour expressions express the dismal camaraderie of utter frustration, the commiseration of insurmountable challenge and impending failure.

Yvonne covers her mouth in denial, gazes at the table, then says to the air, "This is impossible. We're no different than Alan over in Hut 8."

A phone in the corner, hidden behind a stacked trellis, jangles like a bank alarm. Tolkien searches the room, finds the receiver and fumbles it briefly.

"Hello . . . uh?" He mumbles a bit, then blurts out an officious "Hut 11."

"Mr. Tolkien? You have a call."

A click is followed by a familiar voice, breathless and sounding out of context in these surroundings. "Professor?"

"Timothy? How did . . . ?"

"Never mind that now. I've got rather disturbing news."

Tolkien feels panic-laced adrenaline. His family? Edith sick again?

As usual, Lessons rambles on, ". . . as I say, bad news. Well, sort of. Your office, when I went to return your umbrella and your notes, from the Beowulf lecture, well, the door was ajar. Likely the janitor, I thought. But then I saw scratch marks on the lock. So I think this sorry excuse for a door lock was jiggered. Well, I go in. To tell the truth, everything looks fine."

Tolkien lets out a gentle sigh. "Ah, good."

"Well, not really. Only at first. As I looked around a bit more, I see that things *have* been moved. Ever so little, like they were each picked up, examined, then put back down."

"What in blazes do you mean?"

"Well, I'm trying to tell you. Here's what tipped me off. Your special page, the one you always keep in the front of your proof edition of your *Hobbit* book? That you showed me? The one with your scrawl . . ."

"Yes. Yes. What about it?"

Tolkien knows the page. The moment, almost of revelation, comes back. His hands holding the last blasted booklet of a bloody stack of exams. He is all but finished, the grading done in an exhausting grind over three days. The final page of this final booklet is wonderful: it is blessedly blank. He looks at all the empty space, gently pulls the page out of the booklet, and lets it lie on his desk. He picks up his pen. With no idea what his hand intends, as if whispered by a most fecund muse, he scrawls something he is absolutely sure he has never, ever written before:

> In a hole in the ground,
> there lived a Hobbit.

He feels a sharp pang at the likely loss of the page, at something so . . . central to his creative self. He holds the image until it scatters with Lessons' endless chatter.

"Well, the book was on the floor and the page is missing. So I've checked twice, it's gone. You want me to go over it again?"

"No, not now. One other thing to check. Go to my bookshelf. Left side. Next to the window. Eye level. See the journal, red-bound leather?"

"Yes. Got it."

"Open it."

"Okay, yes, well here's a loose page, a list of names. Let's see. Thomson, Robert; Simmons, Steve; Nowlan, Dennis; Streiger, Jodl."

"Hold there." Tolkien is quiet for a moment.

"Okay, go on."

"Grzesiek, Lynn; Lessons, Timothy. That's me!"

"Quite astute of you. That's my little account of my student assistants over the years. But check the volume itself, all the pages intact?"

"Ah! Yes. Seems so. Lots of strange writing. Words. 'Simarillion . . . Hertegest . . . Valinor'."

"Enough! Now when?"

"Whenever you'd like."

"No, no! When did this happen?" Tolkien, as always, feels a severe case of exasperation in Lessons' presence.

"Oh yes, it must have been on the morning of your lecture. There's more. I took the liberty of talking to the University constable. Together, we talked with the janitor."

There was a pause.

"And? For God's sake, Timothy, move along."

"Two men. One tall, one short with a limp. He, the janitor, saw them in the hallway, almost loitering, he says." Timothy imitates the man with his best cockney brogue ". . . if such could be said of proper gentlemen all attired in expensive coats and hats from the likes of Cheatham Row!'"

Tolkien recalls the two men he'd seen on his way to Bristlethorn Hall. "Well, if nothing else is missing, just make sure the lock is secure. We'll get to it soon enough."

"Right-O."

Tolkien hangs up, rolls his eyes at Yvonne, and returns to the scrolls spread before him.

A brooding silence—not unlike the stillness of a deep forest—again envelopes the room. It settles on them like an ominous fog. Time, devoid of meter or conversation, is displaced as if by a spell. A spell, if such it is, that might continue unbroken forever.

Tolkien, used to feats of scholarly concentration, finally gets a handle on use of the key. Tricky, deliberately confusing in aspects, but decipherable. He is getting better quickly, as if the language has come around, wanting to be uttered and understood. He feels intrepid, boldly pursuing its lead, letting it reveal one more chapter of Ara's Tale:

> For the impertinence of her stealth, the Dark Elves condemned Ara to obscurity.
>
> The greater her deeds, the greater her erasure from history.
>
> For mortals, what is there but the memory of their feats? Few

would proceed in the face of such cruel reward.

To herself, if for none other forever, Ara was a heroine. Slayer of the Dark Lord. And yet a heroine not quit of her impertinence.

Her life having once before been spared—in grudging admiration of her stealthy talents—the Dark Elves suddenly found her again spying upon them, indeed entering their council. She even brought with her that vainglorious boaster, Beowulf, slayer of their cousin Grendel.

Amazing! Thinks Tolkien. He yearns to decipher the rest of the passage, but its complexity will not yield, save a last line:

A curse by the Dark Elves can never be undone. And yet . . .

Tolkien struggles. Is he being led down a false trail?

A chair scrapes. Yvonne gets up, stretches, and says, "I think I found out about Mr. Poe's mysterious stone."

Tolkien is absorbed. He doesn't look up.

She puts on her coat. "Helloo! I'm done for now, professor. Going to get some coffee. You?"

He barely stirs. "No, I'm going to stay at this for a while."

As she closes the door behind her, Tolkien's hands begin to shake. They clutch the scroll and key. His mind faces a snarl of twisted logic, twisted branches, twisted intention, all pointing to maddening and deliberate denial! He once again is stalled, and his attention dissipates like an angry man fatigued and lost on a bleak highland.

The blunt truth is, *One who wanders may well be . . . probably is . . . lost.* He is being trifled with something unseen. And thievery is occurring at his office, behind his back! Someone important, perhaps his Mum, must have once told him, "Don't just sit there. Get mad! Get up! Shake the basket!"

And with that voice in his head, something in the professor snaps.

Chapter 15

THE SHARD

—

Lying at Yvonne's end of the table, unnoticed by Tolkien, is a commentary composed long ago by a predecessor in the line of stewards of these inscrutable lays:

Although it is today but a tumbledown of sheep sheds and seep-ponds, the original village of Frighten was renowned for three things. First, the immense gourds that grew from its deep soil. These often exceeded the size, not to mention the capacity, of a man-styled ox cart. Most famous of these, of course, was the legendary Johnny Squanto, from whence came tales that terrify children to this day. Second, it was the home of Aragranessa Flameleaf. Ara, the heroine-savior of the Third Age and, some say, the author of its doom. Lastly, least known and liked least, was the creation of *Readra-Stánas*.

The act of scrying, a tradition since earliest times, often used an object, preferably an artifact of lineage, such as a crystal, or a finely polished sword-blade, or else a medium, such as a vessel filled with sacred waters. The scrying party would claim to see into the past and present, travel across distance and time, and, most importantly, foretell what was yet to be. Crop success or failure, murder, plague, war, betrayal. All could be discovered. The payment of a tithing to the surveyor husbanding such devices would engender from them claims as sincere and credible as a midnight declaration of coming sunrise.

In Frighten, to return to the story, a tradition of crafting *Readra-Stánas* grew to enjoy wide esteem. At first these objects were reviled as cheap, inert imitations of the *Palantiri,* the seeing-stones wielded by Wizards and Elves.

In a world where a surfeit of written languages had become a burden to communication and commerce, where the featherweight of the meaning of a word could at times move a Kingdom's fate, and easily outweigh the value of a trunk of gold, the *Readra-Stánas* came into their own. They could, by means and process now lost to us, enable the surveyors to know the meaning, the true import of words written in foreign tongues. Scores of these were created, of variable shape and color. Sometimes they were fashioned of crystal with tints that mimicked the autumn colors of the Frighten landscape.

With the Final Scattering of the Halflings, the art was lost, and the stones become forgotten oddities. Some say a few examples survived, to be discovered leagues or lands away, perhaps occupying the mantle in an obscure inn, gathering dust along with other curiosities.

One surviving stone, named by men Leasbregda, The Trickster, was associated with Ara's legend. It was deemed dangerously false, purposeful in its deception, somehow related to the Dark Elves. In its interior was a creature, a scorpion or spider that looked as perfect as if frozen in ice. At times, however, it seemed to move. By gazing through the stone, one could seemingly translate the written words of a foreign tongue. In the chaos of the Scattering, it was said to have been destroyed by Ara herself, or at her direction, its shards tossed in fields and lakes surrounding Frighten.

Had Tolkien seen this commentary, it would not have deflected him from his path, down which he is bulling like an enraged aurochs.

As he hoists the trunk over his head, it is much heavier than he anticipates. His voice has become an other-being, an animal sound of exertion. Something he has never heard from himself. With the strength of unsettled frustration he holds it aloft, flips it over, and dumps its contents on the table.

The documents spill, sprawl, slide and scrunch into an avalanche of disorder. They are like creatures, unmoving as yet, though something in Tolkien's mind won't rule that out. They project an almost tangible air of insult.

Which is petrol cast unto the bonfire of his frustration. He turns the trunk upright and slams it down on the table, sending more documents cascading away. *Yes.* He peers down into the trunk.

Empty as the looted tomb of Balin.

Except . . .

A bulge, perhaps always obscured by the trunk's contents, or perhaps just now shaken loose with his slamming, lies deep in one corner. He shoves the trunk across the table, spilling documents on the floor, to get a better light. Then, slowly, he lets his hand descend.

* * *

Yvonne is sitting on the edge of Alan's desk. Her hand traces an idle figure among the green flimsies scattered there. He maneuvers a slide rule along the same path, following her lead. The two of them are silent but obviously in communication. They look up and the moment evaporates as Fleming barges into the room.

"Ah, where's our kindly professor?" asks Fleming, as if she counts for nothing.

Her mood is broken, replaced by a moment of revelation: she is sick of men. Men who are always too much man, or, not enough man. Never just right. "I'm not sure," she cuts. "He's too deep into his little boy storybooks."

Fleming sets his mouth, stares at her.

"Alright. I left him back at the hut. I'm afraid stories, his, ours, this Ara's, won't be much help to us. Want to know one more thing that's bothering me?"

"Of course." Fleming tries hard not to show condescension.

"That prig Lindbergh is mouthing off everywhere. Celebrity makes him an expert on world affairs. Real world heroines, meanwhile, get ignored, erased, if you will. Amelia's been missing since 1937, disappeared. They left her out there."

Turing leans back, looks at Fleming. "Your bailiwick, old boy, you handle this one."

Yvonne continues. "The Japanese are holding her captive, I know. She's a pawn. And somebody . . . somebody around here knows the truth!"

Fleming is surprisingly earnest. "I agree. Wish I knew the facts there. I'm not popular in Hut 6, the Jap Codes boys, er, team. You try them?"

She shakes her head, frustrated.

"I'll tell you more," he says. "Heroines like Amelia Earhart are tolerated, but often disfavored in this world. Too often their fate is simply to be a tale unfinished, or worse, forever untold."

* * *

Ripping the fragile cloth lining in the trunk, Tolkien's hand grasps something and then withdraws it. As he opens his hand, he sees a shard of broken glass. Smooth and round on one side, edges sharp as obsidian on the serrated underside. He hefts it. It feels as inert as a porcelain paperweight. *Just a broken bottle bottom!* he hrrumps.

And yet, as he turns this accidental bauble in his hand, there is a glint, a hint, a nuance of depth. The light that reflects through it seems oddly changed. He holds it up to the overhead light, then brings it to his eye. There . . . there! Something . . . deep inside. More than an image. He studies it from various angles, finding the best view into its depths.

Preserved, more perfectly than in any amber, is a spider. Intact, almost alive. Its tiny hairs, its unholy set of arachnid eyes, its sharp pincers. As he shifts his view, he senses that it is also regarding him. Guarding. Watching.

He blinks and catches an after-image of the spider running, jiggling out of his vision. He jumps, holding the shard away, sure that he will discover the spider has exited the glass and is scrambling up his arm.

Nothing. He looks back, but there is no sign of it. It has perhaps retreated into the depths of light and shadow that go on and on, that now bear resemblance to nothing other than the floor of a deep forest. He can feel the immersion, the glass sucking him in. He resists, trying to deflect his view but is stopped as some angle reveals a man from the back. There is an odd light, like fog on a sunny day. The man wears a tall officer's hat and a black leather military coat. Tolkien hears a voice, sharp, acute in its perfection of English. The voice wears power and threat comfortably. It becomes clearer, vaguely familiar, exquisitely perfect in its rendition of a passage from *Richard II*:

> Against the envy of less happier lands!
> This blessed plot . . . this earth . . . this realm . . .
> this . . . England.

The man's attitude of cynicism surrounds the last word, as evident as his face is unseen.

The image dissipates into a foreboding gloom. Tolkien wants no further part. Panicked, he averts his vision, but it is too late to escape.

His mind falls fully into the realm of the glass shard.

Chapter 16

DREAMS BEGET DREAMS

—

Tolkien's long, dreamy fall is arrested as he crashes through a mesh of tree branches and lands on a forest floor. The branches continue to tear at his arms and face. His senses are alive and exquisitely tuned. The air is moist. It reeks of wood and fungus and moss, a world long since gone to decay.

He fights the lattice of branches. Like obstinate beasts, they grapple with his hands. Grip upon grip. Each shifting for advantage. Squirming and rending his flesh with their rough bark. They are inexorably closing around him.

He knows he will lose this wrestling match. These barked fingers will soon tire of their demonic play and go for his throat. Through the groping branches, he sees the outline of a gate. The ancient rune-covered type he knows so well. A secret gate. As always, he will go through it. To the cursed replay of the Somme? He heaves himself forward, pushes through the gate, and careens into a massive tree. But for his gasping like a wheezing fire-bellows, the world here seems quiet and sill. The trunk, next to which he lies, stretches ever higher and disappears into an obscuring canopy.

For a moment he stays there. His breath settles and he looks about. Across from him, all but invisible in her concealment, is a halfling female. Her intelligent eyes are boring into him, her admonishing finger held upright across her lips. Somehow, he knows this world.

This is Aragranessa. This is Mirkwood.

Her eyes instruct him to look right, and he sees the object of her espionage. Just beyond the thinning expanse of the trees is a small clearing, centered by a fire that flickers and casts huge, over-wrought shadows. Surrounding the fire are uncommon examples of common vermin: stoats, jackals, raccoons, ring-tailed cats, ferrets, weasels, moles, foxes, rats, squirrels, forest hares.

He sees a huge possum, whispering to a wily raccoon.

The hares, with tall, upright ears, stand next to a ring-tailed cat with immense eyes of iridescent yellow. A great black squirrel looks around pensively. Rats are there, of a size and ferocity to empty a medieval village. They are arrayed around a singular figure, a fox standing upright. Soon they are engaged in a Babel-like exchange of squeaks, chirps, rabbit-foot thumps, squawks and hisses, all punctuated by brief, eerie whistles. Whether song, argument, or the casting of a spell, Tolkien cannot tell.

By a nod of her head and stern eyes, Ara commands him to look behind him, deeper into the forest. There, hidden from view from the clearing, stands a group of men huddled about a robust leader. A proud man, yet clearly one in the thrall of Ara. They wait in her reserve.

By his raiment and manner, his broadsword, his helm with crest of boar-bristles, Tolkien knows well the legendary Beowulf when he sees him in flesh and blood.

Tolkien looks back to Ara but she is gone. In a moment she has moved to the clearing, where she is presenting herself to the startled council.

The animals scramble, many shape-shifting into more threatening creatures, badgers and bears. Ara is undeterred and steps fully into the firelight, her small figure captured in lonely silhouette.

Almost out of earshot, Tolkien strains to hear her speaking. The standing fox moves to confront her. Tolkien hears the word *jötocun,* and trembles. He knows of this thing that stands before Ara. It is almost certainly an incarnation of the Crafty and Malicious One. Son of a giant known for cruelty, father of monsters. Described as far back as the Icelandic Eddas and the earliest Germanic lays. A promiscuous shape-shifter. Devourer of the hands of gods.

Loki.

While Tolkien cannot see him clearly, he knows the mouth that speaks to Ara bears hideous scars. Remnants of stitches once commanded by the gods.

Tolkien is mystified. What could impel her to stalk this monster, leave behind her stewards, and walk up alone to face him?

The answer is lost to this moment. Tolkien feels his body, his soul drop slightly.

He opens already-open eyes. Mirkwood, the dream, is gone. He is in prosaic old Hut 11. His hand slipping as a sleep-crutch for his head. The ruins of his tantrum, the emptied trunk, the whirlwind-debris of scattered documents, the glass shard, are before him. Through the window he sees a faint tint of blue in the east.

On the table is also a pen and paper, on which evidently he has been drooling. Fortunately, this is something he never does, and, unfortunately, it suggests to the moment some deep level of extremis. He feels like a haunted somnambulist. On top of the pile is a page of notes, dank, written in his own hand. He has absolutely no recollection of writing anything. Even as the brooding Mirkwood of a few moments ago is receding from him, he feels the empty, used-up malaise sometimes described by those subjected to its spell.

He reads the notes, as if from a stranger and seen for the first time. They are fragmentary, a translation effort by an amateur. They further a story he recognizes:

> . . . save for a flitting light of fame in her own mortal time, the greatest heroine of Middle-earth was to remain forever erased from the memory of all mortals, with one perverse exception: her life might be recorded in the demonic language of the Dökkálfer, the Dark Elves. Yet even that history would be persecuted and harassed into oblivion by the inheritors of this world, men and their meddlesome wizard-allies.
>
> Brave men and women, unsung, their names and fates forgotten, would steward and preserve these obscure lays.
>
> With luck and long years, perhaps the remnant tales of Ara would be read again.

An insistent pounding rattles the door.

Like a wound-up jack-in-the-box, Tolkien vaults out of his chair. He takes a mind-clearing inhalation, scurries across the room, and opens the door. Turing is standing there, alone and breathless. In his hand is a single sheet of green flimsy which he waves as he barges in.

"By God, I can make these machines work!"

Despite the disarray of the documents, which Tolkien has himself created, he feels a moment of possessive anger as Turing splays his sweaty hands and the flimsy across the fragile, rune-filled pages and translation scrawls.

"We intercepted signals from an armed German trawler off Norway. An amateur, a fool for our benefit, was at the Enigma keyboard. We recognized his slovenly work, always signing with the same seven-digit name. We had previously guessed that it was his girlfriend. These are three hundred relatively common girl names in German, of which seventy-four have seven letters. A small task to find it: Ludwiga. Admiral Donitz would have his balls. No U-boat operator would make that mistake. The margins are always where the mistakes happen. Anyway," Alan gasps a quick breath, unable to slow down. "We quickly got a fuller crib of knowns: *August 31, 1939*, and *Heil Hitler!* Then the fool forgets to encrypt his message as he sends it, stops, goes back and restarts the whole message with the encryption in effect. We thus have a huge set of knowns and I let the Bombes do their work. We broke yesterday's code within hours, and listened in on their U-boat directions. You were right with your . . . what was it? Ah, yes, *Palantir* idea, Tolkien. For just a moment, we looked right into the mind of the enemy!"

Turing takes a breath and looks down at his paper. "The most interesting thing is this!" He leans over, eagerly reading his discovery as if the room was short of oxygen:

> From: Admiral commanding U-boats
> To: U99 and U417
>   Naval attaché Washington [lost] impending departure of convoy [lost] from Halifax. HMS Empress of Atlantis, 6000 tons sector AM 23, will join at last moment, bearing high-level American official.
>   Shel . . .

Here it's lost again—maybe 'lby' or 'lton'—three, maybe four letters anyway. Whoever or whatever it is, the message goes on.

> You are directed to locate and shadow the vessel. Upon declaration of war sink the Empress at all costs without regard

to other targets. Ensure no survivors. The Führer will personally decorate the captain that sinks the Empress with the Ritter Kreuz to the Iron Cross. Good hunting [lost] advance congratulations. Defeat England.

"Oh my God!" The gasp behind them is pained, as of one pierced by a sword. They turn and see Yvonne. From her open hand a thermos of coffee falls to the floor like a ponderous bomb. The inner core shatters and the glass and liquid mix in a disturbed gurgle as it rolls across the floor.

She staggers back. "They're talking about my father! I'm sure!"

Alan, caught unawares, stumbles. "Oh! Can't be. I didn't put it all together. Listen, the name is surely off. Shelton. Sherman, Hellman. Who knows? We extrapolated some. How could it . . .?"

"Because my birthday is next week and he's Roosevelt's main ally!" She pauses.

They look at her as if weighing her non sequitur.

"I've got a feeling . . . He's been quiet, like he does when he's going to pull surprises. He loves surprises . . . and he refuses to fly!"

There is no answer that can respond to this.

She gathers her thoughts, asks bravely, "How long does it take to cross the Atlantic?"

Tolkien is still foggy, but he remembers Fleming's warnings. He stands mute, as they talk.

"I'm guessing," Turing mutters, "but I'd say what with assembling the convoy and escorts, the rendezvous, six or seven days to reach England."

"And if the *Empress* left yesterday?"

"Well, there is no war. Yet. The papers say German troops are massed at the Polish border. If they cross, the dominos will fall quickly."

"And the *Empress* will be a fair prize?"

"I'm afraid so."

She puts on her courage-face, struggling to play it off. She gestures to the table, trying to comprehend the mess. "Look, Alan, these documents . . ." They can see her tears. ". . . the . . . the professor and I have been working . . ." She catches her breath, ". . . really hard . . . on them."

Turing cuts her off. "No reason to worry. I'm sure we've got it wrong." He peers again at the flimsy, studying it as if it had betrayed him. "I'll go check on that spelling."

She is not there. Hand on her mouth, she has already fled the room. Tolkien looks at Fleming, shakes his head in resignation, and says to the air, "First bloody steps into Mirkwood."

Chapter 17

A RETURN

—

It was said of old that the birth of a dragon could be felt for miles, across ragged mountain ranges and deepening fjords, as a sense of foreboding. An unease, not quite audible, hovering at the threshold of perception. Dogs would whine and chase their tales, cats would climb trees to irrevocable heights, and men of good nature would contemplate villainy.

This day, when it arrives, cracks open like a dragon's egg. Strange-hued clouds boil forth to tinge a reluctant sun. The dawn feels disturbed and unnatural.

When Tolkien arrives at Bletchley, Yvonne is nowhere to be found. He takes a biscuit and cheese from the BP Canteen and sits alone in Hut 11. Not a proper post-breakfast, but par for a fitful day. A courier soon delivers a note, which reads:

> Professor, sorry for my outburst. I will have myself together tomorrow. I have arranged a meeting at 1500 to discuss our strange collection. Some things I haven't told you about yet. Hope you got some sleep. We're going to need it.
>
> Yvonne

Tolkien dithers with straightening up his mess. He wanders through various scrolls, casually scanning for meaning. Nothing. Desultory, deadening, nothing. As profound a non-message as the deepest wooded glen waiting for a tree to fall, for the metaphysical question with no answer to be asked.

So be it, he thinks. *Let the forest wait.*

Which of course, it obliges only long enough to put him off his guard. He leans back and starts to read the war alarms on the front page of *The Guardian*.

Comfortably shifted just so, he rustles up the paper and holds it out to let his middle-aged eyes focus. They insist upon a more distant vision. Damn! There, before him, on the floor in the corner, is one of the hand-scrawled papers he had drooled upon a wrecked and wretched day ago. On it are the words that had flowed out as if they were his own. He gets up, picks it up, and begins to read. He senses that the words are but a fragment, perhaps portraying an earlier moment in Ara's chronicle:

> In this failed world, much has been lost. With destruction of the evil named "Bind," danger and malice yet survive. They lurk, they reside in many forms, they are malevolent and patient.
>
> Hear now the tale of Ara, greatest of the now-unspoken heroines of Middle-earth. Bound she is for her home village of Frighten.
>
> That most formidable of obstacles, the bottomless reservoir of confusion, again lies across her path.
>
> Myrcwudu.
>
> Before her are its first shadowy eaves.
>
> A small horse, quick and agile, carries her. It is of a kind that would be ridden in later times by the Halfling Border Guards. Tapestries illustrate still how the Guards met their fate at the last stand before the Final Scattering, that marked the end of the beginning of the Fourth Age.
>
> The age that saw the erasure of Ara's existence.
>
> But ours is a story of an earlier time, when victory was still fresh, and the wordwrights that sought to chronicle Ara's Tale had not been silenced.
>
> Halting before those first claw-like branches, she remembers the fears of the year before. The terror of being captured by the Wraith Pazal, of escaping from the ill-fated council of men with the Dark Lord. Her journey as a lost pilgrim entering into the despair of this Great Forest of

Doubt. A place old beyond time, brooding in its depths.

Now, having achieved great feats, having crossed twice the peaks of Everdivide, she is back. Accompanying her are folk of legend—Ringbearers and their companions. And she has one last mission: to find and confront the weasel-faced trickster. The author of her curse.

It is he who speaks, "Do not lurk in the shadows, Ara the Conqueror. Come before us."

So much lore about this curse. To what end?

Tolkien remembers a different end: that he has an appointment to get his identification badge. Spy or not, he may someday need it. He places the pages on their proper stack, refolds the newspaper, and heads for the mansion.

Nothing better than a solid errand to get one back on sound cobblestones, thinks Tolkien. *Away from that calamitous, phantasmagoric forest!*

Chapter 18

MIRROR, MIRROR

—

At 1600 hours, approximately, because it is Bletchley time, Hut 11 is crowded. And dead quiet.

Fleming, Turing, Tolkien, and Shelby are standing in a loose circle. They are like perplexed surgeons, stumped as to the diagnosis of a fragile patient.

The patient—trunk, scrolls, letters—was the day before a disaster of spillage. It now lies dismembered on the table. The oldest scrolls, written in what Tolkien firmly calls "Dark Elvish," lie in one group. Many of them are charred and heat-warped. Next to them is a clutter of vellum sheets, also ravaged, scribed in Old English and related Germanic hands. An odd scrap of rough leather with even odder writing sits on top.

Flanking these is a selection of writings modern in both physical appearance and discernible English language. The letter from Poe tops this pile.

The trunk rests, alone and empty, at one corner.

Lastly, and sitting by itself in the center is the patient's heart. The Key.

Not on the table, in fact severed from the corpus and hidden in Tolkien's pocket, is the shard of glass.

Each of the attending experts bears a distinct facial expression. Fleming, the tireless manipulator, is searching for an angle, a strategy to empower this hopeless assemblage. Turing is frowning, distracted. He has other matters, bloody critical matters that are also in a forlorn state.

Yvonne, superficially recovered and now thoroughly professional in her focus, exchanges sober, unsmiling glances with Tolkien. She covers her nose and mouth. Unlike the tobacco-addicted men around her, she has an extraordinary sense of smell.

Can't they smell it? Not just the oldness, but the residual musk of fear and desperate flight. These documents have meant death and destruction to prior stewards.

Tolkien is biting his lip, head bowed. His arms clutch his chest and his chin nests on one fist. He's the lead physician here and his look is dismal. The gulf, between the physical reality of these strange artifacts and their dimly perceived meaning, is a staggering abyss.

Yvonne cuts through the tomblike stillness, "Gentlemen, we are all in a dark fog. I've got an idea. In fact, I've got a great idea. Leave your stuff here, grab your coats, lock the door, and meet me at the mansion in ten minutes. We're going somewhere. She hesitates. Then adds, "That includes you, Alan, Your Grumpiness."

* * *

The lights dim and Tolkien smiles, savoring the moment.

The darkness, the anticipation, the shared communion, the moment of immersion.

If Fleming thought in such terms he would, of course, say, ah yes, *sex!* Tolkien, however, would hold true for something more meaningful: that hoped-for glimpse of *faerie*, of an other-world.

Yvonne is next to Alan, a current running between them. Fleming senses it, ponders cynically whether it is direct, or more like Tesla's alternating current.

The four of them are, after all, sitting together in a row at the Strand Theatre in downtown Bicester.

The celluloid frames begin to flicker upon the screen. A disturbing overview of the present as Lowell Thomas intones soberly for Movietone News. Adolf Hitler is reviewing the Kreigsmarine fleet. The Führer salutes from a perch on the bow of the massive new battleship *Scharnhorst.* He is framed by a giant Nazi flag rippling in the breeze. At another point, he makes an odd flourish to remove his hat to enter a bulkhead and wipe his brow.

Tolkien studies the face. Trim the wings of the mustache, add twenty years, and there you have it. This is quite possibly the *Meldenganger,* the German messenger Tolkien met in the convoluted trenches of the Somme. The man had made infrequent cameos in

Tolkien's own inner newsreel, his recurring dream sequence of those grim times. Now Tolkien wonders, *Should I have taken that life? Given up my own?*

The moment evaporates as, on the big screen, the RKO Tower emits zig-zag radio signals, introductory credits toll, and the orchestra cues to a waltz. An animated storybook appears. Its pages magically turn.

Once upon a time . . .

Yvonne looks down the row to see Turing, Fleming, and Tolkien. All three grown men, even Alan, are rapt. She sees the light dance like fairy dust across Tolkien's shining eyes.

Ninety minutes later, as they exit The Strand, they cluster below the unlit marquee. It reads "Special Return Showing: Snow White and the Seven Dwarfs." They talk excitedly among themselves.

Fleming is in a playful mood. "What say you, Master Tolkien, 'dwarfs' or 'dwarves'? Who's right, you or Walt?"

As they begin to walk, four abreast, Tolkien answers. "With all credit to Mr. Disney, whose genius I admire with reservation, I find this: he has no interest in fidelity to the past. He ably puts together a fun story, not a myth. A myth has roots, it sprouts leaves. It is part of the great Tree of Tales. So, the answer is simple: if "elves" is the plural for "elf," which it is, then it follows that *dwarves* is the correct plural form for 'dwarf!'"

Even Turing is now amused at Tolkien's flash of enthusiasm. Fleming continues the fun. " I disagree. The Americans have gotten the King's English right for once. Let the Oxford Dictionary settle it?"

Tolkien, having once worked on that tome, doesn't take the bait. "Hardly, Ian, and this is why." He gestures grandly, his arms spread. "It may be bad philology, but my choice *sounds* more authentic. Unless, of course, you want the true ancient form, which was 'dwarrows.' A tad cumbersome. In any case, when in doubt, trust your ear." He pauses collecting a thought, "I really should expand on this at some point."

They advance down the sidewalk, a phalanx of lively conversation. Turing joins in. "Professor, you sound like someone who is desperate to get something done."

Tolkien nods his head, takes a deep breath. "If I could but muster the joy I used to have, the pleasure of not just writing a tale, but of unearthing, discovering if you will, that which exists independent of our own conceptions."

They all look at him.

A car honks somewhere. Their feet clunk and clatter on the sidewalk, as if carrying on a conversation separate to shoes and pavement. "Whew!" says Yvonne. "You absolutely must visit the propeller-heads over in Hut 13. They also have a rather different take on reality."

Tolkien is undaunted. "If something I write has a real existence, as I used to fancy, then getting it right, like dwarves, is serious business. Such matters are worthy of pondering, this name for a noble race now abandoned to Mr. Disney's fairytales. There at least is buried a shadow of truth." Tolkien pauses. "Unlike the gaudy fun we just observed."

"Now I see your reservations about this Disney chap," Fleming observes. "At least he makes his realm *alive*, a world of vibrant, moving images on a huge screen. Something your stories, and that stale pile of obscure scribbles back at . . . our office, will never see. I'm speaking for your critics, of course, a few of whom reside among your fellow faculty members."

Tolkien smiles archly at Fleming. *That's true, of course.*

Yvonne saves the moment. "So, professor, what sort of truth are *you* seeking?"

"Thank you, young lady. Let me put it this way. Take *dwarrows*. I once thought there survived a glimpse of them, perhaps only in their name. One can piece together from such words a history, the saga of a race of smaller beings with superb rock-hewing skills, and powers deeper still. Powers glowing in their hearts as embers from the ancient forges that opposed . . ." Tolkien tries to catch himself, but it is too late. The word slips out with the tone of a believer. ". . . the Elves."

They are all quiet, but no one rolls their eyes. Fleming offers in a kindly, if still condescending, tone, "Don't let them call you odd, professor. Just keep at it, old chap."

"Quite alright, old boy," Tolkien responds. "By the way, you still let the occultists guide your life, or is it weekly séances now?"

Yvonne is glad they are away from Bletchley and getting to know each other, barbs and all. She steps in front of the three men and stops them with raised palms. "Okay. All this talk of fire and forge needs some drenching. Even quenching." One of her hands points a thumb at the threshold of a darkened pub, not two feet away. She opens the door and the promise is kept: light, sound, warmth, yeasty smells, and a dense cloud of tobacco smoke.

Soon they are huddled in a booth. Above them, stretching a dozen feet along the wall, hangs the resplendent, darkened scull and antlers of an Irish elk, last seen alive centuries ago.

"Pulled out of a bog. A wonder, if you ask me," volunteers the barmaid as she nods upward in response to their gawking.

Soon they are huddled over their pints. Yvonne is sitting next to Turing. He is expounding. "The big chap above us, real bone, tells me of reality. The metaphysics of what you're describing, Master Tolkien, are beyond me. But I am interested in a different aspect about what is real. Reality may be only what we decide to say it is. Take computing machines, which I worked on until this bloody, imminent war came along."

Fleming says, "Ah yes, Alan, is modest as always. Turing here has invented, or at least designed, a machine that, well, thinks. It's called, humbly enough, a Turing Machine."

"Preposterous," cuts in Tolkien, "Now who is being fanciful? I hate machines, granted, but to fancy that one *thinks* is absurd."

Yvonne defends Turing as if he were her man. "Really? At some point, Alan tells me, you won't be able to distinguish a machine's 'thoughts' from those of the human mind."

Turing finishes her thought. "And, thus, for all purposes, it will be as real a sentient being as you and I. Don't let the tubes and wires fool you."

Tolkien grumbles, "So much for the old Divine Spark. Better to have magic and speaking trees than these infernal devices."

Fleming has been watching. He savors his pint, wipes the foam from his lips, and says, "It's not just about checking out the Grimm stories from the library. Let's just say, just for a wild moment, that someone wanted to make a movie of your book . . . your hobbies . . ."

"Hobbits! And don't be silly. The book sales are modest, but quite sufficiently gratifying. I'd rather not have a film projector, a *machine*, rendering my story. Reading and words, preferably spoken aloud as of old, that's the ticket."

"Come on, man, think big! Your reviled friend, Disney, thinks big. Now, your book, a cartoon perhaps? Possibly in color? Up on that screen?"

Turing leans in, "Yes, use some midgets, like that chap just did in *The Wizard of Oz.*"

Before Tolkien can respond, Ian tag-teams. "Your sort of world, eh, Tolkien? Across some threshold in the modern day. A passage. Call it a gate, pathway, wardrobe, or even an errant balloon in a twister, as Kansans say. The portal to Oz. Or a faraway, inaccessible place, Scull Island where King Kong rules and terrorizes the natives."

Yvonne can't resist. "Ah, same with the unknown Himalayas hiding Shangri-La in *Paradise Lost.*"

Turing follows. "Some prefer science, the curse of science, as the portal. Miss Shelly's Victor Frankenstein, or Wells' Dr. Jekyll. Even Verne's Captain Nemo and the *Nautilus*. Not to mention time-travel. Perhaps Monsieur Jules Verne wasn't so fanciful after all."

This, of course, touches upon a topic of interest for Tolkien.

"What do you mean?"

"Just go talk to the Hut 13 guys."

The joke apparently is an inside one, as Yvonne and Alan share a smirk.

Fleming excuses himself and heads for the loo.

Tolkien is fully, finally relaxed. He is in good company that differs from the predictability of his Inklings. This, he realizes, is more like the formative moments with the TCBS.

Fleming returns and slides into the booth next to Tolkien, immediately lighting a cigarette. Custom-made, Morland, like his fictitious character. He plumes smoke, then taps his lighter on the table, convening their attention. "First, a word for our wonderful young lady." He smiles at her. "*You are* a wonder, cheering us up, worrying all the while about your father. I checked just now. They tell me the *Empress* should be all right. Nothing to worry about. That's all I can say. Now, let's discuss these infernal documents. Our superiors want answers, fine, but they also lack imagination. They have no plan. I have a plan."

Yvonne says, "you better hurry up, because Denniston and Philby want a briefing from the professor and me. On where we're at with this project. At the mansion, at 0900 hours tomorrow."

Fleming unveils his plan.

Tolkien listens, then silently plans his tomorrow. With the strength of these new friends, he feels a faint stirring. *Enough to try*, he thinks.

Chapter 19

SEA AND HEAVEN

———

Salt spray lashing his face, Senator Shelby huddles in a windbreak just outside the forecastle cabin of the *Empress of Atlantis*. An icy splash down the collar of his seacoat reminds him somehow of happier times: the rhythm of day-fishing with Yvonne off the Chincoteague, lazy drifts in the estuaries of Mobile Bay.

A mile to starboard, scanning the horizon of high swells, the periscope of U-99 cuts the surface like a shark's fin. In less than a minute she is on the surface.

Shelby cups his hands to light a cigarette. On his right hand, the worn but still gaudy National College Football Championship ring, University of Alabama, 1925, always a sure vote-getter. On his left hand, the worn but solid wedding band, a must-have for public office.

The lighter flares, illuminating his face and hands. He takes a deep drag and plumes out the smoke. *Ah, this should help calm the stomach.*

He looks again at the implacable swells of the northern Atlantic. Starlight reveals the trowels of the immense rollers through which they are steaming. *A cold place to die*, he thinks.

The door to the bridge slides open, a voice cries out from the green-tinged darkness inside. "Care to try your hand at the con, sir?"

Shelby bogarts his cigarette, sending a flurry of sparks into the wind, and ducks into the bridge.

The captain, a Scotsman named McDougal, steps back from the wheel. He offers the till to the mysterious guest. "A clear night, a rolling sea. Another few hours and we should be in the convoy envelope.

Unfortunately, the forecast is for the swells to subside. A flat sea awaits us."

"Wonderful, all around," Shelby says as he gingerly takes the wheel. At once he feels the very guts of the sea, like a living animal fighting the rudder.

The captain laughs through a gallows cough, "Flat seas, sir, are no friend to us. They allow U-boats to see us. Let's them move in and shadow us. Big swells are your friend, even with the uneasy stomach."

Captain McDougal will be one of three hundred merchant marine officers and seamen to perish within the year.

As U-99 yaws on the surface, her con is jammed with five officers peering through binoculars into the glowing night beneath stars so breathtaking, so numerous and cold, as to each be gods. Whether stars or gods, they humble the fleeting efforts of men into pettiness and cosmic insignificance.

The men at the con of U-99 are, however, unimpressed. Let the universe, vast and sublime and uncaring, go its own way. The lives of men are but moments to desperately write their own accounts, in deeds, in blood if necessary.

Now is that moment.

One of them sees a mote of red, an unlikely firefly flicker at the crest of a distant swell. They all focus and soon the night-glow silhouettes the stubby profile of a merchant ship.

Otto Kretschner, the captain, is pleased. It is almost certainly the *Empress*. Alone and lost. He contemplates the risks of taking her now. The formality of declaring war will be complete within a day, perhaps two. He looks around and smiles at his officers. "Clear the bridge. Prepare to dive."

U-99 quietly adjusts her buoyancy and slips beneath the waves, leaving the night to the twinkle and shimmer of infinite gods dancing in a dark heaven.

Chapter 20

A TOOL TOO SHARP

—

Tolkien arises early the next morning. Like a pilgrim, banished and now returning, he takes a deep breath and enters the forbidden realm: his office.

In his hand is a carefully wrapped object. He steps gingerly, as might Beowulf himself upon entering a torch-shadowed cavern in which lurks great peril.

He sits at his desk and places a clean sheet of paper in his Remington. He squares his shoulders and sets his mind to . . . create. Long minutes pass. The blank page remains a void, whispering disturbing mutterances. A trackless non-place into which his muse has fallen.

His head drops, cradled in his hands. Despair and guilt, muse-destroying demons, swirl about him.

How did this happen? he thinks.

He knows these wonderful beings, Bilbo and Frodo and the rest, were once alive to him. Now they are wooden. Middle-earth was once as vibrant as billowing, epic clouds coloring from yellow to red with the sunset, as sensuous as the thunder-crack of a summer storm. It all beckoned him.

Looking up, Tolkien feels the full price of his despair. The foundation stones of his cathedral of belief will not be still. They shudder and move. The fire of his creative conviction sputters but will not rekindle. His Tale of the Ring will be as a scattering of bandit leaves in a cold November wind. His pledge to his long-dead Fellows, the

TCBS, will fail.

To add insult, the stinging words of his critics mock him: "Mr. Tolkien's book is about what? 'Hobbits.' Oh? Really. It's all fairy stories, fit enough as childlike nonsense."

He places the object on the desk, then carefully unwraps it. One of the scrolls. He unfurls its first turn and sees, once again, the clever language that has begrudgingly revealed to him the story of Ara.

His voice, unbidden, mumbles into the room. "If I cannot in some way believe this heroine's tale—written by hands that surely believed in it as much as the bards who sang of Beowulf, or as did blind Homer himself recounting the feats of Odysseus and Achilles at the gates of Troy—then I am no better than my own critics. Critics that I passionately despise."

He methodically rewraps the scroll, gets up, and leaves the room. The blank sheet of paper stays, a bitter white flag of surrender. One segment of a colorless wall of mist that obscures the stalking dragon of disbelief.

He prepares for the ride to Bletchley, promising himself that even with his loss of belief in that other-world there is still work to do in this one. *This time,* he thinks, *this new Fellowship shall endure. I will not fail it.*

* * *

It is 0900 hours plus thirty.

The meeting at the mansion is not going well.

Denniston and Philby are looking at Tolkien as if he were a mental patient about to be taken away. His attempts to describe his experience in translating the strange language seem futile.

"I've . . . I've come to believe . . . it appears that this . . . language, is from an . . ."

"Out with it, man!" Denniston commands.

". . . an ancient race. What I always imagined elves to be like."

Up go their eyebrows.

"They," he continues, "this language, is diabolical. Meanings flow and shape-shift, as if revealing a path, only to be taken away. All in the same moment."

Philby picks up one of the charred vellum pages and looks at it, as if to figure out how such convoluted markings could bring the esteemed and eminently rational man before him to such an incoherent rant. "It's obvious," he says, "that this material is a too-sharp sword. If even you, professor, are confused. If it causes this kind of . . . anxiety."

Denniston won't let it go so easy. "So, what exactly does it say?"

"It is, at least on the surface, a story of a heroine. In a world called *mit-gard* by those who lived in it. Middle-earth in modern English. A bounded, yet vast and wild expanse. Her name is Ara."

"Who?"

"Apparently an ancient heroic figure. A female. Of a small and obscure race. Aragranessa Flameleaf."

By their looks, he knows they think he has utterly cracked, but he keeps talking. "At first they, these words, seem like a lyrical day-song. But they are in truth a night-rending thunderstorm. They drown out all other thoughts. They put the mythical sirens to shame!"

His eyes glossed like unwashed windows, Tolkien stares at the page of scrawled writings in his hand. He is dimly aware of his location. Hut 11? At the table. Notepad. Writings in front of him.

No! No! He is here at the Bletchley mansion. The big room. Denniston, Philby, and Yvonne all watching him.

He blinks and squints, forcing refocus.

The markings before him are as foreign as the scratch-runes of some last race of Wild Men, as familiar as his own heartbeat. They are his own. Written by his hand, and yet, he admits, he has no memory of them. He thinks about his cynicism toward occultists and mediums. His sentiments suddenly seem misdirected, even naïve.

His eyes cast downward, he says, "Let me share with you what I . . . last translated, just to give you the flavor." He does not pause as he reads the words aloud:

> Ara's Curse, as it came to be known, was visited upon her by Loki himself. Still furious at her uncanny stealth, he pronounced:
>
> "Your feats, *sneaking* chief among them, are over. Your history, all tales of your vain heroism, will be erased. Just as autumn leaves scatter in fragments before the harsh gales of time.
>
> "Those who may seek to secret away some bit of your history, or, worse yet, discern the meanings of our language, shall suffer a fate at one measure with their hubris, their over-

deep delving. They shall inhale the molded mists of Mirkwood, and thereby be infected with its contagion of Doubt. Tread not there, delve not into Ara's tale."

"Now," says Tolkien, "here is the most interesting part."

Philby interrupts, "Are you really translating something, or indulging more of your own stories. We have a war to fight, professor, and we've no ti—" Denniston lays a hand on Philby's shoulder. They step away. As might consulting psychiatrists, they mumble together amid weighty hums and nods. The matter decided, they return.

Philby begins. "The benefit of the doubt I give to you, professor. This . . . language whatever it is, whatever its fascinating heritage, is not a tool of value in this war. By your account, it cuts everyone, even very smart people, who try to immerse themselves in it. A bag of words for loonies, not an article of weaponry."

The meeting ends abruptly. Tolkien walks from the mansion back to his hut. Yvonne has lingered behind. She catches up to give him the bottom line. "They're shutting us down! Taking it all away and shipping it off to some remote warehouse, far from any likely bombing zone. There it will get lost for another century. Maybe forever." She pauses, "Pity."

Tolkien reflects for a moment. "So what is lost, then, with Fleming's, our, absurd plan?"

"Everything, or nothing. It all depends."

"On what? For God's sakes, they are going to order us!"

"Until then? We make ready for Ian's plan. Look, they'll not miss any of it. You decide what pieces to keep. You have any energy left? Go back to the hut and make some decisions. I'll follow in a bit. Now go! Scoot!"

Tolkien hurries away, in fact *scoots*, as he ponders what it's like to violate the Secrecy Act, not to mention take professional orders from a woman.

Chapter 21

MEN AND WOMEN

—

At 1400 hours, Yvonne jangles the key in the lock to Hut 11, and calls out, "Hello professor. Sorry I'm late. You there? Making progress?"

Once inside, she pauses. She slams the door behind her. Arms crossed, she leans back, feeling the thin plywood give, studying the room. Her intuition says transgressions have occurred and she will not be happy. Even in advance of knowing all the sins, a mental sign flashes the bottom line: *Enough Is Enough!*

Now to the tally.

Her keen sense of smell takes the next measure: her nose crinkles with the acrid tang of charred tobacco. Beneath this lurks a deeper malodor, the stale-mouth, old-dentures smell of a spittled pipe left unattended and uncleaned. Annoying.

Her eyes quickly discover the source and the even greater sin. Tumbled onto the precious documents, from a careless perch on an ashtray, sprawls Tolkien's familiar burlwood. Its dottle is scattered all about, the vellum pages marked by a spray of fresh singe marks.

Eyes flashing, she marches to the table and reluctantly tweezers her fingers around the pipe stem. She holds it up with disgust, as one might regard an odd-shaped stink bug.

The door behind her swings open. Tolkien swoops in with a flourish of good cheer, humming contentedly. He has a lunch sack from the commissary in hand. He closes the door with happy deliberation and then sees her.

She is holding the stinkbug aloft for him to see, her eyebrows lifted in accusation. Tolkien can't help the impression; her glare makes her look like an insufferable schoolmarm. His wits tell him what a man should do. "Oh, my God! So sorry! How careless of me. Here let me help!" He rushes up and fusses, dusting away the tobacco.

She will have none of it. "Now, you sit! Forget your endless lunches. I want you to listen!"

Tolkien is taken off-guard. "I beg your pardon?" He sits, nonetheless.

Yvonne wastes no time. "Now that I've just possibly gotten you in a guilty mood professor, I want to have a frank conversation. About us. What do you think about women?"

He sputters and fidgets. "Well . . ."

"No, come on, no weaseling out." she says. "Just pretend I'm one of your tweedy, smoke-stinky pals, and we're all in our cups with frothy pints at an all-men's club, and I just asked you the same question."

Tolkien knows what this calls for: the deep breath before the plunge. "Well, if you want the truth, you have to indulge me." Maneuvering for mental space, he picks up his treasured pipe, takes out his pen knife, and begins the almost-holy ritual. "The first thing, if you must know, is that I believe in hierarchies and differences. The races, dwarves, elves, men, all have both."

He studiously inspects the cleaned pipe bowl, as if were a fount of further wisdom. "Now, as to women . . ."

Out comes the tobacco pouch, tediously unrolled.

". . . they are companions in a shipwreck, not guiding stars."

Yvonne leans against the wall, hands stuffed in her pockets, unimpressed.

"And to be direct, Miss Shelby, women can achieve remarkable insight, even outside their . . . range."

Her eyes narrows to slits.

Tolkien's fingers pinch tobacco and fill the pipe bowl. Pinch. Deposit. Pinch.

"How quickly women can excel at the tutoring hand of a man, and then when his influence is removed, cease their progress."

Tap, tap, goes Tolkien's index finger as he taps the bowl. *Tap, tap* goes Yvonne's left foot, a metronome of annoyance, as she increases its tempo.

"... a man has his work, his career. A woman has her home and ..."

Tolkien strikes a match. Flare and a lighting. A smugly contented first puff and exhalation.

Across from him Yvonne is a lit fuse edging toward the dynamite.

"... and the bottom drawer. So, you see ..."

The dynamite explodes. She steps toward him, arm extended, finger pointing at his face. "You are truly an ass! And a cad! A masculine version of a coward. In this world of men and women, you are not, sir, a hero!"

Tolkien puts down his pipe. "And women, I say, are ill-suited for heroism, at least of the epic kind. The kind that entails a great journey and a quest."

"You should look at yourself—in the mirror if necessary—and be ashamed. What are you, mid-forties? And so set in your clubby ways. You are, in a word, antiquated. Your Edwardian shows, Master Tolkien, and a new age is dawning. You, the bloody British Empire, and this attitude towards women, will not survive unchanged."

He leans back, seeking in mind and demeanor to recover the inflated air, the labored deductions, the cloaked security, of a pompous academic. It's no use. That refuge is lost for now. He'll have to deal with this woman on her own terms. He glowers at her from a place far removed from his comfort zone.

She continues, "Have you ever even had a real woman friend?"

"To be truthful, no."

"Edith?"

"She is ... let me put it this way: at one with a character in one of my stories. Luthien. A dancer in the glen of my dreams, a fellow orphan, a cornerstone of me."

"I don't doubt your love for her. She shares your faith?"

"Not so much. She resents my devotion."

"Maybe she's right. Christianity has done no great favors for women."

"We all have our place."

"Bloody rubbish, as you folks say. Do you *dare*—just once—to look in that glass I hold up? What kind of world has no heroines? All your school boy games. No wonder your world feels off! In a way, it's right there in front of you. If you believe Beowulf is, in some sense, real, then so is Ara. And vice versa."

The fact of his discouragement, his Grendel of disbelief, is now four-square in front of him.

"Which is it?"

The moment floats like a messaged bottle in a long, rolling sea.

Tolkien often thinks in imagery, in a world where he is every bit *Baggins, Bilbo Baggins.* He sees himself ascending a mighty tree in deepest Mirkwood, clambering up to get a true perspective. He tops the thick canopy and feels the breezes of clean air and clear thinking. A meandering river twinkles in the far distance as he considers Yvonne's voice. A moment ago, it was that of a harpy. Now her words, having made their mark, invite a cathartic glimpse of something unexpected: strength, power, *initiative* in women.

Beyond anything he had imagined, which, truth be told, wasn't exactly something he'd worked at. *Bit of a shocker, yes,* his inner Bilbo says to him.

But, of course, he will never admit it. That would be unmanly groveling.

Accordingly he resumes fiddling with his pipe, recovering his balance with long puffs, feeling his bearings return. "Yvonne, what is really bothering you? Something bigger than just me and my . . . attitudes."

"You want to know? I feel like a pet canary. Locked in a cage. I want to do something real, something that makes a difference. I have control over exactly nothing." She pauses for a reaction. Seeing none, she continues. "Can't you see, I've got to have a plan, a strategy. I need a homerun!"

Tolkien looks up, a quizzical expression on his face. "Ah, yes, *homerun,* your quaint American slang. Odd way of talking, you Yanks. By the way, does it look like rain? I need my wellies." He begins to fuss with his tobacco pouch. Opening. Smelling. Closing.

His curt dismissal makes Yvonne livid all over again. "Don't try to dismiss me! You are hopeless! Caught up in your school boy rituals, and your little ivory tower. She pauses, mentally unsheathing a sharp knife. "And your children's story, the fairytale book? Fan fiction for *Beowulf?*"

The knife cuts and she sees his jaw tighten, his ego wince. Her hands gather scrolls and translations. She puts them in her shoulder bag. His glaring eyebrows suddenly lift and his eyes widen, questioning her.

"Night reading," she answers. She whirls into her coat, grabs the bag, and strides to the door. "Try to muster the courage to create a real story, perhaps with a real heroine. That's exactly what I'm going to do." She stops. "I may not see you after this. Denniston wants you and me to meet with Philby at two. You go. After that, visit Hut 13. For me."

The door closes and she is gone, Tolkien sits for a long time, studying his pipe as if it were an artifact of a world about to change.

Chapter 22

MIDGARSORM
(The Worm of Middle-Earth)

———

Discovery of a curse, particularly one's own, can be a multi-layered, tearful experience.

She may have been turning pages and crying for minutes or hours. She feels the pain ratchet higher with each layer of revelation.

She decides to lay the bare truths, hers and Ara's, side by side.

She strips away the underserved thrill of being a governmental "liaison" at the heartbeat of this hidden beast in a great intellectual— soon to be shooting—war. Her job is nothing more than political patronage, pure and simple.

Her patron, her father, her sole surviving parent, in grave danger.

Alan, her never-loved lover, beyond the reach of intimacy.

She studies a rendition of the large runic sign for Ara, perhaps drawn by some anonymous steward of the past century. Her tears dot the image with six splashes, as of stars in an obscure constellation.

As clear to her heart as it is unprovable, she feels the truth of this intersect of her loss and fear with the tale of Ara. She wipes each eye clear with the back of her hand, then pulls up her own version of the translation key. *Perhaps this will work.*

Later, alone in the room, she knows the truth of Ara's fate. She reads aloud the words she has written, words once spoken by Loki:

> Aragranessa Flameleaf, know the gravity of your fate.
> Mortality is a gift to Halflings as it is to men. It fills the world
> with clarity, color, vibrancy. It challenges each mortal to drive

a stake in the world and declare their existence. It makes all things dear, and so ignites purpose and longing. It is the only root from which heroism grows.

You, however, will be denied that gift. You will drift in a placid and endless river. Like us, the Dark Elves, you will be lost in time and condemned to a ceaseless dimming.

Our cousins, the haughty, self-styled "Fair Elves," walk in the land by day and night and do many things. That is not us, nor is it you. We can do very little, save a few entertaining spells of the kind I am about to place on you. We invoke our policy unto the world by guiding the hands of others. Such as our fabulous, recently departed minion, the Dark Lord and his clever Ring, crudely called "Bind" by such as yourself.

Our insufferable kin soon depart to across the Sea. We remain in Mitgard. For now. We will find a path, a secret gate, perhaps by the very power of our words, to enter the Fourth Age. There we shall resurrect our presence. You, however, will stagnate and drift on the eddied river of time, shorn of the ability to *do* in the world. Apt, we believe, for one so gifted with stealth, so sneaky, so eager to serve your twisted definition of right.

Depart now, be forgotten, and drift in a feckless raft for all your unshored existence!

I declare by my powers that your mortal existence shall be forgotten, save by one account. Written in our own tongue, as uncertain as the forever shifting paths of Mirkwood.

Thus your vaulting ambition shall remain in check. A spell of lingering shall envelope you. You shall drift past the moment of your mortal bones, alone, lost, and becalmed in a sea of time without horizon. Mark well your little remaining time. You shall be undone by the next turning of the moon. You may thereafter be a teller, a scop, a provoker of great feats of art, but never again shall you by dint of action be an instrument of change in this world."

Yvonne looks up from the page. She knows this Cassandra-like curse, this to-be and not-to-be fate. She is condemned to a similar stasis, a mere watcher and thus a non-being in an active, violent, tumultuous world of great destiny.

From the time Loki spoke, Ara had precious little time.

Like me, thinks Yvonne. She returns to the page, her voice unwinding the long-untold tale:

Thus it was that Ara, like an ill wind, fled the boughs of Mirkwood and raced to find her Amon.

Word she was brought of a pestilence of dragons. The rumour uncoiled like a contagion across the fevered nightlands.

Rushing against time, she came to Frighten. There she found her Amon, known in some tales as Eron. She witnessed his famous death-battle with *Brethfirren*, last lineage of the dreaded Midgarsorm. Worm of Middle-earth.

There stood the once-mighty Ringbearer, now dwindled with the weight of carrying Bind. A hero damned also by the ever-festering, fevering, never-healing scar of a wraith's sword-cut.

Nonetheless, there he stood, held up by his mighty beast, once again, for a final moment, young and vigorous and undefeated. A wondrous hauberk of luminous plate and mail made noble his head. A sword singing of magic and lineage in one hand, a blazing shield of long-ago kings in the other.

Confronting him in that night-veil, Brethfirren paused, shifting with caution, testing the defiant stance of his adversary.

The battle that ensued, the burning of the land, the long howls of dragon-pain that echoed like a volcano's anger from across the Northern Seas. The might of the wyrm and the able warrior that opposed him, these have been well-sung and oft-told in the tales.

Little account of the ending survives. Thus it was that Brethfirren, mortally wounded, slowly, sadly let go his last hot breaths from a cold flesh meant to last all of time. The races of Middle-earth, fell and fair, noble and brutish, wise and foolish, all halted and gave witness to a passing that, like so many in these times, would mark a turning. For the loss, the world-to-be would be grayer and less alive.

The ruined body of the Ringbearer was held in the arms of Ara. It was she who arrived as he lay spent, at the mercy of his equally fated foe. It was she who hoisted his shield and turned the last ribbon of fire from the dragon.

They lay there, her final moments before the veil of her cursed immortality descended, his time now marked by hoof beats, like sand falling from the glass, as they were rushed full-horsed to the Sea. There they would depart for the West, and leave Middle-earth forever.

It is said by the poets that on this last battlefield of mortal and dragon, these lovers were at once and forever, the *altar* and the *sacrificed*.

To any who doubt, look low in the eastern sky at autumn's equal of day and night. Let the darkness arrive and reveal the stars of Ara, the Altar. Let the sharp-eyed among you peer closely and see the very dragon fumes of that long-ago moment drifting off as a wisp of star-smoke obscuring the deeper heavens behind.

Know that these stars tell an eternal truth. Dragon slayers did fall, and Ara, the Muse, wanders still.

Hwat! Be not surprised! Lest this tale end in sadness only, without a new beginning, as every worthy story should, you shall hear at another's watch fire that Ara returned, that she would not suffer to be erased, that she would, over the long march of time, whisper and advise. Ara will ever inspire great feats of others!

Yvonne dropped the last page unto the others scattered across the floor like the fallen petals of an autumn flower.

Ara will ever inspire great feats of others!

She snatches the single page with Ara's Rune and the constellation of tear spots, assembles a scroll and a dozen other pages—originals and their translations—and places the bundle in her briefcase. *One, perhaps two more days at Bletchley,* she resolves. *Then I'll light the fuse!*

Chapter 23

SHIPS AT SEA

—

The *Empress* is laboring through heavy seas eight hundred yards straight ahead. The calculation must be perfect. The first shot of a brand new, if not formally declared, war. Kapitan Kretschner, who will become the undersea ace of the Kreigsmarine, will not lightly tolerate a miss.

At the periscope eyepiece, he hesitates, pivots right and sees the bow of an American merchant ship intruding from starboard. It is steaming at full speed, airing black, oily smoke into the air. It acts as if it knows his position, as if it is prepared to intercept the path of his imminent torpedo.

The orders are clear. No attack on any vessel of a non-combatant, especially the Americans. After all, it is well known that Lindbergh and the American Fifth Column is doing better on that score than any fleet of U-boats.

The captain studies the intermeddling vessel. He checks her bow. The letters, momentarily bathed by white sea-spray, become clear. She is the U.S.S, "Ara." A name freighted with lore and well-known to sailors. Her celestial visage on the southern horizon—often as the only constellation visible in a cloudy sky—portends a storm at sea. In any case, she is a fell portent. Derived from the Latin for "altar," she is a place of sacrifice of men and gods against the Titans.

There is not enough time for further adjustment. He returns the scope to the *Empress* and speaks quietly. *"Firen."* The torpedo's exit from the firing tube sends a shudder down the vessel. The vibration is exhilarating. He knows U-99 and her sisters, if properly led, can defeat England. Now the game has started. The communication that ties it all together is crucial, but secure. Enigma cannot be broken.

He sees the torpedo's trail, its prop spray intermittently flashing the surface as it cuts the waves. The vector was hasty and this is likely a near miss. He holds the second torpedo. Caution and patience mark this beginning. This meddlesome Ara, her possible weaponry, should not be underestimated.

He folds the telescope arms and says quietly to his junior officer, *"Tauchen."* Dive. U-99 descends and slinks away. Perhaps, U-417, somewhere nearby, will complete this task.

* * *

"Dumme nues!" Morons! Idiots! exclaims the Watcher, as he looks at the sector map for U-boats. U-417 is moving off its vector. A false directive? Perhaps a lazy breach of Enigma protocol has allowed the English to confuse them! It is too late to turn U-417 around without falling within the nearby convoy escorts' sonar. *"Dis stinkt mir!"* This *pisses me off!*

There are bright sides here, he thinks. *Now I know they are probing our Enigma codes. Blind luck this time but a giveaway just the same. Time now to use our assets at Bletchley.*

He sorts through items his staff has brought to his attention. Orders, directives, press accounts, intelligence reports. One, a hand-scrawled note from the Führer, catches his attention. It is a joke perhaps.

> There have been reports, here in Berlin, on the Wilhemsplatz itself, of vaudeville performers, itinerants, gypsies, training their monkeys to give the Nazi salute. Sedition and destabilizing mockery! Said animals are to be destroyed.
>
> Toten der Affen!
>
> A. Hitler

He holds the note, weighing the mental state of his Führer. *Time to get this war started.*

* * *

Fleming holds up a sheath of green and blue flimsies to an assemblage headed by Denniston and Philby. "Significant, happy information, lady and gentlemen. Hut 8 put it together. The *Empress* was apparently under attack by U-boats this morning. U-99 we believe. Narrow torpedo miss, then, as she took evasive measures, U-417 was in position to finish her off but suddenly pulled away. That's you, Turing, your genius bit of timely misinformation."

Turing dead-pans, "Our guess on their U-boat map, the vector numbers and a limited break on their codes. We had a few hours' window, so we sent out a message, deliberately garbled in parts, to U-417. Sent her packing for parts unknown."

Fleming picks up. "This gets better. The reason U-99 had to quit the field?"

They all stare, dumbfounded.

"You won't believe this. A U.S. Navy *Crater-class* cargo ship, arrived out of nowhere. Came up and shielded the *Empress*. Nice bit of seamanship. The Jerries didn't dare risk hitting an American-flagged vessel. Want to know the angel's name? The USS *Ara*. After the constellation signifying the altar of the gods! It, the constellation, trails a huge cluster of distant galaxies, like incense burning. You can close your mouth, professor."

"So, my father's safe?" asks Yvonne.

"You've got the last information we have. Unfortunately, those two ships, *Empress* and *Ara*, won't be able to rendezvous with the convoy. Those trains never stop. We'll have to wait and see."

"Then they're still alone out there?"

No one has an answer for that.

Chapter 24

PUB PLANS

——

The Irish elk is patient. It presides over Tolkien and Fleming as they sit across from each other in the most isolated booth the establishment has to offer.

Which, this evening, is irrelevant. The pub has only three other customers. They fill up half of the stools at the bar. They look like regulars who spend more time seated where they are than at any flat. No darts this evening. No cards. The blackout and all the worry about invasion and bombs is taking its toll on the drinking business.

They are arguing with the bartender over how much this bloody Hitler is going to cost them in war taxes. "And we being pensioners and all," can be heard from one agitated gent.

"Keep it low, and they won't hear us." Fleming whispers, looking over his shoulder. "And what's more, they don't give a bugger. Look at you, Tolkien, you fit right in. You're as seedy as a tweedy beggar."

Tolkien fakes a lower-class accent. "And you, constable, so fine and done up in your fancy Saville Row get up. And all your airs to boot. You stand out like a dainty fairy princess at a bloody dock worker's convention."

"Does she know where to meet us?"

Tolkien nods, takes a sip of ale and pulls his pipe and smoking kit from his pocket. He places them on the table just as Fleming leans over, splays his hands flat on either side, and says under his breath, "Philby received a message. Verbally. Authorized by Ribbentrop. Bastard still fancies himself as a liaison, able to commiserate with fellow adversaries in the spy game."

Tolkien conjures newsreel footage of the recently departed German Ambassador to Britain. A fat man that could dance with unexpected agility. A man that cultivated contacts at the highest levels of society. He was given to flirtation and intrigue, as his social whirls and whispered alliance with American divorcee Wallis Simpson, wife to abdicated King Edward VIII, would indicate. *Arrogant but conniving fool,* thinks Tolkien.

Fleming continues, "so here's what's interesting." He adopts a conspiratorial tone. "Tell me when Yvonne comes in."

"Alright. Go ahead."

"It's essentially an offer. Like I said, this spy game is still about commerce."

"And tricks . . .?"

"Lord, yes. Good tip, old boy. Sharp, you are. Now hear me out. Have you observed Yvonne and Alan together?"

Tolkien considers this. "Sex and marriage is between a man and a woman. It also means that I know what sometimes goes on, even within my own church. I've no real interest in this. Besides, fraternizing among peers is probably unstoppable in this pressure cooker."

"Hear me out, you know the penalty for sodomy in this country?"

Tolkien looks across, blankly. "No, it's never crossed my mind."

"Sharpen your senses . . . and your wit! Part of spying is spying on your colleagues. Isn't there something more? Almost, how might I say it, *romantic.*"

"Well yes, there seems to be some personal chemistry there."

"It's more than that, and less. A twist."

"I suppose so, yes."

"And?"

"They get along fine."

Fleming sighs and contrives a look of deep disappointment. "I thought you were, at least inside, a bit of a rogue, perhaps not a roué, but nonetheless a man of the world. How can you be a proper spy, Tolkien, if you're not attuned to scandal and sex. That's your best observation about those two?"

"Drop the French, you scamp, and get on with your prattling story."

"Very well, I'll be direct. Our man Turing has . . . homosexual tendencies. They, he and Miss Shelby, considered getting engaged. But then he revealed his inclinations. Now it's still there, close to love, but platonic."

Tolkien checks his pint. "Thank you for the scullery gossip."

"No, no, it's more! The point, old boy, is that if the truth about Turing is revealed, we lose our key man. Too much of a security risk. A prime candidate to be turned. If we lose Turing, we lose prying open Enigma."

"And for Alan, what does it mean?"

"It's simple in its own crudely medieval way. He likely faces prosecution, then lengthy incarceration, or . . ."

"What?"

"'Voluntary chemical castration.'"

Ian pauses, then goes on. "Here's Ribbentrop's offer. They know about Alan. They will not exploit this information. They won't out him."

"You, of all people, believe that? And what do they expect in return?"

"Simple. They believe we have found the *ubersprache*. The bloody old documents you are working on. They would never admit it, but these bastards are so arrogant, probably rightly so, that they believe no one can break Enigma. So they're not worried about our futile efforts, our personnel, our Turing. They are willing to bargain for your musty old cache."

Tolkien sees Yvonne come in the door. He raises a hand and she nods, briskly walking past the regulars at the bar as they pivot to ogle. As she approaches, Tolkien gives Fleming a proper wink. "What does she know?"

"Everything. She's torn in a lot of directions. Protecting Alan. Worrying about her father, probably out there on that targeted ship. The dead ends on the documents. Ah! Here you are!"

She slides into the booth on Tolkien's side, pulls off her gloves and hat, and dives in. "So, where do we go with this . . . proposal?"

Tolkien feels the question is really to him, a fellow steward of the documents. "Well, this . . . as we know, Dark Elvish, is a powerful thing. It has a life and agenda of its own. It'll never work for this war. For us. Or for them. It's useless as a tool. In fact, I believe it's quite dangerous to play with. Even I, used to linguistic complexities, can only bear to translate it in bits and pieces. It's not something you can 'break.' Not because it's big and complex, like Enigma, but because it can control the reader's thoughts. It is beguiling us right now with a story, a great story about this halfling, this Ara woman, but who knows if even that is true?"

Fleming looks over to Yvonne, who is pursing her lips. "I'm in," she says. "I know where this is going. Let them have it, or at least some of it. Let it be sand in their machine." She looks at each of them before continuing. "Let it scramble *their* heads. We each give up cards, we get a promise back. Not much, I agree, but they get a card that's really a Trojan Horse. Maybe we *want* them to have it."

Fleming adds, "We agree, I think. In the right hands, it can royally bugger, excuse me, scramble their thinking." He looks at Shelby, "Your face is one big reservation. Change your mind?"

"Maybe. Part of me can't bear to turn Ara over to these villains. They have no interest in her. They want the Elvish mechanics. They will complete her destruction."

"So what do we do? Nothing?"

"I have an idea. Three things. First, we . . . all of us . . . have to try to save Alan. Even if at bottom it's only a fleeting promise by despicable enemies. Maybe Ribbentrop can be trusted at some level. So, that's a plus for some kind of deal. Second, we—Professor Tolkien and I— think that right now this language is essentially a haunted house. Easy to get in, even easier to get lost in. At some point the person that delves too deep in it may never be able to find an exit. He or she will be lost forever—in the vast Doubt of Mirkwood. It's that powerful. So, I believe, like Denniston and Philby, that it has no *direct* military use by us."

Fleming asks, "What's three?" as Tolkien watches Yvonne with a kind of awe.

"Just what you'd think. It does have a military use against them. We can offer them just enough, a few pages, perhaps. Maybe include a doctored copy of the Key. Promise more in six months if Ribbentrop keeps his silence. That way we keep the bulk of the documents intact, save Alan, save the lost *Beowulf* book, and save Ara! With no benefit to them."

"*And* as a bonus, maybe we scramble their heads!"

"Let's be bolder," she says, "let's ask for something immediate. I say, safe passage for any ships leaving Canada as of the day before yesterday. Before this war became inevitable. They will scoff at that, of course. But maybe it's not a throwaway card."

Tolkien feels like an amateur snared into a high trapeze act. He blurts out, "This will have to move fast. Isn't there some sort of restriction on just *dealing* like this? Secrecy Act? Philby? Denniston?"

"Not to worry, old boy. I'll handle all that. Philby will convey our counter to them. You two decide which pages, put together the package. Finally, a bit of fun and games!"

Yvonne elbows Tolkien. "Now to the chase. We'll go without sleep if necessary, be ready in a day or two."

Tolkien moans, "What's new there?"

Yvonne gets up, finishes her pint, sets the glass on the table with a *thump*, and looks down at them. "Well? There's about to be a war on, you know!"

* * *

Upon arriving at the mansion, Yvonne is handed a note. From Philby. It says: "Talked with Fleming. All plans on hold. Stand down."

She thinks of her father, of the *Empress* wandering the cold, rolling, wave-capped gray wilderness. She sits in her dorm room and removes the bundle of documents from her briefcase. She sees the pages of translation scrawled in Tolkien's inelegant hand. She thinks of his penmanship as a reflection of his professional mumblings. Yet, like his spoken words, these hold the reader's attention in a stern grip. They appear to be the recounting of a bard speaking of Ara as an already-historical figure.

> "We few of the League of Ara know well these words spoken in the depths of Mirkwood were worse than a sentence of death: stranded in this fallen and mortal world, you will remain as an ongoing spirit, robbed of your petty heroics. No longer able to touch and do. You may only whisper, and with that haunt or inspire, but never touch, living mortals. That, Shadow-Sister, is your fate."

Yvonne leans back in the chair. That's me, she realizes, robbed of any chance to do, to be, to have a story!

She reads a side note Tolkien has written to himself. "These Dark Elves are probing into our world under the sun. They want to be here. They use others as their instruments, the Dark Lord of their own time, this strangely living language. Our worst evils, Hitler himself, may now be, or yet become, their minions!"

She refolds the papers and puts them in her bag. Her face is alight with resolution, a plan that will demand sacrifice, yes, but just might save her father, her untouchable love, and, in the same moment, by her mortal touch, infect the enemy.

She finds a card given to her by a member of the German English Friendship Society earlier in the year. A short, bald man with a limp, There! Herman Guass. He had a tall associate. She places a call and takes the rail to London. She walks six blocks to the address listed near Prussia House, the German Embassy. She practices what she will say to two men who are surely remaining emissaries of the Third Reich.

Chapter 25

MASKS

———

Morning light slants across the kitchen table at 2020 Northmoor Lane as Tolkien bustles about. He is freshly shaved, dressed in a sport coat, his brown tie, four-in-hand knotted tightly. This is a time he values, before the day's grind begins, when he can sit with Edith and just *be*.

To just *be*, however, is not in the cards today. On the table are spread copies of the Guardian and the Times. The headlines are shattering:

Germany Invades Poland!
War Declaration Today!

As if the headlines are not enough to bring the terrible prospect of open war fully home, Tolkien gazes upon an even more disturbing sight. Five gas masks rest next to the newspapers. Edith must have waited in line all yesterday to be issued their family allotment.

His mind brings up images of each member of his family, their faces grotesquely covered by the alien, dun-colored mask, the goggles through which peer panic-stricken eyes, the aquatic-like breather over the mouth, the inhuman tube extending beneath it. He has already come to terms with the fact that Christopher and Michael are of age, and will soon be sent into this maelstrom. But Edith and little Priscilla, caught in the claustrophobic nightmare of trying to breathe through one of these! Searching a way through a lingering cloud of lethal sarin fumes.

Tolkien's animus toward Hitler, already robust, takes on a further dimension. This . . . this assault on his family! Now it is personal. He feels vindicated all the more for throwing his lot in with those at Bletchley.

He sweeps the papers and masks and canisters to a sideboard, and quickly sets the table.

Edith comes in and he pours her tea. Holding the sugar bowl, he directs, "Let's talk of this . . . war later. I've got something . . ."

Edith will have none of his patter. She wants to set the day with her thoughts first. "Ronald, I was thinking last night of stern old Father Francis, my nemesis, how he forbade our talking for those three years until you were twenty-one. Those were bleak times, until your letter arrived, posted on your birthday, asking me to marry you. We all need stories, daring escapes, especially in grim times such as these. Don't despair of your writing."

Tolkien is upended, so touching are her thoughts. He responds by just looking at her, seeing the kindred spirit of the orphaned school girl, the young woman, the mother of his children. His beloved.

Time after time, she saves him.

She knows what he is thinking. For a suspended moment they gaze at each other. Just being.

She gently breaks the moment. "Well, say something. Come now, you were about to tell me something important. I know because you were down here early boiling water and setting out the tea."

He can't tell her names, details, much of anything. But perhaps, the bottom line. "What I'm involved with is . . . quite important. I'm sorry for the odd hours. I'm distracted, I know."

"I would say 'And that's news?' but, then, it's more than I've seen in you before. I've seen you terribly busy. This is different. Deeper. Are you in danger?"

"Danger? Hardly. Just a lot of paper and pencils. No car chases or guns, in fact absolutely no adventures for me! Nothing for either of us to worry about. Let's have our spot of tea and I'll be off."

BOOK III
DISASTERS

———

Never say "no" to adventures. Always say "yes," otherwise you'll lead a very dull life.

~ Ian Fleming

Sometimes it is the people who no one imagines anything of who do the things that no one can imagine.

~ Alan Turing

Chapter 26

QUANTUM DREAMS

—

A fool's errand! Tolkien hrrumfs to himself.

He has had only a first breakfast, and he has now wandered to the very edge of Bletchley's park-like grounds. A fruitless search. He is hungry. He is despairing, flitting like a mother bird robbed by some cruel wind of her nest. Mercutio's line plays in the air. *Nay, if our wits run the wild-goose chase, we are done.*

He turns back and stops. There, in a thick copse of trees and brush, hidden from all, unless they are turned just so on this unlikely path, is a modest two-story overseer's residence in a subdued Georgian style. It nestles at the end of a less-trodden walkway, a path long since surrendered to weeds. Hardly the abode of dwarves, as Yvonne suggested. It looks more like a witch's lair in a deep forest.

As he approaches, he sees that the door is strange indeed. Unlike the other Huts. Not the utilitarian, weathered doors, slopped all about with drab paint.

The face of this door is a sprawling work of art rendered in fresh and vibrant colors. *As she said, you'll know.*

At its center is a radiant full moon, its face-like array of craters cleverly incorporating the numerals 1 and 3.

Below the moon is a silhouette of, almost certainly, the grand scull and antlers of an Irish elk. The effect is almost three-dimensional, as the tines cast a faint moon-shadow.

Above all this is a Celtic tree, one side with boughs full and summer green, the other with its limbs afire in autumn red and orange.

All about these, capturing the edges of the door, is the winding image of a monstrous forest. Its roots descend into a soil of ornate rococo shell and wave motifs, jumbled with abstract cubist "rocks" in the manner of Picasso.

He passes this over because he is riveted by the image that covers the background and edges of the door, bleeding, or rather writhing, over to encompass the entire doorframe. It portrays an intertwined life form, neither fully plant nor animal. Organic and vaguely menacing. Perhaps inspired by that strange Barcelonan, Antoni Gaudi, whom Tolkien once met on his grand European tour as a teenager.

The effect is powerful, for in its thickets Tolkien sees Mirkwood itself—alien, convoluted, and chilling in its implacable sense of another world, beyond yet not indifferent to our own.

He hesitates briefly, wishing Yvonne was here. He knocks, timid at first, then louder.

After some time, the door creaks open. A young man's head peaks around the edge. He fits with the eccentric crowd of geniuses at Bletchley: pale, gangly, early thirties, a razor-thin nose and cloudy green eyes. He is, to Tolkien's surprise quite literally, wearing a Cambridge beanie adorned with a small propeller attached to the top. The prop rotates lazily as his head tilts to look quizzically at Tolkien. He asks, "The password?"

"I . . . I don't know."

"Then you shall not pass."

The young man's eyes, despite the dodgy headgear, bear the measuring focus of a guard protecting the keep of his liege. He steps fully into the doorway, his arms crossed. In the ancient etiquette, his challenge must be answered or he will summarily close the door.

Tolkien is thinking of words, incantation, code-names. As if this is one of those secret gates, worthy of some Old English source-word. He settles on the simple truth: "My name is Tolkien. Yvonne sent me."

At the mention of her name, a flash—recognition? respect?—crosses the guard's face. "We have few visitors here. Damn the password malarkey." He steps aside to allow entry. "Come in, Mr. Tolkien."

Entering the threshold of Hut 13, Tolkien takes in a scene he will remember all his life. The interior walls of the house have been crudely demolitioned away to open up the space. There is an array of strange folk occasioned all about: leaning against walls, sitting on the kitchen counter, seated on unmatched couches and chairs in what once served as the parlor. Several occupy the steps of the ascending staircase.

Tolkien quickly counts the assemblage. Twelve. The same number as Beowulf's entourage, as the assemblage of dwarves in his own work, *The Hobbit.*

A chair sits empty and mute in the center, as if waiting for someone to be summoned forth and testify before this strange jury.

A large blackboard stands at the ready across the room. Through the heavy chalk smear of long use, there shows a bewildering concentration of inscriptions: numbers, formulas far beyond his own mastery of Level IV Calculus. There are also runes, of the oldest known variety, he notes. Complex symbols indicate that at least one among these is a mystic of the Shambhala persuasion. A bit disturbing is the sign of the pentagram, as if here lurked a Warlock, a *waerloga*, an oath-breaker of old.

One of the twelve, an older man, gray-haired as if elderly but possessed of an obvious vigor in step and carriage, comes forward. He flashes quick, mentoring eyes as he speaks, "Professor Edenbaum, late of the University of Heidelberg, at your service." They shake hands. "Come in, welcome, sit with us!" He gestures to the lone chair, looming like an inquisition dock.

Tolkien gazes about once more, decides he is too deep in this to retreat, and reluctantly sits.

"Let your eyes relax, professor. We are an odd lot, I grant you. A bit like the parlor of one of those University clubs, where all the rejects are politely tucked away with tea. So it is with us here at Bletchley, except they're afraid to let us go. *Just in case*, as they say. Your come-and-go friend, Fleming, is responsible for our happy band. A bit like your Gandalf character, I suppose."

He winks and continues. "Scoured from all over merry Old England, we are every bit a carnival's dozen: psychics, mystics, students of the occult, medians, magicians, self-proclaimed warlocks, enchanters, beguilers, physicians. Here, here is Doctor Kraus, freshly immigrated from work with Albert Hoffman at Sandoz labs in Austria, an experimenter in strange nostrums derived from ergot, the rye grain fungus." An oddly happy man in a white lab coat nods. "We have all tried this substance." He pauses, testing Tolkien's reaction, then moves on. "A few of us, like me, are quantum physicists. I am also a refugee. A student of Erwin Schroedinger. You know of him? Yes? Particles and waves? A little? No matter."

The man is by now almost breathless. Tolkien sizes him up, an especially odd-duck among a collection of bizarre fowl. "So what is your mission here, all of you together, if I may ask?"

"Ah, precisely the right question. We've discovered that, in a way, we are part of a continuum of thinking on a question of great moment to you, indeed to the philosophies of all times."

"Which is?"

"Why, the oddest, most intractable problem: what exists independent of the conceiving mind?"

"Yes, that's a profound question, one that confounds me of late."

"Yes, well, perhaps a profound answer also lies here. Now, to the really important question."

Tolkien looks to each side. "Yes?"

"Do you like cats?"

A silence hovers in the room.

"Cat got your tongue, professor? Well, here it is. Forget all the tedious stuff physicists are now working with, light somehow being *both* particles and waves. Let's get to the bottom line. Let's get to these cats. My mentor, Professor Schrödinger, the equivalent for our times of an alchemist of old, famously owned one. A cat, that is. Or perhaps not. You see, this is how the real world, the one beneath our pragmatic, ape-brained perception favoring the finding of food and mates, seems to work."

Edenbaum pauses, raises an eyebrow to Tolkien to make sure he is following. "There is a cat in a box. It could also be a particle, a wave of energy, a safety pin, a thousand years of history, or a universe. But let's all just agree for the moment that it's a cat. You don't know if the cat is alive or dead, gray or black, until you open the box. Then, when you do, in that moment of sentient perception, it becomes what it is. Maybe a living gray cat, after all. Perhaps even one of your fantasy people, these hobbits. Follow so far?"

"Not really."

"Well, you should, because the even stranger aspect, I believe, is that this phenomenon will be proven to occur over significant distances of space. Professor Einstein snorts and complains of 'spooky action at a distance' . . ."

"Or time!" exhorts another of the assemblage, a plump fellow holding a slide rule like a wand. "It really goes either way. So the concept of time travel is not absurd. You, Mr. Aspiring Gentleman writer, could be, have been, are now, will be the scop that first creates the tale of Beowulf. Imagine that!"

For a flash the idea catches Tolkien's attention. Then he looks around, checking for signs of sanity among the rest of this "happy band." No luck; they are rapt as acolytes.

"So, professor, be appreciative of the malleable character of reality. The fact that observing something changes, or at least determines, its character. And what is observation but part of thinking? So, to get to your Big Question, belief as reality—having the power to create what is imagined—is not sooo bizarre. Let me offer a bit, a remnant perhaps from some riddle:

Nothing is but what is not.
Nothing is but what is thought.

* * *

The next hour is to Tolkien a spell of similar incantations, spoken by each of the acolytes, Edenbaum finally sounds as if it is a closing moment. "So, from all our perspectives, all of us here in humble Hut 13, other worlds do exist, and all worlds exist in the mind of some sentient creator. If you wish, one with a capital 'G.' That includes you and your childish fairy tales."

Kraus, the white-coated man from Sandoz, speaks up. "I've read your book, professor, and I think the question you ponder is who dreamed up whose reality. Are these characters the product of your mind? Certainly. Do they now have their own existence? Just so. But here's the funny thing. Did they dream *you* up? Who among you and your Middle-earth characters is the dream of another's weaving? Perhaps the answer lies in your great, trackless forest, Mirkwood. Others have braved it and found their way out. Now you must."

* * *

As Tolkien leaves Hut 13, the Sandoz man grabs his arm and speaks to him. "We are oracles, revealing truths. Your man Turing is, however, merely a seer—a dirty-hands man tossing the bones, dipping through entrails and earthly scrap for meaning. Bless him, for the moment and the world's peril under Hitler's shadow! Fear only that his machines one day become the dreamers."

He steps out unto the weeded pathway that leads back to Bletchley proper, and Tolkien feels the loose foundation stones of his beliefs shift once more. His yearning imagination might yield a world that—just maybe, possibly, hopefully—lives.

The day, now at noon, seems brighter, with only one cloud drifting to threaten the light. In a moment it passes across the face of the sun. What if the Dark Elves, conceivers and meddlers on their own, were reaching into this world? Probing with the bait of their language? Relentlessly prying open a secret door?

Ah, poppycock, thinks Tolkien, *just let a pretty, peaceful day be and find some lunch!*

He breathes deep and, enjoying the moment, takes a boyish, skipping step.

The pressure wave is soundless. It lifts Tolkien and hurls him a dozen feet. Remnants of Hut 13 sweep by his vision in slow-motion: a sample of the front door, papers inscribed with Celtic signs, a Balrog's hot breath of dust and dirt, a rotating, twinkling shard of glass that seems like an icy elfin blade, a hat.

The primitive part of his mind registers only that he is—*must* be at the Somme. He curls into a pre-natal ball as he feels something approaching, a shadow dark and cataclysmic in its immensity.

It arrives as a veil of utter blackness. A cessation as if a fell axe had sundered all existence. *I sleep,* he thinks, *forever in the dark. Never to awaken. Never to finish . . . Never . . .*

Ages pass and he stirs as all beings born or re-born must, in confusion. He wills himself to fade away as a mist of sadness, but it doesn't work. He is trapped, a revenant entombed in a cairn of old, locked in a nether-house earthed forever beneath a somber mound.

A barrow.

Ages more pass, a thousand suns, moons, and seasons. Past, present, and what may yet be are a single cavalcade. The procession is inestimably, indescribably rich, filled with vibrant scenes that seem to only vaguely fit together: Bloemfontein, the grove of trees, the loss of his mother, his first tender kiss with Edith, flashes of the Somme, holding in his hands the original *Beowulf* manuscript, his lectures at Oxford, a disagreeable moment with one of his student assistants. Then a bag of darkness, as of a passage. What follows are images he doesn't recognize—a trove of documents covertly placed on his doorstep, flying into New York City and banking to see the Statue of Liberty, talking with a stranger in a pub called The End, a mammoth-sized spider scurrying through an unfamiliar underground, a young American woman, again, and an uttered name, *Cadence*.

He clutches at the name, as if they, or at least their paths, might someday cross. Ca . . . den . . .

But then, he will never leave this vault of darkness.

A ray of light, thin and pale as wheat straw, pierces the dark, revealing a jagged jumble of timbers and debris.

He recoils, crabbing and scuttling away to hide in the dark. He senses distant footsteps from above. They vibrate down to him. *A Trespasser on his barrow!*

There is another kind of light, he realizes, a flowing, greenish fog. A muttering incantation fills the air. He hears nearby moans. These are mixed with muffled sounds from the banished world *up there*. It reminds him, curiously because it no longer matters, that there is but a porous membrane between reality and faerie. Down here, in his evermore home, he senses a rustle, the spasmodic flap of cartilaginous wing, of *something* stirring. Something he does not want to meet.

He knows now what he has become: a *draugr* of old, as expressed in ancient Norse, an *after-walker* that dwells in tombs. Perhaps he will in time shape-shift into a hideous form and rise as something swollen with decay and yet uncorrupted. A fiend of a moonless night that mounts the oxen, the property most precious to every medieval family. Oxen that have grazed on the grass of this, his barrow. These he will harass and ride as the poor creatures run, howling into the night to perish of madness and exhaustion.

He stares at the return of the thin shaft of light, the green fog evaporating at its touch. Soon the shaft widens, and a hand reaches in. It crawls and gropes about like a crab shorn of its eye-stalks. He shifts away, but it finds a piece of his coat and presses its fingers on the cloth in confirmation.

It grabs and yanks and Tolkien is dragged to the light to be reborn from this barrow-place.

As he is pulled out his eyes flinch at the flashlights that beam and dance. They assault his eyes. A face with a blue cap, a fireman, is addressing him.

"Bit of roof fell on top of you, sir. There we find you, just now, all huddled 'neath it. Luck on luck to top it off. Bless the saints, I would sir."

Tolkien's eyes and mind reconstruct this upper world. He realizes he is dirty but unhurt. He dusts himself as he sees flames and smoke boiling up from the pit where Hut 13 used to stand.

"Bloody gas main, I suspect sir."

Chapter 27

UNDOING

—

Kretschner is already late to the wolf-pack rendezvous. Alerted by his radar, he finds two vessels alone and unprotected. He is stunned to see, once again the *Empress* and the *Ara*. He turns from the periscope and laughs quietly to the officers huddled around him. "They wander like Hansel and Gretel lost in the forest."

U-99 stalks closer. This time they will be sure. The running depth and magnetic trigger are set at five meters, just below the keel of the *Empress*. The shock wave will break her in two.

As the torpedo propels from the firing tube, Kretschner thinks *the Iron Cross will be waiting when I return to Wilhenshaven. Perhaps a trip to Berlin.*

His watch, precisely calibrated to the clocks in the Chancellery counts the seconds. Any moment. U-99 vibrates slightly with the distant, subdued thud of impact . . .

* * *

The torpedo's explosion lifts the *Empress*, rips her amidships, and cants her hard to port. Shelby is thrown across his cabin. The air immediately smells of smoke, fuel, and sea water.

The floor rights itself a little. She is listing hard, water pouring into her hold, her ribs collapsing as the hungry sea eats at her.

He grabs a life jacket and clambers up the tilted cabin floor. He manages to crawl into the oblique hallway. The list is now forty-five degrees, the vessel threatening to roll over. He finds the ladder to the upper deck and climbs, his legs dangling down from each rung. He can feel the stern starting to descend, lifting the bow, accelerating the slide into the depths.

He knows that, even if he clears the ship and its myriad entanglements, and avoids the wake that will suck down everything nearby ... that in open water he will have at best five minutes. After that, the hypothermia is irreversible.

He finds the hatchway, sees black smoke and blue sky framed by an off-center rectangle.

The *Ara*, a half-mile ahead, turns hard and makes to the *Empress,* where men are already jumping from her lifted bow into the sea. Foam, fire, and smoke boil the water as her hull descends, her final moments accelerating as she descends porthole by porthole.

* * *

Turing enters the small room in Hut 8, engrossed in reading a garbled transmission. Amid the jumble of letters, just out of comprehension, lurks a fragmented meaning. His head hurts from lack of sleep.

He stops. Something is wrong. He looks up and around.

The silence tells him. The knitting-needle clicks of the Bombes are silent. He dodges desks and overturns chairs as he rushes to the closet door. He flings the doors open and his arms remain frozen in the air. A mangle of wires and smashed vacuum tubes meets his unbelieving stare.

Chapter 28

REFORGED

———

At the far edge of Bletchley Park, the charred ruins of Hut 13 still vent a thin column of smoke into the dawn. As firemen and investigators search the rubble, one MI15 official picks through the debris field, stooping and meticulously recovering random bits of paper—memos, notes, books, journals, much as good neighbors had picked through the aftermath at Ashburnham House so many years ago.

Elsewhere, unnoticed in the lights and sirens and commotion of the night, a procession of cars enters the main gate, the guards snapping off crisp salutes. The cars park in the rear of the mansion.

Within the hour Tolkien is summoned from the Bletchley Medical Clinic. He sits, a bit dazed, in one of the large chairs in the mansion's Great Room, looking at new daylight seeping through the edges of the blackout curtains. His head is bandaged with gauze to cover his lone physical injury, a cut in the forehead. Though slight, it will leave a small scar just above the hairline that Tolkien will wear with solemn pride to the end of his days.

The real injury to Tolkien is his shaken confidence. He knows, as does everyone at Bletchley, that, despite the official cover, this was hardly a gas leak "accident." It was aimed. At a target. Which was, quite possibly, if incomprehensively, Tolkien himself.

A swath of full sunlight suddenly probes the curtain seams and slices across the oak floor. Trousered legs pace through the light. It is Fleming, he is pounding a fist into his hands, speaking to the air, striving to comprehend the string of disasters. "It's so bloody bad!"

"Worse than that. We are done." The response is from Turing. He is sitting in a straight chair, looking down at a note that, by his despondent posture, confirms the end of the world.

Fleming turns to Turing. "Forget the note for a second. Let's go over the message. You got it out, right? Before?"

"Yes, that day. Before."

"And?"

"It was directed at the two U-boats. We re-directed them. No way to know if it worked."

"Did they know we were reading their code?"

"Bloody damn well they knew. The timing of their reaction was immediate. They changed rotors and plug boards settings. Our whole effort is being watched, from somewhere."

"Next, can we rebuild the prototypes?"

"The rudimentary Bombes?" Turing can still smell the tang of metallic smoke drifting up from the smashed vacuum tubes and ripped wires. He looks up, his eyes following Fleming as he paces by. "Time and money are inverse coordinates. The more we have of one, the less we need of the other. Unfortunately, time is not an option. Neither is money. You know that better than I. Things won't hold. And Denniston has already turned down my requests for more funding. Philby is lobbying for flesh and blood spies, maybe gumshoes to prowl the streets of Berlin, maybe gypsies posing as street vendors outside the gutted Reichstag. Ridiculous! I don't trust the bugger. In any case, we're done. I can't go on with pencils!"

A voice, deep and broad, almost grumbling, cracks like thunder across the room. It comes from the dark of a sitting-chair corner. "*Go on?* Success is never final, nor is failure always fatal. Pluck up your courage, man! If you're going through hell, the *only* course is to keep going."

Turing and Fleming are frozen as the voice, like the sudden groan of an ancient glacier, leaves an abyss of silence. A match scratches and flares, and the back of a large overstuffed chair is eerily silhouetted. A cloud of smoke drifts up, freighted with the earthly aroma of Havana tobacco. In a moment, a short, rotund man rises and shuffles at them from the shadows, puffing contentedly on his long cigar.

Fleming keeps his polish. "My Lord, let me introduce . . ."

"Hardly necessary, Fleming, I know some of this cerebral lad. Mr.

Turing wrote me a rather pointed letter, complaining about the lack of resources for his work. This code-breaking machine. Well, Mr. Turing, why should I fund you if you are already defeated?"

"Well, your lordship . . ."

"Balderdash! Now listen to me. Never, never . . . never give up!"

Turing thinks better of saying more. "Yes, Lord Churchill, yes."

"Very well. I arranged to come here before theses unfortunate setbacks. Let us see what's left of your work, Mr. Turing. If you hold a good show, I can arrange for you to receive ample funding and resources. As you say, we have no luxury of time. Now let us be off. My assistant tells me I must return to Whitehall within the hour."

Churchill is abrupt, a man of duties manifold and unfulfilled. He heads to the door, nodding to Fleming as if to an old acquaintance of mixed reputation. Turing follows the way a surly but loyal hound trots after its master. Tolkien rises from his chair, stiff and a bit unsteady. The First Lord of the Admiralty suddenly stops. "Spot-on service to crown and country once again, professor. I'd say your dragons are unquiet. Help us find some better spells to defeat them."

A trail of cigar smoke lingers as the man exits the door. As Turing passes by, he hands Tolkien the note. He does this with an air of unhappy commiseration. "Traitor." Turing whispers, his informing voice low, flat and venomous.

As the door closes, Fleming resumes his litany of doom. "So, as you can see from the note you hold, Yvonne has gone over. Add to that, one of our huts was blown up right under our noses. Seven dead. You, sir, escape by seconds. Our school-ground efforts to untie the Enigma Code with machines is . . . *kaput*!" He slaps his hands and wipes them clean. "Now, to more bad news. I didn't have time to blurt it out. They got the *Empress*. Torpedoed last night. Sunk in minutes. The American vessel, *Aris* whatever, was nearby. No word on survivors. I assume we lost Senator Shelby. The American press will howl. The Yanks will cringe. There goes our war-saving ally."

Tolkien is standing, but his mind reels with the enormity of bad news.

"And the war?" continues Fleming. "The Krauts are pouring into Poland. Parliamentary gears are turning. The King will speak tonight. Our little cabal, you might say, is ill-omened. Oh yes," the next part he spits out, "*she* gave them some of your precious documents." He raises his chin and flicks his finger at the note. "Go ahead, read it!"

Tolkien walks over to the curtains and lifts the note into a pool of light. The words, written in her sweet American-girl cursive, bound into view:

Dearest Alan,

This is goodbye. They tell me they have my father. I do what must be done. For you. For all of us.

Love forever,

Yvonne

Below the note, crabbed along the bottom of the page, is a string of symbols.

He looks through the curtain seam to the manicured autumn landscapes of Bletchley.

Another fellowship cracked.

The next thought Tolkien simply cannot stop. *No wonder there are so few, nay, no heroines of old.*

He looks back at Fleming. "Where did this note come from?"

"Left at the doorstep of Hut 8 by some bloke, maybe a kid, a midget . . ."

"What?"

"I know, daft. Anyways, a little figure. The guards chased but wouldn't catch 'im. Disappeared, stealthy as a fox. One of the Kraut operatives, I suppose. The envelope was sealed, addressed to Turing. The gibberish at the bottom is still a mystery."

Tolkien's eyes cut back to the note, as if seeing it for the first time. He scans back and forth, reassembling, recalling.

"Go fetch Alan!" he says. "I'll be at Hut 11. There's more to a clever message than the eyes first meet!"

* * *

When they gather, Tolkien is engulfed in a rich cloud of pipe smoke, fed by energetic puffs and *uhms* as he pencils words on a pad, consults the "circle and star" key, and ponders Yvonne's note.

Fleming and Turing, like expectant fathers, smoke chains of cigarettes, sit and await word from the delivering doctor. Tolkien finally puts down his pipe and pencil and regards them through the collective haze.

"Clever girl, she is! This is no farewell note. It's an instruction. Here it is, as best I can decipher on the run as it were, which is what we're about to do. Run!"

"Out with it man!" says Turing.

"She says: My note is a lie. I have given them some of the documents. As sand. They are taking me. Uiguenal. May Ara deliver this."

Turing says, "The last part, Ara? Who or what is that?"

"Not important now. The word I don't know is *Uiguenal.*"

"I do," says Fleming. "It's a place, a long, narrow lake in the southern hills of Scotland. Bloody obscure, down a muddy side track from a ruined castle I once visited. A place called *Rodorfiell,* Skyfall."

"And?" asks Turing.

"It's six hours hard driving," says Fleming. "If we leave now . . . ."

"Perhaps we should check with Denniston, Philby." Even as he finishes, Tolkien regrets saying this.

Fleming cuts the matter away. "And spend a week being interrogated? There's not time. We go now or we regret it forever. Are we to be sad duffers at the pub, lamenting our refusal of this call, forever holding our manhood's cheap?"

"And transportation?" asks Tolkien. "Surely not your little imp of an auto."

Fleming shrugs.

"Don't look at me," says Turing. "I'm just a poor, about to be unemployed, mathematician."

Tolkien winks. "Since we're going over the wall anyway, I know of a bloke with a nice buggy, foolishly leaves his keys under the floor mat."

In twenty minutes, they are skulking behind the mansion.

The MLS-7 owned by Alistair Denniston is the newest, biggest, four-seat roadster made by Aston-Martin. Its long, sleek, low-slung persona is unmistakable: the grill, the head lamps, the rumble of its six cylinders.

The guards, thinking it is the director, lift the bar to the exit gate as the car approaches. Fleming, Tolkien, and Turing speed by, turn the corner and roar northward.

BOOK IV
SECRETS

—

But that I am forbid,
To tell the secrets of my prison-house,
I could a tale whose lightest word
Would harrow up thy soul.
> ~ William Shakespeare, *Hamlet*

I am aware of the Official Secrets Acts and that I am subject to them and that there are serious consequences, including prosecution and imprisonment, if I am found to be in breach of them.
> ~ Text of Official Secrets Acts Oath, 1939

Chapter 29

THE LAKE

—

Loch Uiguenal is indeed an obscure, elongated lake hidden in the heather-hills of southern Scotland. It lies north of *Vallum Aelium*, Hadrian's Wall, and is reached with difficulty. Its few visitors experience several hours' drive (or a two day ramble by foot) along a rude, unpaved tract that skirts and meanders through the rising uplands.

In good weather, the lake is also accessible by a small airplane equipped with floats. Should such a plane need to land elsewhere in this country, its only recourse would be to make for the Atlantic, eighty miles to the east, perpetually roiled, windy, and fog-bound.

Along the lake's southern shore huddles a whitewashed cluster of stone buildings. A smokestack bespeaks a small distillery. The plume cuts away from the stack, indicating near total humidity.

The weather today is bad. In fact, there is bloody little weather to see as, a few miles away, the Aston-Martin angrily bounces through the road's water-filled ruts and potholes. It speeds though a world enshrouded by clouds, easily outracing the limited range of visibility.

The driver is Fleming, competent as always but challenged this day by the road and the fog. And time.

"Dammit! Faster, Fleming!" yells Turing from the front passenger seat.

Peering through water-rivulets streaming across a side window, Tolkien leans forward from the backseat to look as a form looms through the mist. In a moment, it recedes into the fog. "Megalith," he says. "Lots of these inexplicable sentinels still guard this country."

Turing is unimpressed. "Forget the travelogue, professor. Check the map? Are we close?"

Their words, shouted, spat through gritted teeth, punctuated by hand slams on steering wheel and seat back, all tumble together like a vicious slide of rocks.

"Damn it!"

"We should be coming on it anytime."

"How in bloody hell should I know?"

"Go! Go!"

Suddenly, they are silent.

The auto, as if sure of its power, soars over a rise and, for a long exhilarating moment, is airborne. Tolkien clutches at the seat and door handle as the beast lands, fishtails and recovers its footing. Fleming momentarily slows the car.

The long-ago voice of a Welshman's wisdom plays in Tolkien's mind, still contesting to be heard against the low thump of exploding cannon shells and the reaping chatter of machine guns.

. . . Trust him! A born jumper, he is! Hang on, laddie!

Tolkien feels the sudden, intense guilt of being, once again and forever, unable to save his fellows. He leans forward and pounds the front seat. "Don't slow down! For God sake, punch it!"

Turning looks at him, then joins. "Quite right! At it, Fleming!"

Fleming stomps on the gas pedal. The Aston-Martin surges forward, the power of its great, laboring six-cylinder heart sending a shudder through the vehicle. It shreds the fog and leaves a vortex of mist, agitated and confused, in its whirling wake.

They rocket through long fingers of fog and erupt into a pool of daylight. The road ahead is suddenly visible, a brown rut leading down through autumn-colored hills, marked by fresh tire tracks.

"There!" Turing points. They see the cluster of white buildings hard against a narrow shoreline. A small dock juts into the water. To it is tethered a floatplane streaked blue and gray with a kind of watery camouflage.

Fleming speaks in a flat monotone, as of someone duly impressed. "Arado 96. The A-3 model, single engine. Long distance scout plane. New to the Jerries." He looks over at Turing. "It can be carried on ships at sea. This one could reach a waiting U-boat off the coast, or fly non-stop to the German border, maybe even Hamburg."

He squints, peering over the steering wheel. "Looks modified. No guns or bomb cradles. Enlarged, maybe to hold extra passengers?"

As they accelerate toward the lake, they see two cars parked near the dock, each with its doors flung open. Arrays of figures are standing opposite each other.

Fleming begins to honk the car's horn.

A moment later, their roadster behemoth slides to a wild, gravel-fanning stop almost exactly between the parties. Fleming is out the door and standing as Tolkien and Turing struggle with their exits and then come up beside him. They immediately sense an exquisite and perilous balance—an explosive admixture of adrenaline, fear and grim resolve. The air crackles, awaiting the spark of fatal misjudgment.

Standing to the left of the newcomers are the dour Mr. One and Mr. Two. Their hands are in their coat pockets. Mr. One does a surprised double-take at the Aston-Martin, then at Tolkien, before returning narrowed eyes to their opposites ten feet away. There stand Gauss and Steerman. The two German agents hold machine pistols pointed slightly up. Between them, inexplicably, stands a fully uniformed officer of the Waffen SS. He is tall and thin. His hat is marked by the scull insignia of the *Shootstofle*. The shiny, downcast visor rides rakishly low, obscuring much of his face.

Standing behind him is Yvonne Shelby.

Tolkien's neck hairs are sprung like hedgehog spines. *God help us! There's no place to hide. If someone starts shooting . . .* Time, so fleeting moments before, slows down. The only sound is the gentle lap of water on the Arado's floats. The air smells of wood smoke, distilled spirits, murky lake and heather. A low wind slithers and churns the mist-bands bleeding past them. One point of the officer's collar flaps. A disconsolate sound. Tolkien and Turing glance at each other then slowly put their hands in their coat pockets.

This brings the machine pistols to stare, directly and implacably, right at their torsos.

Tolkien, feels a strange impetus to act, to reach out and touch the situation, to defuse this bomb. He takes a tentative half-step forward. His voice, quavering slightly, is obviously out-of-step with this array of grim professionals. He looks at the Nazi officer. "Let her go, sir. I insist."

The man, eyes still concealed beneath his visor, turns sharply to Tolkien. By his attitude, he clearly regards Tolkien as a squashable but humorous bug. His English is as precise as it is condescending. "*Insist*, is it?"

He pauses a count, then, perhaps enjoying a possible bit of badinage, looks at each of them. "We're here, I suppose, to negotiate . . ." He swirls one hand in a mixing gesture. ". . . but I already know each of you and where you are coming from. You, Master Turing, you're *confused*. In a lot of ways. We need not belabor those now. Commander Fleming, you're *fixated* on the Big Score, coming from down and stealing the cricket match. Your grandiosity is your weakness. And finally you, Professor Tolkien, you're at once too pompous and too *scared*. You should stay secreted away in your lecture hall, huddle with your precious student assistants."

The last was so odd, Tolkien furrowed his brow and studied the officer. *Something, unclear what.* Impeccable English accent, but he changes it as if it's all a façade.

The man's accent is of a station and class well above Tolkien's. Perhaps Eton or Cambridge. It is spot-on for an upper class gentleman enjoying a holiday of lawn tennis.

It is Fleming who finally responds. "Well, if I remember my Hollywood westerns, this just might be a Mexican stand-off."

The officer replies, "Quite right, sir. A rather bad strategy all around. No need to brandish weapons, now is there?"

He gestures for Gauss and Steerman to lower their pistols. "Besides, the snipers are ready to finish any . . . unpleasantness."

Tolkien and Turing steal a glance to their left, toward the distillery.

The officer nods at the buildings, then continues as if this were all but a minor misunderstanding among gentlemen. "Hope you civilian chaps don't mind a proper uniform among you. I prefer to dress as who I am. Nasty rules on spies these days, no?" He then turns toward Tolkien and removes his hat.

"Has it been all this time, professor?"

Tolkien stares in shock. He finally exclaims, "Jodl? Strieger? How?"

Strieger clicks his boot heels smartly and gives a bowing nod. "Your humble student assistant, Herr Tolkien, Class of '33. Sorry I didn't keep in touch." He is toying with his old mentor now. "You probably just gave your famous *Beowulf* lecture. To be honest, I miss that. The ancient Anglo-Saxon, the Germanic myths. You brought them to life for me, made me think of my Fatherland."

Tolkien can no longer hold his anger. "You're . . . you're a damn traitor!"

"You've forgotten? That, like you, I was born in Bloemfontein? Orphaned and then adopted. I see you remember that much. You never asked about the rest. My father was Dutch, a Boer. He was executed by the British. My mother died in the infamous concentration camp for Boer women and children on the outskirts of Bloemfontein. You remember your father's grove of trees and your mother's rose garden? I remember nothing, save what I imagine from a tiny photo of my family behind barbed wire, dumped at the interment field. But I know much more. Oh yes. Twenty-five thousand women and children died there of starvation! Their burnt forms."

He pauses, then curses in perfect Afrikaans, "*Verskriklike! Jy bastards!*"

The epithet, laden with passion and truth, hangs in the air.

The demeanor of a composed SS officer soon returns. "You see, old chap, you Brits invented a new form of war. Scorched earth, they say. A technique we have now perfected. Perhaps you shall see the other side of it. In any case, I was adopted, brought to Merry Old England, grew up and went to Eaton, then to Leeds. My displeasure with British attitudes, however, was always growing, even as you opened my eyes to my Germanic heritage. One must sometimes choose."

Tolkien recalls the young student, eager, gifted in language. A solid, if irreverent, Shakespearean. None of which endears him to Tolkien. He is, however, enthusiastic about the Neiberlung saga. There was an unpleasant disagreement between them at the end.

"Jodl," Tolkien says, "you could've been someone. Truly. Now you belong in a glass jar."

"Now, now, professor. *Ivory towers, glass jars*, how pedantic! The truth is that I have gone far beyond being one of your subordinate little bookworms. You write children's stories. I get things done. Things willed into action and reality, not just dreamt of. My deeds are part of the thousand year Reich. They will live on. Will yours? *Your* epitaph will no doubt read 'And as for his real actions, after the Great War, nothing much happened'."

Strieger makes a show of checking his watch. Impeccable time. He clucks, then says, "My Führer has an undeserved reputation for impetuousness. Actually, he seldom demands immediate action, save, I must admit, when he wants something personal. So, you see, I am here as his personal emissary to assure that his wish is fulfilled."

Fleming breaks in. "Very well, Herr Strieger, you have more weapons than we. We, however, have you stuck somewhere in the bloody middle of nowhere in Scotland."

"Again, you underestimate." Strieger nods toward the Arado. "We are really very close, mere hours to the Fatherland. That said, this … situation presents a bit of pickle for all of us. Ripe, as I said, for a bit of negotiation. Commerce among spies, if you will."

Fleming is impassive as Strieger continues. "Thanks to Miss Shelby, we already have a representative assortment of the Ara documents, beautifully written in this obscure language. Nonetheless, our skills in reading them may prove poor and tardy. That is why, professor, I must insist that we … resume our relationship. The Führer has a personal interest in the mystery of this language and, since you are here, I can say with authority that he will earnestly desire your services in Berlin. One former signalman beckons to another, if you will. Perhaps, after so many years, you two can commiserate together on the futility and slaughter you both experienced at the Somme. Something not to be repeated this time, surely. The rest of you, after we depart, will be free to go your own way. Let us move along."

Gauss and Steerman move toward Tolkien. Mr. One and Mr. Two pull their pistols, the gun barrels moving like the noses of wary beasts. The machine pistol held by Gauss barks like a small dog. Mr. Two fires an errant shot, then crumples, going down like a strong tower, buckling along the lines of its own joints. Yvonne screams "Nooo!" Mr. One regards the gun barrels aimed at his head, the imminence of his own death, weighs it against the anger, the duty, the futility of shooting now. He keeps his pistol aimed. His is a taut wire, his tensile strength unknown.

A patch of fog shreds and drifts by. The waters lap. A coot utters a quarrelsome croak in the distance. To Tolkien, the moment is a crystalline sense of now, poised on a future that could go in any direction.

Turing, to this point silent, steps forward. "Stop this! Look! Sir! I'll go with you. I'm more valuable to you than all these amateurs!"

Strieger is looking at the unmoving body of Mr. Two with casual disinterest. He turns to Turing. "Ah, Mr. Turing, we unfortunately have only one available seat, and, to be honest, your code-breaking skills, earnest as they are, are of little value. To put it simply, your side is hopelessly out-matched. The Führer has personally concluded that our system is unbreakable. He desires, however, to see and understand this mysterious language."

Yvonne steps up in front of Turing. "Then you've got the wrong translator! Professor Tolkien isn't up to the job. He frets and dithers. I'm the only way you can master this language." With a slow and deliberate movement, she pulls from her coat, a large, folded piece of paper. "This is a copy of the essential key, the only way to decipher the Ara documents. Except I've done my own encoding of the symbols. I'm the key to the key. You take me, you get the complete set. Otherwise, you're nowhere."

Strieger considers, looks at Tolkien, ponders the extravagance of options, and abruptly says, "Very well, my lady, you shall go."

"Yvonne, damn it! No!" Turing's hands are clenched at his side. He is shaking with frustration. "I . . . need you." Then he plays his last card. "Your father is alive. He's safe. You don't need to do this!"

She looks at him, her eyes like portals to her heart. She is at a cliff's edge of life, a precipice which brooks no retreat. "It's too late, Alan. You can tell him. Tell him that I love him. Now, we're all in this moment, and I've made my decision."

Alan, visibly trembling, is about to lurch and renew the deadly exchange of close-order gunfire. She grabs his hand, leans close. "You must stay here. Where you belong. Same with Professor Tolkien. Alan, we both know we can never be together and we know why. We'll always have our time at Bletchley. Now I've got a job to do. Look for me . . . where you see things best. Inside the numbers." She peers into his eyes until the moment is obliterated by the sudden roar of the Arado's engine. Their eyes cut to the sound. Each knows that events cannot be stopped now, that moments missed can never be recovered. They look back to each other. One last look.

The propeller increases its speed, drowning out all but shouts.

"Time to go! *Schnell!*" yells Strieger. Gauss and Steerman slowly point their weapons at each of their antagonists.

Strieger doffs his hat, turns, and then goes over to talk in Tolkien's ear. "Despite my criticism, I love your book. Bringing the old myths back to life. Really begs for a sequel. Perhaps something darker . . . more adult. Think about me, even if unfondly. Perhaps, even as a character. A watcher. Or perhaps only the mouthpiece, his name told in no tale, of a powerful leader."

Strieger steps back, smiles, and takes Shelby by the arm. He leads her to the dock as Gauss and Steerman step backward, covering the exit.

They board the plane, and Gauss casts off the lines. The prop wash pushes the plane away from the dock as Gauss clambers aboard. As the Arado turns to the lake, a backwash of spray and mist covers the dumbstruck retinue standing on the shore.

The Arado taxies out, turns into the wind, and lumbers toward them. In the space of a few score yards, sheer engine power lifts them off the lake, the floats trailing long streams of water. The plane roars overhead, tips its wings in salute, as if offering Shelby a last look at Turing, or perhaps a nod from Strieger to his mentor. The plane vectors east and disappears into the fog, the engine sound dimming to silence.

Chapter 30

TERMINATION

———

Two days later, Tolkien is walking alone down a pathway at Bletchley through a drizzle. He replays the aftermath of the events at Lake Uiguenal: the long moment of standing there in a stunned cluster, covering the body of Clugdahl McCrory, Mr. Two, with their coats, the rain pattering in solemn thunks on oilcloth. Later, transporting the corpse to the distillery, the workers there confused, calling for medical help with their marine-band radio. The arrival of an abbreviated military convoy. The long and exhausting drive in a green Land Rover back to Oxford. The angry look on Edith's face, softening as she sees his silent distress. He does not talk.

When he arrives at Hut 11, the door is blocked by a large, trench-coated man. A light rain drips steadily off the brow of his soaked fedora. His professional glower says here is a comrade of Mr. One and Mr. Two. He demands Tolkien's ID. His studying glare—picture-to-face-picture-to-face—suggests to Tolkien the security apparatus of declared war, the result of the unstoppable gray swarm already racing through Poland.

Mr. Some-Number hands back the ID and digs in his coat for an envelope. Without speaking, he hands this to Tolkien, who now sees that the door to his hut is sealed by an imposing hasp and padlock.

"My possessions, my notes, records?" The man rotates his head in an inarguable *No.*

Tolkien rips open the envelope. It contains a single green sheet, the note handwritten. Unusual for Bletchley, with its endless typing pools and protocols.

He reads the note, looks at the guard, and begins to double-quick his way back down the path.

He has mere minutes to get to the meeting.

At the mansion, Denniston's absence from an event called at his behest is as unusual as the handwritten note.

In his stead, in the great room with the table, is Philby. His back is to Tolkien, and he is standing before one of the large windows. The curtains are pulled back and he is centered in framed silhouette. A perfect still life of a man in deep contemplation. The only movement is the smoke of his cigarette coiling up in a lazy spiral.

At the entry door, Tolkien coughs politely, and Philby's silhouette tocks slightly, like the ears of a fox.

Finally he turns, bearing a flashed and false smile, and adopts his oily bonhomie. "Well, well, professor. Welcome back. What a nasty bit of business, eh?" He doesn't stop for a reply. "Here we are again in this glorified barn of a room."

Tolkien remembers a helpful Fleming-ism. He is quiet and he lets the long moment force Philby to continue.

"Now let's sum up where we are. An urgent need for a special kind of translation brought you to us. The strange documents showed great historical, archival promise, but, in the end, little of strategic military value, eh? Now this bloody war has started, in bloody earnest. Sabotage has occurred in our midst. And lastly, a rather disastrous course of events this week in Scotland. Events in which you, Turing, and Fleming all went off on an ill-advised cavalier's journey. In the director's stolen car, I might add. Without authority and with an upstart story to explain the disappearance of Yvonne Shelby."

Tolkien, thinking of the death of Mr. Two and the loss of Yvonne, has had enough. He starts to speak up when Philby puts out his hand in the emphatic gesture of a hard stop. "Tish, tish, tish, *tish*, professor. Now just listen. Mr. One has been . . . reassigned. Fleming and Turing are under our firm control. You, less so. I'll give you the benefit of thinking that you were a hapless tagalong on one of Fleming's mad adventures. Mr. Denniston has asked me to intervene in this matter and clean it up. That I will. Now, we have initiated an investigation to find Miss Shelby. It will be inconclusive. She is known, it turns out, to have certain . . . instabilities. The senator will be advised that she was boating and drowned, her body washed down to the sea.

"Your two partners in crime will be reprimanded by private letter. You, however, I intend to deal with summarily."

His stare has taken on the unwavering focus of a predator. He advances slightly, enough for Tolkien to feel the menace. "Do you know the penalties for violation of the Secrecy Act? They are not pretty. Capital crimes can be charged. Most assuredly they can ruin a career, overturn a contented and productive life. All in all, create quite a pranging and make the missus quite upset."

"Your expect me to engage in a cover-up? You are quite mistaken . . ."

"Now, tish again. Upset will not help your position. We will be overseeing Miss Shelby's fate quite closely, I assure you. Your role is to forget her and all these misadventures. Her story will never be told. Not even under the guise of fiction. Stay out of the heroine business, Master Tolkien." He stops briefly, then moves to his closing. "You, professor, are now terminated."

"What?"

"Excused, canned, jubileed, cashiered, sent home. You won't be drummed out, you will just turn and go. Your abortive career as a code-breaker is over. All accounts of your business here have already been destroyed. You will never speak of this to anyone. Not Edith. Not your gossip circle at the pub. Go. Resume your life as a teacher, and speak no more of this. Ever."

"The . . . the documents?"

"All in safe keeping, old boy. As I said, perhaps, long after this war, you may see them again. Or maybe not. Who knows?"

He clicks his heels, bows slightly, and offers a final, stiff hand. "Your service to king and country is once again fulfilled. One of your familiar friends will escort you home." He snaps his fingers and sweeps an arm toward the door.

There, escorted by a uniformed guard, is a smiling Timothy Lessons.

"Now, Mr. Lessons, perhaps *you* will quit pestering us with your endless calls!"

As Tolkien exits Bletchley Park forever, Lessons turns to him and says, "I'll take you to the Bird and Baby. A more appreciative audience there, I dare say."

Chapter 31

THE BIRD AND BABY

——

Nothing has changed, thinks Tolkien as he steps into the Eagle and Child pub. *Except me. And, outside, a war.* The depths of the room mellow into murky yellow shadows as he makes his way to the customary table of the Inklings. They are already convened. He steps up and they stand. Handshakes all around.

"Ah, so good to have you back!" Jack's lighted eyes and smile tell it all.

"Yes, quite, we've missed you, having to listen to other's tales." says Charles Williams. Tolkien can tell he doesn't really mean it.

As they settle in, a pint and pipe soon comfort the good professor. He is relaxed.

"Hope they didn't send you on some mad adventure, old boy."

Tolkien dislikes lying, but finds he can acquit the task. "Well, you saw the beginning right here, but in the end much ado about nothing. More than a few unfounded rumors about our Oxford comrades, all nothing, really. And a few crossword puzzles."

"Eh? Say that again?"

Tolkien had been waiting to gently but firmly close this secret gate. "Sorry, Owens, rambled past my Secrecy Act limits even now. Sure you all understand."

A few awkward laughs, followed by a moment of quiet, confirms closure of the topic.

"I do, however, have a new tale to recount. Perhaps a prelude to getting my own work back on its rails. Are you ready, laddies, for a tale from the legendary lost book of *Beowulf?*"

"Hear, hear! Back to jolly-old make believe."

"Or is it?" Tolkien asks the air. His eyes twinkle, the face of someone who has seen things few have.

A shadow suddenly falls across the table. They look up to see a scruffy young man, hair like a moldy haystack.

"Oh, my assistant, Timothy Lessons, who, with your permission, I'd like to join us as often as he might. All agreed?"

Jack speaks for the group. "Your vexatious reputation has preceded you, Master Lessons. Sit, be still, drink much, say little, and you may yet fulfill your secret dreams. Yes, you might become one of us!"

Tolkien breathes deep, all but rolls his eyes. "Now, where are we? Ah yes. Listen! Harken to a time in Middle-earth when the valor of an unheralded heroine shook the world." His voice, its mutterings vanished, rolls forward as his eyes survey the Eagle and Child with renewed appreciation. He has the look of a proud man who can be ordered only so far. The Inklings lean forward and listen:

> . . . Ara, she was called. Cloaked and comfortable in the Wild, she seldom entered an inn. Yet such was the dreadful storm that it washed away all signs on the ground, and left her with the need for the faint track of rumor to regain the trail of her Amon. Cloaked as a male Halfling, she entered the pub known mysteriously as The Lost Shard. There she huddled on a half-bench in a corner, looking beneath the shroud of pipe smoke that obscured the upper half of the room. Other men of the Wild were there, hard men. They were at a nearby table and oblivious to her. She heard their words:
>
> "You've no choice, Barren, we are summoned!"
>
> "Lacklin is right. He has plans for us. Big plans. Something more than just ranger-killing. Bigger even than snaring that upstart, the self-proclaimed King of the Broken Sword. The boasting fool! Bumbler! Braggart! He is ours soon enough. What say you, Barren?"
>
> "By my real name, Seax, I pledged when I was but a boy, swept away from my plague-riven village. I did swear that I would venture far beyond this world. Beyond even the great Wild of lands unclaimed, beyond the depths of even

Mirkwood. Perhaps this is the summons."

"*Seax, Barren,* whatever your name is these days, you're always thinking about some big escape. Other realms, all that rubbish. Let me tell you, my deadly friend, there is only one world in this universe and you are in it."

The man they were talking to glanced over at Ara, surveyed her as a lump in the shadows, then turned back to the other two men as they continued.

"You only have to live within the moment commanded by the Dark Lord's orders—collect the heads of these pesky rangers . . ."

"Yes, collect your bounties on those heads, and die in the traces of his service like the good beast of burden you are. I wouldn't tell your little orphan story to anyone, it only breeds contempt."

"Yessh, e-eshy pickinsh thatsh!" slurred another voice. The speaker, known only as Iker, was shrouded in shadow. He leaned into the candlelight. Revealed was a crude leather mask. Its pieces were rough-cut, its stitches irregular, its shape inhuman, as if it did not fully hide the horrific injury beneath. Blotches of dark discolored the leather where nose and mouth should have been.

His voice was at once wet and garbled, strange in the way a cloven remnant of foreign armory might but hint at its nature. The man's hand went up beneath the drape of the mask, perhaps to adjust some loose part of his former face before speaking. His words came in a broken cadence: "Ah-g, Barren . . . I-g . . . know I'm schluss pret . . . ty-g shless . . . bet-g you shoul-g close your buffoon moth-g."

The third man laughed, swallowed a considerable draught of ale, and wiped his cup-hand on his sleeve. "Don't mind our masked friend. His work is more horrid than his face. The Gracious Eye grants him a generous bounty on these woodsmen that once ranged and ruled this country. The bounty must work well, for he finds them everywhere. Unlike us work-a-day journeymen, he travels with his own pair of hangmen."

The hand of the masked man returned to adjust whatever

shipwreck underlay the mask. Now the voice was much clearer. "Ah, one may see schluss which way I have gone. The trees along the roads wear my livery. Even a wandering halfling's neck I did recently stretch. Hanged rangers are but profit to me, but yield a fine return of fear for our master-g."

Barren spoke, "You may find your wages failing, as these woodsmen are now few. The only prize remaining is the one known as Quicklegs, deemed by some The Usurper, by others, Elf-Lover. They say he trysts with an Elfin maid and consorts with wizards cloaked in grey. No matter; he is mortal. His days are already written and their tally is short. What say you, Baldagis?"

"If the plague doesn't get him first. I hear the Black Ship sails this land once more, gathering villages entire into its limitless, never-lit hold."

"Yes, I know that ship," says Barren. "As a lad, I fled as its blood-darkened sails broached the horizon. I left my village, my family, my best friend. I became a circus imp."

"Well, you've come up in the world, Barren. Unpropertied, untitled, unsung."

"Yushh, now you're an assashinsh-for-hire."

A knife blade swept from Barren's cloak and rested on Iker's throat, testing its exquisite point against his voice box. "Be quiet, lest your foolish larynx join your misshapen face! Besides, Baldagis, Lacklin, and I are summoned by the Dark Lord for a special errand, and, if you mind your manners, I may mention your . . . diligent work . . . to him."

"Don't be so uppity, Barren. You'll kneel to your uppers like the rest of us."

"Lacklin, my friend with the very short-sword," said Barren, "you would grovel even at the feet of his pet wraith, the reeking ragbag called Pazal!"

"*Whatever* I'm told to do."

"Well, it could be worse than groveling. Or better, depending on your point of view. I'm sure you'd like to find out, put your nose up those skirts. Get to be real friends with the Eye's stinky emissaries, eh."

"Up yours, dreamer! Your mouth will get you into more

trouble than you can handle. You got a better plan?"

"I'll wait for my chance. And, of course, as always, honor his command."

"You *better* say that, and mind your letters. We meet him on the morrow."

Evening at the Eagle and Child rolls on, as it always does, to a comfortable corner of the world where the yeasty-smell of a warm pint and the rich aroma of tobacco smoke surrounds all. Tolkien is wrapping up.

". . . and that is all of the tale that I can tell for now. Perhaps ever. The record of her story is now all but lost. It is too late to rewrite my own works—to rewrite *me, the Edwardian prig,* as I have aptly been called. This tragic heroine truly deserves her own account, a written leaf and branch on the Great Tree of Tales. That task I leave for other hands and minds. However . . ."

Lessons and Jack, enthusiasts ever, lean in. Charles, a doubter, leans back.

". . . I am nonetheless inspired. Perhaps I can muster a tip of the hat in my own works to unsung heroines such as Ara and," Tolkien hesitates, his eyes glisten with a flow of unfallen tears, "brave, unnamed women who this very moment sacrifice themselves for us. Women, like Ara, forever unnamed and lost to the world."

Chapter 32

TÖTEN DER AFFEN!

———

Fleming, deciding how to carry on with a lower profile after the disaster at Uiguenal, is reading a report from MI6 on the fascination of Goerring and Himmler with the occult. *An opening for a better project, perhaps. Especially for an occultist like me.*

He checks his message box.

In an unmarked envelope is a single green flimsy. The corner date and authority code scissored off. He knows the format, however. It is from Hut 8. A message decoded from Enigma:

> T6 "Ubersprache" program shows tremendous progress. American translator cooperates without need for scapolamine. She lacks additional material. Scour museums and libraries for remnants of Cotten Vitellus V and retrieve at all costs.
>
> Delay or failure will not be tolerated.
>
> Defeat England!

Fleming pauses, does a double-take as he scans the next part of the translation:

> I have personally directed that all remaining monkeys in Berlin be seized and destroyed. Owners who are uncooperative, who harbor such seditious pests, will be treated summarily under Protocol 7. Medical research will continue

using human subjects. No exceptions to this policy will be permitted.

Toten der Affen!

A. Hitler

Along the bottom is a note in Turing's distinctive scrawl:

"The bloody bastard is cracked! Sand in the Machine. She has gotten your perverse Dark Elvish into his mind. Toten de Affen! Ha! Kill the monkeys, indeed"!

As to her, and all of us, fates we ill-deserve are nonetheless ours. I understand her father was broken but resolute. She left him a note. At least he understands what I also know. She has chosen her fate.

Chapter 33

PROMENADE

—

Three days later, Strieger is taking an unusual afternoon promenade along the Wilhemplatz.

His mind, always bespoke, always sharp in its bearings, will not rest. It seems to roam a labyrinth of false trails. *Scheist! Scheist! Have to clear my head!*

As she promised, the Shelby woman is cooperating fully, almost enthusiastically. Even now, she is huddled with his team. A handful of elite linguists and code-breakers. This strange tongue, *Myrcwudu* they call it, will be tamed to become the *ubersprache*. The Führer is pleased, already asking for additional moments of instruction for himself.

But all in due time. His team is excited, almost transfixed by the subtlety and depth of meanings. The language demands much, it writhes and squirms before giving up its meaning. But soon it will become a trained animal—subservient, ever obedient to the Führer.

The edge of disquiet Streiger has been feeling, almost like being lost in a gloomy forest, seems dispelled by the fresh air and sunshine of this walk. There is excitement in the air. The exhilaration of forging war, of being in the capital city of the inevitable victor!

Up ahead, an organ grinder, a colorful gypsy with his trained monkey, is entertaining a crowd. Jodl approaches to investigate. The monkey, uniformed in red and standing on a little table, takes a coin proffered from the crowd, doffs his boxy little hat, bows, and deposits the coin in a cup at his feet. His tiny hand immediately shoots back out in a supplicating gesture, his almost-human eyes pierce the crowd. A comical little man.

Strieger moves closer, extends his hand to offer a mark. The little monkey-man studies him, sizes up his SS uniform, and suddenly stands upright. Stiff military attention. The monkey reaches into the gypsy's breast pocket and pulls out a little square of black felt. This he holds beneath his nose as he bats his bootless heels together and his right arm pistons out in a perfect Nazi salute.

As Strieger watches, the little monkey holds this pose, his face somehow absurdly serious. Someone in the crowd laughs out loud.

A mockery of the Führer! thinks Strieger. He lifts a hand, snaps his fingers, and two plain-clothed men step forward. Gestapo by their bearing.

"Arrest this man! Dispose of him as . . . his kind should be disposed of. As for the monkey, destroy it!"

The unpleasant matter concluded, Strieger turns to leave. The two men try to grab the monkey. It is not chained. It screeches and writhes out of their hands. A second attempt is met by a stern bite that draws blood.

The irreverent little creature then jumps to the ground and, quick as a squirrel, flashes toward an esplanade of large, closely set trees. Pedestrians jump; the monkey ascends the first tree and glares with perfect impudence directly at Strieger. He then disappears into the multi-colored autumn boughs and perfects his escape. From somewhere in the tree he no doubt peers out at his hapless master being escorted away.

Strieger resumes his stroll and ponders his doubts. Perhaps no living thing, man, beast, or language, can be fully trained. *Oh yes,* he counters to himself, *now that we have this language, we will wrestle it until we prevail!*

A stray thought nags him. *The Watcher? Let others take that dull oversight. The Führer is right. Enigma is unbreakable.*

Still, just let me clear my head.

He strolls on for a long time.

Chapter 34

ARA FOREVER

———

The next few days display a low, gray, swan's-belly sky, then shade to the ever-earlier nightfall of autumn. At last, the weather clears to a brilliant night sky accented by the blackout covering all of wartime Britain. Tolkien peers from his bedroom window, talking in the depth of the stars. He hurries downstairs.

He is unhesitating as he enters his study, sweeps his months-old drafts into a trash pail, and busies himself at this typewriter. New paper, new outlook, new energy to his work.

He has a letter to write, amends to make, and a story to finish.

He inserts a set of papers and carbon in his typewriter, and begins to peck. Within the hour he is wrapping up the letter:

> Of course, there is little that I can say directly.
>
> Ian and Alan, my friends, our fellowship has been tested, has suffered an unimaginable loss, but it has not broken.
>
> It gives me strength to know that some of what we desired was fulfilled. And now I find strength greater still to go forward and complete a long-ago promise to another fellowship, one that lives now only in my heart. Where else will we all reside in time?
>
> In that endeavor, Ara, not my tale, is nonetheless my guide. More than a muse, she is my guardian angel.
>
> Know, Alan, that I believe you will make good on your challenge. Even your machines, for better or worse, I confess,

may someday be as sentient as you believe.

Know, Ian, that you will no doubt find that smart rascal of a character you seek. Handsome, callous, loyal, dashing and dangerous. A formidable combination!

As for me, I have found myself in the Quiet Man in the Big Adventure. You remember? Baggins, Bilbo Baggins, at your service.

I hope this war does not forever sever us, though it may well work out that way.

Farewell, and Your Friend and Fellow,

J.R.R. Tolkien

He pulls out the letter, signs both copies, and inserts a fresh sheet. This is the red meat he has been waiting to taste.

And, even with that hunger, it is not easy at first.

His muse whispers, *Now, in the bitter watches of the night, sit with your debt, lament your prejudice, summon your humility, open your heart, and bestow a token of heroism to a deserving woman in your tale. Write!*

And write he does. It comes in starts, initially an image of a flower alone in a field of snow, fashioned of cold steel, thence to the image of an idled shieldmaiden, fearless of death but terrified of the fate of a cage. A heroine in search of her journey. Yes! A minor but pivotal character. She will be closing with her destiny in a moment of confrontation and sacrifice. He lets his imagination run, his muse whisper, and the character suddenly stands before the twisted Left Hand of Evil:

The wraith-lord was impossibly tall, reigning over a fief of fear flung across the battlefield. Haughty and dismissive of men, he hefted his bludgeon playfully, and the words he sang came as taunting barbs. "No cage for you, little flower. No rest upon peaceful bower. For you the ages of lamentation. Your mind shriveled. Ever quavering before the Lidless Eye."

Shieldless, she extended her arm and pointed her sword at him. He laughed and she spoke in response. "I fear neither you, nor your Master whose unblinking sight is shrouded by malice, nor even the drear watches of regret. All this I have passed. I stand before you, and I shed my helm. Start! Yes!

Your sotten smile melts. For you see I am woman, I bear a sword of noble lineage, and I am your peril!"

He rereads it. A rough draft, surely to be changed for the better. But still . . .

He is interrupted by Edith, with tea and, on the silver tray, a bowl filled with sticky toffee pudding! He looks at her as she pours his tea. "You are my Luthien, My Dancer in the Glen. I am a deeply fortunate man. Let me set my mad typing aside."

She hesitates, her hand on his shoulder, looking down at him. "And the little lady you were once speaking of, this Ara?" her voice sounds just a little jealous.

"Dearest Edith, she is, I suppose no more real than Beowulf, or my hobbits. Beyond that, by penalty of treason, I am forbidden to speak further. Nor of Bletchley in any way. I leave those tales for others to tell. Those with less burden than I, and a steadier will, a . . . a cadence if you like."

Chapter 35

A LETTER

—

In 1947, the Tolkien family moves from the Northmoor residence to a Merton College house on Manor Road. Their mail is forwarded to them for some weeks. The Royal Mail at this time is supremely efficient, often delivering several times daily and offering a kind of same day discourse for those un-fond of the blower.

So it is that this tendril of the Tree of Tales concludes with Tolkien finding an unusually tardy delivery in his mailbox. It is addressed to the Northmoor residence. It is in a hauntingly familiar hand. By its postmark, it had been dropped in a mail pillar some days previous. The stationary, however, is more of a mystery. It is tinged with yellow, as if it had sat about for years. Its edges are dog-eared, as if it was occasionally carried about in a coat pocket or handbag.

He carries it into his new study, lays the other mail aside, and sits in his desk chair. As he stares at the envelope, his eyes momentarily focus beyond, to a foot high stack of manuscript pages centered on his desk. Here is the first complete draft of his opus, *The Lord of the Rings*. He returns to the curiosity of the letter, turns it over, thumbs one of the dog ears, and suddenly knows with certainty who this is from. The thought un-gates a flood of feelings long suppressed. He remembers the sheer sense of loss, of another fellowship sundered. He grits his teeth as he recalls Philby's clawhammer threat of the Secrecy Act. A loss that cannot be spoken of is a wound long in healing.

He has to concentrate on use of his letter opener as his hands tremble ever so slightly.

He slits the envelope and pulls out several pages. It is in the form of a note, without date or return address. It is in the hand of a woman, American in style, and it says:

I write this in haste, though its delivery, if ever, may be long-delayed.

I finished translating what seems to be a lost chapter of Ara's Tale, a time of endings, and so it seemed appropriate for this moment of sharing with you. We never know which ways journeys may turn, do we? Hers, mine, yours, Ian's, Alan's. Here is my rendering of her last chapter:

On the burnt and bloodied field of battle known forever hence as Wyrmslay, Ara held her Amon—Ringbearer—as he died in her arms. Tears cascaded from her eyes as she clutched him and wailed the cry of a lover lost to her beloved.

Condemned to the shadowlands of immortality, she could not follow her Amon in death.

In time, she would accept and acquit her unending and solitary destiny as a muse, though it grew from a soil salted with regret and anger at, not her fate, but her loss.

And, you may ask, how did this moment come to pass?

The force that ties the world together is a form of magic, and all magic, light and dark, is of but one sea, whose tides ebb and flow with the force of belief.

Thus the destruction of Bind, the Great Ring, in which Ara played a vital part, was once celebrated far and wide. But it had consequences, unintended and unhappy, as well.

Held in check by the force of Bind was much of the natural order of the world, and, as we all learned, part of that order was . . . Dragons.

A last generation of their kind, they had slept a thousand-thousand years. Now they awakened. Other forces also awoke. Mingled and confused with these creatures were seething winds, torrential rains, unforgiving drought, convulsions of the earth, massive waves, volcanoes over-spilling with molten anger to darken the world entire and shame the petty fire-hills of the Dark Lord.

The Last Wyrms flew even unto the Far West, to the lands where Ara and her Amon had sought refuge with the Light Elves.

Thus by paths and shores unknown, Ara returned to take a stand in this Middle-earth. Her Amon became known as Dragonfoe.

Save us Ara! Turn back this wheel of time and fortune. Can the shackles of Bind be worse?

Professor, I think you know this Muse. Nameless, she has been at your shoulder all along. I enclose something which I was able to retrieve. May our, and all, journeys be justly remembered,

Yvonne

The last sheet, was in Tolkien's own script. It was the single exam page from 1928, the fount from which many, still-unfinished journeys had begun. On it was written:

In a hole in the ground,
there lived a Hobbit.

INTERLUDE

—

"Psst, the Provisioners arrive! Are you ready to stand down?"

"I can't stop now!"

"Look at me, Montefur, slow-witted twin of another father. THIS is the only time. The world will soon depend on our restoration of the trackway of Ara."

"Again, Plaxe? I knew you'd bring up our past. And you once said these were just musty artifacts."

"I understand more now. Let us report the telling as best we can, with stich and glue and your furious scribbles."

"And the parts scrawled in a tongue unknown to both gods and men?"

"Those will tell their own tale . . . in time."

BOOK V
AMERICA

—

These creatures live to me as I am creating them. Twere I to finish, they would become wooden, lacking in life. Thus, the tale must go on. It is, after all, one belonging to all who would but participate and find its first steps, beside a secret gate.

~ J.R.R. Tolkien, *Letters*

1970: AN ARRIVAL

—

As he deplaned at what was then Idlewild Airport, the old man was scarcely recognizable as the chipper Merton Professor of Anglo-Saxon Literature who enthralled his students at Oxford. His lively gait had slowed to a shamble. He hugged a barrister's document case, its contents bulging, its latch reinforced with knots of twine. His flashing brown eyes retreated beneath brows that sprouted like dark, untended weeds.

He shuffled through a turnstile at customs, glanced at himself in a mirror, and cut his eyes away. His gaze returned to study his image in the glass. Gone were the smile creases that always radiated from those eyes. The forehead, usually noble, now mapped a gulag of deepened liver spots. His hair, typically a groomed roller of white-capped gray, retreating as if into some mythical northern sea, now splayed out like moldy hay.

Why be surprised? he thought.

His trans-Atlantic sleep had been elusive, shattered by dreams of menace and chase. It distilled, as always, into the nightmare of the giant spider—the apparition that had haunted him since he was bitten as a child in his native South Africa.

Moments before, as the plane banked in approach, he had glimpsed the Manhattan skyline rising through a pinkish, fog-shoaled dawn. The World Trade Center towers, each under construction and exotically aglow, regarded him like outlandish stalks bearing glassy, multifaceted eyes. His muse of myth and language hovered near. *Watchers*, she had whispered, *guardians over secret gates.*

He weaved through the crowds to arrive at baggage claim. He felt panicked, as if slipping unmoored into a churning river of people and unintelligible loudspeaker announcements. Two awkward turns and he finally saw the sign. *Taxis, yes.* He fumbled in various pockets and pulled out a note. Despite being jostled, he stood his ground. He held the note outstretched in one hand while his other hand clutched the barrister's case tightly to his chest. On the note was typed:

Algonquin Hotel. 59 W. 44th Street. Four nights

Someone, perhaps his wife Edith or his travel agent, had handwritten below this, "Nice place for writers, a favorite of your fellow Inklings." Then the typeface continued:

Columbia University. 116th and Broadway. Department of Old English Studies.

A final notation was scrawled in his own eccentric hand: "See Os! West Inn (?) Bar. Beware Myrcwudu."

He crumpled the paper against his chest, put it back in his pocket, gathered his other bag, and set out in the direction of the taxi sign.

John Ronald Reuel Tolkien steeled himself. *Go now and bar this fell gate,* the muse breathed. *Before it is too late!*

For a man about whose life it ultimately would be written, "After 1925, nothing much happened," this lion of letters trudged in utter fear for the first time since he was eighteen at the Battle of the Somme.

Chapter 37

2008–2009: DOCUMENTS

Thirty-eight years after Professor Tolkien came to America, the last connecting thread to his visit hummed, taut as a tripwire, across a razor's edge.

In a canyon on the outskirts of Los Angeles, in an unlit room, sat the soulless thing. It adjusted its dark cloak and hood. Its gnarled hands, one bearing a heavy ring dulled by long wear, moved a sharpening stone in a slow, steady rhythm. The stone ground against a steel blade with a sound like teeth grating against chalkboard.

On and on. Screech and scrape. Back and forth.

The Wraith Pazal relished the exquisite sharpness of the blade. He could take all the time in the world.

Eventually, six feet of freshly honed steel gleamed across the kitchen table spread with a worn red calico tablecloth. The sword was notched on one edge, its grain interwoven with ghostly, writhing images. Next to it, Abbott and Costello (in the guise of salt and pepper shakers) observed with horrified mirth. Beside them, a tabletop chorus line of mint-condition Barbies gestured from their original boxes like game show presenters.

Bud and Lou, the mint-in-box Barbies, the hooded figure, the great sword—all convened in stillness. The clocks—even the owner wasn't sure how many there were—ticked and chimed and tocked as if in harmony with the dark and rustling woods outside.

This moment waited for Jess Grande to come home to his leaning, weathered, creaky, dusty—in all, very Topanga-like—little business establishment cantilevered over the creek and known as The Mirkwood Forest. In fact, The Forest, as locals called it, was in its very dustiness and leaning and weathered façade, a perfect reflection of Jess.

Almost luckily, he was late.

Because it wasn't just another fall night.

It was Halloween.

As midnight approached, Jess arrived at the door. He stood and listened for a long time. He wrestled out his keys and struggled in clinks and rattles with the wobbly lock bolt. He opened the door and stepped inside. Even before the door snicked shut, he felt the silence. Every clock had stopped. He quickly reached beside the door and hefted his walking stick, his sturdy companion and fearless "equalizer" for thousands of miles and at least a score of brawls in unnamed saloons and forgotten diners along lonesome highways. He stood ready. The moment, timeless and unmeasured, ran on and on, as if a hushed and expectant mist were gathering. Far away, something bellowed and cursed.

It may have been seconds, perhaps hours, before pain ripped away the fog, and he could again think clearly.

The unexplained wound in his leg seeped an exquisite stream of fire. He hobbled in the colorless light of the gallery. A table fell over. Glass broke and pointless knick-knacks clattered across the floor. Like an incongruous yellow night-moth, a telegram flimsy fluttered down to rest briefly in a swath of moonlight that revealed:

> Cadence: I would like
> Topanga. We have much
> won't leave you.
> Jes

The flimsy lifted again, escaping his shambling steps and hiding beneath an overstuffed chair.

The night of meeting finally had come. Each desperate, lunging step down the hall, each year of the long parade of the last decades, each unexplained late-night sound jerking him awake to a heart-pounding vigil in the dark—all presaged this moment.

A voice spoke, as if far away but approaching fast, "Sharpener, halt!" A glimmering sword point flashed by him.

He stopped, exhausted, leaning against the wall. Outside, to the squirrels hovering in branches, a pale flicker swept through the interior of The Forest.

Inside, Jess sweated and faced his pursuer. The hooded figure was large, standing impossibly there in the prosaic reality of this money-losing, two-bit, little nostalgia shop.

The voice came in a low hiss. "You possess a tale not of your hand, entrusted to you by thieves!"

"I . . . own them. They're just some old scrolls." Even as he said this, Jess felt the sinking weight of a long dormant falsehood finally being confronted.

"Do not trifle with me, Sharpener. Give me the Book!"

Jess remembered the grey-and-white haired old man who had given it to him, the promises made, the secrets long kept, the miles and miles traveled since then. He remembered the little wound of the mind, unhealed through the years, that someday, somehow, to someone, he would have to answer for what he possessed.

That moment had come.

"I destroyed it," he said, summoning a reserve of false courage.

"Your lie befits your life. Will you grovel now? Will you watch us take the girl, the only precious you have left?"

Jess's walking stick was inexplicably missing. He stood empty-handed before the intruder, flat-footed and defenseless.

The flashing sword point rose, poised to plunge deep into his chest, and open the throbbing sack of his heart. As the blade readied for the final thrust, he could almost feel the sharp entry, the chill serum of the burning ice of stars pouring in. The hood of his attacker flared, and Jess felt the last staccato tugs of reality shredding free at the seams. It was, ironically, as he had always suspected.

He almost submitted to the trance, but then fixed on the hateful words: "take also the girl."

No way, he thought, *not my granddaughter. She's on her way!* He held on, trying to think of a plan. Any plan. In the end it wasn't elegant, but it would do.

He fell back through the doorway into the next room, scrambling to find an iron handle set flush in the floor. His hands, blind as moles, found the heavy metal ring and pulled hard. A cover lurched open and Jess dove head first into the black abyss. The cover fell back with a solid, close-fitting thump.

Pazal stepped into the doorway and paused, searching in the darkness that to him was as the noon day sun. His prey had disappeared!

The great sword swung in an arc and crashed into the doorframe, spraying wood and cleaving a rent inches deep in the cheap doorframe.

Along the creek side beneath the trapdoor, the brush rustled as Jess—once known as the Scissor Sharpener—scrambled for his life. He would again travel the long gray road of anonymity.

Behind him a restless wind, precursor to a coming storm, seethed through the trees. A tide of clouds covered the night. The tiny shop stood silent and empty.

* * *

As fall next returned, the missing man's granddaughter sat at a creek-side table on the grounds of the Topanga Commune Organic Restaurant on a pleasantly cool Saturday morning. The table was a half-mile upstream from The Forest. Cadence Grande smiled at the clusters of birds that sang in accompaniment to the low burble of Topanga Creek. She had a bright, happy face framed with shiny black hair bobbed pixie-fashion. A face attractive, if not beautiful, as much for what it said as for its features. A tailored nose and a wide mouth quick to smile, but it was her green eyes that truly spoke. They were arresting, settling firmly on whoever was talking to her, not flitting away. Normally, they said that here was a studier, a person of confidence and resolve. If they now flashed an occasional beacon of cynicism, it was because nothing had been normal since her arrival in Topanga last fall.

As she arranged her table, a tall pony-tailed waiter approached, doing his best Billy Jean dance steps along the flagstone pathway.

"How's Miss Pixie today?" He wiped his hands on his apron already floured and spotted with the morning's bread-making. "The usual?"

"Good morning, John. That would be great. How's business?"

"Not bad, unless you got bills."

She thought for a second. "Ah, do I know that one. Can't pay them, can't ignore them."

He laughed, left, and returned quickly. He presented her with a scone and the signature coffee procured, so the menu boasted, from a tiny Zapatista village deep in Chiapas.

She sat and had her breakfast. It dawned on her, as it often did these days, that she was sitting alone. Not for lack of friends, great and true friends. Not even counting the seventy-plus on Facebook. Not for lack of men either. She had been in a serious relationship, but it hadn't worked out. Now she was seeing a pragmatic young man named Bruce.

No, the alone part was a deeper feeling, something that lurked beneath and unbalanced her confidence, like a giant squid brushing the keel of a becalmed sailboat.

The truth was, like many arrivals in Los Angeles (or, in her case, re-arrivals after a long absence), Cadence had begun to see her life as a movie. Ridiculous but true. And it helped. Helped to put into perspective the main scenes. Her father dead since she was fourteen, his interrupted presence somehow still around here in Topanga. A man whose own death he would imagine as an ongoing journey of the soul.

Her mother, gone two years now. A woman whose own demise she would hold to be an unaccountable accident disrupting a practical plan. The dreamer and the to-do lister. They couldn't have been more different.

Of course, at this point, Cadence didn't get to ask them any more questions.

She let the movie roll to the next scene. Every time it played, it was shocking. Her mother reaching out with shrunken, bird-claw hands. Sitting bedside, Cadence could feel the hot malignancy, loose and raving, burning through the last timbers of her mother's life. A conflagration so extravagant, so unconscionable, as to be beyond reckoning.

And it wasn't the first fire to scorch Cadence's psyche. The truth was, deep down, Cadence hated fire. As surely and profoundly as Ahab abhorred his whale.

She combed her hair back with her fingers. It was a new habit, impatient as if trying to sweep away the mental haze that had intruded on her since returning to Los Angeles. A brume with a faint tang of burning, like the acrid tinge of smoke from an over-the-horizon inferno. She knew exactly when her inner nose first detected it.

She let the last reel of her movie play.

Scene Six. Cadence, the orphan, arrives in Los Angeles. She is filled with hope. She finds a big surprise. Her grandfather Jess, her last known family member, is inexplicably gone. It isn't the shock, or the guilty moment of bitterness. It is the empty feeling. No, a chasm. Hell, it is the Marianas Trench, the Challenger Deep, the Valles Marineris of empty feelings. Maybe melodramatic, but when she looks over that straight-falling edge into the abyss it eats up everything. Just at the moment she found a reason, a foothold, in her grandfather's urgent telegram, the ground beneath her had fallen away. The owner of so many answers to so many unanswered questions . . . vanished. Only that tinge of smoke hanging in the air.

Oh Baloney! Cut the drama and get a grip!

Thank God for the inner voice of her mother's mops-and-brooms wisdom. That would carry her past all this. She took a deep breath and looked at the table.

Before her lay her folio sketchbook, along with something new in her life: a pile of fifth graders' papers. This was good. She relaxed into a smile, thinking of the quirky innocence of her students.

She picked up her green marking pen (red was so last century and so, well, inflammatory). She wrote a gentle correction in the margin: "Abominable Snowman, not Abdominal Snowman." Some of her girl students were taller than she was. Cadence was barely five feet, but her stature disguised much. Men and boys liked her, always deferring to her and sensing a coiled strength in her movements.

She graded papers for a solid hour, but her thoughts kept flowing to the fate of The Forest. The shop, just up the road, was shuttered. It looked neglected from the accumulating roadway detritus of dust, beer cans, and fast-food wrappings. Twice a week she dutifully raked and swept it up, but the road never quit spewing its debris.

Tomorrow she would be back there again. It was like tending a misbegotten memorial for a lost seaman, a place of vigil with no capstone to a life gone without a trace. Her vigil for Jess had elongated without clear reason, one month following another. She wasn't going back home to Indiana. Her mother's ghost, newly formed and restive, was too close back there. Her grandfather—wherever he was—sure as hell wasn't coming back here. She sensed that at least the waiting part was over.

"Missing person, consistent with prior history," was the way the police report put it. She knew better but couldn't prove it, because the very essence of her grandfather had been a magician's coin trick. Now you see him, now you don't. Mostly don't. Like the same venerable coin, marked and dated, that the illusionist gives to one audience participant and pulls from the ear of another selected at random so that there could be no trick. But the trick, as the magician tells the audience, is the coin; it chooses its destination; the magician is only the emcee.

She frowned as she recalled the detective talking to her amid the yellow police tape and the fingerprint techs cluttering up The Forest.

"This is the only picture of him you have?" The detective was holding up a curled and faded little Polaroid, a brittle and ancient specimen from a vanished technology. The man in the picture was blurred and distant, tall with a Fedora hat and beard. His face was shadowed. He was standing next to a road.

"Would you recognize him if you saw him?" he asked.

"I'm . . . I'm not sure."

The detective stared hard at her.

"Not really. Okay, no."

"So you came here right after you got this?" The detective reached over and picked up the sender's flimsy copy of a telegram. "We found this beneath a chair."

"Yes. Three days."

"Uh humm."

"But what about the blood? Prints? DNA? This!" She walked over and put her hand on a three-inch deep cleft in the doorframe.

"That could've been something he did. Sometimes these old loners wig out. I've seen it before. Man goes ape and lights out. Anyway, we didn't find any weapon."

She stopped and just looked at him.

"Look . . . uh, Ms. Grande, sure there are matching prints and some blood drops down the hall, but then they just stop. It could just mean he cut his finger. There are maybe a hundred different fingerprints in here. Retail scenes are tough."

She walked over and crossed her arms, standing next to the now-open trap door in the floor. It opened into a four-foot drop down to the creek side.

"Look, Miss, a door's a door. It doesn't matter which one he chose to leave by. This was closed when we got here. Ms. Grande, let me be candid with you. I've seen these cases before. Sometimes a, well, hobo-type never gets it out of his blood. Roadsong. White-line fever. Call it what you want. This man has absolutely no driver's license history. No fingerprint record. Anywhere. There's not much for us to work with"

He paused, thinking, and then went on. "You know the next step on a missing person investigation? When all the leads come up cold?"

"No."

"You call in a psychic . . . don't laugh."

"I'm not laughing because it's funny," she said, but she was. *Only in California.* "Not at all. It's just . . . is that it? That's your plan?"

"Pretty much."

"I don't believe in psychics."

"Well, there's one other strategy. It's usually the most effective."

"Yes?"

"Go home and wait."

So that was what she did. It had been like riding a slow glacier until two weeks ago, when she found a hidden room in the attic. Suddenly, like a roused animal of great size, the world moved with unexpected speed.

The sheriff's foreclosure sale was coming up fast. Twenty-eight days to go. You couldn't miss the big date stamped in red on the foreclosure notice. Every day a huge legal clock slipped another cog, ratcheting a spear-like hand toward the moment of a final outcry sale on the doorstep of The Forest.

On top of that, the anniversary of her grandfather's disappearance loomed a couple of weeks away. Topanga got into its holidays and gave her plenty of reminders. Pumpkins were piled up and cornstalks arranged at the entrance to the town's shops, even the Post Office. Next to her, one gnarly, old, leaning streamside oak was robed in outlandishly oversized fake spider webs. It looked like the outlier of some treacherous mythical forest now home to creatures unseen by day, hideous and partial to laying man-snares. No, she didn't need props to remind her that the season of ghosts and goblins was here. She kept telling herself that none of it meant anything real. *So bring it on,* she mused, *just don't give me that old black magic voodoo malarkey about strange things happening on the a-n-n-n-i-v-v-v-ersary! Give me facts and proofs. And some money to keep this place afloat. I'm tired of this vigil.*

A freshening breeze swept around her table, bearing the fragile promise of long overdue moisture. The pages of the sketchbook riffled open.

She took out her Schlesinger #5 charcoal. The picture before her was almost complete. *In its incompleteness,* she thought. As an artist, to know someone meant to see and to draw that person. On the page was the image of a man's back, his face turned away, an old fedora on his head and a worn backpack on his shoulders. In the distance, a startled bunch of kids stood around a motorcycle and looked at him. His telegram had touched something raw and needy. She longed to see his face just once. To behold, as an artist, her last living bit of family. She wanted to carefully study his image, now as indistinct as the little Polaroid. But it was all gone. The sketch before her was the thin essence, the best she could render. Call it *Man Leaving.* She drew a few lines, none offering a muse, and then closed the book and pushed it aside.

She had her real work to complete. Organized before her were two neat piles: corrected and uncorrected papers. Repeated in similar cycles over the next decade, such piles would order the stars for the lives of children in her South Central Los Angeles classroom.

Her classroom? Funny how easy it was to forget this was the last week of her temporary teaching assignment.

Up on the road, she could hear traffic increasing. The noise of the stream usually washed over the drone of cars at this spot, but the water had dwindled after months without rain. Sunlight waved through tree boughs across the table. The papers continued to move from one pile to another, transformed from unfocused products into solid, red-marked judgments. Grades etched on each two-page research paper. Generous grades, too, sometimes better than they merited, but determined by what would help that half-formed person move one step forward.

With the last paper shuttled to the done pile, she had before her a blank sheet. She thought of her predicament, of being stalled, of looking at unpaid bills, and ... and ... of the hidden room discovered two weeks ago in the attic of The Forest. Suddenly, without planning it, she scrawled on the paper:

In a pile of papers in the attic hides the key.

She sat and stared at it for a long time, feeling the first breeze of a coming storm.

The discovery had actually been of a second attic, hidden in the ceiling of The Forest. The first was above the front door and conspicuous with its red-painted plywood hatch cover framed by molding. Her first week there, she had gotten on a stepladder, pushed it open, and taken one obligatory 360° peek. That was all she needed. She saw a small, spider web-laced frolic room for squirrels and mice and birds. That checked out, she ducked down and retired from further attic exploration ... until a month ago, when she finally started cleaning the back storeroom. Jess had let this space, perhaps once a bedroom, slide into junk collector's depravity. But it wasn't a hoarder's manic nest. Its contents were a wild ruin of flea-market treasure, rising from floor to ceiling, and offering but a narrow and twisting footpath into its core. The path curved to things unseen around a column of boxes. It hinted that it might close behind an unwary intruder, shift and close and blend her into the junk, never letting her go.

Make of you a Watcher. The thought came clear and unbidden.

Drawing on the weighty depths of her twenty-something cynicism, Cadence decided she was too worldly to get the heebie-jeebies from this.

It was just a junk room.

Until she entered the path and peered around the corner. Standing there was a leering six-foot sentinel. She recoiled even as she recognized him (as would any kid from her generation). There he was. Jasper Jowls, the giant standing Banjo Dog himself, with big, rolling, satanic eyes fixed on her. He was frozen mid-strum, his banjo gone, his skin wrinkly, and his hound-dog ears drooping.

She imagined he had fled from some long-ago foreclosed Chuck E. Cheese franchise hidden deep in the San Fernando Valley. He stood there gape-mouthed and menacing. She was afraid to take her eyes off him. She could feel his vibes. *Come in further, Cadence. You can be one of us!*

Instinct guided her. Cadence carefully stepped backwards, retreated from the room as fast as she could, and slammed the door. Later that night she listened for sounds from the room. Shuffling. Murmurs. But there were none.

* * *

It took her two weeks of sporadic afternoon work to clear a beachhead into the junk. She found green melamine mixing bowl sets, two dozen line-tangled fishing poles, and a hulking metal-bellied 1920 Pullman motorized washing machine with a bulbous metal top and hand-crank rollers, looking evilly robotic and worse for its fifty years in some roofless Midwest garage. Then, beneath a dust cover that made of it a brooding ghost, she found a freestanding Victorian-era oak and brass coat rack. She disrobed it. On it were slung an array of capes—superhero capes. As if it had once stood inside the entrance to some mysterious lair: a Secret Headquarters where a select group of Marvel and DC comic characters came to de-cloak and let their hair down. She fingered and lifted the strange dusty fabrics: red for Superman, light-robbing black for Batman, a ragged burgundy shawl . . . perhaps for Spawn? There was a dark gray cloak for The Shadow and yellow garb for Thor. There were others of powers and provenance unknown.

Once the entry was secured and the escape path cleared, she personally freed Banjo Dog. She got a dolly and moved him and set him out at one of the front windows of The Mirkwood Forest, just to the left of the front door. He stood there, looking straight ahead like some veloured Kaw-Liga, leering at startled passersby. She wiped her hands together and put them on her hips and studied her work. She felt satisfied. Here she could keep an eye on him.

She returned to the junk room, expecting it to be cleansed of the creepy atmosphere exuded by Brer Jowls. It wasn't. Behind and above where he had stood was a second attic hatch, which she now studied. There was a small black hole in the hatch cover that made her wonder if some further presence waited there, watching her. Scores of nails had been awkwardly pounded up to secure the cover to the frame. Some were bent and some were flattened, as if by desperate hammer-strokes.

She got a stepladder and a hammer and pliers and pulled out the nails. She wrapped a clothes hanger around the end of a pole to make a hook for the hole. She stepped back, pulling. The hanger held and the hatch creaked down on unseen hinges and rusty springs.

Within hours she was scrunched over in an attic space that had been covered, every inch, in closely fit pieces of flat metal, mostly washed and cut ten-gallon oilcans. They were all nailed tight and sealed at the seams with slathers of black caulk. The walls, the floor, the joists, everything was covered. The room was critter and bug proof.

And in that space was stored a lifetime's worth of her grandfather's writings. She spent hours scouring the journals with a fading flashlight. Some of them were stuffed with odd notes and clippings. They were string-tied with dates written on the covers in Magic Marker or pen or crayon or heavy lead pencil. June- September, 1984 and so on. The sheer density of it was impressive. It was an exhaustive codex of what? Stories, thoughts? Excuses?

Behind the pyramid of journals, like the square box of treasures often found behind the sarcophagi in Egyptian tombs, lay a peach crate. Its label read SARHOLE PEACH FARMS. She liked the label, a picture of orchards laid out in perfect order in happy colors, a brilliant yellow-orange morning sun shooting stripes of daylight way up into the sky.

In the crate was a battered valise, like a barrister's case. A rude shoulder strap, festooned with bits of faded tie-dyed cloth, had been added to it long ago. In the valise was an odd assortment of documents that were wildly unlike her grandfather's journals. These were obviously old, not by a few decades, but by scores of hundreds of years. They were written in an array of scripts and by many hands. A few words were annotated in English on one of the yellowed page margins—"Ara," and "halfling" and the unintelligible "Myrcwudu."

As she read through the scattered English in the documents, she sensed a rail spike being mauled into the frozen river of her indecision. From it fractures radiated out, the tiny fissures crackling underfoot as they spider-webbed in all directions. The Yukon-scale ice jam that had been her life this last year started to break up.

And that discovery also touched something deeper and more elusive. She felt a jangle, a twitch, something suggesting the body comes equipped with secret tools hidden in secret chests. Faculties masked by reasoning but still capable of lighting up unused nerve trackways. Instincts firing on receptors that understand before the conscious mind knows, that hear drums dim and distant. Cold sweat and heartbeat thuds foreshadowing the approach of rough beasts . . .

Something quivered against her thigh. She jumped. Her cell phone was on vibrate. She answered. It was Mr. Mel Chricter's secretary calling to schedule an appointment.

Cadence listened for a second. "Monday? Yes. Yes! Okay."

A moving van downshifted and backfired on the road above the creek. The report was like a cannon crack, sending birds in the trees to flight.

Hell, yes! Here's the break, she thought.

She packed up her sketchpad and papers and thought about how she would get to the man's office in Beverly Hills. Monday morning was only a day away and cab fare was out of the question.

* * *

On Monday at 7:30 AM, Screamin' Jay Hawkins was on KLAX 83.5. He was moaning raw lyrics at the two million cars stacked into the Los Angeles morning drive.

I put a spelll on you.

The green Jaguar, top down, looked smooth and feline as it cat-pawed the slick road. The rich canyon air mixed with wet seat-leather smells. A light drizzle misted over the windshield. The burl wood interior was aged like a fine pipe bowl.

Cause you're my-yeen!

The silver jaguar face snarled back at Cadence from the steering wheel center. A pleasant low engine roar worked its way up from under the hood. After she released it from its tarp, it had been hoarse and coughed for the first mile, but now it purred. Not too shabby for a '65. Her grandfather, whoever he really was, clearly had a way with fine machines.

Cadence leaned the car into the steep decline and hard, sweeping slalom S-curves of Highway 92. The tires squealed with delight as she snaked down, toying with disaster, following the asphalt serpent down Topanga Canyon. Shooting a straight line through the curves pumped adrenaline into her veins. Her nose filled with an exuberance of smells deep and dank as she heard something, a pattern beneath the wind and engine roar. Almost like whispered fragments of strange and breathless language.

This morning the clouds had rolled in and poured down the first rain in four months. The road was treacherous where water mixed with the oily residue laid down by millions of cars, the slick sweat left by the city's dumb, ongoing toil.

But up here, far from the metropolis below, her eyes drank in the secret beauty that is Topanga Canyon on a rainy day. Overnight, once-brown vegetation had transformed into every hue of green. It was like driving into another world. Waterfalls tumbling from clefts high in the sandstone walls might be showers for sprites, she fancied. The side canyons loomed as places of mystery that no man had ever ascended, their hidden caves fit dwellings for imaginary creatures. Up ahead, the stone cliffs sank into a swirling sea of gray mist.

The road beckoned to her this morning. She hoped to return from her meeting with Mr. Chricter, the for-real agent, somehow a different person. Leaning forward, the wind blowing back her hair, she imagined herself a figurehead on the bow of a ship, bound for discovery. With that questing image, she understood a small part of the faceless mystery that was her grandfather. She understood his sheer wanderlust.

But, of course, he was now her *missing* grandfather, and in that blunt fact was an enigma somehow related to the battered valise full of documents shoved into the tiny backseat behind her. And, more precisely, with the fragmented "Tale of Ara" that lurked within those documents.

In a moment, she descended into the subdued world of the clouds. She could feel the road approaching the bottom, where it merged into Highway One, the road to Santa Monica or Malibu. The sea that today would be a crashing gray washtub.

The clouds closed around her. They swirled and flowed, revealing roadside encroachments of thick brush. She looked at a tangle of brush and saw it. A long-nosed face was looking back at her. Their eyes locked and then it was gone. She heard a sharp, keening whistle. She peered hard into the rearview mirror.

It could have been anything, she thought. But she knew it wasn't. Not a person, not a misshapen tree trunk. Maybe a badger or a coyote. Or well, today, an imaginary gnome.

Out of the mist suddenly loomed a giant dwarf. She stabbed the brakes and the Jag's tires screeched in protest. The dwarf was plywood, a full-color figure of Disney's "eighth dwarf," a clutching, leering "Greedy." The next sign objected to a proposed development in the canyon by Disney heirs. She took a deep breath and blew it out, settling her eyes on the road and both hands on the steering wheel.

The canyon remained an undeveloped gash in the Santa Monica Mountains, despite being at the shoulder blade of the great city. It had a few homegrown shops, a theater started decades ago by blacklisted Hollywood refugees, a nudist colony, and clutches of "creeker" cabins hovering streamside—at least, until the next fifty-year storm.

The triple threat of natural holocausts—fire, flood, and earthquake—still dominated the canyon's existence.

Fire, of course, Cadence knew only too well. Mother Nature's conspiracy of topography, fuel load, and wind, birthed horrific infernos. The names of the recurring beast's incarnations made headlines: the Hume Fire of 1956, the Wright Fire of 1970, and the Pluma Fire of 1985. But the speed and fury of the Topanga Fire of 1993, slouching its molten hide through the ridgelines and canyon corridors on its way to the coast, was unparalleled in a hundred years.

Downshifting as she approached the ocean lurking ahead, she couldn't help but see a few of that fire's hateful scars: blackened, cracked trunks of older trees. These were surrounded by flurries of new growth.

She shuddered and tried for the millionth time to block the images of that night: her father grabbing the spare truck key and rushing out of the house as the red glow in the sky approached—the crackle and whoosh of a wind-driven firestorm—the cries and shouts—the mad scramble down the twisted hillside road as the air prepared to explode into an inferno.

And the insane roar of the unleashed monster.

That was the last time she saw her father.

"So, you see, it's natural," she remembered the musings in one of her grandfather's journals. "Stories of family, of crisis, of achievement—all seek patterns of disaster." One of many quaint chestnuts he left in his wake. Now the waters of his passing were still. It had been almost a year since that Halloween night when he disappeared. Right after—out of the blue—she got the telegram. Yes, the old-fashioned yellow thing delivered for a price for people that distrusted phones, much less even understood the Internet. It read:

> Cadence: I would like to see you in Topanga. We have much to catch up on. I vow I won't leave you.
>
> Jess

It was short and awkwardly to the point. The word—*"vow"*—was particularly desperate. Like a drowning man yelling for help to the only person left on shore who might listen. And she'd arrived to find a disappearance. No pattern leading to renewal, no cycle to redemption. No answers to any of her questions.

She glided through the last turn before the beach. *Dwarves. Spells. Things unstoppable.* When there are no clues, everything is a signpost hidden in the overgrowth.

The only sure thing was the blue-margined court document peeking from under the valise in the back seat. "Essentially an overdue bill," her lawyer, Everett, had told her. "Pay two hundred thousand dollars within thirty days or your grandfather's estate will be seized and liquidated and the money shelled out to his creditors."

That would be it for The Forest, this car, his documents, all of it. After foreclosure and one hell of a garage sale, what would be left? Zip. Nada. The man might as well have never existed. The last trace of him snuffed out of existence before she could even get a handle on him. *An erased person*, she thought, *except for me and his bills.*

She downshifted, catching the green at the light to Highway One, and glanced at the dashboard clock. It told her she risked being late for the lunch she'd pulled every string she had to set up.

Soon she was stuck in traffic on Santa Monica Boulevard, at what must be the world's slowest intersection. The reason was obvious. Huge billboards, upgraded to full digital displays, loomed like monstrous, angry televisions over a sea of gawking drivers. People weren't driving, they were watching. The screens closest to her advertised the newest, epic remake of *Tarzan*. It flashed the word "Ju Ju" in immense red letters, and she could just hear, over the traffic noise, deep thuds of jungle drums emanating from the screen. She shook her head in disbelief, saw a sudden lane opening, and gunned ahead.

By the time she got access to Little Santa Monica Boulevard, missed the ivied entrance to the Peninsula Hotel, and inched around the block, she knew she'd have to dig deep into her purse and valet park. And still be late.

She pulled to a jumpy stop, handed the keys to the attendant, and opened her purse to deposit the valet ticket and gather her thoughts. She looked at her purse. It was from Macy's, some obscure brand called "Borunda," which sounded like a country in Africa. It cost twenty-five bucks. It had never held more than a few hundred dollars. In twenties. This purse that could never save her grandfather's—her—property. She closed the latch and hefted the valise and tried valiantly to slow her nervous walk. She wanted to run. Her heels clacked as she entered the tiled foyer and saw the restaurant. "The Belvedere Restaurant in Beverly Hills," to be exact. She tried to gather her thoughts. Everett told her that Mel had recently fallen on lean times, but still had one hell of a Rolodex. He was once a journeyman editor for a publishing house in New York. A description that suggested sepia-tinted days when stacks of manuscripts would wait patiently and whisper: *Bide your time. A well-told tale is timeless.*

A waiter escorted her to a table flanked by palms amidst the gauzy, canopied white light of the restaurant veranda. At the table loomed Mel. He was twiddling a business card. A hefty amber drink and an iPhone sat by his right hand. He had a face made for print media. Thinning hair, angular features that formed a kind of broken reef, in the middle of which rose a prominent, craggy island of a nose, a great bumpy nose, long-battered by waves of single malt scotch. He had peculiar blue eyes, like the ocean, like salt and wind and sun-fade. They beckoned in the peculiar way of a very perceptive drunk. He looked as if he had squinted and seen some distant light, some rare existential truth, through the bleary long lens of booze and ill fortune.

She recognized the look. From long ago, from her own dad's eyes. Cadence smiled nervously at Mel across the breeze-rippled tablecloth.

Calmly, he continued to twiddle Everett Marlowe's business card. Everett, Mel's roommate at Duke, Class of '83, was Cadence's attorney as administrator for the estate of her grandfather, recently declared "Missing, Presumed Deceased." The lawyer was, as they say out here, *a close personal friend* of Mel-the-Agent.

Suddenly, like a conductor's initial baton flourish, Mel tapped the card on the table and poised it in the air. He turned his right side toward her and his right eye gave a peculiar knowing squint, like that of an old conniving pirate. It was a look that offered intimacy and demanded candor. "So . . . Cadence," he paused. "Everett told me about you and your . . . interesting find. But first about you. You're just out of school?"

"Yes. I graduated last year from Colorado State . . . University." She felt more secure adding that last part. "I was an art student, with a film studies minor."

"I see." His iPhone came alive and vibrated across the tabletop. Mel's hand deftly silenced it. "Cleveland State. Fine school." She grimaced like a good alum, but held her tongue. He glanced at some text on the screen. "You got family?"

This was awkward territory for her, but that engaging eye made her feel she could confide in him.

"No, not really. My mom passed away two years ago. My dad, he . . . died when I was younger. So my eccentric grandfather was it. And now he's disappeared." Mel put Everett's card down and took a drink as he studied it, as if there were still some deeper meaning to its sparse information. Cadence looked into the depths of her iced tea for some normal conversational tidbit to throw out. Finding none, she waited until he looked up, again with the narrowed eye, and spoke.

"Everett said you have something interesting to show me."

She fumbled with the valise, nestled like a Pomeranian on her lap. "Well, yes, I found . . . my grandfather had these manuscripts, actually." She dug into the papers in the valise. "I found all this in a peach crate in his attic. I, it, I think it's . . . some of it's by J.R.R. Tolkien."

"Hmm. You and everyone else *wish* they could find just that. I'll share some things with you in a bit. Hmm."

A cloud passed over the sea-swept atoll that was Mel's face. He looked at her like this fifty-buck breakfast at the Belvedere was a very expensive use of his very valuable time. In other words, The Big Favor was being bestowed. It was time for her to deliver.

She ransacked the valise for a moment, stopped and looked at a small, brittle page with handwritten lines, then thrust it at him. Mel sighed and took the page. He squared in his seat and put on his reading glasses and his eyes began to track down the yellowed scrawl. Ever so slowly, his focus steadied as he read:

I fear that I no longer have the will to withstand their presence. They conspire to have me destroy all that is contained in these writings. Much of it they believed destroyed long ago. Now they will spare nothing. They will return. So that these pages are not snatched from my own hand, I hereby set them, through my new friend and purveyor of sharpening services, into what I hope will be a sea of conflicting currents and untraceable tides. On these shores in New York City, I hereby gift these manuscripts to Jess Grande for safekeeping.

JRRT

Mel's right eye inquired of the worn leather valise, pondering the raggedy shoulder strap attached with bits of tie-dyed cloth.

"So what else is in there?"

Cadence looked up, her hand already forearm-deep in the documents. She swept out another page, this one torn and frayed as if it had spent years trapped in the corner of a desk drawer. Mel took it and read:

The halfling entered his room, quietly humming the singsong tune of the elderly. The sun slanted in, motes of golden dust in the air and a perfectly halfling-sensible bed looking out of place amongst the draperies and refinements of the chamber. A robed and hooded figure was sitting there. On his bed! With his book! His special precious book. The figure was tearing out pages and smearing others with a sheep's wool wad of ink.

"I beg your pardon sir, but you are intruding in my quarters!" Anger rose in the halfling's chest now. Then the figure looked up and pulled back his hood.

"Old friend," sighed the wizard. "I left you to tell the tale, not dress our fellowship in wasted details."

"Details? What may those be?"

"We have spoken of this before. Your story will be

measured and preserved only if properly told."

"Told? I have only reported the truth."

"Not . . . about *her* . . . ," choked the wizard, continuing to tear and smear.

Their breakfasts came. Mel took a call. Cadence ate while keeping the valise on her lap, awkwardly guarding her grandfather's trove of scribbles, runes, and ornate writings from many hands. Whatever it was, someone, or multiple someones, had gone to extraordinary lengths to create it.

Mel's iPhone vibrated again and he picked it up, studying the caller's ID before declining. He held the phone out importantly. "These new touch screens, sensitive as hell. This thing keeps dialing people up on its own. Dangerous, huh?"

She nodded. She didn't want to talk about her own phone, the rudimentary little freebie Nokia that came with her basic prepay plan.

"Cadence, let's get down to our business. I understand you need money to save your grandpa's place. I wish I could help, but this seems like bits and pieces. You got anything that we can frame into a whole story?"

Okay, try your last, best card. "How's this?" Across the table, she slid another ancient-looking manuscript, creased and stained with candle wax, in a readable but archaic script.

He began to read, and then put down his fork as the words unwound before him:

Herein lies the account of the Fourth Book.

In the last days of Middle-earth, when the Ascendance of Man was assured, and many plots wove through the separate ambitions of all races, there was lost a fourth volume to the Red Book of Hertegest.

Unlike the three "known" volumes, of which many copies were scribed and long cherished, the original and the few secret copies of the fourth volume were doubtless destroyed in the hopes of erasing the contents forever. The effort was successful, and little of its tale escaped save as unexplained lapses and obscure references in what readers, now far removed from those elder days, presume to enjoy as truth.

It was only in the deep to the south of the world as it was then recognized, where the dimming of all the other races and their powers was swift and complete, that Azakuul, Third Caliph of the Realm, extracted much of the tale. It came to him from Orontuf, most quiet and humble of the Great Wizards. The Caliph, proud of a long lineage of learning and knowledge, was adept at collecting both information and power—by charm, by the bribe, and, if necessary, by ruthless cruelty.

And so our story has a source, but we know not if the giving of it was willing. The grim circumstances of the Confession of Orontuf are little known now. As he was, by reputation, not inclined to speak to mortals, we may surmise that His Brownness, Master of the Plants and Harvest, was coerced. So also does the unflinching character of Azakuul the Beheader testify that most certainly not all was voluntary.

Such was the time: halflings dwindled, elves fled to their havens, dwarves toiled ever deeper into the mountain fastness, yes, even as orcs became extinct from a noxious plague of their own foul making and trolls grew smaller and hid under bridges. So too did the Wizards of Old change forever. Gone now was their power. Orontuf, it is said, survived his unfortunate stay with the Caliph, and became a wanderer in the Far Lands. Legend has it that his nature was changed, such that he began to speak to Men and ended his days as a mortal, quietly growing the best potatoes in all the region.

The Caliph, himself beheaded, quite lost his grasp of the tale. Thereafter it passed through paths unknown until it lay, long dormant and unnoticed, in the personal library of an ale merchant that collected, but never read, what were even then ancient manuscripts. Then once again it disappeared into obscurity.

It drifted on tides of ebb and flow for a long, long time.

Mel held up another page, similar in appearance, and read:

It is said by ancient sources that, at its core, the events that came to be known as the Saga of Ara span but thirty days between two full moons before their terrible conclusion. These were marked by a . . . WONDER.

Her journey began with a full moon that was a great fat coin of harvest time. The next full moon was discolored and bruised, a battered shield of war hanging in a sky fumed with anger and strife.

And in between those so different moons, the great red star Narcross grew large and hove close to the land of Middle-earth. There it grew progressively brighter until it filled the intervening run of dark nights with a deep red gloaming.

Narcross stared balefully over the land like a watchful eye. People fretted, fearful of portents that herald a return to the dark legends of the past. Seers and auguries in multitude arose. Owls in twain crossed that angry red star. Beasts misshapen pulled by night carts laden with unknown cargo that fouled the air for leagues about. Crows cawed in sentences and sat upon the heads of docile children.

People shuttered their windows and barred their doors. Folk of design both fell and fair withdrew to refuge common to their kind. Within keep and hut, smial and cave, underbridge and deepest forest, sheltered eyrie and simple hole, all huddled and hoped. Please, please let this likeness gaze only with harmless envy on lands untouched by its evil purpose.

In the span of a week, the celestial intruder dimmed and receded into the twinkling tapestry of the night.

But something had stirred, great movement was afoot, and events came to pass that shook the world. Ara, as all the world once knew, moved at the very center of this tumult, and by her witness the Long Age ended.

Mel put the last page in his lap and took a deep breath. "You know I'm close to both Houghton-Mifflin and New Line. Bernie Alsop and Maxwell Karis are personal friends. That's the little morsel of good news. Want the seriously bad news?"

"Okay."

"You'll probably never get this stuff published."

"Why!"

"Two reasons. First, publishing as we, as I, know it, is gone. It is the Great Auk. It is going bankrupt. Almost no one will take a chance on an unknown like you."

She listened, slightly stunned, waiting to finish getting hit with the one-two punch.

"Second, one word: lawyers."

She caught the whiff of threat, could see the long unspooling of a tangled thread of hassle and delay before anything got done. It pissed her off. "All right, so tell me first about the publishers."

"In truth there are only a handful of big houses left, mostly foreign-owned. And they are fragments of bigger conglomerates. I work this street. I know. I haven't done a decent deal in six months. This industry's worse than General Motors because it's broken and it won't get bailed out."

"But won't it all come back soon? This can't last too long."

"It will never come back, not the way it was. What's coming is what you see everywhere else—a digital tsunami overwhelming the old ways. Newspapers? Dying. Magazines? Falling like flies. Big label music and CD's? Gone. Broadcast radio? So last century. TV. All sliced into bits. Now, clunky old hard-copy paper books that are hauled around from warehouses to dying brick-and-mortar emporiums? And then back again. No way. The whole industry is compressing to a few survivors. People are getting laid off, budgets cut, and that's not a great time for unproven writers. Hell, even I got rejected this year. Totally. My first book."

"What?"

"Yeah, and I went to Iowa for chrissakes!"

His tone opened a little window into his psyche. He suddenly reminded her of a boyish, sputtering Luke Skywalker. "I . . . I'm not a half-bad pilot myself!"

She started to let it slide, but something told her to push him back while he was in this vulnerable zone. "So, with these Tolkien documents, I guess if all else fails, I could go on Oprah?"

He leaned back, the momentary look was priceless.

"Just kidding, Mr. Chricter. Okay, so what about the legal stuff? I'm only trying . . ."

He recovered smoothly. "Hold on. Just suppose some of these documents *are* real. Then *you're* a threat. Worse, you're a sinner against the god of money. Forget kindly old Professor Tolkien. He's wonderful but irrelevant. This is about something unowned, uncontrolled. *That's* a threat. That's where I come in. Without me, you know who you'll see next?"

"Well . . ."

"Intellectual property lawyers. They are terrible. They are the bloodless low priests—our friend Everett excepted—who have the sacred access."

"Access to what?"

"To the blessing that all stories that want to get told must procure. Copyright. It's a genie, a jealous little god that can bedevil people like you for a century or more."

"But I'm not *writing* a story. I just bet this is the real thing. The Ara that these talk about," she patted the valise for emphasis, "is a heroine in somebody's world. A world no one, not even Tolkien, has ever really seen before. She seems to have made a huge difference. It looks to me like this may be all that's left of her. This . . . orphaned story." Cadence bit her tongue. She went on. "It belongs to everyone . . ."

"Bullshit. Nothing is real and nothing belongs to everyone. This is either nothing or, just possibly, a question of . . . very precious property."

She sat back, thoroughly dejected.

"Let me give you a little story, Cadence. You know movies, of course."

"Yes . . . I think I do."

"You like monsters?"

"Not particularly, especially if they're fiery."

"Well, you know the movie *Alien*? You know, 'acid for blood'?"

She nodded, unsure where he was going.

"Well, you know where Ridley Scott stole that idea from?"

She looked puzzled. "No."

"You should. Every good story steals something from the past. Anyway," he shook his head and clucked in disappointment. "Look it up. And one other thing."

"What?"

"Take some friendly advice: don't bet your life on a movie trivia contest."

She felt the growing heat of being lectured to, and couldn't stop it from slipping out: "Thanks, Dad. I'll remember that." She didn't skip a beat. "So where am I? I do what, just take the peach crate and put it back in the attic? No one ever reads it?"

"It all depends on one thing."

"What's that?"

"Provenance. Proofs. Is this stuff real, or just somebody's scribblings?"

She waited, sure he would continue.

"Then, of course, if you're right, if it's real, some people will want it and some people will try to stop it."

"So, I'm stalled."

He paused. "No. But there is another way."

"Somehow I knew you would say that."

He leaned conspiratorially forward, his squinting eye focused on her. She leaned too, her left eye narrowing in rapport, her silk blouse grazing the breakfast halibut on her plate.

His voice fell to a stage whisper. "Look, there is a bigger story. Perhaps a tale of which these fragments are but a part. Use their evil genie against them. The sparse contents of this peach crate are not the real story here. You're the story."

"Only one problem," she whispered.

A moment of unexpected silence; he wasn't following.

"I don't have a story to tell," she said.

"Bullshit, and I don't mean that about what you have to say. Tell what really happened. Start with the start. Where'd this stuff really come from?"

"I . . ."

"And if you don't know, find out."

Yeah, she thought, *as in find my grandfather after a year of a cold trail. I might as well find out who killed JFK and where Jimmy Hoffa is. I'm no good at this.*

Cadence looked at him, certain he was following her dismal interior dialogue almost word for word. She steeled herself for a dismissive wave of the hand.

Instead, he softened and said, "Everett told me you were pretty lost about what to do. After you got to L.A. with the disappearance and all." His demanding eye narrowed. "So, what are you doing now?"

"Keeping house at his property. Ignoring his creditors, and . . ." she brightened, "teaching school. Fifth grade."

"Saints' praise to you."

She rushed on. "Yeah, L.A. public schools. Raynor Elementary. I like it. I hope I get hired back. But for right now, I'm here. I'm ready to do something."

His lean fingers once more tapped the edge of the business card on the table. "Look, Cadence, "I can tell that you really want to find your grandfather or, excuse me if I'm too indelicate, what happened to him. So if he's the one you gotta find *and* the one who knows about these writings *and* Tolkien, then you need to go look for him. What's an angle you haven't tried? Tell me something new."

They were both quiet. Then she said, "Well, you wouldn't believe all the stories about him."

"Oh? Try me."

"Well, here's the root of it. He was a scissor sharpener."

"A what?"

"You know," she held up two fingers and brought them together several times, "for cutting. Meshed single-edge blades? Really hard to sharpen? I'm sure you'd just throw them away, but that's not how they used to do it."

He nodded.

"Sharpening them used to be a wayfarer's trade. Scissor sharpeners travelled all over. Like gypsies." She was warmed up, talking faster now. "You see, my folks said he had a valise, probably this one, that he carried all his stuff in, a folding grinding wheel, whetstones, a few items for sale. He hopped trains and hitchhiked and walked through all the big towns and half the small towns in America. He kept a journal every day. He's sort of a family myth."

"I'd be wary of myths. What's the real truth?"

"I don't know . . . at least not yet. I never met him."

"Okay, take a break and eat your fish. I've got a call to make. Then I want to know all about your grandfather."

Chapter 38

INKLINGS I

—

Timothy Lessons, a student at Oxford, was the first in a long line from Exeter College who intermittently recorded lectures of J.R.R. Tolkien—possibly surreptitiously—and even meetings of the writers' group loosely known as the Inklings—undoubtedly surreptitiously. These meetings, which occurred from the 1930s through 1970, traditionally took place on Tuesday evenings at a pub called the Eagle and Child. Tolkien, often called Tollers, was a member. His close friend, C.S. Lewis, author of the Chronicles of Narnia, and known to friends as Jack, seldom missed a session. Like each of the surviving tapes recorded by Lessons and his followers, this one is undated. They are placed in rough chronological order, earliest first. What follows is a partial transcription:

Noise. Shuffling and scrapes. Coughs. Approaching voices.

"Here we are again. I'm late and still no ale?"

"So, Tollers, back from a visit to Barrett?"

"Bit of a holiday?"

"Even better, Charles. I had a fine time roaming about the hills. All of a summer day. Just at evening, I came to one of my favorite growing-up places."

"Well, don't dawdle. Our thirst grows restless."

"Madame Sarah, your indulgence, please!"

The clanking of freshly filled pints, presumably dark and topped with brown foam, sliding on a sheet of ale. The sound of jostling around the table.

"Now you may tell us!"

Tapping of pipes all 'round—except for Charles Williams, the sole cigarette smoker at the table. Scratching and flare of matches. Sucking sounds and tiny grunts of contentment.

"All right, I will. Sit close and listen. Imagine a place that somehow didn't change over a long, long time. Not much of that left in our little isle today. And what's more, it's not only still there, but it's still working. Now, grown older—I have, that is—and finally unafraid, I just went in."

"I've got it. A house of fallen virtue. Ha!"

"No, but this place is the more strange for still being in working order. Imagine an old mill at Sarehole. Tall stone wheelhouse so ancient that no one alive remembers who built it. It sits beside a stream. Inside, a grind and creak that is like a voice worn with time. The labor of water, wood, and stone continues. Full-span belts of ox-hide, sutured and sized as if to hold up the pants of giants, whirr and slap. Mighty shafts that once were tree-sentinels in some Mirkwood now lost to us—these turn and shudder with power. Miller's dust everywhere. Water glides from pond to pond. Quiet and calm. Green and deep and dark. Each gathering its fill of unreleased energy. Suddenly the water pours into the race. It tumbles down the sluice with irresistible momentum. Wooden gear teeth mesh into morticed slots in the rolling cogwheel the size of this room. It turns and the grindstone rolls. All this is overseen by a miller named Roos with a long black beard."

"And you finally made his acquaintance?"

"Well, it was his father that I saw as a boy. But the name and the measure of the man remain the same. I listened, and delved, as best I could, into the names and lineage of his family and the place."

"Ever the philologist you are, Tollers."

"Give me a name, and I can find a story. Give me a language, and I can find its bones."

"Give you ale and your pipe and you can talk all evening."

"Aye, from my view, Tollers, in the case of our English, the bones are a bit jumbled, wouldn't you say?"

"Much has been lost. Yet much may still be seen, if dimly."

"And your invented language? This dwarvish tongue? "

"Elvish. Not invented so much as, well, found."

"Since we're picking on our good Professor Tolkien tonight, let me ask him a personal question. For all these . . . myths you explore and populate, you yourself never seem to change. Jack here goes grayer by the month."

"Or the week."

"Or the pint."

Laughs and the sort of snorts that come from older men in their own company.

"Don't be foolish, Ian. People can change. Why, I even brought Jack around to a Christian point of view. No mean feat that. But here's the lesson, and listen close . . ."

Hush and the creak of chairs.

"Never underestimate a man's ability to transform himself, especially when he travels the borderlands between myth and reality."

There is a sound of movement, as if someone, perhaps C.S. Lewis, leans further toward him.

"Tollers, as much as I admire your intellect and your pursuit of this hobby, there are those at the college, the newer of them I admit, that ask if you should not be working toward publishing something more, well, scholarly."

"And you, Jack, of all people, should listen to them?"

Someone can be heard dropping his pipe.

"So, you continue to dream of inventing this mythology for England?"

"For my own small part, yes."

"You said at our last gathering that you aspire to replicate the Finns. They had a thousand-year head start on you. Lonnrot only compiled the Kalevala, he didn't write it. And the Finns didn't mix in with the Romans and the Normans along the way."

"Nonetheless, now that we are all well bound by our ale-oaths, I tell you I find myself unable to stop. I'm not even sure if it's made up any more. It seems to be a tale less invented than discovered. The thing is rather unstoppable in its own way."

"And at last that is to be published?"

"That, Owen, remains to be seen. I have a fine, growing collection of rejection letters to vouch for my diligence and some critical advice from these no-longer prospective publishers."

"Such as?"

"'Too extravagant.' 'Hard to follow.' 'Silliness. Let it go.' And my absolute favorite, 'Hobbits . . . really? ' I could go on till our next round of ale."

"How do you feel about that?"

"If a tale inspires, someone will seek to destroy it. It's the way of the world. What are a few snide publisher comments, anyway? Great epics of heroism and adventure have been rubbed out routinely. The victors write the history."

A pause. Murmurs.

"It's not my tale anyway. It is a lost tale, partially rediscovered at best. I'm happy to unearth it as I go. Besides, my children enjoy all its bits and pieces. It may fall to others to finish it because it goes on and on, backwards and forwards. But enough of my ramblings . . ."

"Jack, tell us of your holiday."

"I will, just as soon as we are relieved of all this miller's dust and language-bones of our forefathers. Sarah, bring a round full-drawn of fresh pints, if you please."

Chapter 39

OCTOBER 16

———

An hour after the meeting with Mel, Cadence drove home with the Belvedere's breakfast special, *Halibut Sous de Mar*, drying on her blouse and flopping in her stomach.

Under the spell of Mel's eye she had told him almost everything she knew about her grandfather, which, all in all, wasn't a lot.

For instance, she told him about sitting in the still, muggy, old-peach-crate smell of the hidden attic on that hot, never ending afternoon of Indian summer. She told him about opening one journal after another. How she would note a place, a famous name, or a strange word. She told him how, looking at the brittle yellowed pages of his personal journals, she realized her last flesh-and-blood relative had traveled a very, very long way.

For reasons obscure even to herself, she didn't tell Mel one fact: that her grandfather's story involved a secret riddle.

Cadence had noticed it as Everett wrapped up the paperwork of declaring her the administrator of the estate. There was a poem in her grandfather's handwriting, scrawled across the outside of the same envelope that contained his rudimentary will and named her executor:

> Cast in truth, stolen early
> Hidden well from yearning eyes
> Bears the tale of Ara's role
> Thieved by hands that shun them all.

It was as enigmatic as the man himself.

Her current road however, was plain and practical. She needed to come up with some serious money, and she was driving on empty. There wasn't a gas station until the Topanga turn.

Her cell phone beeped. She answered. It was Bruce, her sometimes boyfriend.

She was flanking the shore and approaching the turn into the canyon mouth. The signal would be lost as soon as she turned. The southern reach of Topanga Canyon, before it spilled out into the estuary and beach, was one of the few dead spaces for cell phones in the five hundred square miles of the city of Los Angeles. Vertical canyon walls barred all radio signals in the canyon for a six-mile stretch.

Bruce's voice warbled. She half listened as Mel's insistent questions kept replaying in her head.

Where'd this stuff come from? So find out.

She multi-tasked, downshifting, steering into the turn lane, thinking of where those documents actually might have come from, trying unsuccessfully to say something to Bruce.

"Helloo? Cadence, you still there?"

"Yes, sorry."

"That's sort of the problem, isn't it? What's with you?"

"I'm . . . worried."

"About what?"

She caught the green light. Second time in a row. Lucky on the small stuff. She crunched the transmission into second and accelerated through the turn.

Now she could talk. "About everything, Bruce, every damn thing. My job is ending. I'm out of school, and I can't get a permanent job. I send in my resume and they ignore it or they laugh. 'Art' or 'American Culture Studies' I don't even know where to begin in L.A. You have to have connections, relationships."

"I'll tell you a quick story. I was *raised* by foster parents. No easy gig. When I was eighteen I used to gripe and whine a lot. Cars, job, school, you name it. One day the old man, who was *really* old, pulled me down by my ear. He said, 'You little shit. You know what I was doing when I · was eighteen? I was inside a Higgens Boat with thirty other scared bastards, headed for the first wave on Omaha Beach. So shut up the damn whining.' I never forgot . . ."

The first missed bits of digital signal.

"Anyway, speaking of relationships . . ."

"Listen, Bruce, this thing with my grandfather. It's hard to explain. He's all I've got. And The Forest. I have a court-ordered sale notice on the seat next to me."

"Cadence, get out of yourself. Let go of the dead and missing. I'm here, alive and accounted for."

"You don't know what I'm trying . . ."

"I know it's not about us. That's a problem."

They had stepped into terrain they'd been avoiding. Still, his response was a little quick. "I've been think . . . out us."

She held the phone closer to her ear, twisting to get some signal. Then she heard, "So . . . think we . . . through."

"Bruce? You're breaking up. Hey . . ."

Dead air, their conversation was over. *You're breaking up.* Did she really say that? She'd laugh if it weren't true. She'd both delivered and received Dear John's before. His tone, even the dropouts, said it all.

"Damn!"

She realized she had missed the gas station.

"Double damn!"

She gritted her teeth and prepared for the S-curves, pissed off at the uncertainty of the meeting with Mel, and now the drama with Bruce. Her mood spawned the unwelcome thought that had been swirling on the edge of her mind. It came forth, a dark metaphysic, fully formed and dreadful.

Erasure.

This is how it happens, she thought. *Nothing dramatic, just a string of deducts until there's nothing left.* She mentally checked them off. *My dad, my mom, now my grandfather and the answers only he knew. These documents, The Forest, Bruce, my so-called career. Me.*

Since her mom had passed away, the dilemma of self-discovery that every twenty-something faced had taken a dark turn. A term kept creeping into her thoughts, one used by the dwindling subcult of fans of the Disney movie *Tron.* The few new recruits in the subcult being occasional film students. The term was "de-res," meaning de-resolution, ultimate elimination. But it wasn't just that. The crueler fate was never really being someone in the first place. Aside from fire, this was her greatest fear.

She held the transmission in third and felt the rpm's rev as she accelerated up the canyon. *To hell with the gas.* The tires squealed as they bit hard to edge away from the yawning canyon rim. Her head roared in tandem. Gravel sprayed off the canyon edge. Her clenched hands put squeeze marks on the steering wheel and she thought, *get off your ass. Do something, like Ara.*

As if fanned by the wind, pages of the strange documents whiffed before her on a mental screen. She thanked good ole Colorado State for her last semester, throw-away elective class in "Cursive History." It helped as she tried to read the antiquated, almost Elizabethan, English scrawled in secretary hand on a few readable pages stashed in the peach crate. The sharp up and down marks finally revealing simple words like "is" and "the." These built into phrases. Then, as if coming alive, they formed whole sentences that gave up their meaning, despite strange spellings and word orders. She still felt the thrill of reading something that may have been secreted away for centuries. The show-stopper had read:

> Gatherad here iS all that remains of the Accounte of Ara, the Saviurre of All from the clutches of the Dark Lourd. May peace find her Soule.

Her intuition concurred. The valise contained the entire surviving record of Ara, gathered up and secreted away for some unknown purpose. The tale was exquisitely fragile, one step away from total de-res. And yet Ara, her story, seemed determined to live.

She wants to be.

She fought through the built-in barriers, the warnings that whispered, "Be careful what you wish for! Don't believe in fairytales!"

The wind roared through the convertible as she punched the accelerator. The car cat-pounced forward, fishtailing dangerously and pushing her back against the seat. She surprised herself as she suddenly unleashed an exultant scream into the din.

The wind ripped the sound away. Embarrassed, she felt like a YouTube replay of Howard Dean, red faced and screaming without reason. She slowed down to a controllable speed. Her mother's voice-over, cover for all the admonitions in the world, regained the upper hand for now. Cadence resolved to go back to her default mode. Slow and steady. She would start by figuring out the truth about this Ara.

When she got to The Forest, that warning feeling, subtle but still jangly, came back. Like delicate, neck-walking fingers. As if far distant juju drums portended an unknown danger. Something bad. Something hidden.

She looked around and knew something had changed. The change was small and elusive, but there. It took her an hour of bustling about to notice it. She was sitting in the back of the store at the battered roll top desk that had served as her grandfather's office. She had cleared a small working space in the clutter of expired catalogues and aged receipts. A coffee-stained Amtrak voucher peaked from under the pile. She happened to glance up toward the front of the store.

Jasper Jowls had moved. She was almost certain. He was on the right side of the entrance. His head, which she was almost sure had previously stared out the window, was turned slightly to the left, as if trying to overhear her doings back in the store. She was sure no one else had been here. The store was closed. Only Everett had another key. Maybe he had stopped by. He kept bugging her for an inventory of anything she found that was really valuable. She said she'd get it done, but she hadn't. There was nothing really valuable here, except, just maybe, the documents. Still, he might have come by and poked around and shuffled things, looking for the list.

She regarded Brer Jowls with suspicion, but then let it go. She would ask Everett later and go from there.

* * *

That night she unwrapped one of the first documents she had taken from her grandfather's valise. It had been bundled in linen, as if especially dressed to draw attention. She had set it aside until the right moment, which perhaps wasn't now, but now would have to do. She sat up in bed and opened it carefully, unfolding the stained coverlet to reveal pages ripped at the edges, as if torn in haste from an antique binder. They were the compliment to a dubious late-night strategy of white wine and lemon pie with whipped cream. Threading through passable cursive, she read:

> His spoken name was Barren. Like others of his kind, he had secret names, seldom uttered words that evoked his origin among the ancient animals and their spirit hosts. He had come to this place fresh from hunting Woodsmen. They were an entertaining quarry. Their pride oft betrayed them. To one of

his night-stalking skills, they were clumsy.

He knelt, head glistening with oil, eyes like black marbles. He bowed deeply before the Dark Lord. Estimable captains, Morath, Baldagis, Lacklin, were arrayed in similar poise beside him. Their tunics blended in seamless weave with the shadows.

Lacklin spoke first. "What errand, Master, would have you draw us to this hidden dell and save these slinking Woodsmen from our sport?"

"My loyal shadow-stealers. Your service is now of most timely need. I would have you deliver one in particular of your chosen prey. As Brothers in Darkness you have left the numbers of these far-seeking rangers, these meddlers, greatly dwindled. There is one, of descent most irksome, who craves power and pretends to a throne that has stood empty since the time of my . . . interruption. You know him well. He goes by the name of Quickstep, apt for one who flees at the very rumor of your approach."

Morath responded. "He is elusive, and yet his trail tends now to one direction. He consorts these days with a lesser wizard and the two of them conspire to grow their heads to great size. So bloated is his with dreams, that now perchance he will slow his flight from me and let my snare of dark-within-dark take him. Do you wish him alive and able to grovel before you in confused and drooling pleading?"

"Bring him to me, and you shall each have the reward of watching my special treatment for this bothersome pretender."

They bowed their heads in assent.

"All save you, Barren." The hunter looked up in surprise.

"For you, a different quest. With aid of the token sealed in this small pouch, are you prepared to burrow deep, wiggle and squirm into the constraining rock and there transform yourself in appearance and time to emerge long hence as one with the tasteless mien of your quarry's heirs?"

"I . . . am."

Barren reached up and took the pouch from the Dark Lord's spindly fingers.

"In your retreat from this world, my servant, you shall find in that pressing cleft a pool which you shall enter and from whence you shall emerge. There you shall retrieve a clutch of writings and rid them of a young woman that is their steward. She plucks and worries at them in search of some fantastic truth. A truth that is best left to those of a higher realm."

"Yes, my Lord."

"And, a further direction."

"Yes again."

"Others have been sent before you. Many of my emissaries now people that world. Some I have sent and brought back, including the bumbling Wraith, Pazal. They have all failed their quest. They perhaps have been stiff and ill-suited to their task. You, Barren, are the quick learner and the quiet hunter that blends with all. You shall not fail me, nor be turned by the petty distractions of that realm!"

"Neither minstrels nor sweet fare nor drink shall unsteady my hand from the pull of the bow nor my eye from the gaze that has ever been death to my quarry. This I swear!"

"Go then, and return to me with these scribbles entire and bloody showings in hand."

An unease settled on Cadence as she read, the vague sense that this was not just a storybook. Who was the "young woman" that was "steward" to "scribblings"? Ara? The words, cracked and distant, muttered through time and places long lost and pointed a finger right at her chest. If so, what "fantastic truth" did they hold? She turned to the remaining pages as juju drums echoed, dim and far away. The first page had a short passage, almost like an entry in some ancient encyclopedia:

The one known as Barren was originally called Seax, which means "knife." As we all know, only free men may possess knives. Thus should his later actions be judged.

He was eleven years old that spring. As soon as the muddy wagon roads became passable there came into his village a carnival, an itinerancy of rude apothecaries, alchemists, and jesters. In their train came a circus of caged beasts not of these parts. Great short-nosed bears, immense lime-green vipers with huge yellow eyes and hissing mouths that were obscenely white or light-robbing dark. Four legged serpents and talking birds from southerly climes. Monkeys that resembled little, angry caged men.

Within two days there dogged the carnival a parade of penitents, scabbed and feverish, moaning of some great god that had forsaken them. The villagers blockaded the roads with bonfires and barred all they could. But it was too late. The Great Itinerant, the Plague, had arrived.

The strange circus, rushing in fear ahead of the pestilence, swiftly moved on. With its passing it took the boy.

The next page, in a close-scrawled hand she hadn't seen before, returned to the previous parley with the Dark Lord:

As always, Barren did the Dark Lord's bidding without question. It was not that he lacked the will, but that he lacked the questions.

Once, early, he displayed temerity. Just a slippery step down the path toward questions. He had walked forth on a rocky promontory overlooking a vast and wooded wilderness. The morning, much like this one, all gray and clammy, a predawn full of imminence of change. There he felt through the very soles of his feet the intimate, slow mechanical grind of all being. Deaf to questions. Just the unanswering grind.

He took that for what it was, and he did not again think beyond what he understood. His was the pursuit and the kill. Since leaving his village as a strange and troubling child caught up in the throng of a minstrel troupe, hunting was his skill consummate, and so that he became.

He was naked save for a small leather pouch tied on a cord around his neck. Fog lay close about him; earth and moss clung to his skin from the narrow clefts in which he had spent a score of moonless nights. Foodless, drinking dew that beaded on the granite that rooted and contorted down and down to the center of everything. He lay bent and still until he was ready.

Before him beckoned a pool. From its depths he could smell his prey.

With sound less than a limb falling far away in the pre-dawn forest, he cut the water like an otter and disappeared from Middle-earth.

She reread parts of it, then put it away and fell asleep. The juju drums stopped.

Except that something made her get up to check on Jasper. In the blue light that flowed like glowing liquid wax through the front windows, she approached him. His back was to her and head was still cocked as if to hear her sneaking up on him. She reached out to touch his shoulder. His head turned mechanically to greet her, big evil-doll eyes and bigger teeth. His body pivoted and his clubby-fingered over-sized paws came up and closed around her neck. She tried to scream. The worn velour of his paws felt itchy and harsh as they shut off her air. She jerked and tore at him.

OCTOBER 17

Cadence convulsed and gasped and woke up. The demonic Jasper Jowls receded into the gimlet pool of dreams. She got her breathing under control, exhausted from trying to outrun a freight train laden with nightmares.

She got up and walked a few steps and groped blindly for the light in the bathroom at the back of The Forest. The room and wall felt unfamiliar. She clawed the wall until harsh fluorescence filled the room like a gray-tinged sickness.

A horror mask leered out at her from the mirror.

Sunken pits for eyes. Hair astray. A sadness in the mouth and a weight dragging the shoulders to the floor. A being withdrawn and frightened. The face looking back at her in the flat gray-green light at three in the morning was not the Cadence she knew. Some hallucinogenic fiend had obviously entered from the other side—the Anti-Cadence that dwells in the soulless land of flat reflection and eternal doubt. This, she told herself, was not just a precursor to a bad hair day.

And why should it be? The week, commencing with rain breaking the fall heat and so promising of discovery about her grandfather, was already frustrating. What might have been a helpful meeting with Mel turned out to be inconclusive. Then there was the non-conversation and mini-lecture from Bruce. Then the troubling, accusatory reference in the documents to a "steward," not to mention the scary Banjo Dog. But worst of all was the nightmare that preceded it. *The* Dream. The one everyone has but never talks about, the one that threatens to open black doors where no sane person voluntarily enters.

She tried to steady herself. *I should be able to handle all this better.*

She had always managed her way through bright beginnings that turned to disaster. She recalled her freshman year as a member of the crew team. She had rowed her single scull into a morning fog that quickly clamped down around her and would not lift. She knew that roped buoys marked the only dangerous area in the entire six square miles of lake: a great black hole that was the spillway. This round, concrete maw swallowed tons of water along with trees, rowboats and swimmers that got too close and were pulled in by its current.

Soon there was zero visibility. She could not even see the water or her oar tip. She tried rowing one direction, then another, then shipped her oars in the oarlocks and listened as she glided along. Everything was deadly silent. She yelled, but it was like screaming into a feather pillow. The fog did that, muffling everything. The few sounds she heard were hollow and distant, coming from nowhere.

You're all mine, the fog seemed to say.

Then she did hear something recognizable—the rush and fall of water. It was the full, throaty roar of the spillway pipe somewhere out there as torrents of water poured into the long, dark fall down to something … very bad, maybe a mesh of angular jagged steel leading to a compressed sluiceway far beneath the lake.

She couldn't pinpoint the direction, but it was getting louder. She readied her oars. Her heart rate jumped as she panicked. Should she row backward? Forward? Was she drifting sideways toward the inescapable current?

The roar grew louder.

She dug timidly, turning her head every direction in the swirl of blank grayness. Then she felt the scull start to move. Her body, imbedded in the hull, was intimate with the slightest nuance of the water—current, waves, temperature. The quickening feeling around her only punctuated the reality that at any second she would see the spillway mouth looming through the fog, and her boat would tip and topple down as the torrent opened up to take her.

She had to guess. All that existed was the roar and this moment of decision. She rotated the bow with her right oar, dug hard and felt the pull of current against her effort. The hull lurched, gaining only an inch with her utmost effort. But that was lost as she was suddenly pulled backward several feet. An enormous tree limb swept past her, one branch reaching up, splayed leaves parading along level with her eyes. She dug again, head down. She had trained for six months, three hours a day on the rowing machine. If there was ever a time for that training to pay off, this was it.

She rowed for a long time, lost in the effort and the blank light that blended perfectly with the water. She was like an airplane pilot that lost sight of the horizon. Forced to go solely by the treacherous instincts of feel. Maybe she was gaining, maybe she was losing.

At the point of exhaustion she checked her stroke. The roar had receded. Her hull was making smooth wake in the glassy stillness of the water. She rested for a moment and an orange marker buoy slid past her. How had she not seen them before or felt their connecting safety ropes drag beneath her?

The fog opened like a curtain pulled away, and she saw her instructor and other crewmates out on the lake looking for her.

The power of decision never left her after that, at least until recently. She could peg the moment exactly: it was her arrival at the doorstep of The Mirkwood Forest, bag and hopes in hand, to find nobody home.

The face in the mirror seemed incapable of choice. It had already entered the anxiety lane, merging toward the panic exit.

Her father once said that three o'clock in the morning, a time he embraced and inhabited most of his life, was the time when women and children sleep the sleep of the dead and men's souls awake to reflect in a bitter pool. He was cribbing F. Scott Fitzgerald, she later realized, but underneath was the truth. It was for him the time to ponder the quiet desperation of a failed life, often with a tumbler of bourbon in his hand.

The Dream was a visitation from her father.

He was a younger man in the dream.

She knew he had been a roadie, working on tour with obscure 1980s hair bands with names like Twisted Forest and Drop. Promotion of the bands, if any, amounted to grainy Xerox pictures of scruffy longhairs pasted on cheap, three-color flyers stapled to utility poles.

He helped with setups, sometimes also working the sound or the light show. She'd seen the torn and creased posters and the flyers in a box he kept in his closet. He had also worked as a carnie, which was pretty much the same job. The caravan of battered trucks and trailers would pull into some small, nameless Midwestern city park late on a summer's night, and immediately start setting up for the next day's opening. The Ferris wheel was the biggest job. The riggers started on that first, assembling the wheel spoke by spoke, then hoisting it onto the two steel support towers that were mounted into the trailer chassis.

In Cadence's dream, it was the proverbial three in the morning. Her father was at the top of one of the support tower ladders, connecting the lighting cables to the copper rings at the hub. The whole trembling exoskeleton was held together with spliced, crimped, and frayed support cables; stripped bolts; and big steel bars hammered into place but lacking the cotter pins that could ensure they wouldn't slip out. The Ferris Wheel was a big creaking disaster waiting to happen. Moms and dads would that very day entrust their children to the swinging gondolas, gaily dangling a hundred feet up in the air.

Standing in the center of the wheel, sixty feet above ground, Arnie Grande felt strangely apart from the others. The work lights below made everything either blinding white or opaquely shadowed. But one of the lights suddenly went out, and he could suddenly see everything in surprising detail: trucks like toys, people milling about . . . and there he saw his father, Cadence's grandfather, the Scissor Sharpener himself. A man Arnie had last seen five years before, when he was sixteen. The man was walking away from him along the midway. There was no mistaking him, with his old fedora, his valise with the leather shoulder strap, and his solid, steady gait etched into place by years of walking, walking, walking.

Arnie Grande yelled, screamed, and pointed, but no one could hear or cared to see. For just a moment, the man below seemed to pause, as if he thought he heard something, but then kept walking. Arnie tried to keep him in sight. He last glimpsed the man stepping between partially unloaded trucks.

Arnie shot down the tower ladder and hit the ground running. *Where'd he go?* He ran desperately, zigzagging around the garishly painted horses, swans, and camels that lay like victims of an improbable massacre beside the eerily naked merry-go-round.

The sludgy movement of dreams took over, and the horrible truth emerged: his father never even heard him, and was gone.

She splashed water on her face and looked at her reflection again. It was beat up, but still looking straight in.

Looking at herself, she felt certain there was a mis-weave in her own tapestry. If only she could but undo the knots and pick out the errant weft and reweave it all into sensible order. If only she could but find the careless hand that moved the shuttle. Yes, her grandfather. Jess was out there. She would find him. Perhaps in a place of refuge, candled window light spreading out to greet her. They would talk dispassionately about life's hows and whys and she would understand how to set the order of things.

But to find him, if ever, she faced a chartless reckoning. Save for a few clues, she stared at a whited map. The documents and a reference to New York City on a note from Professor Tolkien were about all she had to go on. In maps of old, such unfilled regions were wastes where monsters thrived.

No matter. Mel's backhanded encouragement had spawned the idea of taking a trip. She could make it happen or just slink away and surrender.

She searched for the Borunda handbag, wondering if her one unrevoked credit card would finally just dissolve this time, like some prop from *Mission: Impossible*.

She fished out the credit card and called to check the balance. There was two hundred left on the credit line—not enough. She remembered a clutter of papers on the roll-top desk. She rushed to it, rifling through slots filled with junk. She found a drawer full of aging bills, shocking in number, and combustible in their yellowed brittleness. Finally, she found the envelope with the AMTRAK logo, just as she remembered. It was a voucher for travel to Anywhere, USA. She scanned the fine print until she got to the expiration date. She stared at it like it might change.

She swept it up with poetic flourish and sat down with her computer, Googling for AMTRAK.

She made the reservation and organized her bags. The valise, all the documents, the few clues to her grandfather, these would go with her. The rest was incidental. One backpack and a roller bag held all the overflow.

Standing there at that unexpected, six in the morning, deep-breath moment, she wondered what Ara would do. Would she have embarked on this sudden and uncertain journey? Cadence sat down and opened the valise and pulled out one of the scrolls. She unrolled it and looked at an expanse of sweeping, rune-like writings, as unintelligible as the fissured bark of trees—trees that might once have stood in the trackless depths of ancient Mirkwood itself. Scanning rapidly down the scroll, she came across annotations in antiquated English written in a tremulous hand. Etched on the thin leather, next to the runic language, was the now familiar riddle:

> Cast in truth, stolen early
> Hidden well from yearning eyes
> Bears the tale of Ara's role
> Thieved by hands that shun them all

Another turn and a couple of loose pages un-spiraled from their hiding place in the scroll. They were well presented, carefully penned, and readable. She sat down and began to read out loud: "It was, Oruntuft said, a time of great—"

"Haste!" cried the Bearer. The hoof beats of warhorses, powerful and relentless, were already upon the road as it turned from the village gatehouse.

A ragged, chill dawn greeted them. They stood in the lane before the inn, confused, swords drawn, a pale light, like red forge-flames, suffusing their razor-sharp blades.

The Woodsman knelt down and examined the hoof prints. "Steel shorn, with a great point in the front. Only the steeds of the Wraiths," he spat, took a breath forced upon him by fear, and continued, "have . . . have their hooves armed such, and bear these runes and tri-faceted nail-heads."

The halflings looked down at the print, saw in its relief the cruel pattern.

One of them turned and gazed dazedly at the east. Another bent over, looking at more hoof prints. The Bearer stood still, closed his eyes, and smelled the terrible reality of this new day. He could feel the raw edge of his life sundered forever from his past. His faithful friend hovered near, looking about with sword in hand, fearful and vicious at the same time. How dare they!

If any others watched—and there were some, both evil and fair—the halflings, with the Woodsman kneeling nearby, were painted in stark tableau. The light of this morning was harsh and unforgiving, casting their faces and clothes in orange and purple.

They were wrought in brilliant hues upon a break-of-dawn canvas of deep, textured grey. In the background, the ruined East Gatehouse, now a pyre of fire and smoke, lent a mocking counterpoint.

"Where is she?" he asked to the air about him.

As always, the other halflings hesitated.

"Are there others of your company?" interrupted the Woodsman. "Speak now! We must stay together or perish by the swords of these enemies one at a time. Have you no loyalty?"

The Bearer looked to the gate. "She insisted on staying there." he said, pointing. The gatehouse was ablaze now, the barriers broken and cast down. A plume of smoke, pink and grey, rose into the lightening sky. The air smelled of smoke.

At that moment, the innkeeper came running up, all sweat and terror, and began to ramble between gasps for breath. "They . . . took her . . . grabbed her . . . up . . . like a doll."

The Bearer grew still, and then sank to his knees. He pulled his small sword where he fell, and double-handed, stuck it deep into the earth.

The harsh judgment of the wizard—"Do not take this woman!"—echoed in his ears. Why had he not paid heed? He listened again to the now hollow wisdom that had guided him— that Ara, alone among the halflings, knew from experience the woods and Outlands. That she alone possessed the conviction and resources to guide them through the world they were about to venture into. A world beset by war and the conflicts of wizards, men, elves, dwarves, orcs, perhaps even the six-armed brudarks.

Whatever he might say to please the wizard or his dear cousin, how could he, a normal, perpetually hungry halfling, deal with such demands? And so he had chosen Ara to accompany them, to be his confidante and resource. He had even shown her . . . it.

A lie, he thought, *why did I think that?*
I even let her keep it, if just for a moment.
And now she is gone.

He looked up. The dawn's chill raced and swirled about

them. They had left their homeland, and everything it had meant, forever. This new day contained creatures of terrible power, creatures whose greatest passion (or, at least, greatest command) was to kill them.

An eddy of dust filled his nostrils. Bitter. It was a taste little known to halflings. The Bearer, for perhaps the first time in his young life, tasted the bile of despair, borne out of the certainty of a long journey ahead that had now gone very bad from the beginning.

The Woodsman rose up. The same morning chill brought the approach of autumn to his nostrils. Despair he also knew but seldom acknowledged. So ingrained was it in his being after those many years that he bore it like a battle scar from the long past.

The ruby red and deep gold leaves of fall in the northlands swept about them, chattering down the lane in a current indifferent to the cares of mortals.

Going on to nowhere.

Like us, thought the Bearer.

At dawn, Cadence paused one last time in The Forest, standing in the small screened-in porch that had served as her grandfather's bedroom. Everything was in order. Slanted light played through the creek-side oak trees at the back of the building, splaying in odd patterns on the bed like a waving sea fan, highlighting squares of cloth cut from gentlemen's suits, pajamas, blue jeans, all stitched together in a frayed depression-era quilt. An heirloom, perhaps? A forgotten pattern to forgotten family ties?

On the chest of drawers, next to an old leather jewelry box bearing someone else's initials, stood the only thing in the room that didn't look second-hand. It was a faded picture in a wooden frame, probably from J.C. Penny's or Sears or some other department store photo emporium. As always, Cadence picked it up and studied the subjects. Posed against a stock blue-neutral backdrop, they stared out at her with startling familiarity. It was hard to believe, but there it was, frozen in an incongruous moment as rare as an alignment of stars: her mom Helen, her dad Arnie, and a baby with a pacifier.

In the distance, another world away, she heard a dog barking and a car horn honking out on the road. *Time to go.* She put the photo back in the same spot and re-hefted her bags.

She hurried through the dimness of The Forest, squeezing along the tight aisles of comic books and retro psychedelic T-shirts. She thought about the police tape and fingerprint dustings, now long gone. It had annoyed her they had left that for her to clean up, but she did and kept everything else intact. On her way through the kitchen in back, she stopped for a final look. On the calico-covered kitchen table, the Abbott and Costello salt-and-pepper shakers stood waiting. So were the mint-condition, boxed Barbies her grandfather might have bought at a yard sale along with miscellaneous collectables and vintage rock band posters. Banjo Dog had not further strayed from his post. She knew fine dust would settle over all, impossible to stop since it incessantly seeped in from the road.

She sighed as she surveyed the clutter, wondering if the trip she was about to take had an end point.

She checked the lock on the back door and then checked her cell phone for messages. There were two. She punched them up.

"Cadence, Megan. So, I know you say you don't believe in luck or fairy tales. Well, I'm telling you, missy, I'm counting right now five thousand dollars I won at Vegas! The trip you didn't want to go with us on Friday? So don't be a stick in the mud, and let's go together. All of us girls. Like soon! Let you cut loose and try that old time gospel mystery of the slots. Oh yeah, you won't believe what else happened! Don't you not call! Bye."

The second one was from Mel. "Listen Cadence, I got your e-mail from last night. If you're going there, okay, I'll help you. Go to the Algonquin Hotel, mid-town. A-L-G-A . . . anyway, you'll find it. I'll make arrangements. Now look, I've been scratching my head over this whole thing. I've been talking to some of my people, and well, there's more here than I thought. I'm having research done. In the meantime keep this secret, all right? I suggest you leave the documents with me for safekeeping. At least take them with you. I'll call as soon as I can."

She saved both messages, sidled down a cramped aisle to the front of the store, and backed out the front door. The air, already giving up its moisture, felt tired and reheated. A morning bee droned somewhere along with the growing road sounds. Cars clipped by every few seconds. The keys jangled in her hand as she worked the troublesome deadbolt.

"You fear a trial of fire!"

The voice came from nowhere. Not sure if she heard it right, she froze, her hand still holding the key. Then she heard the rumble of a low growl, like a heavy gauge spring being compressed to the point of powerful, uncontrollable release.

She whirled around. A black dog faced her. If it *was* a dog. It looked pure Pleistocene, the kind of wolfish creature that lurked outside the glow of a Neanderthal campfire. Its long, black fur stood on end as if electrified. Huge, yellow teeth curved like arthritic fingers below yellow-pitted, greenish demon eyes.

Where's the leash? some part of her mind questioned.

It stopped growling just long enough to breathe, and when it did, saliva roped down its impossibly long red tongue to muddy the dust at its feet. It took a step forward. She tensed, slowly bringing her bags around in front of her. Their eyes locked in stares, no question about who was prey.

Another step forward.

"Docga! Heel!"

The dog stopped mid-step, its eyes unwavering as its master appeared at its side. "It's okay," the man said. "He's never attacked anyone when I'm here."

Somehow that wasn't reassuring.

The man seemed at first glance to be a typical Topanga creeker. Black T-shirt. Dirty jeans. Sandles. Black beard and hair. Druggie lean. The kind of man you'd see living in a tent or under one of the rock outcroppings just below town.

He looked directly at her and said the oddest thing, "Beware, Graymalkin. Your soul embarks ill-prepared for your need-fare."

She was so surprised she laughed. "My *what?*"

"A journey that must be taken."

"Who are you?"

"Never mind who I am. You will receive offers."

"Okay, get out of here."

The man didn't seem to hear. "Remember, on a journey one always faces temptations to abandon the path."

"You're crazy, go back down to the creek."

"Each offer reveals that which you most desire."

Now she listened. Not that she understood, but he had her at *what you most desire.*

"You've shipped many an oar I can see."

"You know nothing of me."

He paused, and then looked directly into her eyes. "The truth is, caterpillar, there's not much about you worth knowing. At least not yet. Except for one thing."

"How about my boyfriend comes out and kicks your ass." Cadence was not above a bluff.

"Don't you know that heroines are always orphans, in one sense or another?"

"That's it. I'm going back inside and he's gonna come out here and pound you good."

"Attitude and loud talk can't help you on this journey."

She picked up a rock, and the dog leaned forward.

"You still don't know what this is all about, do you, Cadence? Can't you smell it? Change is coming. Like smoke borne in advance by a hot wind that propels the fire."

She just looked at him, wondering how he could know to touch her fear of fire and say just *that.*

Having said his piece, he turned and walked away, whistling. The dog followed placidly at his side, tail doing happy puppy dog swishes as they moved away.

She knew of Graymalkin, a malicious spirit in the form of a cat. It was the familiar of the first witch in Macbeth.

She also knew what time it was. *No time*, she thought, *I'm late. Very late.*

She picked up her bags, looked over at the parked, tarp-covered jaguar, and headed down the road for the corner bus stop. The bus was there, the driver impatiently checking fares at the door.

The waiting, at least, was over.

* * *

When she finally got to Union Station in downtown L.A., only one ticket window was open and the line would not move.

Cadence was finally next in line, her packed roller bag attending like a faithful companion. There was a lot riding on this voucher. There was no name on it. Just the instructions: "Present to your Amtrak agent by . . ."

Her backpack was chafing her shoulders so she moved the straps a bit. She had stared at the ticket agent behind the security glass so long that she started composing his life story. How he ended up caught in this glass cage. It depressed her so much that she imagined she was not in the Los Angeles Union Passenger Terminal at ten in the morning, but in the Getty Museum critiquing a modern art installation behind glass. Maybe one depicting the slow drowning part of hell. It would be titled *Gray Tidal Slurry of Boredom.*

"Next."

She stepped up to the window, shoving the ticket voucher into the depressed slot.

The agent swept it up and placed it to his left for a quick study through his wire-framed spectacles. He wasn't an old guy—just the first wee-sprouts of serious gray in his hair—yet he wore a green eye-shade and leather cuff-protectors, something she hadn't seen outside of old movies of the thirties or forties.

He picked up the ticket, his finger running along the text. Puzzled, he turned it over, then found what he was looking for.

"This is five years old. Almost expired."

"Yes. Almost."

"Tomorrow, in fact."

"Yes."

"When do you want to travel?"

"Today. Now."

He leaned back and looked at it more intently, as if it trying to detect some evidence of a crime. Unconvinced, he got up and spoke to a female supervisor. They talked. The supervisor looked at Cadence covertly, then walked over to the window.

"When and where do you want to travel?"

"Today. New York City."

Cadence watched the supervisor study the voucher again, and only then scrawl *OK* on it. The supervisor's initials followed on the lower left corner. The whole thing was obviously a tremendous inconvenience, requiring extra steps they didn't want to take. Besides, it wasn't as if she had actually paid for her ticket. The voucher was the equivalent of Amtrak welfare, and Cadence could damn well wait. The supervisor walked away, the agent again took his seat on the high stool, shot his cuffs in preparation, and gave a sigh that indicated that a long, laborious process was about to begin.

Tap-tap. Tap-tap.

He was a two-finger typist. As Cadence glanced at the clock, something inside her died.

A clunky printer got to work, spitting out three tickets onto a tray.

The P.A. boomed, "AMTRAK 14, SIERRA SUMMIT, BOARDING NOW THROUGH GATE 10!"

"Is that me?"

"Yes ma'am."

She thought about squeezing her hand under the grate and grabbing for the tickets, but the clerk was not finished. He pulled over a stamping device that looked like a loaner from a transportation museum. Cadence watched in agony as the process ground on. He worked slowly and with great deliberation, as if following instructions whispered through an earpiece: Put the tickets in the little hand-press one at a time. Apply palm sharply. Stamp. Check the stamp. Repeat.

"SECOND CALL, AMTRAK 14 . . ."

The only other place this slow, she thought, must have been the Bulgarian Railroad, circa 1930.

Stamp. Check stamp.

Now a rubber ink stamp came out.

No better example can be made of the layering of technologies that burdens progress, she thought, *just add on—never displace.*

"LAST CALL, GATE 10 . . ."

"Is this going to take—"

The clerk smiled and shoved the tickets into the trough. "Have a great trip."

"Thanks!" Cadence turned and sprinted down to the platform. People were hurrying, blocking her way with bizarre collections of luggage. Red hard-side Samsonite Travelers, army duffles, BlackHawk Assault backpacks, string-tied boxes, greasy brown paper grocery bags.

She found the right car.

The conductor was ready to pick up the footstool.

P.A. rumbling. "TRAIN 14 DEPARTING . . ." She stopped and looked very deliberately at the steps.

"Ma'am?"

She took a step, her eyes following her foot as if it belonged to a stranger. She climbed aboard, then turned to watch the uniformed conductor. He looked at her, then smiled and slowly pulled away the stool. He did this grandly, as if his secret job was to create life's points of no return.

She wrestled down the aisles and found a window seat. With the nesting instinct of travelers embarking on a long journey, she deposited her backpack on the aisle seat. A mark to ward off strangers. She secured the rollerbag packed with the valise and manuscripts on the floor.

She looked down the car and smiled. Not crowded at all. Maybe eight out of thirty seats occupied. But the headrest smelled musty.

Arrival time at New York's Penn Station was four days away.

The train lurched and the platform outside began to act strangely, sliding backwards from this oddly immobile perspective. Redcaps glided by with empty luggage carts without walking. She closed her eyes to reset her perspective. There followed a slow, accumulative creaking sound as hundreds of tons of metal protested against scores of train couplings.

The world soon reordered itself to the eyes of the mover. In less than a minute the great upside down U of the station mouth opened to spill into an outside world of endlessly parallel and crisscrossing tracks. She squinted at the maze of rails shining brilliantly atop the black lines of metal, as if some monstrous spider had spit out ferrous webs to ensnare some fantastic prey.

She liked this exercise in abstraction—the high contrast, the confirmation of order and art in all systems derived from life. Flowers, whelks, the faces of mites, whale cochlea, sermons, movie genre rules, journeys . . .

"Excuse me . . ."

She jumped.

The man in the aisle looked to be in his late twenties, well-groomed but in wrinkled clothes, his hand extended toward the opposite row.

"Are these taken?"

"No, feel free."

The man began to do his own nesting, but with the air of practiced routine. He plumped his pillow, tidied his books and newspapers the seatback, stashed his eyeshades just so, and nestled his radio in the open bag down at his feet. The bigger bag went up above, and she somehow knew he wouldn't have to open it during the trip. She half expected him to wipe his hands together in satisfaction, but he abruptly turned to her and asked, "Want anything from the café car?"

She waved a no thank you and turned back to watch the rail web and the trashy backside of Los Angeles dissipate as the train gathered speed. This was a chance to get some perspective on the rude and strangely fascinating ass-end of the city, and she gorged herself. Vines, trash, dumps, back entrances to seedy shops and bars. Inexplicably, she saw the lost graveyard where a thousand rusted and battered supermarket carts trundle off in the night, squeaky wheels and all, to gather and die.

Finally bored, she rummaged for something interesting in the valise. Clues to Ara seemed to come and go in this pile. Even the documents seemed to shift around. She found a small piece of paper, shaped as if sliced by a knife from a larger page. She pulled it out and held it up to catch the strobe light of a passing bridge. The paper contained a bit of verse:

> Down roads long and weary
> Past borders high and far
> Through gates shut tight
> Each to the other vow
> Together to spy that dark blue sea!

A rather simple and affected halfling limerick, she thought, barely qualifying as a riddle. Of no magical significance or power whatsoever. All in all, a trifling thing.

Or was it? It was, after all, a *vow,* something far weightier than a promise. Whoever "each to the other" were, it was *theirs.* Cadence pondered whom in the world "they" could be. Ara? The one called The Bearer? In this pile of scrap it was doubtful she would ever know.

The train slowed and came to rest in a maze of tracks and warehouses. It lurched and stopped, again and again, as if queuing in an unruly line of racehorses at the starting gate. Liquid metal slams cascaded along its length. It rolled forward and gained speed.

Soon enough, the sun was setting in the ocean, far beyond Topanga and the quiet and shuttered remnants of The Mirkwood Forest. That place receded from her mind as evening shadows swept forward over the shoulder of the train. Her view flew past the dusty tracksides of San Bernardino. The country was thinning out.

The neighbor across the aisle had not returned.

She watched with the pensiveness of one accepting the lockdown of a slow journey while other events ran at full speed. The train rumbled on, finally approaching its maximum velocity. Cadence opened one of her grandfather's journals, one she had packed after thumbing through it and finding that a part of it had been written on a train. Her attention was diverted, though, with a whoosh of air compression. Looking up, she saw a long row of salvaged doors riffling by, very close by the train. Hundreds of doors, it seemed, were all nailed side by side to make an endless color-chip fence, a bright sampler book of discarded gates to unknown lives.

As she watched the kaleidoscope of doors pass by, she thought of the many houses she had lived in. All the bedrooms and bathrooms . . . and back doors.

The procession ended abruptly with a de-whoosh and a return to slightly more open spaces. She thumbed through the journal, put a bookmark at one spot, and fell into a ragged, dreamless sleep.

* * *

An unwelcome consciousness came to her, stiff and crumpled. Bleary, gray, morning light fused with atonal flatness so that all land and sky were a single-hued haze. The Great Salt Lake stretched off to the north. A porter came by with coffee. It was hot and cheap and surprisingly good. She set it on the next seat's tray table and opened the journal again. Each page or so had a heading and entries in her grandfather's jittery script, etched with different instruments—pencils, exhausted Bics, fine-lined points of apparent pedigree. Finally she found the entry she was looking for:

> Lakeside Ballroom, June 12 '74
>
> Hopped off the D&RGW last night. Slept in dry culvert on the ROW. Saw strange building mile or so off toward the lake. Went over and found huge abandoned resort and ballroom, maybe from the 1920s. Then at the shoreline, now stranded half mile inland. Looks funny there, standing on huge pilings. 20 foot ceilings, 3 stories. Grand staircase all gray and forlorn and crusted and scary as hell. Easy to get lost in there. Always sounds going on. Birds fluttering in and out. Wind moving non-stop, like an off-key organ with only a few pipes left. Echoing so

the sound is amplified. Old boards clapping somewhere in the wind. Put it all together and it's like ghost music resonating eternally from past revelry.

Too sad for me. I hoofed back out and caught this westbound. Am huddled inside a firewood boxcar now. Snug here, writing by slats of light. Vienna sausage for lunch.

She watched the lakebed stretch away as minutes and miles clacked by. There! That had to be it! Coming up and passing by in the distance was a pile of burned timbers and a high framework of tottered concrete beams. Those gray-black remnants had to be the ruins of the Saltair Pavilion. It was used as a set in the 1965 cult film *Carnival of Souls*. That, along with *The Cabinet of Dr. Calagari*, were her favorite progenitors of zombie movies.

Okay, she thought, *that right there touches it. Everything so damn academic with me. No substance, just the look, the special effects, the trivia. Life as just a movie to watch. The image but not the touch. The picture but not the danger. The illusion, but not the magic.* Her mind wouldn't stop.

Worse yet, I'm just a trained observer, a student of, what, movie history? Pop art? Comics? God help me, television? I'm really just a librarian, an archives clerk. How far removed from life can you get?

Well, maybe it's not removed at all because, to quote somebody, that's all there is. If you don't believe in magic, all you'll ever see is the pragmatic, maybe spiced with a few cheap tricks for entertainment. After all, that's why they call them "shows."

Her mother's voice came to her, timbre-perfect: "Two generations of romantic misfits. That's the men in this family!" That voice was imbued with yearning for a touch of normalcy that marriage never dealt her.

The voice echoed away as the train wailed out a long whistle, decelerating to the station stop in Salt Lake.

She reopened her grandfather's journal at a bookmark:

Montana summertime with high cumulus ranges and big blue-sky days to knock your eyes out. I'm looking at this good luck charm given to me this week. I did a favor for a man who needed help. The favor's not important now, though it was important to him. He searched me out and said maybe he'd give me a blanket, but that was too easy. Then he said maybe a beaver skin, which could have magic aplenty but was too heavy to lug around. Then he said he had something that was just right. He knew, he said, because his father was a shaman. He'd been off the rez too long, but he said he still knew what it was all about. So he gave me this thing. Said it was good luck if I used it, but serious back luck if I didn't use it and keep it sacred. "Not like rabbits' feet where you can take 'em or leave 'em. You got to be one with this," he said.

I told him I wanted to give it back to him, but he said that was also bad luck.

Then he leaned very close. "Not only do you got to use it, you got to change your ways." I dreaded what he was gonna say next. "Your spirit is lost. You got to quit wandering like a man with no home."

Maybe someday I will. But that's a scarier thought than hitching rides right now. I'll keep this thing safe and maybe pass it on. If I ever get home again, that is.

Anyway, I'm sitting in a truck stop, just finished eating lemon pie, and I'm looking this thing over. It looks kinda special. It's ivory and it's old. Looks like a tooth from a giant bear maybe, back when bears were twice as big as they are now. Maybe like Alaskan bears in the museum except beefed up even more. There's a spot for a hole to be drilled and a key chain, if I had any keys. I'll keep it and hope my luck doesn't sour. I sure as hell can't let go of it now. I guess whoever has it has to figure out the truth it's trying to say. Even if, like me, they know bad luck is their own damn fault.

Cadence looked into the mirror of the train window and studied the part of her that were her dad's features. His, of course, were an echo of the man whose journal she held. She unzipped a pocket on her backpack and took out a tinkling assemblage of keys and chains and little gewgaws, all of it anchored by a polished tooth four inches long and punctured by a hole with a small welded chain, looped though it.

A talisman with interrupted history.

Up till this moment, all she knew was that it had been her father's. He used it for his truck key, but couldn't find it that fateful day, so he grabbed the spare off the key hook. The fire's orange glow was already spilling over the canyon rim and sending Halloween shadows through the house as he gunned the truck and took off. She knew the story of the fire line and where it happened. She still had videotape of the news reports, including interviews with firefighters who had been there. One of them even spoke at the funeral.

Three years later she asked that man to tell her what really happened. He told her there were two dozen men and three pumper trucks lined up at the narrows at Old Topanga Canyon Road where a cluster of cabins stood. The canyon walls were steep, closing almost to creek side. The fire had already crested behind them so they couldn't retreat more than a half mile. The fire crew chief said, "This is where we'll fight."

The fire was coming fast, the wind shifting and blowing its furnace-breath down the narrow sandstone corridor into their faces. Still unseen, the red monster stalked up around the canyon bend, its shadows dancing clear up the orange-lit walls. Then it turned the corner. It bellowed and raged like a furious living thing, then gathered force and marched forward.

They'd cut a line up the canyon sides, their fire hoses quickly draining a rubber dam placed in the creek. Three pumps sprayed huge plumes of water into the air, challenging the beast.

It stepped into the first plume. Hose-drenched trees erupted like match heads. The water boiled in the air as it arced, steam hissing as the beast thrust out a fiery arm. The spray only angered it, like acid on the back of rippling red flesh. It lashed out another tentacle, and the next moment they were surrounded on three sides by walls of Day-Glo red and orange.

Arnie was there. He had said he was going to help his friend defend his cabin. It was so like him, trying to do right but never getting it together. He was driven by something he could no more discern than a meteor understands its destiny before it flames out in the silent night sky.

Six men died that night—Arnie and five firemen. The fire finally grew impatient or bored, skirting a last piece of canyon and sparing the cabin en route to once again confront its old nemesis, the ocean.

Thinking about it rekindled her utter hatred for fire, the abomination, the true rough beast. The recurrent dragon that stalked her inner landscape.

Chapter 41

INKLINGS II

—

All evening the group had discussed issues of faculty and politics, and only at the end came about to literary topics.

"Jack, I want to return to this term 'Mirkwood,' of which you are a fan. What does it mean to you?"

"Tollers, whose absence to the loo will at least allow me to get a word in, is the historical authority. But to me, it is the place where tracks disappear and no line of sight exists. Once you are in there, it becomes the Forest of Doubt."

"Yes, Cambridge, exactly."

"Now, now, let's not stir up that rivalry."

"Well, sounds like life sometimes."

"Exactly, we all stray into Mirkwood now and again. Getting out, into the place where belief can exist and be a proper guide, is the trick."

The sounds of footsteps, shuffling of chairs.

"So I heard you speak of Mirkwood. Bandying ancient words in my absence could be dangerous."

"Well, then to you, Tollers, since you borrowed the term from Jack, what is the essence of Mirkwood?"

"Hah! He's the pickpocket of my purse of ideas! But to your question, I'll skip the lecture on its deeper roots, its role in Eddic Poetry, its references in Scott's *Waverly* and elsewhere, and get to its essence. It is the physical embodiment of Elvish language."

"Oh, well that's a turn then! Anything else to add for those of us less learned in such?"

"Yes, we've heard you talk of both, but never together. What do they have in common?"

"Elvish, I found, has aspects deeper and wider than I thought as I sought to, well, reinvent it. My poor linguistic attempts, Quenya and Sindarin, are just that. Real Elvish is far deeper and more mysterious. To call it a language is to gravely, perhaps dangerously, underestimate it. Elvish and Mirkwood are alike, because each has paths that shift before you. Each beguiles and hides its truth. Dangerous things, Elvish and Mirkwood."

"You seem to have some new thoughts on this. You were, ah, telling us last week about this . . . trove of documents?"

"Ah, yes, I suppose I did mention them. I've sorted a bit of it. It's mostly a collection of bits of history that I've yet to decipher. The pages look as if they were torn out of many sources, Old English, more recent scribblings, and, the bulk of it, pieces of writing that indeed seem to be a form of Elvish. Curious, really. I'll get to the bottom of it in due time."

"Sort of an ancient clipping service, eh?"

A sigh of exasperation.

"I suspect, Edwin the Inquisitive, that it is more a bundle of writings about some forbidden topic, all literally ripped out of ancient libraries.

"Related to *Beowulf*? Hello?"

"I pause only because I'm not sure. That remains to be examined."

"Perhaps these are from . . . your 'Middle-earth'?"

"Well, the name is not mine to begin with. It is a term of long pedigree – *mittle-erde*. It is found, surprisingly, in the earliest existing fragment of Old English we have, called Caedmon's Hymn. A line that goes like this:

A softly spoken song, perhaps in Old English, is sung by Tolkien. There is a period of silence before he begins talking again.

"It means 'Then the guardian of mankind the eternal Lord, the Lord Almighty, afterwards appointed the Middle-earth, the lands of men.' It was scribed as the monk Caedmon sang it, *aet mude*, "from his mouth" in about 680 AD. It is, put simply, our centered Northern World, with all its legends and myths. In a sense it springs fully developed from *Beowulf* where, if my count is correct, it is mentioned a dozen or more times. Indeed, if you recall from Jack's reading of a few Tuesdays ago, even he has created adventures in a similar Middle-earth. Sadly, one peopled by his poor take on me. In any case, it is no one's invention and no one's property."

"Returning to your find of these strange documents, they must have been someone's property. How did they come to you?"

"I have to be careful here. Old obligations, the war, all that. I can tell you they came to me, this time, like an orphan, a changeling, left swaddled in a barrister's valise on my front stoop."

"*This time*? Mysteries, Tollers, always mysteries."

"Well, at least they were free."

"Like you fancy this ale will be tonight, Edwin. Pony up the tab and let's be off to home!"

Chapter 42

OCTOBER 18

———

After the stop in Salt Lake City, Cadence plumped her pillow, reclined the seat, and settled in for the moving picture show of cross-country rail travel. September rain splattered the window, soon to beget snow in the high country—that same day, in fact. The train labored up Soldier Summit, passing tight side valleys, some desecrated by mining waste. She watched one roll by, complete with a leaning wooden mill and tailings pile. New gingham curtains in the windows of a cabin were a poignant touch, though barely noticeable among the yard cars and wrecked pickups and a garden that had gone to yellow and droop with the first hard freeze. A trail of smoke cut sideways off the stovepipe chimney in the dank cold, as if it couldn't leave this godforsaken place fast enough.

She turned to a page from the valise, all spidery scrawls. She got the feel of it and read:

My Dearest Amon,

The harvest moon begins to fill and we have not seen each other. Remember the glade?

Your wizard came today, and he sat me down with my father and my mother. He said you will be going—leaving! And that I must simply wait for your return. I remained quiet, though he looked very directly at me. I did not tell him of our plans, or of my knowledge of your precious, the gift from your cuz.

I will see you by the waxing moonlight at the Catpaw Bridge.
I will not fail you, and we shall be together.

My love, Ara

P.S. My father draws forth a group of the most stalwart of
our village. "Trouble in the south," he says.

So, Cadence thought as she shook the page in delight, Ara had a
lover!

For the next few hours the mystery of Ara kept unspooling. The tale
slowly assembled itself from the brittle scrolls and battered pages. One
historical account revealed a chilling secret:

Horse and Rider

The father of Aragranessa, Achen, was keen to instill in his
daughter the wisdom and lore of the wild places. "Wild," of
course, being a term reserved for the relatively close and
relatively safe woodlands surrounding their home village of
Frighten.

True, in those woods known locally as Portic-wud, the
Sanctuary Wood, vagabond creatures might wander down from
the North, and travelers on errands untold were known to
camp. Even elves were whispered to pass beneath their boughs.
Yet her skills were competent to detect and avoid trouble.

Ara's vision was renowned as particularly keen. Her father's
early test of this was to direct her gaze to a special point in the
vast starsprent vault of the night sky. "Look for the Horse," he
said, "for its yellow color like the steeds of legend." As she saw
the yellow point of light and described the arrangement of other
nearby stars, he said, "and what, if anything, does the Horse
bear?" She stared hard at the twinkling sky. "A Rider," she said,
"it bears on its back a most faint and tiny star!"

Thus Ara passed the most acute test of eyesight known to
halflings.

One last question she had for her father that night, and she
made him proud in the asking. "Will my sight give me the vision
to see truth and honor as keenly as you?"

To this tale must be added another. The very year in which
she spied the Rider, she came late to an edge of the Sanctuary

Wood. The most subtle of movements caught her eye. With worthy stealth she approached, and saw what at first appeared to be a gathering of animals. Creatures roughly her own size, upright standing, but with faces akin to badgers and ferrets and wolves. Even as she watched their faces shifted into a common pattern of dark, acute eyes over long noses. All held up by pointed ears. She knew she was seeing what few, perhaps no, halfling had ever seen—a gathering of elves. Perhaps even Dark Elves.

They seemed unaware of her presence. She crept even closer and heard the indecipherable music of their native speech, punctuated by high, sharp whistles. Their conversation grew more intense, as if arguments were brewing. She thought she heard one of them say "anginn," an old world, used by elder halflings to mean "source."

Then she froze as all the elves grew quiet and turned their heads toward her at once. They regarded her as if she were sitting in the village square on a dunce high chair with a ridiculous dunce hat.

One spoke to her in her tongue:

"For your subtle woodcraft, a reward. You may tell of this secret, for none will believe your wild boast and every retelling will filch more of the good name of your house. For your uninvited presence, though you understood none of what you overheard, a price. All things have consequence. This is your tithe: every unselfish step you take hence, every worthy deed you undertake, shall each draw your fate closer and more certain. Your good acts will only dim the memory of your passing. Put all others before you, unsparingly risk your life, and your tale will all the more certainly be erased and forgotten for all time. Go now!"

Ara fled in fear and confusion and never told a living soul, save her Mum.

Cadence found herself leaning forward, clutching the last page. She took a breath and eased back. *So*, she thought, *Ara and I each have a burden. Hers was a secret curse that doomed her for heroism. I'm lucky. I'm just chasing a question mark. No one's out to de-res me . . .*

"I don't think," she started to say out loud.

The connection of long journeys now seemed almost palpable. She reached over and got her grandfather's journal and opened it, picking out a passage that seemed to be notes from another east-to-west-coast hopping of freight trains. It described pure old- time hobo-style travel:

Grand Junction. June 14, 1980

Worked at a diner next to the rail yard. It was called, simply enough, "EAT." The sign stuck up on the roof in flashing red neon. So I think now that "the Eat" or "Eat at the EAT" must be a national chain targeting the raunchy and low-down spots. A kind of niche. Anyway, this one had only six counter stools. No tables. One person running the grill, waiting tables, busing, doing dishes—the whole thing. Got my standard job. It always works. He paid me to clean up the garbage out back, cut up some boxes. Got five dollars and eggs, taters, toast and coffee.

It's hot. Laid up in the cool of some big abandoned icehouses next to the rail yards. They're basically big wooden boxes, five stories tall, made up of foot thick timbers. No windows. You could fit a basketball court inside each one of them.

The man at the EAT said these things used to hold ice for the fruit transport. This valley is world-famous for its peaches. It got that way cause of the icehouses. The railroads and the orchard people figured out that you could get big, fresh, ripe, sweet peaches to streets in New York or Philadelphia in three days if they were iced down.

So, before air-conditioned boxcars came along in the fifties, those icehouses, made of foot-thick wooden beams laid tight into big boxes fifty feet tall and a hundred feet on each side. No windows, one little door. They were the way they stored up ice supplies for the late summer harvest. That's all over now. They're just sitting there. There's still plenty of ice in them at the bottom and the corners. 15-20 feet thick. Ice maybe 50 years old. Just outside the open door its 108 degrees, easy.

Anyway, I lay up all day watching them make train. They use a hump yard. That's a little hill the tracks go up and over. The switch engine pushes cars up the incline, they unloose the coupling, and the car goes careening down the other side.

The rolling cars are switched to different tracks. You can hear them shunt over. Then they crash into the couplings of the cars waiting there. That's makin' train, and that's my custom ride. All day, all night. Cu-Chang. Each noise echoed 10 or 20 times by the cars jamming together down the line. Kind of like music.

Course I got my own music. Right here in my teeth fillings. Only I can hear it. Although once I had little Arnie put his ear next to my open mouth and he could hear it too. Tonight its playing K-O-M-A Oklahoma City! 50,000 Watts Serving the Heartland! ("Playing tonight at the National Guard Armory in Elk City, Spider and the Crabs! And at the Fairgrounds Pavilion in Olathe, it's Ray Ruff and the Checkmates!") The other day it was K-E-E-L Shreveport dishing up southern fried top 40.

I'm thinking about Helen and Arnie. What am I doing here? I keep dreaming I'm outside looking in at them. A dream that I can't shake. That's my fate. Always outside looking in. So I succumb. I'm here and they're there.

Hell, maybe I'll try a new name today. Keep even myself guessing.

Cadence sat, stunned, holding the man's confession in her hands. *So I succumb* . . . The crime scene—a remnant family. The confession—a note from the road . . .

    Before she could get too angry, the man across the aisle rustled, saw her awake. "You know the sounds?"

"What?"

"My name's Julian. I was asking if you know the train sounds."

"Nice to meet you. I'm Cadence. Yes, I'm hearing them, if that's what you mean."

"But if you know them like I do, there are subtleties. There are actually three signature sounds of trains."

"Okay, tell me."

"Well, there's the sing-song click-clack of the junctions in the rails. But listen. Listen. No song, right? Now it's more like a delay, maybe ten seconds, then just one click-clack. Hear?"

The train rumbled, and then the isolated double-note came and went. It seemed like a rare passing comma in a jargon of flat and unintelligible steel on steel.

"Yeah, there," she said.

"That's not the way it used to be. Used to be every second or two, an almost constant beat. Up-tempo, sort of. You know, Chattanooga Choo-Choo, Pennsylvania Six Five Thousand, Orange Blossom Special. That's all gone now, cause they changed the rails. They put in longer rails so there's only a tenth of the junctions there used to be. So it's a backbeat now, is all."

"The other sounds are still there. It's kinda like the Doppler effect. Another train whistle or clanging crossing signal, depending on where you are. It comes and jams together and then fades away. And there's that long, lonely whistle going away in the night. The stuff of country songs—Hank Williams and Johnny Cash. Of all the ways people get around—cars, boats, planes—there's only one, railroads, that has the music, the joy and the sorrow. So, what do you think?"

"I think I don't know. To me it's just trains. Nothing magical about it."

"Don't dismiss it. Magic sometimes comes in little packages."

Cadence listened.

"Well, what's your story?" he said.

"I'm going to New York to find out about my grandfather."

"That's great. That's where he's from?"

"No, it's where he met someone famous. I have some documents from there."

"Was *he* famous?"

"No, he's . . . was kind of a bum. A drifter. He left my grandmother and my dad."

"So why are you looking?"

"I don't know. Just to find something true about myself, I guess. How come he left. How come my dad was the way he was. You know, that family thing."

"At least you got something worth looking for. Me, I got nobody much to worry about. They know I'm here, wherever that is, but it's *here*. On the train."

"How's that?"

"You know, like the Kingston Trio song about the guy on the Boston Metro Transit Authority. 'Did he ever return? No, he never returned. And his fate is still unlearned.' Only I'm here by choice."

"You live on trains?"

He scooted over to the aisle seat. "Since 9/11."

She scooted over to hear better. "Okay, let's hear your 9/11 story."

"I was in D.C. I watched it, or rather felt it, hit the Pentagon. I felt the boom, the ground shaking, the big mushroom and then the plume of smoke. Suddenly everyone was in the street. Traffic stopped everywhere. The whole city stunned. I was outside the Willard Hotel, a couple of blocks from the White House."

"Pretty scary, I bet."

"Yeah, unreal. Strangers all stopped to talk to each other. We heard that more planes were headed to D.C. to blow up the White House and the Capitol. Then I heard it coming."

"What?"

"Jet engines coming in full bore. I looked over toward the White House and the guy next to me. They were coming in to blow up the President. We all started to hunker down. I said to the guy next to me, 'Shit, watch this.'"

He took off his watch, holding it in his open hand like a wounded butterfly, like it had been traumatized by the same experience he was describing. He massaged his wrist nervously.

"We were all crouching, some on their hands and knees, helpless, hearing it coming. Then it came, right flat overhead maybe two hundred feet, twin F-16s roaring over us wing to wing. They topped right over the White House, like they were saying, 'This is ours and we are ready!' The sound crushed all of us. I think I ended up curled up like a baby."

"Then what?"

"I went to a packed outdoor restaurant with a TV wheeled out front and watched the towers fall. The traffic was jammed. I just wanted to get out of there. So did everybody else. There were a thousand people trying to get into a single Hertz office. Fools waving their Gold Cards— it was a joke! Cell phones were jammed. So I left my bag and briefcase in a conference room. I never went back. I walked to a highway that had some traffic moving. A guy in a convertible signaled for me to get in. I ran and hopped in as he was moving along. He said hang on and we cut traffic, onto the median, on the side lanes, heading, it turned out for Barksdale, Maryland. He took me to his house, we got on the computer and snagged the last reservation on a west-bound Amtrak leaving in six hours. It had been turned around before getting to D.C. He got through to his wife and kids by landline. We had beers and leftover fried chicken and he drove me thirty miles to the little train station. I got on. And I never got off."

"You mean you *live* here?"

"I've been living on Amtrak ever since then. The first three days after I got on, I slept on the floor. I bought this little polyester blanket—you know, with the official blue Amtrak logo. This one here." He held up a worn and travel-stained once-white blanket, limp with use, its edges frayed, folded carefully like an heirloom quilt.

"I slept on the floor, like I said, 'cause there weren't any seats. We all gathered in the bar car the next night. Maybe a hundred, two hundred people. Told our stories. Shared news. Got raucously drunk, sang songs, you know. Felt the kinship of disaster.

"So, when I got to Denver, I just kept going. Never even called in to my job. Then on to Portland, then Seattle, then back across to Minneapolis, then south to New Orleans. I had a long leash on my credit card, so I just kept on buying tickets. Until a ticket agent clued me into the MegaPass. Unlimited travel, one annual fee. I picked up bits and pieces of life in the railroad stations or a few blocks surrounding them. Toiletries, clothes, stuff to write letters with, books . . . it's simple."

"You're still afraid?"

"It's . . . deeper than that. I just can't really get off. I scuttle to those stores to get things, then come running back. Literally, running. I'm safe here I guess. Sort of hiding while moving. Funny, I travel hundreds of miles every day . . ."

He left the sentence unfinished, his voice trailing away as he turned to the window. She noticed his watch. The sweep hand didn't move.

Around dawn she awoke briefly and watched the gray world relentlessly trip by her window. She wondered how the man across the aisle felt. They were all strangers here, thrown into this long, shunting tube of aluminum, speeding on wheels of steel. She was grateful that, at some point, she would get off the train.

The next day, Cadence felt the change, the long, slow ascent out of the Mississippi drainage. They passed the continental cleavage, and she felt the easy strings of the West loosen and the verdant tugs of the East take hold. She was coming to pick up a trail, even if it turned out to be a cold and fruitless one. The fact of going and standing on the trail itself was enough for now. It was doing *something*.

And what was this train ride, this meandering stumble in the dark? She recalled the odd phrase used by the stranger at her doorstep three days ago. *Need-fare. A journey that must be taken.*

Her thoughts ran to Ara. *Of course she's not real, Just a story.*

Then she paused.

Hell, then I'll take the story.

Cadence pulled out her sketchpad and pencils. She remembered a line from one of her instructors. Our artists' conceit is that, ultimately, nothing is real unless it can be rendered—described, named, painted, photographed, *drawn*.

Well, so be it.

A muse was flitting about, ready to land on her shoulder, whispering a sketched composition with pounding horses and the waning moon that was a clock running on Ara's fate.

She sketched for an hour and dozed and looked out the window. The countryside rolled along, telephone lines arcing from pole to pole, looping the land together like big stitches. Fields with crop rows whipped by, hypnotizing her to sleep. She awakened to the first reds and yellows of fall, flashing by in the boughs of trees. As darkness again settled in, she sped past decaying bridges thickened with vines that seemed to harbor small, leering faces beneath. For the next few miles, a gauzy, grey twilight hugged the world and was punctuated by a series of bonfires that burned merry hell in open trackside fields. They belched up smoke and flame, as if they were signals for some invading night army. To Cadence they were especially disturbing because they were wild and untended and uncontrolled.

Four years she had spent at Colorado State, pledged Tri-Delts, did the events scene, went out with football players, and never once went to the big pregame bonfires. She would get sick just thinking about it. She turned away from the window and nestled and closed her eyes to dream of more pleasant things.

She awoke to the sound of thunder and angry spanks of sheet rain punishing the train window. She looked around. It was still night. Her heart was pounding. Somewhere, somehow, the change she at once coveted and feared was coming closer. Drum beats rumbled in her mind and mixed with the noises of moving steel and wind.

She put her face to the window and cupped her hands around her eyes. She peered out into the flickering nightmare of a Class V thunderstorm. Lightning rippled across the sky and gave substance to the silvery veils of rain. Passing pools of water glinted in the flashes and watched her like the eyes of passing strangers. Then, as a core of ragged bolts created a kind of flickering openness to all the unpeopled night, she passed a country crossroads where five cloaked horsemen circled inward in council, their mounts pluming nostril smoke and strange blue light. One rose in the stirrups and pointed a finger at her, his outstretched arm moving, keeping dead aim on her as she sped past.

Then, as if it never existed, the scene passed.

She abruptly pushed back from the window. Just black glass now, complete with smeary hand and nose smudges on it. She stared at her reflection.

There would be no more sleep this night.

The train outraced the storm, streaking toward a new dawn of breaking purple and yellow light. After a while, she heard the clink of rails followed by a highball wail mimicking those tones of sadness and regret. *"You know the sounds"* the man had asked. Now she knew.

She listened and heard a wheel-click, suddenly tripping into that rare short-rail click-clack, click-clack for a minute or two.

She was approaching something that had been kept from her. Maybe it was just some factoid about the Tolkien documents; maybe it was another puzzle-piece about Ara. She hoped it was some truth about her family. *Not magic, not a fairytale. Just gimme truth*, she prayed.

Chapter 43

THE POOL

—

The water here, like the light that seeped down to this deep, sub-street level, was a thin, greasy gray. Both found their way through the street grates to fall into the hairline cracks in the concrete. The resonant drip-blip, drip-blip had resumed its endless, lonely cadence.

Across the littered concrete floor pooled a great splatter of water, as if something bulky had heaved forth from hidden depths.

A darker shadow hovered now in the corner. So very still, but alert to its strange new surroundings.

This thing warped into the shape of a man, whose very breath was the moan of windswept crags, whose walk was the grass-rustle of treacherous heaths, whose voice was the crack of bones. This thing—this man named Barren—had come for Cadence.

The name New York City meant nothing to him, but he would learn. Fast. That was his talent.

BOOK VI
PROVENANCE

———

The book sits still, waiting for my eye to glance away. There! Did it not shift ever so slightly? Does something sprout along its spine? A ripple runs now beneath the cobbled skin of its cover. Words have power. I dread it, but soon, in the day, I will pick up this tattered volume. I will read and another world will exist.

~ The Scissor Sharpener (Journal)

Chapter 44

INKLINGS III

—

The discussions this Tuesday evening wandered from academic standards to gardening, and then faltered altogether, until the following exchange:

"Well, not to jump into politics this late, but what about the story in today's *Guardian?*"

"Today's what?"

The sound of a folded newspaper being opened and scuffled to fullness.

"Here, Ian, you troglodyte. Today, July 16, 1962, page one, 'Government Unveils Cambridge Five As Spies. Great Damage Done.' It gets worse. 'Kim Philby, a graduate of Cambridge's Trinity College, revealed as double agent for Soviets'."

"At least not an Oxford man."

"Don't be too proud, Clive, there are foxes in every henhouse."

"My God, what's happened to Queen and Country, and all that?"

"Tollers, you're quiet. Why the down face? Jack, you tell us."

"Well, as his friend, I know some of this, but it's up to him."

"Eh, Tollers?"

"Come along, we are your fellows here."

"I worked with him."

"Who?"

"Kim Philby."

A long, questioning silence.

"All right, now that you've wilted the spinach, tell us. Enough of myths and old men's tales for tonight. Come on."

"Very well. Hardly Top Secret anymore, I suppose. Much of it is already declassified. Here it is—just before the last war, I was briefly an agent for the government, for her Majesty's Secret Service."

"You rascal! Another of your secret gates, Tollers."

"As you know, I published *The Hobbit* in 1937. I had what I thought was a modest reputation for scholarly work with languages. I was recruited by S.I.S., as part of their code-breaking effort. I was assigned to Bletchley Park, the cypher school. Alan Turing, who finally broke the Enigma Code, was there. Hitler's agents were scouring the world in search of a 'living cipher'—an organic language that changes its apparent meanings on its own and is thus immune to code-breaking. He was understandably concerned with his security, and so wanted an impenetrable code to be used by his personal cadre of bodyguards."

Someone takes a big slurp of ale, sets down his glass, and belches.

"Keep going, we're on pins."

"During that first month I was part of a team that followed reports of far-flung Nazi agents studying obscure tongues—Ket in Siberia, Na-Dene in Arizona, Vandalic in Prussia. I remember some jokester in our group passed around a compilation of Burrough's language of the Great Apes, as spoken by Tarzan. Things soon got very serious, however, when I was unexpectedly approached at my Oxford office by two gentlemen. They claimed to be scholars of Norse mythology. They said they wished to explore the connections between *Beowulf* and older Norse legends. They spoke in particular of a collection of ancient documents that told of rings and elves and orcs. I told them such were staples of ancient Norse and Old English texts. They added that these documents displayed a 'living language'."

"At their urging, I looked briefly at one example, an apparently ancient document. It was fascinating but something told me not to let on. I told them I could not fathom its meaning. I reported the encounter to my superiors. One of the men that debriefed me was Philby, already a shadowy triple agent it seems, with known links to Von Ribbentrop and others in the Third Reich. He asked about their collection of documents. Sometime later, having completed my pending projects, I was relieved of duty without explanation. I didn't ask questions, and happily returned to Oxford."

"And then?"

"My life was very busy with teaching and writing. I didn't think any more of my S.I.S. experience until recently . . . yes, Clive?"

"Sorry to interrupt, but Sarah tells us we are past our curfews."

"Excellent, for there's little else for me to tell."

"Next Tuesday, then?"

"Ah, yes, Clive will be reading. We'll no doubt forget where we were just now."

"Goodnight all. Don't forget your hat, Jack."

Shuffling and packing up and goodbye sounds.

* * *

The following teletype was discovered in declassified files of the Government Code and Cypher School (GC&CS), now a museum, at Bletchley Park, north of London:

September 6, 1939. Field Report. Station X. Documents referenced in Tolkien, J.R.R. interview retrieved from subjects Glaus and Spearman. Said subjects, formerly members of Anglo-German Fellowship Union, likely Nazi operatives. Documents in their possession comprised of archaic parchments and scrolls with much runic text, believed stolen from historical collection of Lord Grivenhall at Ashburnham. They are deemed unlikely to contain "ubersprache" sought by Hitler under his Seigfried Directive. Subjects turned over to S.I.S. for interrogation. Tolkien status with GC&CS compromised. Documents retained in original barrister's case and stored at Loch Uiguenal with notation for possible later delivery to Tolkien, who will be relieved of duty. Philby, H.A.R. 794XGCCS.

Post-script: Spearman had in his effects several 8 1/2 x 11 B&W photos, apparently movie-production stills, signed by Leni Reifenstahl, with her compliments to Joseph Goebbels. Her inscriptions translates to: "I trust we can soon complete the Fuhrer's movie project, Nacht der Dökkálfer." That means "Night of the Dark Elves." Unlikely this is a code, so I consider it to be a curiosity for another time.

The movie stills, and the referenced movie, have never been found.

Chapter 45

OCTOBER 18

Barren had been in New York City for one day. At first, he hid in a doorway, covered in a filthy blanket, studying the onslaught of noise that was as the clash of arms on a furious, never-ending battlefield. He traced the many sounds, each to their sources. He even saw the rampaging red beast of a machine that emitted wails and whoops as if it had been wounded and refused to die. He had an infallible instinct for danger, and here he quickly felt safe. More important, there was little magic to be worried about. He moved into the streets. The things that surprised him most about these people were . . . well, where to begin?

Their faces were an obscenity, scrubbed and as bereft of hair as the arses of babies. Most of these moonlike visages were topped by hair that framed the face in ridiculous lengths and shapes, and the hair itself was often painted with dyes. As if that were not enough, some humans wore devices like sticks tied together and holding pieces of glass or obsidian before the eyes. Many wore blinking shell-like objects, clinging to their ears as they talked insanely to themselves.

The smells were worse. They were overpowering, so redolent of alchemy and artifice that it gagged him. The faces all carried an odorous trail of exotic unguents to make the natural stink of man and beast seem like perfume on a warm spring night. Barren was used to reeks that would shame a buzzard off a gutcart, but this was worse. He would, as always, adjust.

He stood, draped in his blanket in a long underground grotto filled with people scurrying like a disturbed nest of termites. His study was progressing well. These beasts were soft, obsessed with themselves, assaulting each other with the obscene displays of their faces, but seeing precious little, so that he could move among them without worry.

Later that day, he waited in a partially wooded expanse, surrounded by the noise and crowds. Swans and geese swam in a small lake. Autumn still grasped root and branch as it was pulled once more into the coldness of the earth to make way for the oncoming Snow Giants.

Here he was as invisible as a tree in a dense wood, and for just a moment he closed his eyes and let rest enfold him. He dreamt at the edge of sleep, hearing bulldrums echo and talk in the far distance. Summons to an ancient mustering.

But his instincts told him otherwise. He roused to wakefulness and studied this park.

It reminded him of a place he'd been as a boy, long before a troupe of dark minstrels had come to his hamlet. A place he knew before he had gone away, half out of fear of the plague, half seduced by the wonder of escape from the drudgery of long toil and early death that was his family's lot.

Once in that long ago, on a brilliantly hued autumn day with smells that were colors all their own, he sat beside a lake. He half-reclined in a bed of straw grass three feet high so that he was almost hidden at the very edge of the water. The sun dipped toward day's end. The sky was so blue and beset with soaring cloud ranges of white and pink and purple that it made him ponder the very miracle of each slow and sonorous breath. A flight of elusive Lórien ducks, bespeckled in black and white with eyes of gold, circled and then came down in formation, cupping their wings and landing without a sound on the water not ten feet from him. Their leader looked at him with eyes like yellow diamonds in the angled sunlight and floated sideways, drifting with the slight breeze. At that moment, through the mutual submission of their gazes, he knew he could master any animal—for the hunt or the table, but most of all for the sheer communion of taking life.

That was the day that defined the axis of his being.

Today, however, had present duties. Some deep instinct, informed by the Dark Lord's direction, told him where he might search. *It is time,* he thought, *to dress and act as these fools do.*

* * *

Unfortunately, he didn't perfect his act quickly enough. Clad only in the stained blanket he had stolen from a sleeping form in a doorway, he was picked up by two city policemen at 9:00 AM on Tuesday, the 19th of October, 2009.

He could have killed the officers without effort, but he knew that would attract more attention than was wise. He was familiar with these types of village officials, reeves or wardmen or whatever they were called here, and cooperation with them was easiest at this point. The language spoken here was strange, loud, and simple. He knew he could master it quickly.

They bound his wrists with chained bracelets and took him into one of the large boxes that moved mysteriously, without the aid of beast or slaves. He soon learned a few new words: "loitering" and "Riker's Island."

He declined to speak for a long time, even as he was shuffled before petty officials. A woman asked him questions, but she grew fearful and left. Within a few hours they took him across a bridge to a place where he felt more comfortable, a drear and decaying keep made of red bricks. He guessed the sign above the gate read RIKER'S ISLAND. Inside was a warren of rusty steel bars and metal doors. They freed his wrists and led him into a larger room filled with a score of men. Later, they showed him a cot for sleeping.

After the guards left, one large and tattooed man scowled and offered a particularly and universally expressive pleasantry. Barren intuitively understood. Amused, he approached the man. In a few moments, no one in the room would speak to or come near Barren. The larger man crawled on his belly on the floor like a cur put to the whip.

Barren spent time observing what he learned was called "TV." It was a portal through which images of small people and things and events could be observed. He watched and studied without sleep: movies, news, reality shows.

By the morning of the third day he had learned much. He conversed with some of the men in the room, who quailed at first but eventually cooperated. One showed him his collection of little illuminated manuscripts. "Comics" the man called them as he began to show them to Barren.

Barren now absorbed this world with voracious appetite. That evening he was approached by a guard. He was handcuffed. He was taken to a small room. A man came in—tall, lean of frame, cropped blond hair, and dressed in fine cloth with a colorful bit of fabric at his neck. He was not a guard. The man began to talk, most of which Barren could understand.

"My name is Bossier Thornton," he paused. "Detective, Criminal Investigations. You have the right to remain silent."

No reply.

"Can you speak?"

Silence.

"What is your name?"

More silence.

"Do you know where you are?"

Barren studied the fool in front of him. He could read him as plainly as aurochs tracks. The man was stupidly ambitious, and therefore worthy of contempt. Barren decided to play with him.

"I'm in . . . Riker's Island?"

"Good. Now do you know where that is?"

"It's either in New York City or a place in a . . . Mar-vel co-mic."

The detective leaned back.

"How do you know which?"

"I'm learning to read. Co-mics. I'm here. The guys have them in there. I read that Riker's Island is a place that holds bad guys and . . . super villains."

Bossier was an ardent fisherman of the shoals and bays of the criminal sea. He sometimes took the Riker's duty out of curiosity, just to see what sorts of people were getting caught in the net. This was an odd fish.

He flipped through the thin processing file for this detainee. "Where are you from?"

"The Source."

Bossier looked up, prepared to give this guy the don't-be-a-wise-ass speech. He stopped. With the certainty of a mug shot or a positive DNA and prints match, or a rap sheet of prior convictions—none of which existed anywhere for this man—Bossier knew that here was a killer. He knew it from the man's eyes. They were steel marbles, glistening ball bearings, that saw everything as prey.

"What do you do?"

"I'm looking for someone."

"Like?"

"A . . . dame."

The sneery way he said it was so stupid it was funny, like a bad amateur Bogey-impressionist.

The man was creepy, but there was no basis to hold him. His processing form made that clear. This one would have to be thrown back in to the sea.

"You want to get out of here?"

"Yes."

"All right. Looks like you'll be out tomorrow afternoon."

Bossier got up and left.

A guard returned Barren to the group lockup. Once there, Barren persuaded one burly inmate to retrieve some scissors stashed in a wall crevice. The man, a hardened felon who specialized in brutalizing his victims, cut and snipped Barren's hair with the careful detail and pandering chit-chat of a docile barber. He fashioned it as Barren indicated, pointing to a cluster of detainees with Mohawks. He then used soap and a little blue scraper to meticulously shave Barren's beard.

Thus transformed, Barren sat on the edge of his cot, feeling the strange tingle of newly exposed skin and the anticipation of a stalk. A hunt that would result in his prize.

At ten the next evening, after four days at Riker's Island, Barren was released back into the city. He was now equipped with an educational jumpstart, second hand clothes, and twenty dollars in his pocket. *Ready for primetime.* He was even starting to think in modern vernacular.

Chapter 46

OCTOBER 20

———

Just as Barren emerged from Riker's Island, the train carrying
Cadence plunged into its last night run before arriving in the city. She
fidgeted and worried. She was happy to be getting there and anxious
about the strangeness that seemed to stalk her.

She looked at the black glass and cut her eyes away. *Don't stare out
that window. Not after last night.* She put her head on the Amtrak pillow,
relaxed into the gentle rocking movement, and sought the refuge of
sleep.

She awoke at five in the morning, stirred by something vague,
perhaps only the train jostling, and obscured by an urgent need to pee.
She leaned up from her reclined seat and looked both ways down the
aisle. The overhead lights were dim and the absence of reading lights
meant the few passengers were all asleep; 9/11 Man was a snoring
shadow sprawled across his seats. She eased up and looked at her own
nest. She shrugged and got up and then stopped. The valise was in plain
sight. She leaned over and pulled it up and moved it down two rows and
shoved it beneath an empty seat. She pulled a blanket from the overhead
and disguised the valise as a dark pile. Now she really did have to go,
and she headed for the women's bathroom in the next car.

As she slid the lavatory door shut, the light flicked on and the mirror
over the sink caught her movement. She looked at it. It was blighted
from the inside with some amoebic gray sprawl that ate the upper left
corner. She sat and her face moved down and stared back from the
mirror bottom. It seemed to loom up from the sink, obscenely

decapitated and somehow balanced. Just to be sure, she made full eye contact. A woman knows her face, and the one looking back at her was ever so slightly off. She thought about talking to this image but hesitated. Who knows what truths might spill out in such an encounter?

She stared for a long time, then changed her mind. She inquired out loud, "*Why* are you doing this?"

Her voice answered, "Because if I don't, I'll stay like I am now . . . empty. When you are an orphan, when that full truth dawns on you, all the other truths you don't know and can never ask about get really big. If Jess is alive, he's the only shot I've got. He's someone real to ask the hows and whys. Maybe he's even someone to blame." She thought for a second and came to her bottom line. "If I don't do this now, I *never* will."

"And?"

"And, there's something else going on. I can feel it. It's like . . . there's something out there after him . . ." Then she let it slip out ". . . and me."

She stopped, embarrassed but mostly fearing that the image might actually take up its half of the conversation independently. Thankfully, seeing no further response, she retreated to her old cynical refuge. She pursed her lips and raised her hands, palms up, and gave her reflection a taunting "who knows?" shrug. She finished her toilet and her image duly rose as she stood.

She turned her back to the mirror to unlock the door. It was stuck. She jiggered it and then slammed the door with one knee. Beneath the banging and the metallic rattles, she heard a splash of water. This was followed by a liquid, squelching sound, and a soft *splish*, as if a foot was stepping carefully into water. Her mind imagined that her "second" was crawling out of the mirror and wash basin to meet her. Only it wasn't anything like her own image anymore. It was some deep-sea gargoyle rising behind her. At any second a pallid, fish-fingered arm would piston out to grip her shoulder. She couldn't turn to look. Not to see that. Her hands jiggered the lock over and over, like some dumb wind-up toy, until it fell open and she stumbled out. Turning to kick the door closed, she saw only an innocent wet spot on the floor.

Nerves, she thought, *just settle down.*

As she re-entered her car, she heard the doors at the other end swoosh. A small figure, not a child, looked back from the shadows and disappeared into the next car. She looked at her seat row and began to move fast down the aisle. The train rocked and creaked. She made her way toward her seat, two-arming along the aisle seat backs for balance; 9/11 Man was still snoring. She looked down at her nest, her sanctuary. Something was wrong. Her backpack was now on the seat next to the aisle.

Her hands were like frightened birds as she reached down and picked it up. Makeup and toiletries spilled out of the newly open side pocket. Her pocketbook, still with money and IDs, lay on the floor. Jess's journal had been rifled, but appeared to all be there. Then she panicked. The valise! For a moment she forgot where it was. She edged backwards to its hiding spot. She tore at the blankets.

It was exactly where she'd left it. She checked the clasp, then opened it. The contents were just as she'd left them. She blew in relief and took it back to her seat. Just a petty thief, she thought.

She pondered this for a few moments, and then went to the emergency phone and called the conductor. After a while, he arrived and conducted a desultory and inconclusive search of the train. She didn't talk about the valise. She didn't tell him that, just maybe, this was no random snatch and steal attempt. Who would believe such a thing?

Maybe someone who believed in these ancient documents and the Dark Lord's words. Someone who knew about his goals and his many emissaries. *But that's not me. I'm jumpy, but this is just a storybook,* she reassured herself.

* * *

At dawn the train, chugging and spent, labored into Penn Station. The platform was packed with day-trippers, commuters, and visiting families.

As other passengers began reaching for their bags, Cadence stayed nested in her seat, tidied up now and still opposite 9/11 man. They exchanged knowing nods and smiles in comment on the passengers walking down the aisle toward the exit door.

When it was time, she got up and reached out and shook his hand.

"Julian, it's been nice traveling with you. I hope you find your place to finally get off the train."

He smiled in return. "You know, I'm feeling more confident about that. I'm going back to the Midwest. Maybe . . . oh . . . Topeka. That seems safe."

"I think it would be great. Who knows? Take a day and sleep in a bed at a hotel or a bed and breakfast. Let the train just go on without you. Listen to it click-clack and whistle away. Leave your burden on the train. Just let it go."

He nodded. People were waiting for her to clear the aisle.

"Bye."

"Bye."

She trundled down the aisle, hesitated at the exit door. Below her was the step stool. *New York, here I am!* She stepped down and kept going along the platform, her feet already lighter.

Rumbles of other trains and the incomprehensible sounds from the P.A. speakers mixed with the shuffle of the crowd with rollerbags and sneakers and clackety heels. The crowd broke; she saw daylight and headed for it.

She surfaced, bag in hand, to meet a mild Indian summer afternoon. A sweep of fresh air, alive with moisture and carrying the myriad smells of the city, swirled around her. As she breathed in the energy of that wind, she felt the city's trademark, the palpable, buzzing presence of possibility. Anything might happen here. There would be no easy bargain but there would be commerce. That alone gave her hope. Here, her pent-up energy could be focused. She could get down to the real search.

Her little map from the Algonquin website said the hotel was less than ten blocks away. After four days locked up on the train, this would be easy. She picked up her bags and struck out due north. Once she got there, she would unload her stuff at the hotel and go directly to her first clue.

As the breeze kicked up and the sky darkened with an incoming thunderstorm, she found the hotel. The Algonquin was a spritely, fourteen-story dowager built in 1902. It looked smart and well-taken-care-of. She checked in on Mel's tab, got organized and immediately left. It took her less than an hour to find the place she had travelled two thousand miles to see.

She stood alone outside the West End Bar.

A raw wind whipped sudden rain along Broadway at the corner of 110th Street. She looked at the yellowed scrap of menu in her hand.

The place right where it should be. Cadence wrestled the door against the wind and stepped inside. The place was busy, shadowy regulars installed on their usual stools. Behind the bar a man with Popeye arms bulging out of rolled-up sleeves, bathed in weird glow-light from under the bar. Gruff and balding, he fit the place.

She felt unexpectedly at home in places like this, where the dark wood-paneled walls had absorbed maybe seventy years of tobacco and beer smells, giving them back in the day, taking in more at night. Gin joint sounds filled the air—small talk, jukebox, clinking and washing, liquid pouring, imported beer bottles gasping into life as their caps tinkled off the opener.

She saw an empty bar stool and claimed it as the door opened again behind her. She could feel the wet street air swirl in and mix with the saloon smells. A figure moved in hitches and starts from the door over to the back corner, melting into a booth.

The barkeep moved toward her. "Yes, ma'am?"

She fidgeted with her bag, ordered a Manhattan, and looked up to see two things. First, the guy's face lacked a left eye. A deep vertical scar transected the socket. Second, the hands placing the beer and glass on the bar lacked a finger. Left, ring.

"Uh . . ." is all she could get out for a second.

"Relax, ma'am, I'm not near the ogre I look." His voice was friendly and low-key, which only lowered her blush to a paler shade of vermillion. He moved off to another customer and she looked at the menu scrap again:

WEST END BAR
14423 Broadway
New York, NY

June 14, 1970
Daily Specials

Meatloaf Dinner, all the trimmings
$1.89
Chicken Pot Pie with salad
$1.29
Hunter's Stew with salad
$1.49

And there it was scrawled along the bottom:

I must depart for England tomorrow. The burden is now yours. I have helped by hiding the key, the heart of the power that lurks in this trove. This task I completed today. There is little else I can do now. I fear they are coming. Keep it secret.

JRRT

"So what brings you here?" The barkeep had returned.

"Well, can I ask you a question first?"

"Shoot. First one's free."

"How long have you worked here?"

"Me, on and off for fifteen years probably. What, you writing a book?"

"Close, but not exactly."

Something dawned on her, looking at his left hand splayed across the bar wood. The missing piece of finger might be tied to the eye scar, like his hand had shot up to ward off whatever happened. Whatever *had* happened, he must have seen it coming.

Who would mess with this guy? She thought and then answered, s*omeone with a big knife.*

"The reason I asked, you came in here like you were looking for something besides a drink. Or company."

"Okay, I'm trying to find out something about this . . ." She slid the menu scrap in front of him. "It concerns a relative, my grandfather, the person who got the note at the bottom. Probably looked in his twenties then. Any ideas?"

He was clearly charmed by the vintage menu. It was a few moments before he answered. "We still do a Hunter's Stew special, but otherwise this is way before my time."

"The owner maybe?"

"Nope, they're an investment group now, buying up distressed places around the Upper West Side."

"I hear this place was something of a landmark."

"Still is. Lots of odd folks come in here—me excluded. Students, writers, tattoo artists, Nobel laureates, Columbia nerd-types, retirees, and invalids living in rent-controlled apartments who show up once a week. They order cocktails no one remembers—Sidecars, Old-

Fashioneds, you know. They all come in and out. Gets to be a pattern from this side of the bar."

"So, what writers?"

He pointed. "Kerouac wrote *On the Road* right over there by the window. Jay McInerney supposedly wrote parts of *Bright Lights, Big City* in here. A bunch of music types hang out from time to time. Bono had lunch here with some save-the-world type. Harold Ramis and Bill Murray hung out when they filmed *Ghostbusters* up the street. Oh yeah, the guys who made up Sha-Na-Na. They were in the *Woodstock* movie. Definitely before your time."

Cadence nodded, recalling greasy, juvenile delinquent rockers on stage. She pointed at the note again. "Well, I think the JRRT initials are Tolkien's, you know, the *Lord of the Rings* writer."

"Huh, sure, but never heard anyone say he'd been here."

"But he has to have been, don't you think, from the writing on the menu?"

"Yeah, yeah . . . Hey! You may be right. The bartender that retired from here, Vincent, once talked about how some famous English writer, I think it was Tolkien or Tidwell, was in here. The guy said the place reminded him of his pub back home. Had a regular thing there with a group of writers, I guess. The Inkspots, I think it was."

"That's a singing group. How about the Inklings?"

"Dunno. If you say so. I just remember the part about the pub. Which means he probably came in here several times. Vincent always kept track of the quasi-famous types who wandered in here."

"So, any thoughts how to pick up a trail on this?"

"Colder than that well digger's ass in Montana. Or a . . . oh well you get it. Let me think on it." He drifted away, doing a turn at his job.

Cadence looked around, observing people moving here and there. There was something odd about the place, and the next moment she noticed a dark shadow in the corner that made her neck hairs stiffen.

A sliver of light from the swinging kitchen door played on and off the crumpled figure. He wore a ratty ski hat and old coat. His head was oriented like he was looking out at her. In truth, she realized, he looked to be a homeless person who had come in for coffee. The bartender brought him a glass of water and a cup of coffee, saying a few words. Cadence gazed out the window at a taxi pulled curbside, its hazard lights blinking madly in the rain.

"Ma'am?" She jerked, surprised that the bartender was suddenly back.

"Coats says he can help."

"Who's that?"

"You were just looking at him."

She looked over there again. Same mysterious, neck-hair-raising gaze from a pool of shadow.

"So what'd he say?"

"For you to quit talking so loud and come over there."

As she slowly got up from the bar stool, she was watched by another.

* * *

Since his release from Riker's Island, Barren's search had taken the remainder of the day and into the night, until this very moment.

Arriving outside a few minutes ago, he knew it was an inn from the mingled smells of alcohol, smoke, and the urine of human woe that swirled at the rain-sotted threshold. He pretty much understood the words inscribed above the door: WEST END BAR. He went in.

He had no need of weapons—not yet, as he was armed with passing command of their language and knowledge of their vanities. His hair was cut short except for the crude ruff striping front to back. He sat down at one end of the bar.

Just as a stag in Mirkwood will twist its ears and raise its antlered head above the oak brush to satisfy its curiosity at an interloper, so did these people twitch before the threat of his very presence.

The young black-haired woman at the end of the bar fidgeted and looked behind her anxiously. She was in all likelihood the one. She talked to a scarred innkeeper and then they both looked at a bearded figure hidden at a table in a dark corner. He was different, not one of the moon-faces, but no threat.

Barren bent his head slightly to eavesdrop on their discussion. Satisfied, he got up and went back out in the rain and entered a waiting taxi. It was time to learn to drive.

* * *

As Cadence approached the booth in the corner, the fragrant derelict reached out and literally yanked her into the seat beside him.

"Understand that you will be watched!"

Whether it was the words he whispered or the overwhelming stink that startled her, she kept her composure. She could see his face better now, even with the ski hat pulled down. He was a caricature of the Big Apple Homeless Man—unshaven, his face deeply fissured, hiding within layers of dank old coats—with barely enough money rattling in his pockets to get by, even if the city shelters were his home every night.

"I . . ."

"I know what you seek." He quickly leaned to the side, peering at her from tabletop level. "Acoustics. Sitting here I can listen to every conversation in this room. That's why this is my spot!"

She nodded in vague understanding, following his darting, conspiratorial eyes.

"Your grandfather I knew. Tolkien I knew. Not since those days of chaos and revolution have I spoken of this."

"Yes?"

"Listen carefully, for if you have come here with this clue, you are no doubt in possession of a tale that will stretch and entangle with its root and branch. Beware of this: There are things evoked by lost stories, by words even, that have a life and a will of their own. Seek out a tale's origin and you are likely to find another. Keep searching and you may stumble upon that realm where the word and the beast mingle as one."

She was torn between the crackpot ramblings and the rational look in the man's eyes. She decided to sit for just one more minute.

"The Eye and the Shadow may have been vanquished, or like the swirl of smoke that enwreathed all ere it passed, may have diffused into new form. Like the banal evil that accumulates in our time. But other eyes remain, many with places and powers that have not yet come into focus. I perhaps know something of these documents you possess, and I know also that their rediscovery, even after so long a time, will not go unnoticed."

Now she was surprised. "But how could you know?"

"Quiet! You know so little, you will bring them here again just by your blundering questions! Be still and learn! Your grandfather was but an errand keeper picked at random. He was sent away with it, precisely because even he didn't know where he was going. He was, however, a respecter of both ancient lore and secrets of his times. Thus he was entrusted with the last remnants of the tale. Perhaps only by chance, he came to play a role far beyond his natural destiny. Beyond that I can say little of his path, save that your presence here tells me much. Perhaps not enough, however. Tell me why you have come here."

"I . . ." She paused to swallow; her mouth had suddenly gone dry. "I want to know where he is, and whether some documents he left, sort of a missing account of a famous heroine, are authentic."

"Authentic? You mean real? If it's a tale, it has a truth of its own. We are all sent down paths and live in worlds that we can only know as 'real' by what our heart says. We can't exist except by believing. What you mean by your question is, I fear, something more . . . base. Something smelling, perchance, of profit?"

He stopped and stared at Cadence. His insinuation made her even more uneasy than his lunatic ramblings.

"Perhaps you have these documents? Are they in your possession?"

Her guardian senses were up. She felt, could smell, the low-grade fear that was enveloping him.

He went on, "Time works against us. You must trust me this much. Go out of here now. Do not walk around. Come to the library at Columbia tomorrow at the second bell. It is my day house. Then I will tell you more. Nights of swift rain and lightning claws are no place to risk encounters with the creatures of this realm or any other. Now go!"

Cadence got up. She glanced briefly at the bartender. He nodded knowingly, and she walked out to face the hawk, the swooping wet wind.

The rain and whipping gale had gotten worse. Luckily—amazingly, she thought—a taxi still waited at the curb, its hazard lights blinking, its wheels resting hubcap-deep in water that threatened to flood the sidewalk. She ran to it, opened the door, and piled in.

With a lurch, the taxi took off. It surged into southbound traffic, heading for midtown. No questions, no hellos. She wondered if the driver even knew she was in the backseat. Through the scarred Lexan partition and the erratic light flickering across the smeared windshield, she could barely make out the figure hunched over the steering wheel.

"Hello!" she said, knocking on the partition. No response. The cab swerved left and right through the traffic as if, plausibly for New York City, the driver was hired fresh from a country without cars. Water cascaded on either side as the taxi boated and crashed through the overrunning street and deep-pooled potholes.

It slammed to a sideways stop at a red light at West 75th Street. Cadence knocked again and the figure turned, fumbled with the partition, and slid the window open.

"Yes?" he said.

"Do you want to know where I'm going?"

"Yes."

"Algonquin. Forty-fourth between Fifth and Sixth."

"Yes."

Approaching headlights played over him in flowing bands of light. His hair was cut down to the scalp, except for a low rough Mohawk cresting over his head to a peak that accented the cross-strip of his opaque Wayfarers.

"I'm ... Travis. Just relax now." He looked to be in his mid-twenties, despite his creased features and mature demeanor. *Military maybe*, she thought. The problem was, the picture that stared back at her from the driver ID pocket was of a man who looked, if she had to take a wild guess, Ethiopian. She looked at the meter. He hadn't turned it on. At West 40th Street the taxi finally had to stop. She didn't say a word, just threw a twenty at the driver and jumped out.

The light turned green and the cab lurched forward, kicking and swerving like a whipped horse.

* * *

By the time she stumbled into her room at the Algonquin, the cold and wet had seeped down into her skin to unleash rounds of shivers. This wasn't the first day she had expected. The cab ride, the loony people at the West End, the sudden change of weather, all foretold some fever settling over her body and her search.

She left her drenched clothes in a pile on the floor of the room, turned on the hot water in the tub, and poured in the entire mini-bottle of complimentary lavender bubble bath.

A froth of bubbles began to grow, and she went to the closet. There, behind the extra blanket and pillows on the top shelf, she had stashed the valise. She pulled it down and put it on the bed. She sorted through a few of the documents and stopped at a page filled with baroque Spencerian flourishes. With some concentrated effort, this was readable. She got in the tub and relaxed, holding the page above the bubbles as she read.

In a flash she sat up again, the bubbles splashing over the tub's edge. She thought about the story gleaned from the scroll a few days ago. Days that now seemed distant and wasted in that vigil-land of grading papers, hanging out at The Forest, and waiting for the impending foreclosure sale. Her heart galloped as she read and heard the rising din of horns and hoof beats . . .

As the ancient warning horns blew, Ara cast a torch upon the signal fire outside the gate, drew her sword and leapt to the center of the lane. Turning to face the darkness out of the east, she felt vindicated. Just as she had at the foot of the Capturing Tree. The others had eaten too much, no doubt drunk too much, and fallen asleep in the inn. And now the Wraiths, or some group of them, had come to this crossroads hamlet.

Suddenly she heard them behind her. They had entered the village! She turned to see them approaching.

A black cyclone, a wall of shadow and thundering hoof beats came up the lane. Sparks ignited from the clash of iron shoes on cobblestones. Streaming manes emerged from the dust and she quickly backed away to the gate bars, holding her tiny sword in two-fisted defiance before her.

On they came, a torrent slashing at village folk who stumbled out from their homes as the great horns blared.

As clear as full moonlight, she saw a skeletal hand emerge from the blackness of the foremost Wraith, marveled at the radiant, jeweled ring heavy upon one finger, and saw a power of angry red light emerge from that hand to blast the gates asunder. She was thrown aside, tumbled and rolled, and only regained her feet to face the Wraiths as they swept past. "Halt!" she cried.

To her amazement, the last of the Wraiths suddenly reined his horse and turned to her. The horse's nostrils poured plumes of smoky breath in the chill air. The Wraith spurred and came before her. He bent over, long robe flowing down, his face obscured in the shadow, and hissed, "A halfling-lass, is it?"

She tried to take a swipe with her sword, but her arm moved like honey in a Frighten January. She felt herself being lifted by some force, like a cold, grasping cloud all about her. The power drew her to the cowl beneath which hid something she did not want to see. She stared into that blackness as the bony hand slowly pulled back the shroud.

She had no voice to give release to the terror she saw.

The bubble bath slowly collapsed and the water grew still. Cadence sat thinking about the unspooling mystery of Ara. Who was she? Did she survive? *After what she's facing, who am I to fret at storms and cabbies?*

Chapter 47

INKLINGS IV

—

The sounds of books and leather bags being unceremoniously piled on benches, followed by an irritated voice.

"It's gotten a bit under your skin, hasn't it Tollers, that the Times called your book a 'mere fairytale'?"

"If the staff is the distinguishing mark of the wizard, and its possession empowers the holder, wizard or not, to flash it about, then these fools are worse than slacking apprentices!"

"Is that an answer, or are your feathers just ruffled?"

"It doesn't bother me at all. There is more in the world than those who sell words by daily tonnage appreciate. I start with words, and with the knowledge, wrought from my own learning, that one can often feel one's way back from the word to a story from an earlier time. After all, what better guarantee can there be that a thing exists, or at least did exist, than the fact that it has a name? And if it has a name, then there must be a history, a story, attached to it."

"Hello. I'll raise a glass to that, whatever it means."

"What it means, Ian, is that we can remember something long forgotten by attending to the very word that once referred to it. I would hope that my stories yet leave room for other minds and hands. That, anyway, is my intention and my hope."

"Very well, to those future stories!"

Clinks. Slurps. Ahhs.

"I confess, tracking words has been a consuming passion for me. Many names in my stories are borrowed or, at least to my mind, discovered."

"Isn't that a bit cheeky of you?"

"Cecil, you and I are bosom friends, so I take your own cheek in good spirit. The answer is yes. I borrowed 'Middle-earth', 'Mirkwood' and ring-giving from a deep well of Norse legend, 'orcs' and a lot more from my beloved *Beowulf*, and, I dare say, 'hobbit' from a list of imaginary creatures I found in the Denham Tracts. There are many more. Perhaps too many, but I treat them as drill bits. Names are something to bite into the bedrock of myth that belongs to us all—even to you, Cecil, as you clutch your empty flagon!"

"From all the bits of stories you've read to us here at this table, I would've thought the 'Middle-earth' you describe was your own invention."

"Hardly. It was there all along. Some part of it, I suppose, I have peopled. Much more of its territory remains for others to fill. As we've discussed before, the term is a wonderful, evocative linguistic artifact. It is a land of vaguely menaced borders, dim dangers lurking just beyond our ken, and moors distant from the light of the keep. A place bounded by monsters that refuse to flee."

"Perhaps, Tollers, your stories should start with someone to warn the reader 'Beware the spell of words. They are unstill. Sleepless they are, bearers of meaning deeper than you wish to delve. They hunger. They wish to evoke stories unbidden and feelings foreign and troubling.'"

"I have already have met this oracle. And I fear I know the truth of this message all too well."

"Tollers, let me ask this respectfully, is there more here than you are saying? This document trove, of which you tell us little, has clearly upset you. What is your disquiet? Do those 'words' whisper to you, separate from their voice on the page?"

"Cecil, I detect your cynic's ear. My answer is yes. Better still, we have with us a witness, quite able to testify on this strange aspect. Here! My summer assistant, Mr. Osley, whom you have met, has had to sit here and slurp his ale double-time to keep measure with you and Jack."

"Here! Here! Don't be shy now, not becoming to a Yank. Speak up lad!"

A new voice is heard, barely audible to the hidden microphone.

"Well . . . uh . . . since you ask, I know this. Professor Tolkien has asked me to work on organizing and translating an unusual collection of documents. Some of them are in a language that I would say is—I know this sounds odd—true Elvish. It is not invented or imagined, but as real as Mr. Lewis's breathless prose. It is a proper language in all respects except this: it is alive. The more we study it, the more . . . restless it becomes. Meanings change. They scurry on an unstill path."

"Well, young master, you learned to dance well at the foot of your mentor. May I offer one compass for your stay here at Oxford?"

The sly winks and nods are almost audible.

"Why, yes sir."

"On those forest paths, stick hard to the real trail. Keep your feet on the ground and your nose for those six points of Sheaf's Stout to which Jack has introduced you. I have no doubt that, in the morning, the sheer size of your head will keep you grounded."

Chapter 48

OCTOBER 21: MORNING

—

By 9:00 AM, Cadence was eating breakfast in the Algonquin's Round Table Room and taking in the ambiance of the hotel. It truly was a grand old great-aunt of a place. It was partial to dark wood paneling and presided over by a highly competent if entrenched and fussbudget, staff. The hotel manager brought her the *New York Times* and unfolded her napkin for her and asked if she was enjoying her stay. He exited with a professional grace. Just as her orange juice came, she settled back and opened the paper.

Her cell phone rang to the high brass notes of Aaron Copland's *Fanfare for the Common Man*. She muted the sound and checked the screen. The display read CALLER ID UNAVAILABLE. As she accepted the call, the voice launched right in.

"Any progress?" It was Mel.

"Sort of. I'm here having breakfast at the Algonquin. Thank you for that. I went to a strange bar on the Upper West Side. Remember the menu I showed you that's initialed JRRT? That place. I met a one-eyed bartender. Oh, and I talked to a madman, a street person who speaks bad Shakespeare, like a C-list Marvel Comics character. Anyway, he says he met both Tolkien and my grandfather. He's a loon, but he may be all I've got. I also got rained on big time and had a weirdo for a cab driver," she added, even as she could already hear Mel's fingers drumming on a table. "Not much progress, huh?"

"You've been there maybe twenty-four hours—relax."

"Oh yes, it seems Tolkien, or someone pretending to be him, hung out at the West End. Years ago."

"Uh huh. Listen, don't despair, because I've got news about our good Professor Tolkien."

"Like what?"

"Get this. The critics at first hated him, then, as with all successful writers, they adored him. But they all call him the Great Borrower because he treated prior stories and sources like, as they put it, a dragon's horde—something to be routinely looted. Or more politely, to be ransacked at will and without attribution. His stories are populated with creatures, proper names, places, happenings from works by Shakespeare, Finnish literature, Sir Gawain, you name it."

"Yeah, I thought that . . ."

"Here's just a few examples of the borrowed names, nouns, and other stuff. I jotted them down for you. For starters, the word hobbit. Then it goes from there: Frodo, Bilbo, Gandalf, Middle-earth, Bag End, Hasufel, Edoras, Mirkwood, Midgewater, Wormtongue, Meduseld, ents, wargs, balrogs, woses, and roughly two-thirds of the various dwarf names. The list goes on and on."

"Okay, but what's wrong with borrowing when he used it to create such great stuff?"

Her waiter unobtrusively placed her breakfast before her.

"Precisely, my dear. Tolkien felt no unease in this. To him, every name and every tale was a place to begin a new story. Which reminds me. Hell, I'm just a professional middleman, but I'd say Wagner's opera, *The Ring*—about the one ring that could rule the world, and the remaking of the mythical sword that was broken—all sounds pretty familiar. Except Wagner wrote it in 1869. In any case, as Tolkien said, the road goes on and on."

"Yes. So?"

"So it means we've got the moral high ground. Tolkien's view was that any story that borrows from older stories is a fair and natural part of the process. You see, creativity and innovation thrive on borrowing."

"Mel, don't take this the wrong way, but your inner poet must be trying to get out. You don't strike me as one to rely on moral high ground very much."

"Very true!" he laughed. "Nor will the ones I am about to talk about. They are the wielders of the power. They will seek to stifle and destroy *anything* new that is attributable to Tolkien even if it is authentically his."

"Well, if you read what's barely readable in this so-called fourth book, it looks like *maybe* he wrote, or at least translated, some small part of it, but by far most was written by other people, maybe at different times in the past. As in long, *long* ago. If you read it literally, it comes from some very strange place. Not his story book Middle-earth, but someplace different. The real one. The one he tried so hard to imagine. Ninety percent of it needs translation, if that's even possible. It's just runes and stuff."

"Let's don't get carried away. Parts of this may seem a little strange, but no matter."

Cadence turned away from a nearby table of patrons and hunched over the phone. She dropped her voice. "'Strange' seems to be *the* operative word here."

"Well," he said, "I could have said 'curiouser and curiouser.' In the vein of odd things, though, I just learned an interesting factoid about our Good Professor."

"I can't *wait*. No, honest, I want to hear it."

"He was a spook."

She rolled her eyes and laughed, as if he was a pure nut case. "You mean Tolkien's a ghost?"

"No, stupid, a spy, a secret agent. As in Her Majesty's Secret Service. Because of his linguistic skills, he was recruited as a code-breaker at the beginning of World War II. You know, deciphering the Nazi Enigma Code, all that movie stuff. Anyway, he only did it for a short period. It's a blurb in the news today. Declassified by MI6."

"How in the hell is that going to help me?"

"I don't know. Who knows all the twists and turns in this? To answer your question, it probably doesn't help. Only you can do that, with support from me."

Cadence sat back and stared at her rapidly cooling scrambled eggs, wondering if things were about to get a lot *curiouser*. "You know, Mel, I'm not sure what all this is about either. What I really care about though, more than anything, is finding out who my grandfather was and what happened to him."

Cadence heard a voice in the background on Mel's phone, "Mr. Chricter, Mr. Jackson's office on two."

"Hey, uh . . . Cadence, hold on. I'll be right back."

She heard him put the phone down, get up, and talk on a speakerphone somewhere else in his office. It was dim but clear.

"Yeah, its Mel. Look, tell Peter I'm onto something here. I've been approached with something interesting. Yeah, I know they had to rewrite Tolkien *again*. Gotta have those ingénues. So this should also be interesting. Heck, maybe there are already clues somewhere. Where? The Narcross scene? I *know* you only want stuff that puts legs on the franchise. Okay, okay, so talk to his people. Talk to Guillermo. I'm on a call."

He picked up the phone again. "Cadence? Fine, just keep the faith. And don't get into any strange cabs. This is big-time stuff and who knows who, or what, may be watching you."

She hesitated for a moment. "Okay, I'll be careful."

"One more thing."

"Yes."

"Since you're having breakfast at the Algonquin," *and I'm covering your bill,* she heard in his tone, "you're in the Round Table Room. Back in the twenties, that was the meeting place of the American counterpart to Tolkien's Inklings group. All the *New Yorker* magazine hotshots and Broadway luminaries traded jibes there. So it may be a sign, right?"

"Right. Maybe some good will come out of that. If I can't find the tracks of good ol' spymaster Tolkien, I'll just switch to Robert Benchley and Dorothy Parker."

"Chin up. You're on the right track."

"Yeah, I guess I need to decide on my next move."

Mel's voice hushed. "Remember one word."

In his pause she thought he was actually going to say "Plastics."

"Provenance, Cadence, provenance. Is this stuff authentic? Prove that and we can get a deal."

She wasn't sure any more that she even wanted one of Mel's deals. She said goodbye and hung up. What was her next move? She amused herself with the wry image of being marooned in a pathless forest, with discarded road signs leaning askew all about. "Secret Gate This Way." "Moon Clock Running." "Provenance and Proofs. Information Booth Up Ahead." She especially liked the one that read "Homeless Man Advice. Next Exit."

What she didn't like was this feeling, like a pair of eyes peering at her from deep in that same imaginary forest.

* * *

Barren was studying his prey carefully now. He knew where she grazed. He would let her get comfortable and slack in her vigilance. He walked the streets to lower Manhattan and in time he came to a great excavation.

Instinct told him a great tumult had happened here, a fall of towers and a killing of innocents. From his own experience, he could sense the embers of panic and fear.

Now, however, he had a mission to conclude. The only question was: where are the scribbles, the documents his master desired? He felt an easy confidence, having donned their garments and mastered much of their speech.

He walked north up the canyons of steel and glass, and came to stairs leading down into a tunnel entrance. It was just as an oracle's entryway might be, he mused. This, he knew, was the roadway for their strange, noisy machines. He went to the ticket kiosk and bought a fare card with money he had pilfered from one of the bright-faced people. They never felt the gentle slip of his hand.

As he waited on the platform for the E train to arrive, he assessed his advantage. In his walking about, he had seen things he innately recognized from his past life, vestigial relics, like broken shell bits betokening a once great ocean. Now they were powerless fragments of magic and illusion. The power in the token in the small pouch slung about his neck far outstripped all the remnants here. It had, after all, served its purpose. It enabled him to learn, swift as an arrow.

So, if there was little magic to use here, he would still manage. He first had some distractions to take care of.

* * *

As Cadence left the entrance to the Algonquin, passing under the distinctive A's, she looked for a Starbucks. She found three of them, all visible from the same spot. She chose instead an independent, Grousin' Grounds, with an angry caffeine addict logo on the door. She ordered a triple macchiato and handed over her credit card. It felt ever thinner. This time, inevitably, it would be the dissolving prop from *Mission: Impossible.* She bit her lip, praying it wouldn't be declined.

The clerk slid it through the reader, and then said, "Hey!"

Cadence quivered. "Is it . . . okay? I can pay cash." She began to fumble in her purse, jockeying it with the valise that hung from her other shoulder.

The guy held the card out to read it. "No, your name. Grande. You're named after a size of Starbucks coffee?"

She exhaled with relief and took the card. "Actually, it's the other way around."

"Then you should sue them for trademark violation."

"Yeah, that sort of thing seems to be goin' around. Thanks."

Toward the back she found a booth with a big table. She opened the valise and spread out some of the documents at a safe distance from her macchiato. She wanted to find more about Ara. Was she really the "Her" so detested by the wizard in the earlier fragment? Was she the one who was being erased by ink smears right out of the elderly halfling's book? And most important, why?

She sipped her drink slowly, thumbing through the documents until, at last, she found a cluster of readable pages bound by some rough sinew. There was a small mark, perhaps archival in intent, in the lower right corner of each page. The annotation at the top of the first page said only, "Found at Delvrose, Year 64 of the Fourth Age." It read:

Ara's Rune

The one known as Ara, it was said, was learned of letters and utilized a grand and distinctive rune in the likeness of an A with eyes that watched over all. She was of average height for a lady halfling, but possessed both beauty (as her kind measures it: simply) and wit in full measure. Her eyes are described as large and expressive of thoughts beyond the ken of many a simple country halfling. She had feet more elegant than most halflings, and often wore her long, dark hair tied up in a manner unusual for those times.

She came, it is recounted, from an obscure hamlet known as Frighten. Residents thereabouts were regarded by other halflings as "a tad off" in the way an eccentric but loved relative might be. Even their names were odd. They called themselves by words favoring the fall: Spookymore, Pumpkinbelly, Gourdnose, Fallglint, Catspaw, Heatherlook, Yellowoak, Flameleaf, Firstfrost, Harvestcart, Orangemoon, Mapleflow.

This much is known: Frighten was a village of proper halfling dwellings and husbandry settled among gently rolling hills creased with sudden clefts filled with dark, tangled woods. In the fall the oak and hickory trees turned brilliantly hued, and the land transformed into expanses of hayfields, dotted with ricks guarded by the most notable product thereabouts: the Giant Pumpkins.

These Great Gourds stood man high or more and weighed on average a hundred stone. They were transported by sturdy wains and stood sentinel in every field and on the doorsteps of most halfling homes. As the final gibbous moon of the harvest waxed to fullness, the pumpkins were carved into fantastic, leering faces illuminated from within by beeswax candles. And so, of a crisp autumn night, the land was dotted with these laughing, leering, grinning, howling, Frighten sentinels.

A note is in order here. Along with the few remembered "inventions" of the halflings, such as the cultivation of the enchantment plant, *hoernes*, and the fine points of their various dwellings, there was another, quite curious matter: the practice, or as they called it, the fine craft, of brewing pumpkin beer. Restricted largely to the region of Frighten, it was originated by the great-grandfathers of Ara (agreed by all to be of an offshoot of the inimitable Flameleafs—or Flameleaves if you want to get picky) and often described by the "outsider" halflings to be a cult of the pumpkin. This practice was not utilized in what we might today call worship, but, as with all their crafts, a happy and complete appreciation and use of the great gourds.

Those visiting the region in the late fall, particularly during the Great Celebration, would oft imbibe the pumpkin beer and declare loudly and with hearty belches, "Best south of the North Downs!" This was invariably met by the exclamation "Puts to shame the dregs they pass off at the Golden Sheaf!"

Those who recall these boasts also recall whispers—of a pumpkin bigger than anyone had seen since warm summers before the Long Winter, of a girth not surpassed by the largest hay wagons of men: a giant, renowned pumpkin known as Johnny Squanto. Its seeds each year produced equal giants, fat, deeply fissured, of a deepest orange, growing by a hand's width each day in the long, lolling days of summer. To this day the saying survives among serious farmers and the crowds at county fairs, "Now there's a genuine squanto, that is!

But we wander from the path.

Some records attest to an Aragranessa being crowned Queen of Frighten in 1109. Of her family it is known they were also of the line of Swallowhawks that gave rise in later years—beyond the span of this tale and even after the end of the Last Age—to the heroic stand of halflings at Wrandy before the onslaught of the Orc-Men. That, of course, led to the Final Scattering of the Halflings.

But of this tale, it must be surmised that Ara first met him . . .

Here Cadence stopped. Yes, the tale finally gets to the *him,* whoever he was.

. . . Ara first met him after a series of the Great Parties (for births and holidays tend to be clumped in spring and fall in this land). He was quite lonely. He was no doubt looking for someone, yet perhaps afraid to venture too far in search.

It is known that the one in times hence known as the Bearer had taken to long walks, even days of wanderings, about the far reaches of the little corner of the world then known. It was in this period, perhaps, that he met Ara. For one element of Ara's character is—if "consistently told" is a reliable witness—well known: she loved the wilds and often visited the less trodden frontiers of the Far Forest. She was spoken of for her lore and wisdom even onto the far edges of their domain. She doubtless had, at times, passed well beyond those unguarded borders.

From this account, little can I glean of her in later times, save this: a promontory often described as "Ara's Watch" or "View Rock" was marked on maps for years, even into our times. It lay at the far western guard post of the Old Land, and from its vantage the dark blue sea could first be spied. Less reliably, it was said that in local lore it was regarded as a place for lovers to share their vows, earnestly ignorant of the namesake for the place they had chosen.

As sadly, are we.

Your humble scribe

The legible text ended here. Cadence put the bound pages aside and searched until she found another bundle with the same archival mark. It was a thin crescent, as of a new moon.

She was looking for what happened to Ara after the village gate. She found the trail. The documents gave up their story and Cadence sat, engrossed:

When Ara awakened in the waning light, she jumped in fear at the memory of the burning gatehouse and the Wraith. Then she settled and looked about. She recognized the place as Signal Hill. She found herself bound with thick, rough cords around her wrists. They were crudely tied, fair game for the cleverness of a halfling skilled in the logic of knots. But first she had to see more. She sat up, prepared to relive the fear of the night before, but realized that she was a spectator.

She was on a small, grassy rise, below which there was an assemblage of black-armored men plumed and regaled in finest battle gear. They stood quietly in a line, their postures suggesting a serious and dignified purpose.

Across from them crowded a swaggering, jostling band of orcs. A small drum was entertaining them as some danced with crude, off-rhythm jerks. Some of them were immense, taller even than the men.

A Power Troll with huge muscles and gnarled canines stood to one side. A creature of some apparent distinction, his tattooed arms were festooned with gold and bejeweled crowns of murdered kings and princes, worn now as bracelets. He held in each taloned hand an array of leather straps used as leads. Those in his left hand restrained a snarling pack of great Dire Wolves. With their overdeveloped shoulders, long red tongues dripping wet pools of slather at their feet, they were shivering in fear and deep loathing. The Troll gave their leads a sharp jerk to curb their whining, his crown-bracelets clinking as the muscles rippled down his arm.

There was ample reason for their fear. Held by the thicker leads in the Troll's right hand was a witch's count of heavy-breathing brudarks.

Ara was stunned. She had seen drawings of them before, but

no halfling had ever seen the horror of a brudark and lived to tell the tale. She blinked at them, not believing her eyes. They were leashed and hobbled, in one of their six pair of legs, before her . . .

Suddenly, like a wind, a presence approached to her left. The men bowed, removing their helmets. The orcs fumbled, stepping on each other's feet in their confusion. The troll simply stared intently as what first seemed like a cloud quickly became a solitary person walking up between him and the terrified orcs. The person was clad in the hue-shifting robes favored by wizards when appearing in public. But the hues in this cloak were subtle in their range, like the variations of darkness in approaching storm clouds—deep, troubled grey shifting to the wisp of a misty white mare's tale, then folding to a weather waif's tattered dark skirt of approaching rainsqualls, and finally they darkened to the angry blackness of a tornado's heart. He bore no crown and no staff. A simple, rustic chair was brought out and on this he sat.

It was clear that they were assembled there to have an audience with others not yet present. The entire group was arrayed roughly along two sides, with this un-wizardly wizard sitting in his chair in their midst.

Encumbered by her bonds, Ara rose quietly to her feet, unnoticed. She looked around and saw, on the far crest of Signal Hill, the black horses that with their riders had come upon her at the village's east gate. She stared at the waiting Wraiths and thought better of trying to escape.

Horses neighed in the distance and the growing hoof beats announced the arrival of a mounted vanguard of men. Within moments they appeared, their mounts hard-ridden and sleek with sweat. They were arrayed in once-bright battle-tarnished armor and cloaks bearing the signs of great realms of Middle-earth. The yellow outline of the Tree of Council and the Elvish rune for M swept across their banners. Ara looked for the Woodsman, but he was not amongst them. A group of them, well-armed and fearless, dismounted. Sturdy men, swaggering and cavalier in their manner, they walked halfway to where the wizard sat and stopped, whilst their leader approached the wizard directly.

Only the slatted breathing of the brudarks marked the silence. The leader spoke, his voice edged with disdain as he knowingly committed the slight of not introducing himself by name and lineage. He said bluntly, "I come as ambassador from the race of men as liege under the Great Houses and the offended One City. I bear this message to thee, Dark One, as well as thy errand-boys and minions gathered hereabout."

The Dark Lord! Ara sank to her knees in shock.

The speaker paused to let the insult sink in. The line of black-armored men stood fast and did not acknowledge it. The orcs remained oblivious. They were struggling just to follow the words.

The man continued. "We come to deliver this message, lest you misperceive our resolve and by the stroke of error deliver your lands into ruin. We are prepared to resolve this matter, and to allow you by the labor of war upon other lands, to forget our just reprisals for the grievous offenses you have committed against us. Our offer is thus: you must retreat from the lands west of the Long River, forego all rents and tithes from peoples under our dominion, and accept the contents of this letter as our last, final and permanent tribute."

With that, he stepped forward and dropped a yellowed parchment unto the lap of the still-seated wizard. He then stepped back and stood, his feet apart in a wide stance, his hand posed firmly on his sword hilt.

The wizard looked at the package in his hands, and then began to open it up with calm deliberation. The sides folded back, then the top, then the bottom. He looked at the opened parchment. It was empty. He let it fall gently from his hands, its tiny, awesome, crackling sound as it landed on the dirt filling the assembly with foreboding.

Seconds ticked by like hours. Finally the wizard stirred and rose, almost wearily. "My gracious Ambassador," he began in a quiet voice, "Wizards, and those that still honor them, and indeed even the misguided elves, have posed this conflict as one of great causes. Of momentous times, the 'Passing of the Age of Middle-earth' it is said grandly by some."

His arm swept about in a mildly mocking gesture.

"Unfortunately, but inevitably," he continued, "men such as you view it from a mortal's perspective, as something to be won or lost in terms of territory and dominion and perhaps a few score years of kingly power. You see it only as power to be clutched at," he clenched now his outstretched fist and then relaxed it to openness, "even as it evaporates into the transitory airs of your lives. I regret your perspective, but I can respect it. I ignore your arrogant and foolish jest with this letter, and I forgive it."

He paused. "What I had earnestly hoped was that this council would be summoned amongst us without distraction and, forgive me, the shrill whisperings of those lawless insurgents known as Quicklegs and his outlaws. Let me speak clearly here. That man is a cruel usurper! He pretends to a crown only to rule you all for his own selfish purposes. And also blessed are we to meet this very eve without the, again forgive me, fear-mongering of this lesser wizard known as Stormhue . . ."

He leaned forward and lowered his voice, as if confiding, "Who, by the way, brings bad news to cover the bad luck he spreads everywhere like a disease. This council, then, I hoped would avoid the dialogue of 'great causes' and also the, forgive me one last time, the pettiness of settling things for a few generations of your race."

He marked this moment with a deep breath. "Let there then be no cavil as to the terms that can divide us bitterly or embrace us both to greater purpose and most blessed peace. I am prepared humbly to accept your terms, if you will but render me one small token. To fill up a parchment such as that unkindly gift of empty space and unfeeling heart which you earlier bestowed upon me. The token I ask is but a small ornament, suitable as a trifling pendant or ring. Plain, of little value to others yet sentimental to me and my lineage. Just as your lands and heraldry are . . . shall we say 'precious' . . . to you. Help me find this bauble, give me this which is mine, and I, along with my supporters—" he gestured to the lines on either side of him, "for as you can see they are neither slaves nor minions, but worthy men of principle and allies of orcs who have been unfairly harassed and ungentled by your houses from time immemorial—these all shall withdraw. The Long River shall make us good neighbors and its waters reflect unguarded borders, rather than warring camps sending forth boats of fire and war, from this day forward."

The visiting ambassador waited a moment to respond. He was cold and unyielding in his manner. "We know not of this token, save by vague legend bandied about by those who pretend to have memories longer than my many grandfathers' lives. But if you value it so, it may be of greater value than you admit, or perchance of use only to those of your kind. In either case we care little. If we possessed it, we would in all likelihood deliver it unto you as ransom alongside your fear of defeat, and seal this offer. But we possess it not, nor shall we divert to aid your search for this trinket. You have made war upon our lands and now amass your armies at our borders, and indeed stand here at this moment upon some mission of secrecy deep within our own territory. You summon to our vicinity those hated dogs of terror known as the Wraiths. We shall not take the bait of your soft words. Quit our lands or we shall evict you by defeat and death!"

The Dark Lord did not regard the man. He simply sighed and said, "May you feel such fear that your balls turn as brittle as stones."

In response, the company under their proud emblems pulled forth their swords, their sudden ringing like a cry of metallic harmonies. Shiiinnnggg! The swords reflected the reddening light of day's end.

Just as suddenly those in the forward ranks shrieked. The troll had let slip the brudarks. The ambassador was torn into pieces in a moment. His sword and helm spit into the air like mere twigs and crumbs. The stunned company turned in panic, gave spur to their mounts in retreat, and then suddenly reined them in.

Ringing the path of their escape were five mounted Wraiths.

"Finish them, and bring me their banners that we may use them as rolls in our latrines and sop-rags in our banquet halls!"

With that, the dark knights and the orcs fell on the hapless few who quailed now between the Wraiths and the brudarks.

Here the scribe's hand failed, as if interrupted. There were scribbles, scratch-throughs, question marks, and re-dos of various symbols. There was half of a note, something about a trap awaiting the Bearer, then an arrow leading to the words "The trap is set for the next full moon!" After further space, the writing again gathered momentum toward Ara's fate:

There followed hoarse shouts and the screams of men and beasts, clashing and banging, the dull thuds of weapons on bodies, and a hideous brudark roar. As these subsided, the howls of Dire Wolves, now loosed to search out survivors, filled the glen.

One approached Ara's spot, picking up a scent and eager to tear into a quailing prey. It pounced at a darker spot in the grass. Its jaws set upon the limp and empty chords of her bonds.

Ara was gone.

Maddening! Cadence looked at the clock and then leafed through the pages until she found once again the sign of a sliver moon. She read with a flash of energy as she saw whose paths had crossed:

Ara had been here. The Bearer felt it.

He stopped, smelled the freshening air that rushed down this glen, and knelt facing the pathway before him. The breeze sang gently of distant snows and the awakening of the Winter Giants far to the north as it rippled in wavelets across the expanse of green grass. Sunlight and shadow danced an ensemble as the nearby trees swayed back and forth.

The patterns of light caught a glint.

There! Gone. There again!

He stretched and pulled from the grass a necklace of gold. It was broken, and dark stains painted its delicate links. It was Ara's. Its lineage traced back to the treasure hordes of the Last Dragon. He had given it to her as their first exchange of gifts. (He had received from her a green *Sibhaet*, the distinctive hat of travelers of the Great Road.)

She had been here. Perhaps only hours before!

He leapt forward holding his Sibhaet tightly in his hand, his feet compressing the shallower grass of the path, and left that place forever.

There was a note in the margin of the passage. The note-maker scribed these lines perhaps centuries after the original document, yet still of a time lost to antiquity:

Where this most famous Halfling thus passed—proudly wearing his Sibhaet as portrayed in the famous Tapestries of Ulmarest—he was intent on his search for the footprints of Ara. The grass grows there even today in similar long-bladed fashion. The wind still ripples across this expanse, just as it did then. The earnest aromas of spring still arrive there yearly. The rich, sad smells that herald the onset of fall are identical there today. The hares and marmots of the nearby rocky hillside reside there yet. And to those who say Middle-earth has passed on, let them stand here! For they are shown the lie by this moment.

That world exists still, for any that would kneel down and smell the simple earth, stoop and partake of the plain and honest work offered by a fine summer's vegetable garden, or gaze to the snow-crested, blue mountains that beckon one to adventure.

If, of a moment, you next linger in such a place, perchance travelling a rude and simple country road, ask thyself who trod this path before? What errands did they seek? What stories did they live? Where did this path take them in their long journey?

Indeed, where does it take thee?

Cadence read on, obsessed now, and came across a context for the evil toward which Ara's feet carried her:

An Account and Prophecy.

By Gifol, Historian of the Third Age in the Court of Hrothulf.

My Lord,

The tale of Ara and the single moon cycle which ordered so much of the end of that world and the beginning of our own, cannot be fully understood without the history of the Source and its Embodiment. Unfortunately this comes to us in tatters, rife with dispute and contradiction. Was this embodiment merely a ring? Or, as various sages maintain, a shield, or sword, or symbol? Was it a secret incantation, with the story of a ring attached merely as a myth? Ruse and distraction infect all history from these times.

A review of its popular names from antiquity tells us little. "Un-still" it was sometimes called in the south, but by far it was known, universally and simply, by one name: "Bind."

I repent now that my long research in the few scattered archives that survived the wreckage of those times is complete. This is what we know: there was an Embodiment of a kind. It was called Bind. It was most likely a pendant or a ring. It was indeed destroyed. With it went much of the magic of the world, along with a pernicious concentration of evil.

Alas, the nature of evil is that it lurks and gathers. It is a seed in the hearts of men.

Magic is more fragile. Have hope, my lord, for I believe it too has survived. The makers at the Source made another Embodiment. Its fate is at present unknown. It may conceal itself as a ring, a book, or perhaps a secret gate.

But to your charge to me as historian of the Court, this I foresee: Evil will once again stir, as leaves gather in the eddy of a stream. Long hence, a holder of that other surviving token from the Source shall emerge. The ancient and esteemed tradition of ring-giving shall be revived. Magic shall be renewed and—"

It ended there. She leaned back and took a deep breath and slowly exhaled. *Maybe another round of espresso,* she thought, *just to rev things up. Yeah.* She hid the valise under her table and went up to the counter, glancing wearily back. She returned and sat down and took a few contended sips. Her hands leafed through page after page of runic lettering. Then, like a wizened gold-panner, her eye narrowed as the black sands of unintelligible inscription revealed another gleaming nugget. She teased with the meaning and it unraveled easily. It shared key threads with what she had read already.

From the Histories of the Ara Society:

Not surprisingly, as the Fourth Age spread across the world, much was made of the power of rings. They became baubles of fashion that marked idleness and sloth as much as fealty to policy, tribe, and guild. The market displayed false relics in all forms. They became counterfeit, tawdry, and trifling.

Ara, it was said, did acquire in her travels a ring of some power. That ring was imagined during the next century by untold numbers of cheap imitations sold in stalls in every market. Even as this common vulgarity of fake "Rings of the Third Age" spread, a few true copies bearing her unique rune bore witness to a secretive "Society of Rings." These groups were in time banned as the last histories of her life were hunted down and destroyed.

And what was the power of her ring? That truth is lost, but one suspects it was but a symbol, a repository perhaps, for her own inner strength.

The text ended abruptly. Cadence could feel the cumulative effects of the shots of espresso. It was like a bubbling hot spring, welling up inside her. She sat upright in her chair, fidgeting, toes tapping, a jittery tempo surrounding her. Looking at the stack of documents, she knew that at best there could be only a few more readable pages. Then the story would dissipate, like a ship faintly seen and passing away in the fog. Her nervous energy told her to take a break, relax, and just draw something. She got out a sketch pen and a piece of stationary from the Algonquin, and let her hand run free. Soon a rough-out of a mysterious gate, perhaps a secret gate, encrusted with vines and roots, began to form. She put her pen down and looked at it. Nice, but the most telling thing was that it was closed tight.

It is telling me something, she thought. She got out another blank sheet and doodled for more answers, her pen performing like a farmer's dowsing rod. It whooshed a few lines and circles and, faintly, she began to see an image of ponderous mechanisms. Her mind's eye quickly outstripped the pen and paper. The picture was too big, too dynamic, too *cinematic.* Beyond feelings and intuition, her guts told her that she was about to lay her hands on the starter crank of some vast, dead mechanism. Something that had sat ice-entombed for centuries. If Leonardo da Vinci and Tim Burton had collaborated on the concept of an Early Industrial *Transformer,* this would be it. She saw her hands grasp and then turn the crank, felt it whipsaw back viciously, heard the dead clank inside. She tried again, and again, creating a pattern worthy of her name. Finally it coughed. Another crank and it sputtered and vomited coal-black smoke. With the next crank, it stuttered and found a jagged rhythm of pistoning heartbeats. Steam, or whatever life force drove it, was rising in its pipes. It was coming alive, and its feet were breaking free of those bitter winter-welds.

Cadence looked at the documents and knew that the engine and its elusive crank lay hidden within those indecipherable pages.

The vision began to slide away. She scavenged the pile for a moment, then found two pages in an elegant and coherent hand:

By wager of battle goes victory, and with it the power to name. This alone, over the long expanse of time, may be worth the test. Kingdoms come and go, lines of noble blood are thinned to whelped vassals, castle keeps wear and tumble. But more enduring, surely, are the word and the name. What lost tales and feats of valor are tethered to simple names? Think only of Cragmoor and Selharm and Vitus! Middle-earth itself. Those coming long after will ponder such names and search for the tale of the victor.

So the protagonists of the Great War ultimately fought, in the long march of history, to brightly name their lands and mark their foes with enduring labels of dishonor.

The Valley of the Dark Lord, now long resigned to the stain of foul names, once had a more pleasant designation. 'The Source,' it was called, and a bit of its lost history tells much.

The one place in the world where the most basic elements

of the world come together, save where ice and fire live as one on islands in the far, far north, was the Valley of the Source. Here forests and meadows and stags the size of three war horses once flourished, along with steaming vents and great geysers of boiling water. Beneath the valley floor, the very essence of Mother Earth dwelled. From a single great cone at the center of the valley, a place known as Fume, she periodically burst forth and poured molten rock down its slopes.

In this valley long there lived a cult of making, and the rich array of exotic minerals, plants, and waters led them to continuous learning. Rock pictures on the valley walls tell of the first nameless physics who here sought deeper truth. Along the way, the art of tanning, the making of inks not much different than that by which these words are scribed, paints and dyes, even the explosive powders secreted by the wizards in their fireworks—all were here invented.

So, deep in thought and process they delved, and The Source provided the materials and energy for their work. Their goals were noble, seeking to transcend by some metaphysical solvent the base diseases of imperfection, corruption, and dissolution. To create the gold that is alive, that imbues the water of life and provides panacea to all ills—that is the quest toward which all their powers were bent.

They tinkered and toiled, kept great scrolls, wrote books without words, and invented humors and elixirs to cure much malady in this world.

In time one among them, a secretive hermit of great wisdom, claimed to have created the Philosopher's Stone, the noblest of substances, the gold that is not dead and that contains the force of life and destiny itself. His study was a cave in the bowels of Fume, and the substance he discovered was al-bimiva, the Quintessence. This he fashioned into many things, but chief among them were pendants and rings.

Fume awoke one day and belched a vomit of lava across the valley. By some miracle unrecorded, the old man that resided in that mountain of fire survived. His study, holding years of careful records and incantations, was destroyed. He managed to save a collection of tokens, each made of al-bimiva. They were precious to him. One in particular, the lost and legendary artifact known as Bind, was the very symbol of his power.

His lifetime secrets lost, he sought out and stole the libraries of others. But he coveted most those tokens. From these he would rebuild. He vowed to control as much of the vulgar world as he could with these tokens.

Of course, as for the Quintessence, it was not yet totally pure. In its flaws melded the imperfection of the world with the corruption of the hermit.

That bent figure, be he human or wizard (for in those days they competed in the quest of alchemy), became the Dark Lord. He returned to Fume to guard the Source and rebuild his library and plot his machinations.

His real name was erased in his vanquishing. In its place are evil names, some with damning *mor*- designations, and others of simple descriptions: Glutter of Crows, Lord of the Slain, and the like.

The glowering red ellipse at the summit of Fume's soaring cone became known as the Glowing Eye.

Another surprise page seemed to jump forward or backward in time:

The ending of our age has begun in earnest.

It has, in the span of a generation of men, become a time of deepening cold. Springs arrive late and summers fail their promise with chill rains and early frost. The Great River as far south as Allnoon stays frozen half the year. At the winter solstice we dance the jig on the river like a gala of berobed skeletons. All weep at the frail forms of the children. Final stores of turnips and grazus [a form of lumpy, twisted, pale carrot – ed.] expire and the stock will go and then the people. All will be gone if the river's thaw again slackens till the end of a long, drear spring.

I fear a turning is upon us, the scars of which will mark all lands and all peoples.

She stopped and checked the time on her cell phone—almost two o'clock. As she packed up the valise, she felt as if Ara and her tale were actually unwinding in real time. What was happening to her *right now?* She didn't have time to search further. The second bell was about to sound at the library.

* * *

As Cadence rushed to catch the subway, Barren entered the West End Bar. He went up to the bar and waited for the ogre-man to come over. He watched him in the mirror, a man built like a warhorse. Certainly a potential nuisance if not taken care of now. The man approached as Barren sat, head down.

"What'll it be, pal?"

Barren looked up. "Be?"

"What would you like?"

Barren just stared at him with his glistening dark eyes.

The big man stared back. He stood no-nonsense still, his huge nine-fingered pair of hands splayed across the expanse of copper bar-top.

Barren slowly said, "Medu."

The man smiled wanly, doing his best convivial barkeep imitation. "If you mean 'mead,' you're in the wrong century. However, if you like weird old earthy stuff, I've got something for you." He turned and retrieved a dark, dust-covered bottle from the back shelf. He put it gravely on the copper bar, label out, as if for inspection, then picked it up and poured a shot glass full. It was a deep brown. It smelled like overturned earth. "Fernet Branca. Italian. I don't know what's in it, but I think it's a liqueur made of loam. You know, dark garden soil. Try it. On me."

Barren looked at him and slowly took the glass and smelled it and drank the liquid. It swirled and stirred a flow of memories, the smell and taste evoking the very earth on which Barren had so often lain in ambush. He put the glass down and looked dead center into the barkeep's single eye.

"Your days behind this bar are over, Cyclops." He watched the big man stiffen, observed the knife scar across his face. "I've got some advice for you—leave this place. Now. Don't be here when I come back."

The man started to reach for a whiskey bottle, neck first, but something flashed in front of him. Barren's knife hand sprung out like a viper's head, cutting the two top buttons neatly from the bartender's shirt and then whisking his throat. It was a teasing scratch, but not a cut.

The buttons rose in the air in slow motion, the man's lone eye rotating up and then down to follow them.

When the buttons clattered on the bar-top, he looked for the man with the knife. The bar stool was empty, the door already easing shut and cutting off a slice of afternoon light.

The one-eyed ogre-man flipped up the bar partition, walked away from his job that very day, and disappeared from this tale.

* * *

Six blocks away, Cadence was late and hurrying. She watched her feet as she quick-stepped up a massive set of stone stairs. She stopped and looked up. Her first impression of Columbia's Low Library from the outside: Monticello on steroids. It towered up and forward, glooming over all that approached by the twelve immense casements of steps. The doors were massive wooden guardians, fit for a great keep that could withstand a hundred Grendels. She inquired at the door and was quickly redirected by a student. "The working library is the Butler Library. There." He pointed to another stern edifice across the quad. She scurried over, entered, and stopped.

The Reading Room stretched on and on, its roof soaring up into hazy dimness. It made her wonder about the heating bills. She gawked her way to the entrance desk, where an officious-looking student served as minion. His overseer watched from an elevated plinth, half-walled in mahogany and gleaming brass. This man, obviously the head librarian, was thin and bent, long-nosed, with too-long gray hair thinned out on his pate. The whole effect was of a well-dressed, oddball hound dog. He looked impassively down at her over his bifocals, his bony hands resting on the ivory knob of an oversized, dark cane.

Students were coming and going in a stream, navigating through a turnstile activated by electronic ID cards. She approached the desk.

"Can I come in?"

"You a student?" Officious was right, she thought, but well dressed. His nerd-heroic style was straight out of Central Casting.

"No, just a visitor." She sensed tentacles of red tape creeping toward her as he sighed and pulled out a blank form.

Half an hour later she was in. She walked around the Reading Room, looking back once at the head librarian. He stared down at her and then over his nose to inspect the form she had filled out.

The homeless man from the West End Bar was nowhere to be found.

Then a hand, barely extended from a rumple of coats, beckoned her from the far end of the room. Yes, she saw, that was the man hanging back behind one of the book stacks. Before she even got there he had turned and was disappearing down a long line of overburdened steel shelves. He had a distinctive limp as if dogged by sharp pain. She followed him to an alcove and a heavy oak table, its surface scarred like the back of a long-lived sea turtle.

"Here," he said, "we can talk."

She sat, feeling a strange security in the ancient grain and bumpy knotholes in the wood.

"Now you can ask some of your questions, Miss Cadence Goosebumps."

Good, this was going to save her some time. "Look, until I find some clues about my grandfather, I'm here to get some proofs, to find out the, well, provenance of these documents. So, who exactly are you?"

He replied, rolling his eyes and muttering to himself, "Why have I allowed my indulgence to be so tested?" Then he took the weary breath of the patient saint.

"Very well," he said. "For reasons I can't disclose, I can tell you only so much. That being said, in 1968 I was a newly hired teaching assistant here at Columbia. My field, which I was faking, was Marxist literary criticism. Those being the times, I was in high demand. Like any good Marxist, I had come to despise all storybooks and their writers as distractions and opium dealers, respectively. I was offered positions at Princeton and Yale. But, feeling an . . . uh . . . urgent need to be outside the U.S. for a bit, and being adept at manipulating the systems of academia, I managed to get a one-semester teaching fellowship at Oxford. Once I got there," he feigned the world-weary traveler, "I realized the stint was really a glorified go-fer position serving tenured professors. I looked around and grabbed a spot with the most fun guy around . . ."

"Who?"

"JRRT himself!"

He looked around, as if realizing he was being too explicit and too loud. He hushed his tone and hunched over, "Anyway, I spent six months in his company. That understates it considerably. I learned in a short time an immense amount about some very . . . obscure things. Then . . . it was over. I came back here."

"So you went back to teaching . . . Marxist theory?"

"It's . . . a little more complicated. I brought back some shadows with me. Hell, I was scared. More of that later. In any case, teaching, as in sitting behind a desk, was suddenly irrelevant. The revolution, you see, like the old mole Marx described, was popping up here! So I jumped in feet first, went to the barricades, embraced the vanguard of the movement, and helped shut this place down. Boycotts, marches, riots, the whole schmear. You don't remember, child, but that was a glorious time. Along with the tear gas, you could smell change in the air. Within the year, what with the precipitous drop in alumni contributions, that evading arrest thing, and my own refusal to support the system by teaching even one of my classes, I was, to use their term, removed from employment. Bastards. Anyway, that seemed to affect me more than it should, being a revolutionary and all. A kind of malaise took over from there. I ended up living on the street. A vanguard itself in a way, wouldn't you agree?"

"I guess, but—"

"So, I learned the way of the downtrodden, mastered its perks and shortcuts, figured out how to survive the cold, the dehydration, the looks of disgust. I became used to the lifestyle. It wasn't the first or last time I morphed my life. They even let me come in here now, as long as I don't fall asleep. Now even that meager privilege is being questioned, I know it, by the new head librarian."

He rolled his eyes to give direction. "You saw him, up on that station. I hide in the stacks now."

"So how did you get to know my grandfather? And where does Tolkien fit in?"

"Charity, my dear, cuts through all distinctions. Your grandfather— an incurable Good Samaritan, you should be proud to know—offered me a meal, even held open the door to the West End Bar for me to pass before him. This despite his own meager purse. Do you remember him or know what he looks like?"

"Not really. I was really little, and he didn't leave behind any real pictures."

"Ah, a shame, really. Anyway, times being what they were, I accepted. At the table, right where I told him in my letter to meet me— at the very booth in the West End where we sat the other night—Mr. Tolkien was sitting. 'You look a wreck!' he said to me. We all ate and talked."

Steps echoed down the corridor, heading their way.

"Silence!" he whispered. The steps stopped, then continued. A student, complete with backpack, came around the corner. He stared, bug-eyed, obviously surprised to see two such dissimilar people huddled in conversation. He hurried on, his steps echoing away.

"Now we must hurry to the heart of it. Tolkien was afraid, but as he said, not afraid enough."

"'Jess,' he told your grandfather, 'As you well know, I am an author, an unexpectedly successful one. I invented languages. I toiled to wrest a history from the barest artifacts of language. But underneath, something beyond and older than me or my father's father was stirring. It far eclipses my modest tales. It . . .'"

"Stop just a second. Before this second lecture gets going, tell me at least the simple stuff. What's your name?"

"They call me Coats on the street. My real name I'll save for now. Anyway, I remember that, like you have done, your grandfather stopped him there. He said something like 'Professor, you look, well, flat-out scared!'"

"Then Tolkien sighed and said, 'Yes, perhaps I delved too deep. There are many forms of good and evil, and there are many things that render our definition of those words irrelevant. I thought evil in my time had grown beyond measure or hope of redemption. I saw its hand when my closest friends were killed during our first month at the front. I saw it drag its loathsome, dripping form up, not just in Grendel's dam, but in a million acts of atrocity, until it no longer had a face. And then, as I struggled to explore it in these stories . . . this I fear you will have trouble understanding . . . something began to stalk me and demand changes in what I had to say.'"

"Was he really afraid?"

"Yes, and don't interrupt now. Tolkien was saying 'Then an . . . event occurred. A trove of documents came to me unbidden. Some in the form of an Elvish writing that, while superficially similar, was far deeper than those which I had been inventing. Like a pool of true deep water compared to a rain-filled pothole. Elvish, as you know, is a powerful language, of much depth and misdirection. It often whispers to you things which it does not literally say.'

"He was visibly shaken at this point, and Jess told him to just say what he wanted to say, and to take his time about it.

"Then Tolkien nodded sadly and said, 'This, Jess, is where you come in.' He then grabbed your grandfather's hand and whispered hoarsely, 'I want you to keep them. These documents. All of them. It is you, traveler, whom I ask for help.'

"Your grandfather was as startled as I was. He laughed and said it was a preposterous suggestion, but Tolkien was insistent. He said, 'Many of the stories were not mine to begin with. Take them away, you must! Haven't you heard a word I've said? These forces beckon me to their service. They urge me to edit away a truth. It has all gotten to be too much for me. I feel like a character in my own books, baffled at the end or just wanting it all to go away. Enough. I've told my tale as best I can. Let others pick up the clues where I have left them. Save this!' And here he drew himself up, closed his bushy eyebrows together like twin hedgehogs, and talked as a man resolute in actions.

"'There are many kinds of hidden gates', he said, 'and for these documents there is a special one. A key. An Elvish 'Rosetta Stone' in a way. But it is more. It is the beating heart of this trove. Through its powers I have unlatched this gate. Yet its true power and purpose remain obscure to me. The very use of the key draws this presence, as yet but a shadow, which would rob the world of all these tales! Thus I have resolved to hide this key away. Still and separate and secret. As for the rest of the documents, let them now be swept away with your travels, my sharpener friend! May they and their key be long separated, and their meeting, if ever, not be an accident!'

"And that's pretty much where it was left. Your grandfather chose his own way."

"What about Tolkien?"

"We'll get to that later. Now I have to go. I will be back tomorrow. Meet me at the Archives desk. Heed my warnings until then. Good day."

Struggling to get his balance, he heaved himself up and departed in a hitched, painful flourish, leaving behind a scent of damp coats and body odor that reminded her of a wet dog.

She stayed for a while afterward, staring at the scars etched across the table's oaken back. The cracks in it were deep: they ran in long lines that joined together in tight fists of knots, like crossroads. She put her hands on the whorls and closed her eyes. Her grandfather, gone by a year and untold miles, had once vectored to this crossroads, sat at the

West End, met these people. He seemed almost . . . here. Just a few more puzzle pieces, and some picture would appear.

Tonight she would concentrate. She would read more of the documents. She would find some new element. Maybe, she would sketch. *Something* would happen.

She opened her eyes and stood up, weightless as an elf, and almost ran for the library exit.

* * *

In no time, Cadence was at the Algonquin. The valise sat empty on the floor. Her bed was covered with documents. She made piles of rough categories: stuff she'd already read or tried to read, then stuff she would look at more carefully. From there she separated stacks into readable English (small), non-readable stuff like Old English and maybe Norse (medium), and a large pile of what she thought might be Elvish scripts (large).

The latter included the scrolls, seven of them. They were brittle and resisted unfurling, as if they did not wish to be read. One or two had clever locks on the spindles, which she finally figured out. She regretted that she had not fully organized the documents before. She noticed again that some of them had little marks, not exactly numbers, but small symbols in one corner or another as if made by some monkish archivist. They sure looked like symbols for moon phases. After all, Ara's journey had been set by a kind of moon-clock that metered her unknown fate. The archival effort was touch and go, as if it had been started but was never completed.

She cleared a spot for one of the scrolls and slowly began to unroll it. It resisted like the others at first, but then its tension relaxed. She gently led the finished hide back to reveal . . . a wonder. It was inked in perfectly beautiful script, long, elegant traces that led into and among the lines above and below. If ever there existed true Elvish writing, here it was, so precise and composed it seemed to glow in its balance of form.

She unrolled another turn and gasped.

There, in a huge hand that dominated the page was an elaborate runic "A." She knew instantly that this was the sign of Ara.

Her muse was hovering there, anxious and eager. She took out her sketchpad and began to draw. She had to capture this moment. When it was completed she wrote at the bottom: *Discovering Ara's Rune.*

She unrolled the scroll another turn. Tucked inside the curves were separate sheets. They seemed to be a working translation in English, perhaps of this very scroll. The notes spoke haltingly, of Signal Hill and the Dark Lord, and then picked up strength as they recounted more of Ara's journey:

> Beneath a moon that now nightly shed more of its rind, hidden in the deepish woods into which she fled from the Dire Wolves, Ara curled in a rugged burrow in a tree trunk. Taking warmth from a fire barely the size of her own cupped hands, she thought of returning home.
>
> Slow and bitter came the truth. Her home, the small village of Frighten, would be all the more mocked if she straggled back in failure. She heard the shrill cries of other children when they had visited the Great Fair: "Frighten, Frighten, weird and wary."
>
> As all halflings know, if the truth be straight and fully told (as it is sometimes not, out of politeness), the residents of Frighten were viewed by the rest of their kind as eccentric and "keeping to themselves." Whatever the positive traits of her own Flameleaf clan—resilience, persistence, and natural inventiveness—they were as nothing against the harsh judgments the residents of Frighten mete out to their own. The failure of her quest would be regarded as a folly, a black mark against them all.
>
> She spent the night watching the darkness, the waning moon spent, and Narcross glowing its red dusk across the land. The bloody hue of night became one with the embered glow of her campfire, the smoke mingling with her doubts. As she fell asleep, she knew that here, at this moment, was her last chance to turn from this uncertain path. Now was her chance to flee toward home.
>
> Dawn came swift and bright, dispensing the few clouds and unfurling a fresh breeze that swept away Ara's doubts as if they were dandelion tufts. She left to another time the toting of grievances. She had skills to use and clues to find.
>
> Perhaps all's a journey, but most are as the errands of shopkeepers. Very few, and never by volition or knowledge foretold, slip the slope that funnels them into a quest. Even so,

with the road offered, the heart in all its mystery will weed out those unsuited. Ara's heart was true.

The next evening she hovered at the threshold to an unnamed byway. She was at once fortunate and ill-fortuned. A current of air wended down from ragged purple mountains to the south, sending leaves skeltering along the path.

She stood for a long time at this crossroads—primitive tracks spun forth from great well-trudged roads. Roads were now her enemy. Roads like this had taken her away from home, ripped her from her comrades. Before her several loomed now, brooding and silent, save for the saw of the wind. Each path provided only a dumb way, withholding guidance to the itinerant who must choose

She studied the four directions. Narcross had not yet risen this night. Soon, flickering points of light saturated the sky, overwhelming the fine lacework of black. One by one, a few died and fell in long arcs. For each one so lost, a thousand more flashed into view. The heavens were alive and breathing.

And moonless. Ara knew that soon it would emerge as a sliver, a battered fingernail eroding nightly until it was gone. From there, it would reemerge and wax swiftly to fullness that would seal her Amon's fate. She knew that every day meant miles to go to a destination she had never seen, save in dark legend.

This week in Frighten, the great lamps of the Giant Pumpkins would be lit. She knew she would never see them again. She could hear her Mum, wise beyond even the village elders foretelling her destiny, "For some children, the front step, once truly left, can never again be found."

With that thought, Ara stepped onto the broken and forked track that led away from her home. She walked south, watching a row of thunderheads illume and quiver against the distant mountains before being sucked away into the endless starry night.

Cadence put the manuscripts down. Exhausted, she took the blanket from the closet and flopped on the couch. Tomorrow would be tomorrow.

She met sleep halfway, and in the surreal, liquid seams of that union, her mind concocted a Technicolor dream. Intrepid Professor Tolkien, old and white-haired but all dressed up like some elderly Indiana Jones, and the Fearless Young Heroine, Ara. Armed and steadfast, they were surrounded by a lurching, drooling, moaning multitude of the Dark Lord's zombie monsters.

The crazy scene froze mid-frame. Heartbeats passed. Any moment Tolkien's face would mutate to something evil, and he would be one of *Them*. Catchy synth bass notes would punch in, a great multitude of hands would clap in unison, and the professor would break into the funky song and dance routine of *Thriller*. It was ordained; he had succumbed to the Dark Side! Ara and all the Heroines would be lost.

The dream fizzled out like a spent sparkler, closing with Ara defiantly sweeping forth her cutlass to confront them all.

Chapter 49

INKLINGS V

——

The recording of this meeting of the Inklings captured episodes of a competition to see who could read the famously bad prose of Amanda Ros for the longest without laughing. Toward the end of the evening the discussion turned to other matters.

"Charles, as a historian, you have lectured us about the tatters and fragments and competing versions of 'truth' that underlie what we today call the King James Bible. Despite that, is there not an essential truth to the varied tellings of the tales of Jesus?"

"I wish I could be of more comfort, but the truth is that many of the gospels, wildly variant in their accounts, were systematically tracked down and destroyed, especially, as we all know, after the Council of Nicea. The accounts fell prey, along with their followers and those who possessed the documents themselves. So what you are left with today, is not justified by its history. Only belief will carry one through . . ."

Part of the tape is lost here. It resumes with clanks and knockings on the table, perhaps a call for ale as the group huddled about in discussion. C.S. Lewis is talking.

". . . I have a hero, modeled after Tollers here, who is in one of my books. Sort of a philologist-adventurer. A swashbuckling professor of ancient languages. He discovers things, because he is not afraid to believe. What, Ian?"

"And where does this discovery occur? So often we speak of breakthroughs and journeys. Tollers speaks of hidden gates; you Jack, speak of passages through the doors of old wardrobes. Why such devices?"

"These are the stuff of tales not by literary convention, but because they mirror the way we form and test the very art of believing. Mark this: true belief arises only from a passage, after a long and perilous journey. The terrain may be of Fear, call it dragons or demons, or Despair, a desolate waste, but it must be traversed."

"Speaking of journeys, and having duly ravaged poor Madame Ros, let us do justice to the true doers of heroic deeds, heroines."

"Some might say we, all of us male prattlers of tales, do not do enough to acquit that justice."

"But there is a void of the feminine heroic, is there not? In your 'discovery' of your myths, Tollers, you read to us little of heroines. Why so?"

"Speaking within those myths, I suspect many heroines existed, but were rooted out by censors with different agendas—none more persistent than the wizards, of all stripes and colors. And yet, there are intimations of one, a tale lost in the root and branch of many languages. A legend of which I am slowly seeing more. A saga that barely survived. A heroine that may have changed the entire course of history in a real place, a place I have seen only imperfectly from ruined foundations."

"Well, so be it. I, for one, suspect that, if history be told straight and true, our heroes, and thus we, owe much to heroine counterparts. In fact, I would wager our fare tonight that . . ."

The tape grinds down to unintelligible drunken growl sounds, presumably as the battery ran down.

Chapter 50

OCTOBER 22: MORNING

———

Cadence awoke on the couch, stiff and groggy. The remnants of the Tolkien and Ara MTV dream video dissipated like strands of mist. She could hear traffic, the distant warble of a fire truck, the deep hum of the city imploring her that worrying over these documents was a delusion. She was on a fool's errand, they said, maybe stumbling toward a precipice. Her body agreed. Fuzzy as she felt, her neck hairs, her heart, and her palms all forewarned of disaster.

She got up, rubbing her eyes, and went to the bathroom. She splashed water on her face. She came back to the bed fully awake and took a deep "start-over" breath. She surveyed the documents on the couch still in the rough groupings she had assembled. She picked through them, seeking a trail that had gone cold. Page after page of Elvish gibberish passed beneath her fingers. Finally, she went back to the small "readable" pile. The first page she picked out had long ago been ripped apart and reassembled with resinous glue. A rust-colored stain hung at one corner. It read:

> The hawk, gray topside and mottled white on the bottom, stood one-legged in the middle of the road. One wing jutted out from its body, torn feathers splayed like fingers, a pitiful wave for help or possibly a giving of directions. It gave the lie to the latter as it jerked about, hopping left then right.
>
> She looked about, the red and orange leafed hickory trees and yellow brush crowding flush to each fork of the pathway. A

place for ambush? Her instincts said move on, head south and pass this place in haste.

The bird stopped and looked at her, eyes sharp and focused past a deeply curved beak. It balanced oddly, in compensation for the askew wing, and, as if in completion of its survey, hopped directly toward her.

Now Cadence rustled around for more clues. The readable pages definitely seemed like bits of a single story, told and retold over long expanses of time. She found another scrap of rough paper that had been folded many times. She guessed it was hidden for some part of its long history:

The halfling feared, deep down, that her choice had been wrong. The world had fallen and cracked like an earthen pot, and she was picking through the thousands of shards without ever having seen the pot whole. But of its dimensions and nature, she had a sense.

This she knew. Her Amon was the Bearer. The object he carried could only be destroyed at the place of its creation.

Perfect, Cadence thought, so they *are* a pair! Her eyes raced down the page:

If she knew him at all, she knew he would not part with it, nor would he abandon the journey to destroy it. She had seen the direction of the Dark Lands and a few other places on a map the Woodsman had briefly shown.

On that map, a great, purple-veined, granite mountain range called Everdivide ran east to west and severed north from south. This barrier she must somehow cross in order to follow his way.

She also knew that she was racing against a moon-clock, as certain as the pouring sands in the day-glass kept by her village elders. This run of the moon to bloated fullness, now well underway, measured the trap awaiting the Bearer. All else, the who and the how, was mere detail. She still had a choice—go forward, or go home. She could not bear the long, tedious hearthside wait for the unlikely return of her loved one. All her family were doers of the first order—on a scale impressive only to halflings perhaps, but "all's the measure is what we have, so eat your porridge and go to work!" as her Mum would say.

She took stock of her meager kit. No provisions, only her cloak and a small knife handed down from her grandfather. She turned to the fish-catching hawk sitting on a log a few feet from the fire. She said to it, "You're a long way from lake, stream, or sea, my friend."

It had hobbled to her on the road yesterday, and that had touched her heart so that she finally knelt and offered her arm. She stared at those exquisitely sharp talons powered by strength that could stop a millwheel, and the quick, yellow beak that, in a flash, could render her blind. At that moment, the world closed down to her forearm fixed in the steady gaze of the raptor.

It stood uneasily on one leg, reached out, and slowly curved those terrible claws around her arm flesh. She belonged to it. It squeezed down hard, then deftly lifted the other leg and sat on her arm, gazing about rapidly in all directions.

The fire was now just embers, casting up lazy sparks. She stared into it knowing, as does anyone that has spent fireside nights in the wild, that in each small blaze lives the memory of all such fires.

Each an augury of the past and the unknown to come.

Above the unlikely fireside pair, the heavens twinkled madly in a riot of uncountable stars.

"Hafoc, I name you," she said, looking at the hawk.

She travelled efficiently, equal to the most adept and durable of her kind. She was unheard and unseen, keeping to the brush-sides of trails and the stream edges as her furred feet travelled tirelessly across rocky plains and through shadow-banded days.

Always to the south.

Cadence took a long breath. So, Ara too felt the doubt, the disquiet of a blind advance toward a ledge. She had stayed her course.

Of course, the grinding city hum countered to Cadence, *because she's only a fairy story.*

She gathered up the documents and stuffed them in the valise. She buckled it up and got down on the floor and squirmed under the bed.

As she struggled among the dust bunnies to wedge the valise in a hiding place behind the headboard, she reconsidered her doubts. Picking up the decades-old trail with Coats was a heartening break. She would stick with this; she would walk toward that ledge. *A few more steps,* she resolved. *Just a few more. I want to unravel one more knot in this mystery. I want to see my grandfather.*

Chapter 51

1970 AGAIN: SEPARATE, STILL, AND SECRET

On his fifth and final day in America, Professor Tolkien was hunched over in the long aisle between tiers of steel shelves in the Teachers' Archives section in the basement of the Butler Library. Looking over his shoulder every few seconds, he turned sideways to catch the tepid light from a bare electric bulb down the aisle. He had in his hands a pen and a few pieces of paper. At his feet sat a small cardboard letter box. He scribbled some more notes on his papers and surveyed his work.

As he corrected a word, he knew this moment, this trip, should be completed in even greater haste. His muse whispered: *Hurry. Where the boundaries between realms meet, it is dangerous to tarry. The gates may shut and the lax be caught forever!*

He started to put the pen in his pocket and hesitated. Ever the editor, he reviewed his note one last time:

> To Whom May Follow:
> Be warned! As a "spell" means both a story told and a power over men, so I write this note to close and bar a gate behind me. I am leaving a perilous realm not just of my imagining. Time now makes me blunt as a peddler late to his errands.
> Take heed, because things of which we weave tales in fact are true, and exist independently of our minds and purposes. As

I have imagined and written Elvish, there are Elves. As I have woven a mythology, it exists. It has a living form and color.

And it *does not rest!*

Like a changeling infant abandoned on my doorstep, a box of ancient documents was left on my threshold one day. Its heritage was anonymous and perhaps untraceable, save for the unease of having seen a sample of similar material before the war. In any case, I studied these documents, and from their depths grew rumors and a disquiet that would not leave. They stir, and like the moors and fen beyond the keep, they breed monsters that slouch and bellow just beyond my reach.

And yet, within this wreckage of ancient histories, there were fascinating tatters, fragments, and even full scrolls. Many of these were written, I no longer doubt, by Elvish hands, masterful hands now long departed from the world. These—precious (I will leave the word, yes) writings have a power of their own. They twist and turn and lead the mind down shifting paths as if they were the very essence of Mirkwood itself. Their language, vast and deep, makes my poor scratchings as but the work of whimsical ants before the soaring range of those mountains they call Everdivide. I have glimpsed this through the agency of a single document, a key that is like an Elfin guide through Mirkwood. I cannot bring myself to destroy it. It is hidden here with this note. May it long rest undisturbed in this musty graveyard of unwanted archives. To whoever may read this note, beware! The key is dangerous, for these phantoms sense its power.

For me, these vague monsters do not depart. They stalk me, and seek not only this trove, but to intervene even in the tales I would tell. Tales that have been unearthed, I thought, solely from my own imagination delving into the bedrock of myth.

The other documents have been sent away. As with these few papers I leave here, I could not be the author of their destruction. I have entrusted them to an itinerant who is fated to wander. These are actions I once held unthinkable.

Now I bury the last, push close the gate, and take my leave forever from this shore.

JRRT

P.S.: Other materials, fragments of Old English poetry, only slightly less disturbing, I have also included here.

He folded the paper and stooped, putting it in the letterbox that the library staff had already labeled with his name. He was nervous. His pipe fell from his coat pocket and scattered dottle and unburnt tobacco all about. He picked up the pipe, sealed the box with tape, lifted it to the dusty shelf, and squeezed it between other file boxes marked with other names and dates. Most were unreadable. *Just another ossuary in the mausoleum,* he thought. He studied his pocket watch in the dim light, knowing that the taxi to Idlewild would take two hours, cutting close his departure to Heathrow. His work here was done. It would be so good to be home.

He studied the location of the box, the burial ground of the Elvish key, one last time. He was confident that it would never be found. As for the rest of the documents, the sharpener of scissors who carries them was adrift where none could track him—carrying his burden into the untraceable byways of the Great American Night.

Chapter 52

OCTOBER 22: MIDDAY

As Coats foretold, Cadence found him again in the library. Alarmingly, he was already talking, and not necessarily to her. She sat down at the table without disturbing him; he continued.

". . . and yes, this library, not quite the Bodlean at Oxford, but close enough, is the very lair of the beast that woos and confuses us all." He pointed his finger down hard into the wood, as if this place were ground zero for all he feared. "Beware Learning! It is a dragon. It resides here, in this great book-barrow, and is wise with the hoarded lore of long and eventful ages. It places a spell on all who wander its labyrinth. If you are keen to its wiles, you can see its vestige here, in the smooth-rubbed trails as it heaves its swollen bulk along the well-worn pathways. Places like the Reading Room, the frequented places where students slave and worship its corpus of closely catalogued wealth."

He stopped and looked around in his suspicious way. He continued speaking as if she had been there all along. Cadence couldn't help feeling dismayed. The last time they had met here, he had seemed relatively sane. Now he had reverted to the same overblown speech he used at the West End Bar. It was wasting her time. She made ready to leave, when he said something that got her attention.

"There are far finer riches it buries in the deeper places here! In hoard-rooms unvisited, you smell its presence in the dust and the air tinted with the scent of lost stories. Indeed, many a tale it hides from us, in the holes of extravagant, musty negligence that pocket this lore-locker. Listen and beware. It is cunning. It plays games and metes us just enough wisdom to cause us to desire more. It places no value on that which it hoards, save for the hoarding itself. The worm reveals truth in tiny, meager draughts so that it may yoke us to the quest. It lets us know, my dear Cadence . . ."

She was surprised he was aware of her presence.

". . . that we are mortal, that we have lost much and can find little. It infects us with a profound sadness. It gloats in its longevity and all-knowing power."

She furrowed her brow and nodded solemnly, with no idea what to say to such a sad crackpot.

"But . . . it has forgotten something."

She tried to nudge him down this path.

"What?"

"In this immense lair are treasures wantonly piled in corners, troves outlandish and arcane that bear great value to one such as I. Thus do I humble myself to the keepers of this entranceway." He looked directly at her. "Perhaps it holds the keys to the truth you seek. In the basement deep below where we now sit, the Professor's Archives lie, all unguarded, save for the watching silence that enshrouds them. Are you prepared to go thieving for the truth, into the untended depths of this marble learning-vault?"

Now he seemed to be saying something useful. "Yes! Where are they?"

"Listen, and I will guide you, though I cannot venture there again. An intruder who dares a second visit to that place double-dares the unrest of the dragon!"

This was at least amusing. She nodded a vigorous yes, set her mouth to a look of grim determination, and put both hands flat on the table. Then she leaned in and said "Okay, I'm game. Tell me."

"Fine. I will continue. This, our whispered conversation at this oaken table, is what our good Professor Tolkien called a 'making.' In ancient parlance, a 'telling,' a creation of words that are the foundry works of stories. You have, my child, made a crossing, stumbled into a story. You are embarking on a strange and dangerous journey."

"Look, whoever you are, however you got here, you're hopeless. Maybe we could just stick to facts and let the story part take care of itself. I just want to gather some information and then go back home and get on with life."

"'Get on with life?' People would die to have the privilege of peeking into the window before you!"

"I appreciate that, really I do. But there's only one piece of essential information that I need to figure out. What happened to my grandfather? For the moment, though, I'll settle for your answer to a more practical question: who are you and what are you really doing here?"

"Too big a question, my child. But, as I grow older, my fears change. A great irony. I used to fear discovery. Now I fear dying anonymous and missing the chance to know those dear few in life who are left to me. Even worse, leaving behind a great debt, unpaid and gathering interest for eternity."

He almost stopped but then regained himself. "So here are a few clues that I have not spoken of in decades. My name once was Osley."

"Great. Very nice to meet you."

"And one other thing."

"What's that?"

"I know Elf."

"Elf? Come on!"

"Yes, the language. But only the written part."

"I don't suppose Berlitz offers a total immersion course. You converse in Esperanto too, I suppose."

"No need to be cynical."

"What do you mean you know 'Elf'?"

"I hinted at bits of this before. As I told you the other night, I was teaching here. I had to . . . leave the United States for a while. To let things cool down a bit. A fake passport was the easiest part. I used my University levers and spent a time at Oxford with Professor Tolkien. He introduced me to these documents and to the Elvish language. I was, to put an image to it, very much The Sorcerer's Apprentice. I became lost in the Mirkwood of these documents. Dreams replaced the thin skein of reality I'd managed to knit together. That's why, as I've told you, when I returned here things weren't the same. They are never the same. Later, I marched in the aimless army of the homeless. Deep beneath these streets I found places utterly lost to the diagrams of the city engineers. Doorways to hidden rooms."

"You mean you live underground?"

"Did. These days, I sleep in city shelters and eat in soup kitchens.

Listen, by the time I was nineteen, I was part of the revolutionary vanguard, one far-out chemical proselytizer. I wore my hair long, adorned my face with wire-frame glasses, and made the phrase 'Tune in, turn on, drop out' an achievable goal for everyone that cared to open the gate. I was the Henry Ford of psychedelic drugs. If I was that kid today, I'd be an entrepreneurial geek. I'd own EA or Narcross Ventures. I'd be inventing computer games that make millions. Such is the tyranny of the Five Percent Departure."

"The what?"

"The Five Percent Departure. In life, as in geometry, what starts as a slight alteration of direction seems like no big deal, just a deviation. But as the lines lengthen, as time moves forward, that five percent makes a big difference. You end up a long way from where you thought you were headed."

"So where's Elf fit in?"

"Ah, yes. The professor had worked out several invented Elvish languages from remnant sources, the Welsh Karbindoos for one. But these documents only showed that his languages were a pale imitation of the reality. The power and breadth of true Elvish, even slightly comprehended, is breathtaking. It captivates the reader like a fly in a web. That's why I came back to the United States. I was overwhelmed. I fell away. I had to. The professor, stalwart to the grit, stayed to his task. But I've disclosed too much already."

"So you still remember how to read it?"

"You don't 'remember' this thing. It's really a logic path, and a dense one. Not unlike the organic chemistry I once knew. Of course, as I discovered, there are deeper subtleties. Elf can be playful or diabolical. It deliberately misleads. It hides. It reserves its true import for the, shall we say, native speaker. So grazing on the most amateurish level, I can translate some and do a passable, if unsophisticated, job. If you've got someone else for the task let me know."

Perplexed, Cadence tented her hands, bit her thumbs, and looked back into those sad eyes. The man behind those eyes wasn't needy, he was *lost*. She decided to take a chance. "Great, so you can decipher some of these documents?"

"Look, I still am the novice on this, which is to say, the wise king in the world of the utterly clueless. Which is pretty good. I can probably translate the ones in basic Elf. The ones that look like Old English or

Anglo-Saxon, that not even Chaucer would've found readable, no. There was once a kind of key, and to get anywhere we would need that."

The fall of a book in some nearby stacks, like an angry clap, startled them both.

Osley leaned down to the tabletop and whispered like a wind battering against the eaves. The voice of the prophet returned. "We have talked like fools! We must leave at once. First I, then you follow."

Then he stopped. A curtain inside him seemed to part. "Those . . . long ago things that stalk and edge closer. They have reappeared. They grow desperate enough to approach the watch fire of our diligence. Cadence, be careful. I will tell you more when I can. I will see you at the West End Bar. Tomorrow at ten."

"In the morning?" But he was gone. This guy had tedious way of coming and going. And he never told her where those archives were.

That evening Cadence found Osley's trail on Wikipedia, the article dated March 2, 2005:

Osley, Ludwin A.

Legendary elusive genius and fugitive chemist, Osley was a follower of the LSD cult of Dr. Timothy Leary ("Tune In, Turn On, Drop Out"). He pioneered the mass-production of lysergic acid diethylamide (LSD) in the early 1960s, while he was still an undergraduate at the University of California at Berkeley. His academic records, partially missing, state that he was admitted to UC Berkeley at the age of 16 from Los Gatos High School. He had a double major of organic chemistry and linguistics. Osley branded LSD capsules he mass-produced as "Osley's Blue-Dot." He operated out of mobile laboratories hidden in semi-trailers that crisscrossed the United States.

Sought by FBI and state authorities in numerous jurisdictions, Osley was reportedly nonviolent and apolitical. He associated with "psychedelic" rock bands such as Lothar and the Hand People, Country Joe and the Fish, and Electric Banana. There are no known photographs or fingerprints, and his California DMV records are missing. He frequented legendary venues such as The Family Dog emporiums on Filmore Street in San Francisco and Colfax Avenue in Denver.

Osley was last seen in August, 1967. He was dropped from

the FBI Ten Most Wanted Fugitives List in 1975.

Cadence fidgeted with the Wikipedia article, checking the footnotes and clicking through links to old articles in the *Los Angeles Times* and *Rolling Stone*. She leaned back and sized up her situation. For some reason, she was sure he posed no danger. The danger was in the terrain they were traversing.

She felt like a small forest animal, easing through the one-way gate in a camouflaged live trap. She was inching forward, tantalized by the elusive, irresistible scent of a secret.

Chapter 53

OCTOBER 23

—

The next day Cadence had a hunch. She decided go back to the library to check on her own on Professor Tolkien's brief visit at Columbia. Charming an intern at the research desk paid big dividends. In that random way that old records yield clues, the intern found a batch of index cards, held together with disintegrating rubber bands, crammed in a drawer. There, miraculously, was a card for the professor's materials left behind when he departed the University so long ago.

An hour later, she stood, backpack and notepad in hand, at the entrance to C-ar-47. The notation, inscribed like runes over the arched brick entrance, was itself a relic. It predated by ages the cataloguing systems of Mr. Dewey and the Library of Congress. The intern told Cadence the code referred to the seldom-visited "inactive archives" section of the library. "You know, where they keep the stuff no one ever wants to see, but they're not supposed to throw away?"

"Like what?" she asked, milking him for more information.

"Like old handwritten notes, lecture transcripts—there's a box or so for every professor who ever taught here or even just visited and didn't take it with him. Sometimes the boxes are books and office stuff, you know pictures, paperweights—that kinda thing."

"So, how do I find something in particular?"

"Alphabetical, by last name. If it's not there, then by year. If nothing turns up, try by subject or just snoop. It's all a mess."

"Ooo-kay, but . . ."

"And here's the catch. After I unlock this door," he had his hand on the steel cage door that ran almost to the top of the arch, "you're on your own. There's a sort of diagram of the place over there on the wall, but don't trust it too much. When people do come down here, they're always complaining that they got lost. No one's scheduled down here through this weekend. Not many people know it exists. Anyway, this door only opens from the outside. Entry, no exit. The only way out is down at the far, far end. You'll find it."

She wasn't so sure. He turned the key and pulled open the door with a disquieting heave. After a squeal of rusty iron hinges, he extended his arm to usher her in.

He shut the gate behind her, wished her good luck, and left.

The diagram was in a dusty frame on the wall and wasn't very helpful. Several labels had been crossed out and written over. She studied it anyway, especially the long corridor that seemed to lead to a stairs down to a warren of stacks that was a virtual maze. Then she stepped around a corner and saw the corridor. It led off into an indistinct haze. Occasional high windows, mullioned and unwashed for decades, dotted one side of the corridor, filtering a thin, grey light past a barrier of dirt and cobwebs. Dust motes floated lazily in the few intact rays. The shadows of tree branches moved like snakes across the linoleum floor.

She stood and stared. This undulating floor, leading down this mystic hallway, was a crossing. Her heart thudded in tandem with jumpy internal juju drums that talked up and down her spine. As she prepared to move forward, she knew her steps, once taken, could not be retraced.

So here I go! She stepped forward with an explorer's panache.

She made it all the way to the end of the corridor, and then down the dim stairs into the maze of shelving, before she heard the sound.

Like a doe hearing a fallen branch, Cadence froze. In the waiting silence, she recalled and interpreted the sound: the furtive movement of feet and rustle of clothing by someone *sneaking*. Now the only sound was the hiss of a radiator. It was as if they were waiting—each for the other—with the infinite patience of the hunting ritual. Cadence the Hunted held perfectly still. She looked carefully and made out the shadow of a bookcase, tilted and surreal, along one wall. There was a silhouette attached to it. Tall and thin and still, as if waiting. A man. No mistake.

She couldn't wait anymore. She grabbed a heavy book off a shelf and stepped forward. Provoke the thing. It did not move. She stepped again and came around the corner of the bookcase. She was met by an untended cart, laden high with books and boxes and casting an improbable shadow. She laughed out of fright. After a moment she turned around to look at different rows of boxes, squinting at the labels, realizing time was moving on. Q . . . R . . . S . . .

Tolkien's box, when she found it, was exactly in place and disappointingly small. It was sealed with masking tape that had long since given up its glue to the dry heat from those creaky radiators standing as derelict sentinels along the walls. The tape fell away as she pulled on the lid. As she opened the box, she smelled, amazingly, the earthy scent of pipe tobacco. She saw clumps of partially burned tobacco scattered over a stack of papers, as if carelessly left there by a harried pipe smoker. On top of the papers was a note, precisely placed and long since yellowed. It was scrawled in an unsteady hand that looked like the professor's. She turned and moved over to catch the light from an incandescent bulb that looked like it had burned without interruption since Edison.

She unfolded the note. It began, "To Whom May Follow." She read the note, uncomfortable as an outsider witnessing a private ritual. She paused over Professor Tolkien's warnings. *A "spell"* . . . *take heed* . . . *a key* . . . *Beware* . . . *monsters do not depart.*

She fingered down through the other papers. There was an article dated 1967 from the University of Leeds Review:

> A remarkable document has been discovered in the collection of antiquities found in the estate of the late Grivendall Thurston, Earl of Haymart, and attributed to the library of his great-great-grandfather, the (at the time) notorious eccentric, and now merely famous, "Mad Librarian," Sir Robert Cotton.
>
> The document apparently was saved from the great fire at the improvidently named Ashburnham House in 1731. The world's only original of *Beowulf* also partially survived, scorched and brittle and mingled with other documents, to be lost again for nearly a century. The particular document in question here has been authenticated as an example of Old English poetry dating from 860 AD.

"These things surface from time to time," said Allison

Mansur, the head librarian at Columbia University. "After all, *Beowulf* itself, so far as we can tell, lay lost and unread for seven hundred years, from the time of the Norman Conquest until its discovery in a Copenhagen library in 1815."

"But," he continued, "this specimen is rather remarkable for both its age and its potential place in Anglo-Saxon studies. Some of the material has yet to be translated, due to the strangeness of its symbols, a system not heretofore seen. In a nutshell, it appears to be a lament written by an ancient king in his own hand. The manuscript, as part of the bequest, is housed at Columbia University, where the Earl maintained close ties since his days as an exchange student."

Stapled behind the article was a page of notes by the professor:

The manuscript, which I have now translated, is by all indications authentic. That means that it is well over twelve hundred years old. The unaccountable fact, unless I have misplaced my wits somewhere, is that this poem echoes elements of my forty years of writing. Perhaps my musings and myth-creation have not been far off the mark!

Cadence was hungry to see the actual translation. She found the pages and stepped further down the aisle, directly under the bare light bulb. She whispered out loud the professor's rendering of those ancient words, the hushed sound spilling over into the empty stacks:

So, the tale of a King can ne'er better be told than by his song.
I am Pazal and this is the ballad of my bitter truth.
Before victory's wealth brought to me overfilled stores, and slavery and fear to my foes,
Princes, strong of limb, tall and fair, stood with liege-gifts
before me in this great hall.

She skipped down and started again, reading what seemed to be an important passage:

> By the rites of ring-giving and vows attendant did we
> confirm our just roles.
> Oh, even by Valar's measure, was that mead-hall fit for
> the clouds.
> Taller than the trunks of the greatest fir-trees did its
> timbers soar,
> Smiling ranks did my Princes array, even as they spoke
> with a mighty voice,
> "Hail King! Liege-Lord and Defender!
> Generous to us beyond our worth's measure!"
> Thus ran the years, in our Kingdom hard by the
> Western Sea,
> Where stood we our sentinels on rocky crag, at forests
> edge,
> and far to the North
> On beaches barren but for the sea-monster's bleached
> bones.
>
> Hard it was!
> The war-scars long stitched my bone-locker with pain
> that renewed itself, each day ever fresher.

Tolkien had scribbled a note here: "The blunt energy of these lines, the gold of men of old, enmeshed in woven spell, is the bard's gift to us today."

> Waiting for the enemy that came only by rumour
> As creeping fog and distant sounds that give no battle
> But unsettle as no din of war could ever muster!

Here Tolkien had underlined portions of the text:

> One day in my great hall, proud of my mastery,
> I admitted, in courtesy, an errand from another
> kingdom.
> Sweet words, echoing my own boasting estimate, did he

speak,
Visions, of power greater, did he lay before me.
And the Source that would its certainty insure
An ancient Ring of Spells.
A token of an alliance of equals, did he offer,
The rites of ring-giving were registered,
The Vow of Protection duly scribed
Like the unthinking swipe of a broadsword to bloody
some last innocent at battle's end, I spoke hastily,
"'Tis done!" said I,
And no king would take back words so spoken.
Now of fell work to full grasp filled were my hands.
To other kingdoms did I travel
And extolled the virtues of the Ring-Giver.
And others sought to repeat my grand alliance
So that, in time, less than a double-handful of us,
esteemed kings of lineage and grace, did compare and
carefully assay the wondrous craft of these tokens.

The professor's own words followed: "Much is lost here. However, in the same hand on separate parchment and perhaps much later in time, the poem continues. My translation is as follows," and he continued the verse:

Generations of the lives of men have passed.
I wear the tattered robes and horror-geild
As once I did strut with finest fur and emblazoned
shield bright with honor,
The banners of my kingdom have long rotted in the
seeping drench of storms and roofs unmade by fire and
ruin.

My bone-locker gone, replaced by this mist of a body—
A bitter turn for one so proud of his limbs, sword-
stewards that could unleash such havoc in battle!
Of my own folly was I ensnared and unmanned by this
Ring!
Mark This! The Vow of Protection lies unspent and

unfulfilled—The <u>leather writing</u> in which it resides,
moldy and ragged, now forever lost.

She finished and held the pages. A final note of Tolkien's translation
was at the bottom:

This poem found by I, Thygol, leader of the Cerian Band of
the Free, in a pouch on the stinking carcass of a winged beast on
the plains where we fought the Black Army.

Cadence searched the rest of the box. At the bottom was a separate
manila envelope. She opened it. It contained two items. First was a
small, rough piece of hide inscribed with runes as obscure as they were
magnificent. On a second, larger piece of leather, as thin and supple as
doe-skin, was an elaborate diagram, an intricate wheel with scores of
spokes interwoven with Elvish characters. This had to be the translation
key—except for one problem: it looked more indecipherable than even
the Elvish. Finally, at the very bottom of the box, lay a disintegrating
napkin from—she paused and smiled ruefully—*Ye Olde West End Bar*.
On it was scrawled a sort of map:

Take 1 train / 137th stop

137th ===130th (Old Stop) ===
door (padlock/key hidden) == the pool

This last was perhaps nothing or, if she believed just a little, finally a
real bricks and steel rails clue. She pocketed all the documents, put the
empty box back, and, looking behind as she went, set out to find the
only exit.

* * *

Hours later, she found Osley in the familiar corner booth at the
West End. She sat down across from him and eased her newfound
documents under his nose, just as he was pondering the apparently
curious remnants of his blue-plate special.

He began reading, carefully studying the professor's notes and the
poems. He sat bolt upright when he opened the manila envelope with
the wheel figure.

"Where did you find this?" He sounded excited, almost angry.

She told him. He reflected for a moment before taking her hand and looking her straight in the eye.

"Cadence, you must be careful! Don't go off on your own like this." He held the translation key up in his hand. I haven't told you some things because . . . because I want to protect you. This all has to be sorted out carefully. One day at a time . . ."

"I don't have a lot of days."

"Stop! Please. This is becoming very dangerous." Then he added, "And I'm sure we will find your grandfather. I will help you."

She was astounded at his tenor, the light of a real person breaking through. He was like a man imprisoned in his past, struggling to get a message out, even if he could never escape.

He patted her hand. Then he took it back and shook his head. The prison warden in his mind was back. "Now, for what you have found in your foolish venture. You indeed discovered some leavings of good Master Tolkien. And you have with you fragments of a lost poem, a tale by one of the Wraiths. Do not come here and wheedle that you have nothing you can put your hands on, that you lack still your 'proofs.'"

"But what have I got?"

"Quiet! Be still! Proof enough you have of something more important than these documents. Your own heart and courage! Descending to that dank hole in the library was no idle holiday stroll. Now that you have proved it, you need not do so again."

He stirred in his seat, presumably looking about for spies. Then his eyes stopped at the bar and she followed his gaze. The one-eyed bartender was nowhere to be seen. That seemed to make him more uneasy, as if his back wasn't covered. He leaned across the table and continued. "Let me tell you something—whether you believe it or not— of the errand they have sent you on. But before the 'they' and the 'errand,' you must understand what you are really dealing with here. And let's get something straight about your grandfather. Never seek too hard for someone that intentionally disappears. No pics, no prints, no DNA, no records. That says a lot. If you need more proof, look at me. If they couldn't find me, a Top Ten Fugitive—yeah, I'm sure you've figured that out— how could they find your two-bit, itinerant, derelict, legend-in-his-own-mind relative? The borderland of fable and reality is hard country to track a man."

He waited, letting it sink in, and then continued. "Now, that being said, the day your grandfather departed with the documents, Mr. Tolkien sat where you sit and told me of his deepest thoughts, which I have long remembered but never repeated to anyone. He said—"

Osley's eyes seemed to deepen and he spoke as Tolkien would, gazing directly into Cadence's eyes.

"With my work I carved a window through which could be seen portions of a world. In that world there are things older and grander than I have been able to discern. But they are there nonetheless."

She nodded, almost believing that Professor Tolkien was speaking to her.

"My journey is closing. It is for others, perhaps, to find and tell those tales. Let others follow, root and branch, where they may lead. After all, Middle-earth truly existed long before me and will exist long after."

Osley paused here, gathering his memory even as it seemed that Tolkien might have gathered his thoughts.

"That is precisely why this trove of true Elvish—priceless beyond measure—remains so important. For now, however, let it sleep. I fear it will again grow restless and by its very being summon the restive hauntings I fear.

"This was the night before he left," Osley said. "He spoke those last words with sadness. But just before getting up from that seat, he smiled a bit and said in a tone that almost seemed to wink with relief—

"'The moon's the same body one sees from my home on the coast at Bournesmouth. It waxes full here at its proper time. I take that as proper reckoning and a portent for good. To my dear Edith I go now and let these mysteries take their own path. I hope Jess, the Sharpener, dispatches his errand well. You have been a good friend. Good-bye.'"

Osley seemed spent by the effort to recall (she was afraid to think "invent") this long-ago conversation.

"And with that we shook hands, and he left. I never saw him again." Osley paused in thought. "I miss him. He was a great and just man. He was better to me than I deserved. He once said he could not tell if this . . . gift was from the Dark Elves. If so, it might be laden with purpose and peril far deeper than we realized."

Osley stopped and looked up. "But let us now turn back to you, Cadence. What of all this so far can we make sense? And what is your next step?"

She thought for only a second. "Simple. Do I stay or do I go? Like the song."

"The prudence of going may now be best," he said. "Your mom would have approved of that."

She looked at him, wondering how he might have so astutely pegged her mother. Before she could say anything, he rose, said "Very well, good night," and left.

Chapter 54

OCTOBER 24: MORNING

———

Cadence woke straight up, and screamed, "SHIIITTT!" The alchemy of a decent night's rest made one thing crystal clear: she was falling into a trance with Osley and all this Mirkwood-Elvish hoodoo stuff. She had to get down to business.

As if on cue, Mel called. It was 8:00. That made it 5:00 AM in L.A. He jumped right in. "Cadence, here's the situation. The original manuscript of the complete *Lord of the Rings* lies in a secured case in, get this, Milwaukee. It's at Marquette University, a gift from Tolkien. That single product has generated over six billion dollars in revenue from books, movies, action-figures, lunch boxes. Not as much lately, but the revenues continue. It is, in the parlance, a franchise."

She interrupted to save her ear. "Mel, it's safe. It's secret. Is that what you're asking?"

"No. Just listen to me. The tale, hence the franchise, is dwindling. It is, as we say in the business, losing its legs. Beyond making a movie or two out of *The Hobbit*, there isn't much more of Tolkien left that's got sustained commercial value. I tell you this because, if you are right, you have possession of physical and intellectual property worth millions of dollars. The very existence of these lost manuscripts may actually enhance the ongoing value of the franchise. Dispute means buzz. Controversy means buzz. The entertainment business *loves* buzz. Any mystery begets buzz, which generates more buzz."

She took a break and held the phone away from her ear. He was sounding like an over-excited bee. She waited. When she listened again,

"... the market is still keen on alternative scenes and alternative endings. The Director's Cut. That, in essence, is what Tolkien gave your grandfather, and ..."

"Oh come on, Mel, you're way ahead of yourself. No book cover with foil dragons just yet. No Oprah plug. All this could be totally unrelated. It could be part of another story altogether, or just historical mishmash. I've even got people telling me that parts of it change as you read it. How's that for provenance?"

"Who? You're not talking with another agent?"

"No, Mel, relax. I found a translator of ... uh ... Elvish. He also says he knew Tolkien. He says ... well it's all pretty weird. I'll leave it at that."

"Well, where does one thing begin and another leave off?"

"That's the question, isn't it? So, you say, we should be happy?"

"Of course. At least so far."

"Well, I'm not. So far, I'm not sure I'm any closer to finding my grandfather."

"Don't go there yet. Let's stay on track."

"That's what I'm saying, I'm feeling off track."

"Here's what I'm saying. Stick with the story-side of this. These documents may be perceived as a threat. Like some kind of surprise bastard sibling who's horning in on the inheritance. No doubt there are some in the business who would want them destroyed. Smart money would promote this find, but who knows what's at work here."

"Okay, Mel. You're paying my hotel bill. I'll stick with the program for a few more days. You definitely sound more upbeat than before. Why?"

"I read it, Cadence. I mean I read the whole damn LOTR thing. Usually I fake it, but I did a lot of homework this week. With the new Hobbit movies coming up, well ... well ... this could be huge."

"Great. So when does your part, the Huge Contract, happen?"

"Soon. Don't worry. Your job is to answer the same question posed at the Council of the Wise, 'May we see the proofs?' So tell me, how's your search really going?"

"I don't know. It's tough to tell. Tolkien was here, but was this stuff really his? It could be something authentic or just lunatic ramblings. I feel stymied."

"You're distracted. Forget about your grandfather for a while. I mean don't *forget* about him, just lighten up. You'll learn something about him out of this for sure. But let's focus. Cut to the critical path. If you won't put the documents in my safekeeping, let's at least take them to some experts—maybe that scrap with Tolkien's note, and some of the Elvish writing stuff—and establish the proofs. Okay? Otherwise we're wasting our time."

"All right, what do you suggest?"

"Thank you. It's all arranged. You will meet Monsieur Brian de Bois-Gilbert. He is head of L'Institute des Inspecteurs, the world's leading experts on detecting forgeries and fakes. They have done all the big stuff since the Hitler Diaries fiasco. Documents, paintings, vintage wine, you name it. If you're ready to find out the truth, he's your guy."

"When and where?"

"Good girl. Ten, Sunday morning. They made a spot in their schedule. That's day after tomorrow." He gave her the address. She wrote it down quickly on a room service card.

"Mel?"

"Yes."

"I'm not a girl. Also, one last thing. If this is real, if it is an authentic collection of lost manuscripts somehow relating to Tolkien?"

"Yes?"

"Well, I have this feeling that something in it is beginning to tick."

"Let's hope it's a money counter."

"I'm not sure I buy that, but if it saves The Mirkwood Forest from foreclosure until I can find out what happened to my grandfather, so be it."

She hung up and got down on the floor and checked the hiding place for the valise. Someone would have to tear the room apart to find it. Even if the mattresses were pulled, she didn't think anyone would see it.

Everyone was saying forget about her grandfather, but that only fed her determination. She would find some clue about what in his life had led him to this place, and from there she would trace a connection back to the here and now.

Just then there was a tiny knock on her hotel room door. She ignored it.

Another knock.

"No, thank you," she yelled.

Two more knocks.

She got up and padded shoeless over to the door, mumbling dire imprecations she had picked up from her L.A. fifth graders. She peeked through the peephole and was stunned to see Osley fidgeting suspiciously in the hallway. He had on his usual worn ski hat and tattered greatcoat.

She opened the door. "How did you get in here?"

"Apparently an understaffed hotel, despite its pedigree. I walked right by the front desk."

"And my room number?"

"Cadence, there's no time to quibble. Something even more dangerous than I anticipated is happening. May I come in? Please?" He was looking up and down the hall.

She pondered this, reflecting a moment on his FBI Wanted List pedigree. He seemed harmless. "Okay. Just stay there while I get dressed."

She took her sweet time, just to make a point, and then let him in. He swept past the threshold, turned, and locked the door.

"Cadence, want the good news?"

"Okay, the good news."

"Elf! I got to thinking about all this. With the key, I really should try to translate some of these documents. I mean it's been a long time and all and I'm rusty, but I ought to try."

"Before I let you do that, what's the bad news?"

"There may be something, well, *lurking* in these documents."

"You said that already. As in . . .?"

"As in a bad presence, a spirit or demon."

"Yeah, it's called greed. Hey, it's morning and right now, I don't believe in spirits or magic stuff. But go ahead. Have a seat over at the desk, and don't weird out. I'm going to crawl under the bed for a second."

Squirming back under the bed with the dust bunnies, she thought *who's weirder here?*

Not an hour later, with several manuscripts spread before them on the room desk and bureau top, Osley told her much of the text was indeed written in Elvish. She was impressed that he managed to say it with a straight face. "Unfortunately," he said, "much of this is in a dialect and style now beyond my powers of translation."

"Os, that sounds a little too convenient for your first test."

"Don't despair! There does seem to be a name for it: *Myrcwudu*. It refers to both a forest and their language. Now, there are other writings, as well as extensive annotations. These are apparently by a historian who wrote hundreds of years after the events, later in the Fourth Age but still of times ancient by our reckoning. They are in a rude style of Lower Elf that lends itself to our reading."

Her skepticism about Osley waned as he became very solemn and began writing on a yellow pad. Then he switched to hotel stationary (the Algonquin was over-generous in that regard). He progressed with the starts and stumbles of a rusty translator. An hour passed as he repeatedly consulted the key. Finally, he offered to tell her what the ancient scholar wrote. His words grew steadier, and like a weary gate, a tale of another world opened:

> From Hertegest Historians (remnant):
> The lesser race of Great Wolves is the Ulf-Ragen, sometimes referred to as warkylgen or wargs. They are the wolf-steeds of orcs. Once rogue outlaws to their kind, they now grovel before the orc fires.
> The master race of the Great Wolves, purer, nobler and seldom turned to any will save their own, are the true Dire Wolves. They are Descendants of Amarog, the Yellow Eye, also known as Evilglint. Dire wolves stand six feet at the shoulders; they are stronger and more perilous than living man can imagine; and they bear a cunning wisdom, equal in their element to that of the Wood-elves. The last reported droug, or pack, was in the northern forest before the coming of the Great Winter that signaled the end of the Third Age.

"There's a break here, let's see. Yes." His words soon trod the main path of Ara's story:

> Within an hour of passing through the last of the aspen groves, the road deepened into a gorge that rose up on all sides. There she felt a presence. Something, or rather several somethings, were moving stealthily behind her on both sides of the shadow-casting cliffs. She feared that Dire Wolves had

found her. She hurried her pace, doubling back waist-deep in the dark brook. Soon the cleft opened into a plain that ran all the way to the blue teeth of the far mountains dividing the world. Only the hawk, soaring alone, cut the air with movement—that and the ash-like shadows of clouds that seeped from the mountains and dissipated to the west.

She camped in fear and without fire on an island in a broadening water flow. Better to wait there than further announce her presence by her smell on the road this night.

A bright moon-rind rose late. On the near shore, Ara saw them. They were phantoms silvered by the light, their breath rising pale in the cold from some primitive inner furnace that drove them to contort and leap in their solitary completeness. They stood on their hind legs and danced.

They licked and nuzzled and growled and yelped. They stopped all at once, one balanced upright on two legs like a dancer, one with forefoot raised in the air. Ears twitched. Their uncanny knowing spreading out to touch her.

Just as quickly, perhaps sensing other prey, they began to howl and loped away as the edge of the world ate away at the falling piece of moon.

All of it was so strange and perfect. Ara thought they were as beings self-designed, without need save as fit their own plan.

In the gray light of pre-morning, Ara once again heard the wolves howling, far away. She listened in the drawn-out stillness. Dew dripped off leaves, the water gurgled nearby, and a low sonorous bellow of frogs' matings hung in the air. The hawk fluttered its wings. Beyond these she heard something else. She turned her head to the side, holding her ear just so. After a while she was sure the wind carried the sound of blowing horns. But these sounded elaborate and full of meaning, not like the blare and blat of orc horns. The sounds soon faded, and the hunters, if such they were, passed on and out of this tale.

Osley ended his recitation and they stayed silent. Ara was stunned by his quickening facility to translate. *No one could make this up on the fly,* she thought.

"Snap!" she said. "That reminds me. I've got something to show you." She dug in her purse, sorting through the papers she'd stolen from the Tolkien archives box. She put the napkin with the strange subway instructions back in her purse, but handed him a small piece of browned hide, perhaps four inches by five inches. On it were proud runic flourishes.

"Where did you get this?"

"My trip to the library basement that you were so worried about. Now, what've we got?"

After a studied moment, he held the fragment up, as if for a throng to see. "What we have here, my dear, is of vital importance. Despite its battered appearance, this is no ledgerscrap. The High Elvish inscribed on it withholds its full meaning from me as yet, but I know the main word. Here." He pointed at a flourish with long trailing legs. "This is the symbol for 'Vow,' a word not to be taken lightly. It perhaps is related to the Vow of Protection in that archaic poem by Pazal, the king-turned-wraith. In any case, it may be of more importance than the rest of these scribbles. Where you found it is telling." Again he waved the piece of hide. "This is, if I trust my first judgment, something held precious by the best authority on deeper Elvish translation, Professor Tolkien himself!"

Chapter 55

INKLINGS VI

———

Part of the recording of this session was corrupted by, of all things, a melted Cadbury bar. The transcript begins somewhere midway in the evening.

"... no great imagination to believe that there was once real magic in the world. What is certain is that it no longer exists, save perhaps in little glimmers of wonder. It was lost, shattered into fragments. And with that shattering the world changed. Heroes and their feats were fated to shrink to misunderstood words garbled into turns of phrase and dusty poems. Things of great moment became mere lists. Heraldic honor rolls became names without import, save to stir troublesome feelings of something sadly lost. We are left with vague recollections of more vibrant times when each day mattered. What say you to that, Tollers?"

"Quite so, Charles, but even if such was the fate of their feats and their names, their tales deserve better! My goal, at least, is to resurrect some of that moment before the Loss of Magic. Who knows, just as characters in a story sometimes know they are part of a tale, so all of us might someday be in a story. Even you, Jack!"

Laughter.

"Now the ale is full to your taps, that's for sure."

"And we would be idiots to believe our ramblings benefit anything other than the cleaning rag that will follow our empty glasses."

"If any of our musings were remembered by the listening walls and this stout-hearted carving post of a table . . ."

"Better yet, recorded so your outlandish remarks could be tallied against you in the future, Ian!"

More laughter and indecipherable banters.

"Perhaps, but regarding one's life as a story, whether ultimately preserved or in time utterly forgotten, is still not the worst of philosophies."

"So, how are your actual writings coming, Tollers?"

"Not so well. I have aspired to write a 'philosophical thriller.' Something a bit deeper about the nature of reality, perhaps. Put all this myth and legend into a modern time, let the struggles happen in a contemporary world somehow connected to the old. Yes . . ."

"And, Tollers, just last week you said that in the fantasy world you visit in your tales . . ."

"I said, to be precise, 'In that world you are not dreaming, you are in a dream of another's weaving.' The questioning of this story-cauldron is about perilous realms and their shadowy marches. To put a point on it, whether elves are true and exist independently of our tales."

There is a moment of silence.

"Are you in jest, Tollers? You would have us believe that?"

"Your beliefs are your own, Ian, but I'll wager a show of hands around the table will fall to the elves' favor. Very well. Let's see who agrees."

Shuffling, mugs being put down, a rustle of clothes, mumbles of agreement.

"The bet also was for our bill, and so we'll add another round to Ian's burden before Miss Sarah sends us home!"

"Ha! Hear, hear!"

Laughter.

Chapter 56

OCTOBER 24: AFTERNOON

——

After more hours of brooding concentration and scribbling, Osley began to open up. "Ara definitely is on an epic journey, headed south. Here's a typical passage that I can pretty much read on its face. Bear with me."

He held up the page and read it to Cadence.

Ara struck due south, and before she realized it, she was lost in Myrcwudu, the great remnant wellspring of mighty Mirkwood itself! A darker forest, perhaps, than what may lie even in the full depths of that haunted realm. All life that could flee, even the great spiders, had long ago abandoned this drear world. She stumbled forward in the pervading gloom that would not give back its pathways.

To either side were immense, desiccated tree trunks, like beings frozen in writhing torment. Their numbers faded into the mist. At her feet, the leaves rustled like a living membrane as they parted to create a track before her and forever close the one behind. She had no choice but to go on. Hafoc flitted from branch to branch, afraid to fly more than a few feet and nervous at resting on the old limbs that seemed to reach out with grasping fingers.

She trod warily, resigned to the single, winding track the forest offered. She sensed that time was forgotten here. In the far world outside this gloom, events would run their due course and leave her far behind. The waxing moon would grow and gloat over the trap set for the Bearer. He was already moving fast to his fate while she was caught in the black heart of the Forest of Doubt.

Here the unlucky traveler contended with the most terrible of foes. Not the dim murk that seemed to flow before her. Not the legendary troops of man-sized spiders that guarded the outer reaches. No, here she faced something darker and more subtle.

Hemmed in by fallen trunks that, to her, were as walls many times her height, shadowed by a murky gloom that only grew thicker, and watched by a presence implacable and unyielding, she quit the false trail. She crawled away and curled into a frightened ball. A veil fell across her eyes. A false veil, for it portrayed that her Amon was lost forever. She imagined his face, his eyes grey-hued like a morning mist with the sun shining through. Eyes she would never see again.

As the darker dark of evening came to Myrcwudu, a glistening fog seeped from the forest floor. It pooled in the dells and flowed among roots that spread like the gnarled fingers of dirtied and downfallen giants. Ara got up and stumbled, directionless, lost in a desolation of spirit that seemed to whisper, *You are vile and pointless. An insect. Scurry now.*

The terror of her insignificance built itself in her mind, like a cairn of rocks heaped up one by one. The very idea made her both fearful and infuriated. If it meant anything to be a Halfling from Frighten, it was to carry a wounded pride. She was wretched and thus she was dangerous. She tried to resist the fog, but it was unrelenting. She stopped, for no apparent reason, as a cockroach might, and waved the antennas of her soul in a desperate search for direction.

Myrcwudu's answer was no answer.

She scurried forward. Deft footfalls paced on either side. Things unseen scuttled and rustled. Once, Ara heard, far ahead, a long, plaintive sound that was something between a whistle and a cry. But for the stillness, it might have been the saw of the wind through a knothole. She froze and waited, but its maker, if there was one, did not reveal itself.

The opalescent gloom thickened until she unconsciously put

her hands in front of her, as if parting cobwebs. She had to find shelter. She peered and groped until she discovered a massive, upended tree. The base of the tree was covered with roots, like a snarl of dirty hair. She could just see within these a mouth-like entrance that beckoned her. She parted the roots and, heedless, put her head in the gaping mouth. She tumbled in. To her surprise, the interior was clean and dry. It felt safe. She summoned Hafoc to perch on a limb near the entrance and she squirmed inside. There she curled into the thin comfort of her cloak.

Huddled there, like some subterranean grub, Ara listened to the night sounds of Myrcwudu. It was an ominous, horrible orchestra. Whisperings of gibberish mixed with anguished cries, as of some passing column of sad and penitent beings. An owl screeched as it passed high overhead. A raucous warbling of some unknown bird cut through the ongoing creak and groan of the giant, ruined trees. In time, the haunted melody swirled into the eddies of her dreams.

As she slept, the sounds collected in a black sack in her mind. The sack bulged and swelled and refused to spill out its contents. Ara writhed in her sleep until she felt silent hands, perhaps her own, but leprous and scabbed, feel their desperate way across her cheeks and plunge hungrily into her mouth to grope for that foul bag.

She awoke with a gasp. Her heart thudded. Her ears sensed something. A dim, gray light, precursor of a faraway dawn, seeped through the entrance. Her small and delicate hands, this time unquestionably hers, pulled out her knife as she coiled in readiness.

Then she realized what had awoken her.

The silence.

No birds, no wind, no moans or whispers or creaks or groans. She sensed Hafoc was gone. Everything was waiting, and something had arrived. She held her breath and stretched her eyes wide, straining to hear or see. Or smell. She flared her nostrils. Floating in the air was the waft of some creature rustic and unwashed, fouled with the stench of raw meat. It was close.

Ara's world closed down to that gray-lit entrance. She knew

this was no dream. She watched in horror as, beyond all her imaginings, a ghastly arm—large and knobby and bristled with hair—finger-walked through the opening.

As she held her breath, a dark bulk followed the arm, filling the gray mouth with a deadly intruder. Her own movement surprised her. She uncoiled her body and, quick as an adder, drove the knife into the shadowy form. It screamed and fell back. The sound cut into the forest like the thudding bite of a sharp axe.

She crawled out, parting the roots and blinking in the luminous mist. Before her lay an orc-captain, his throat bleeding in spurts. He coughed but could not speak. His eyes locked on hers. Dismay, regret, sadness were all there. Whatever had brought him here—perhaps the same inexorable spell that had controlled her path—their fates had at this spot thrown the dice together. Her heart broke as she watched him fade, his orc-life ruined. Her sorrow sliced through the sack in her mind, and the loathsome spell of Myrcwudu gushed out.

Now she could focus her fury. She looked up and around, and thought, *I am no insect, and I will not quail before you!*

She struck out, heedless of direction, and wandered, whether for sleepless hours or days she knew not.

At last she came upon a clearing, shot through with lances of sunlight. These bright shafts highlighted the immensity of the trees. She stood in awe, her gaze climbing the trunks until her neck ached. At her feet, amidst a riot of aurochs-sized roots, a puddle of water caught the light between floating leaves and twigs and created a vicious sparkle that assaulted her unadjusted eyes. She held her hands to her face and looked down between her fingers. She realized she had a bit of magic that might get her out of this place. She knelt and cleared the debris from the puddle. She felt in her cloak and found the small leather kit hidden in a pocket of its folds. This she opened and brought out a tiny, flat bit of wood, no bigger than her fingernail. She lifted from the leather fold a splinter of rock. It was dull gray and each end tapered to a point. One end had been marked with white chalk. She put the bit of wood in the pool and let it float freely. Then she placed the rock splinter on it. It turned and twirled, and came to rest with the white end fixed in one direction. The opposite end was south.

She restored her kit and set out, climbing over and scurrying beneath the deadfalls that lay like repeated hedgerows across her path. There were other puddles, and these she used to float the bit of magic, the intelligent stone her father had given to her. Thus she renewed her direction and felt the fog of despair fall away. In time and events unknown to this scribe, but perhaps recorded by others, she escaped the drear boughs of Myrcwudu, and came again to travel the footpath of this tale.

There Osley faltered. "This place, Myrcwudu, was the black heart of it all. The pathless place. The trap that sets us to turn on ourselves and cycle away our days in false reckonings and petty errands. I'm worried, Cadence. I'm also famished. I feel like I've been stuck in there with her and can't get out."

Cadence smiled. "I'm not worried. She kept her head and she got out. So will we. Let's start with that fuel." She called room service and ordered breakfast and coffee. After eating, Osley gathered steam, feverishly jotting words. Pages of scratches later, he handed her three sheets and said. "Get this . . ."

Cadence read the first one:

Freed from the suffocating eaves of Myrcwudu, Ara was soon in sunlight, crossing a grassy plain leading to a series of hills. She felt exposed and watched, and so she moved as swiftly as possible.

Hafoc, had recovered well. First a few feet, then a dozen yards, then a stone's throw it flew. At the beginning it followed in the direction she was heading, but now it seemed to provide guidance when she was uncertain of the path. It would wheel upward, surveying the land and then alight within her sight.

Watching it float almost motionless on an updraft and then drop out of sight, she guessed that a precipice lay ahead. She passed dual ranks of stones propped and unturned by long ago labors. They were like guiding fingers forming a massive V across the plain. Suddenly, where the V closed to a narrow opening, the ground dropped away in a breathtaking sheer of several hundred feet, ending in a boulder-strewn streambed. The boulders were covered with a latticework of what looked like thousands of giant bones.

So steep and abrupt was the cliff that it took her an hour to pick her way to the bottom. There she stood, ant-like, surveying the confused wilderness of giant, white bone. The skeletons were all of the same kind, all immense beyond her experience, diminishing even the great-horned bison of the North. There were tusks exceeding a dozen arm-spans of men in length, and rib cages through which teams of horses could pass three abreast.

A jagged lens of ice protruded from a seep at the shaded foot of the cliff. From it protruded a mass of wrinkled hide with long tufts of orange-red hair.

A clearing among smaller bone fragments and flint shards told her of an ancient butchery preserved as the stream wandered off to the other side of the canyon. Sitting atop a pile of boulders like a lost and imperial edifice, presided a huge skull. Its long curving tusks would easily encompass a village feasting table fully laden and seated.

After a while, the smell from the ice lens and the lingering sense of disaster left her uneasy. The hawk departed straight south, and she followed.

"Don't stop reading, cause I'm on a roll now. Look at this!" He thrust several more pages at her.

Ara traveled now beneath a growing hunter's moon. It was in the desolate foothills, on a path lost to the memory of even the Woodsmen, that she found the lost wives.

She had traversed Knarch, the Long Downs, and passed into a land of scrub and sinkholes etched unto the back of a great limestone karsk. There she arrived at the first full knees of the Goat Mountains. Above the tree line was a defile no wider than a halfling's shoulders. Through this she squeezed and squirmed, sometimes looking up to a thin slice of skylight blue. At length, she entered a great rift valley. Oriented to the south, it opened up into a bowl of light, sheltered from the storms and north winds, and fed by cascading streams plummeting from surrounding cliffs. At its far end, it narrowed again but remained open, leading to a plain obscured from her sight by copses of trees.

As the sun warmed the air, the sea-hawk circled above her and rested on a cliff. Ara fell asleep without realizing it.

Awakening with a start, she was encircled by them. They were tree-like, but of varieties more supple and wan than their stiff and thick-barked mates, the Treoherd.

"Who are you, intruder?" She heard this not with her ears, but from a sensation that traveled up her arm where a tendril grasped it. The tendril led to a branch that was part of one of the tree-like beings.

"I know you!" said Ara. "I have heard tales of how they were separated from you, from themselves really. They have been searching for you for centuries too many to count."

The creatures stood still for the longest time. Ara began to feel foolish, she had been talking to the air. Then the tendril coiled one more loop and the meaning rushed into her.

"Yes. We came here long ago, beyond and before the time of the many races of mortals that walk on two feet and learned to burn and hack. Before animals began their endless procession across the face of the world, we were there. In those elder days, our kind, plants that grow on dry land, migrated by their generations to fill all these places-above-water. This is our earliest memory. It was our purpose it seemed, for we were never told another. At least, it was the purpose we became the most comfortable with. We furthered this march of green inland from shores so ancient that even we could no longer recognize them. "But that is not how we ended here, in this valley of imprisonment."

"Why don't you leave? Nothing kept me from getting here."

"Be cautious with your bravery, small one. There are grim perils here." The warning passed through Ara with a shudder and she understood the depth of terror that kept the lost wives of the Treoherd within the valley.

"There yet lives but one Worm known to the world outside this valley. Grimmer and more terrible than all others. His lair is unseen by any that walk on two legs. He is hidden in perpetual fog. He sags forth to tear and rend.

The lands beyond this valley, bare and bleak, stripped of trees for a thrice-score of furlongs, are his domain. But that is not all."

Ara shivered in the dawn chill. She felt a fear, throbbing through these now clutching tendrils, limbs that had lasted a thousand years.

"It has allies, a plague of locust-like hornets, red-striped and each the size of a sparrow. They bite and chew as well as sting with a bitter venom. They ensure all is ruined. Though a multitude, they are as one. They live as a single being even with the Worm. They fly in a great black cloud that turns and wheels as if guided by a single instinct. They are his eyes and outliers. Worst of all, they confuse and disable his victims by their constant buzzing and stinging. For their reward, they are his scavengers. Perhaps we are wrong in this. Perhaps it is they that control the Worm as their own instrument."

"But where does it live?" Ara spoke, but somehow felt that she could now pass this thought back through her body.

"Where? Once, a great army of men sought the answer. They marched into these lands. Marauders. Strong and well-armed with the greatest machines of death. They came in search of his lair and treasure. They were wise in their plans. The plague of hornets they lured to a herd of bison, which they drove before them. The wheeling multitude came to test and harass, and stayed a moment to feed. That was their undoing, for the Men had poisoned the carcasses. The insects died with their jaws full of torn flesh, and others fell from the sky as they escaped in panic, realizing this trickery. A scant remnant of the dark cloud blew away eastward, against the wind."

"And so the men found the Worm?" Ara questioned.

"No. The Worm found them. The next night, camped near the shore of the Flat Sea, a dense fog rolled into their camp. It extinguished their campfires. The handful of survivors who fled into the high war engines where they had the vantage of strong timbers and a view unto the camp below, later described the encounter to us:

"'The Worm came in the stillest moment of the night, and was everywhere at once. His tail and taloned wings, and the great sail on his back we saw above the white shroud. The cries of our comrades and the clank and hew of their swords we did hear, but only for a moment. Then all was still. The night and the fog receded in equal stealth, until the dawn saw the bitter remnants of a massacre. Weapons and bodies were strewn in great confusion. A trail of blood and discarded parts of men, bisected by the groove of a great, lazy tail, led unto the sea. We wept at this sight and fled in panic back toward the Misty Wood. The insects, though fewer in number, harassed us and picked at one warrior at a time until he fell. Then they would select another. Five of a force of two thousand did survive. The rest sleep the sleep of the sword, and their spirits float in the slop and gore of this evil thing.'

"Thus do we believe that this thing abides beneath the salty face of the Flat Sea."

"And you stay here?"

"Yes, for the Worm knows we must pass unto his barren soil to make good our escape. Some have tried this passage and none returned."

"Maybe they made it to safety."

"Perhaps, but none other has dared leave in many lifetimes of great trees. And so we stay here. Arriving by folly, we are contained now by fear."

Ara responded, "Do you not think that this, too, is folly, for in time you will lose all by your fear?"

"As have you. You left with a mistaken heart and now are as lost to your loved one as we to ours."

"No," said Ara, "for with your leave, I am departing this valley to find him. Now! "

He watched her finish, then said, "Okay, enough of dragons. Here is something more recent." He handed Cadence fresh pages of ink-covered Algonquin stationary.

It is said by a few bards, though vigorously disputed by the dwindling guild of Scholars of the Red Book, that the famous halfling traveler Aragranessa learned much of the secret lore of trees. Of her wisdom the details are all but lost. Only the dimmest reference to the Lost Vale survives as a lyric in nursery rhyme.

One surviving fragment, however—attributable to students of the self-proclaimed wizard Colorfall—tells of the orphans of the wisest and most agile trees, the Treoherd. As these "keepers of the forest" became indistinguishable from old and surly trees, and their mates were lost in time, so their last offspring, perhaps never more than a few in number, wandered the forests as unlearned orphans.

In time, some of these tree-orphans longed for discourse and company, and so grew closer to men. They attended men's parleys and the tellings of sagas. They put down deep roots and spread immense sheltering canopies. In time they became known as "council trees." They hosted many momentous meetings and came to have esteemed names. Some were ascribed a spirit of their own.

Should you or your heirs visit one of these last sentinels, perhaps ravaged and cracked by long years, honor them as venerable orphans that chose their own destiny.

From an account in 1720:

After the Scattering of the Halflings some centuries ago, and the recent opening of the Froelboc Mine, there remains in this area, in a park surrounded by low hills of coal and hardscrabble mine tenements, a single, immense ash tree. It is gnarled and oddly shaped where predominant limbs have cracked and fallen. It bears its leaves late, and old men wager as to whom, it or they, will survive another year. But every year, like the sluggish steam engines working nearby, it finally warms to its job. It slowly drives sap to the highest branches and a nimbus aura of green emerges. By late summer it bears a rich canopy of leaves. By the second week of frost, it is the first to go scarlet and drop them all.

It stands in the unmarked park known locally as Shirecommon, and is called, for reasons unknown, the Party Tree.

Osley held up the original document, which had angry smears across it. "It isn't just cut off here. It's obliterated by black dye. Maybe we'll catch up with it later, but this part is lost."

* * *

Cadence babysat Osley the rest of the day.

He had shed his coat, and his stink was only slightly muffled by the new long-sleeved T-shirt he was wearing, as if he dressed up for the occasion. He was in a zone of intense concentration.

Looking at him, she could see remnants of the young chemist focusing on his lab work, developing techniques. Yes, the spark, so long diluted with psychedelics, and God knows what else, was still there.

There was more, too, a heavy pall of sadness, but this was well hidden. She wondered how many different lives one old man could hold. She decided to quit hovering.

"Os, I'll be back in a little while. You all right?"

He turned and smiled, saying, "Yeah, I'm great," and then turned back to the papers. Scratch, think, write, his free hand pumping out some long ago rock and roll rhythm on the desk.

As she left, Cadence felt good. There had been progress. In the quiet lobby, she took a bouncing skip and step and edged through the ponderous closing brass doors of the Algonquin. The doorman fussed belatedly to help, but she was gone.

Outside, she inhaled the city smells and heard the city noises and saw the city bustle all around her. Horns honked. A siren wailed a few blocks away.

At that moment, several things happened.

Across the street, a dented, city-worn delivery van was pulling up, intending to double park. Its color was some faded, lesser version of green. On its side it bore what had once been an extravagant image of a sunlit garden, overlaid with arching, three-dimensional letters that read "SANTI'S VEGE'S."

Cadence's mental sketchpad took in these details, adding verisimilitude to the scene that was about to unfold.

The van slowed. The street was otherwise surprisingly empty as down at the corner, two taxis labored around the turn from 6th Avenue. Before them lay the wonder of an entire block of empty Manhattan cross street. Taxis in such a situation could proceed with caution, or they could proceed at the posted speed, or they could take the imperative third choice: Gun it! Both taxis complied fully. Their drivers simultaneously jammed on the accelerators and jockeyed for position.

Meanwhile, a kid, skinny and good-looking—he could easily be one of Cadence's fifth-graders—stepped toward the slowing van, silky smooth and confident in a motocross jacket. He casually moved in front of the van, collided with its last bit of momentum, tumbled head over heels, rolled once, and lay dramatically still. The van nose-dived and screeched as the driver stood on the brake pedal, and the tires skidded the last foot before stopping. The driver, a balding man in his fifties, jumped out, his arms making hysterical waving motions. A terrified and somehow sad "AAAaahh!" cycled from his open mouth.

While the van door was open, quick as a shadow, another kid appeared, reached in, and grabbed a small leather bag from the front seat. The size and shape suggested it might hold cash receipts. He fled down the sidewalk.

The taxis were coming fast.

The fallen boy got up, seemingly fit and healthy; the van driver grabbed the kid's jacket with one hand, using the other hand to point in the direction where his moneybag was evaporating into a crowd of pedestrians. He yelled a futile, "Hey! Hey!"

The boy was sizing up his escape route as he tried to slip the driver's grasp. Cadence knew fifth graders; she could read his eyes. At any moment he was going to bolt out into the street in front of her.

The taxis were hurtling toward them.

Cadence didn't think. She ran. She flashed in front of the first taxi and collided with the kid. This time, his backward flip was unpracticed. They both rolled clear as the taxis slammed on their brakes, swerved, skidded, and fish-tailed past them, tires screaming, white smoke boiling, the air filling with the tang of hot, abraded brake pads.

The long teeth-grinding, shoulder-wincing sentence stopped, leaving a void. The inevitable punctuation mark—the hollow whomp and glassy jingle of impact—didn't happen.

On the pavement, the kid looked at Cadence. His eyes were saucers overflowing with fear and, that most fleeting thing, kid gratitude. He scrambled up and was gone.

She pulled herself up, slowly, legs like rubber. She brushed herself off and reached down to pick up her Borunda bag, surveying the deep scrapes along the sides. The driver scurried around her. A cluster of passersby milled for a moment, but the event was just a close call, not even meriting a decent gawk. She stood there, received five, maybe ten seconds of New York accolades—the maximum allowed in this City of Haste—and it was all over. The taxis moved on. The van driver had gone somewhere. The Algonquin doorman, fussing and faithful, stayed with her.

It dawned on her, as she replayed in her mind the high-def tape of what just happened, that she had probably saved a life. She was wrong. She had saved two.

* * *

Thirty feet away, Barren milled with the crowd. He had seen it all unfold. The kid with his accomplice, practicing the bump and roll to fake an accident. The stuntman's art of timing a slowing vehicle, bouncing with it, and topping the move with a fine comic book death sprawl. Then the playing-for-gold part, his buddy's quick reach and grab heist. They were pretty good!

Just like he had been at that age.

A memory rushed through him. He and his best friend. Inseparable, they were destined to escape their little village and conquer the world together. They stole from the first incoming circus wagon, Barren got caught, and then the circus suddenly packed up and took him with them. Barren remembered the stink of the dancing bear's urine and feces and its low grunts as he lay tied next to its cage. He remembered the lolling wagons and ox carts trying to out-pace the plague. He remembered leaving his best friend behind to dance with the Black Death.

The memory passed. Barren had stationed himself here to complete his task. *Return the scribbles entire with bloody showings in hand.*

He looked at Cadence and felt a hunter's admiration for his prey. She was quick to move and selfless. A fair steward—worthy but fated— to the vile remnants of the Saga of Ara. For this moment only, he would stay his hand.

* * *

Cadence thanked the doorman. Her adrenaline was still in full flow. She needed to move. As the crowd dispersed, she decided to walk for a while. What she really needed was to jog, find that solid, earnest conversation of feet and earth. But that would have to wait.

She walked the streets for an hour, then came back and sat in the hotel lobby. She was coming down. The adrenaline fading into an exhausted, pensive mood.

A cat, evidently a perpetual guest at the hotel and probably a mouser, watched her from its perch on the check-in desk. She purposely ignored it. Resting in the big, plush chair, enjoying the quiet and comfort, her thoughts turned to her father and his own absent, almost mythical father. She closed her eyes and felt a desert wind.

The man who was her grandfather and who was almost always gone, so the story went, sometimes came home. At those times he was quiet. Not morose, exactly, but subdued, as if gathering strength between the legs of the unfolding journey that took him, like an alcoholic, to drink on months-long benders of wandering in search of his soul. How his soul got lost was a story untold.

Nonetheless, in those times at home he had a country man's eye for simplicity and unspoken elegance. Things he pointed out to his son, as simple as a knowing glance or a nod, were passed on, gesture for gesture, through that soundless language, to the son's child. So might it be for generations, a kindred nuance, none knowing the source.

There was a day's drive from their home in Western Colorado a sagebrush desert. It was set amidst low broken hills cut by tumbleweed-clogged arroyos that flanked the high green massif known as Grand Mesa. These hills and gorges, known locally as the Dobies, grew into larger canyons that dropped to the thick willow banks lining the brown flow of the Gunnison River. In some off-road spot, amidst these low hills, Jess pulled over. The jeep, rickety and open-topped, waited like a panting horse. He cut the engine and the tick and gurgle of the radiator measured the minutes as he and nine-year-old Arnie just sat there.

The air was warming up to the century mark as the shadeless silver gray desert readied to endure another blast-furnace day. The man sucked his pipe, got out and knocked out the dottle on the fender. He fingered the pipe, letting the calabash knot bowl cool, its seasoned yellow familiar in his hand.

He put on a battered straw hat and nodded. The boy got out, hefted the water bag, and they began to walk.

They went toward the river, with its distant promise of cool breeze. A high tumble of sandstone clefts—giants' play blocks—stood in their way. There were scores of narrow cracks, man-sized and water-worn, leading into the maze of baking rock.

The man stood and looked and then picked one, otherwise unpromising and indistinguishable. The word for such, lemon-squeezers, was not said. Usually compressing to nothing, these openings offered just enough room to wiggle in sideways. Once in there—and one exhaled to squeeze in—one's breath mingled with the smell of rock. Sometimes there was just enough room to get in and get caught, so the fear of getting stuck was always there.

Some hikers had tried this solo, gotten lodged in the vice, and felt the illimitable strength of all the earth pressing closer against them. Mother Earth's strong hug refusing to let go. Adrenaline and panic expanding the body, cementing their imprisonment.

But the passage chosen by the man did not close, and they wriggled left, then right, as it turned and jogged. They came into an opening, a perfect secret hollow of a hundred foot radius, cut improbably into the middle of the tumbled rocks.

The top of the walls leaned inward, sheltering the sides. On these were etched thousands of pictographs: lizards, scorpions, eagles, vultures, people with two heads, bison, elk, deer, big cats with long teeth, rising suns with splayed rays. Archetypes of a world ruled by privation and magic. The library of a people that long ago decamped, never to return. Some of the figures were twenty or thirty feet up bare sandstone cliffs. Not a sign of "Jim Bob was here 1929" or "Class of '42" or the like.

Dotting the enclosed field were large yellow-topped mounds. The yellow was the remnant rock layer left from eons of water and wind erosion.

They stopped at one of the mounds. It was full of shark's teeth—big, medium, little, tiny. The sharks that left these ranged from Jaws down to trout size. The bigger teeth would span your palm, the serrated edges as knife sharp as the last day they tore into flesh, millions of years ago.

Holding such a tooth in your hand brought the picture into full definition. One saw a flat sea-lagoon stirred by warm breezes, lapping at a palmed shoreline, perhaps a fresh water tributary spilling in nutrients to create a cove full of life. Then the sea retreated one summer, never to return, and the cove transformed into a small lake over-populated with the sharks as alpha predators. The lake became a pond, concentrating all life as the food chain began to eat itself. Soon sharks ate sharks. All that was left was some boiling cauldron of thousands of thrashing sharks.

The teeth, the only hard parts of a shark, survived. And now they were left in a fossil hot spot in an eroding formation beneath the merciless sun.

As relentless curators, the ants were doing their thing—mining the gravel, creating ant hills of tiny teeth as meticulously cleaned as if worked by a lifetime of tweezers beneath a magnifying glass.

The man and boy picked through some teeth, each selecting only one. Then the man reached into a pouch in his khakis and pulled out a small, washed jar. This he filled with tooth-laden gravel, sealed the lid, and gave to the boy.

They returned to the jeep by mid-afternoon, looking back once at the small mountain of boulders and the lacework of lemon-squeezers.

Not a word had been said since they left home at seven in the morning. It was in the boy's mind as perfect a day as he could imagine, and as he would ever experience.

The jar of gravel, its label inscribed in crayon by the boy's hand to say SHARKS TEETH, with kid drawings of sharks on either side, sat sealed on a mantle in the house for years thereafter.

There was a companion to this day, years later, when Arnie took eleven-year-old Cadence to this same spot. Same parking area, same walk across the Dobies. Same searching around for the right lemon-squeezer.

Once he recognized the entrance around the rocks, he turned to Cadence and said, "Let's stop and eat lunch." They rested in the shade of the rocks, and he opened their backpack and took out two wrapped peanut butter sandwiches and two coca-colas. Sitting together with their backs against the cool sandstone, he pulled out a dog-eared paperback book that had lost its cover through long use. She looked at the first page, saw "Ace Edition" and the strange title: *The Hobbit.*

"That's a silly word," she said.

He looked at her, "Yes it is, but I think you'll like it. Let's read a few pages while we eat. We'll start it today, and maybe you will finish it later, even if it's a long time and a long way from here. After we eat we're going to squeeze up in here and get some shark's teeth!"

The cycle of the moment and the place rolled on years later. After she had created her own series of dog ears though its pages, she lost the book. But she never forgot her own version of The Perfect Day. It was marked by another, a more modern style of jar, filled with that same gravel and labeled in Cadence's neat fifth grade lettering: ME AND DAD 1993.

The desert wind blew.

She woke with a start, feeling the cat's tail loop and caress her ankle. She looked around and saw the cat on the check-in counter, still watching her. She did a stare contest with it. Who hated whom the most. It didn't blink.

Okay, cat, you win, she thought. She got up and headed for the elevator.

"Heraclitus."

"Huh?" She looked over at the desk clerk.

He scratched the cat's neck. "He's the resident philosopher."

She stopped and put her hands on her hips. "Got it. I'm dealing with another one upstairs."

When she came back into the room, Osley was walking around, gesticulating and muttering. He started in as soon as she sat down and looked at him in the cautious way one regards a lunatic. "I've been thinking," he said. "Professor Tolkien believed that every one of those pages he wrote was a promise of something real."

"But he made it all up!"

"Hardly. Virtually everything in his stories was already out there. Straight out of Northern Mythology Central Casting. Wily dragons, wraiths, Merlin-like wizards, marching forests—remember Macbeth? Birnam Wood? Rings of Power—a staple of Norse mythology. The 'Fell Winter' echoes the historical fact of the Little Ice Age in the twelfth century. So, you see, a name is a covenant, as is a story." Osley let out a breath and sat down. He suddenly seemed subdued, like a messenger burdened by ill tidings. He looked away from her and held out a handwritten page. "I finished this a few moments ago. The word *haknuun,* Elvish for sharpener or grinder, caught my eye."

She took the page and began reading, involuntarily collapsing to a sitting position on the bed.

He was taken captive. He told them he was no more than a travelling sharpener of knives. They took him before a horrible band of orcs. The chieftain, grim and gaunt, put him beneath a long blade. "Tell me any information you have, tale or stone-cold fact, about a trove of writings. Perhaps it was given to you by others."

He told them little, save that he was a wanderer who had gone far astray from the stars of his world. The chieftain listened, then nodded to a guard. "He is useless. Kill him."

"That sounds like Grandpa Jess!"

"Yes, so it would seem."

"They're going to . . . *execute* him!" Cadence began to stutter and flail her hands. "This ca-can't be true! It's crazy! How, how can this . . . end up in here, in this pile of writings, when he disappeared in Topanga a year ago?"

Osley stood up. "Cadence, don't worry. Not yet. I don't know what this means or how it fits, but I'm going to find out. I'm . . . I'm sure . . . he's not there. But I would go there. In a shot, if I could."

"Now don't tell me it's just something on paper. All this bullshit about the word is the promise of the thing. Then how'd he get there?"

For once, and disturbingly, Osley was without words.

The room's slanting light behind gauzy curtains was spent. She sent him away, telling him to come back the next day. She needed down time to think about the bizarre reference to the itinerant sharpener. She needed to find her own splinter of magnetic ore to match Ara's, and so make her own compass out of this murky landscape.

She needed a plan.

Chapter 57

OCTOBER 25: 8:30 AM

The next morning Osley got stopped at the front desk. Cadence came down and, seeing as it was Mel's tab, rented a separate room for Osley. She was frustrated. Old-fashioned discipline had to be brought to this situation. As she held up the plastic entry card, she said "Os, look at me." She kept her eyes on his, following them as they shifted evasively. "See this. This is not magic. It is real. As in soap and hot water. Now, I have a plan and here's your part. I can't save, even find, my grandfather until we get organized. First thing you do, give me your clothes sizes. Second, go take a shower. Third, order room service. I'm going shopping, and I'll have new clothes brought up to your room. Meet me in the lobby at noon. Lunch is on Mel. Oh yes, here is the translation key and some more pages to decipher. Let's get to the bottom of this."

He was waiting there at noon sharp, cleaned up with new khaki pants and a simple pastel shirt, his gray hair pulled back in a ponytail. Best of all, no smell.

As they sat down to eat, she decided not to wait. "So, where is he now?"

"Who?"

"My grandfather, come on!"

Osley was caught off guard, "I . . . I'm sure he's okay. Don't believe . . ."

"Look, you're babbling! You are translating this, talking like this imaginary world's real, so how do you know he's not caught in . . . *there*?"

"Well, I *do* know, Miss Sarcasm; he's not in *there*. I have more to figure out before I can go beyond that. Remember, these writings are treacherous. They can force the reader into mistakes, take us down lost paths. Let's just take it easy. I'm working on this one passage now. I've been trying to figure out this one term. It seems to be *orrour* or *errour.*"

She ate quickly and got up. "Keep on working, Os. I've got things to do."

"Cadence?" His hands were on his knees. He looked at her like a helpless bystander about to witness an accident. "Be careful."

"Thanks. I'll be back."

She was determined to follow her own action plan, right or wrong. She would cut the Gordian Knot of all this hocus-pocus. Wherever her grandfather was, she now had one solid clue, and she was going to follow it. As she walked out of the door, the napkin-map from Tolkien's archive box in hand, it marked the last time she would consider herself a cynic about what was real and what wasn't.

* * *

The far end of the subway stop at 137th Street had been left unscrubbed for years. The walls were so overwhelmed with black, purple, red, and pukey green graffiti that it hurt her eyes. A few stray travelers were waiting for the next train—a Dominican family of five on a jaunt somewhere, an Eastern European immigrant with lunch pail in hand, a bedraggled student, refugee from last night's partying. Cadence wondered about their stories. The roar and screech of steel wheels straining on steel tracks barreled down the subway tunnel, along with a gusty change of air pressure. She walked to the front of the stop. She would get in at the front of the train. She would watch the view whizz by and try to find the place on the map.

She already knew there was no 130th Street stop on the 1 train. Not on the maps, not in any brochure, not by any indication on the streets. She had walked that entire corner and several blocks around and found nothing but asphalt and buildings and the nonstop blur of life at the intersection with Broadway.

The next train came in all its shabby glory. As it pulled up, she locked eyes with the conductor in his cubbyhole at the front. There was no way to talk to him, sealed in his control room. She got on and sat down in a seat that afforded a good view out the front window of the train. The door rattled closed, and the train began to move into the dark. She got up and looked out of the front window.

There were a few yellow lights ahead, but they quickly gave way to the dark. The train gained speed, its headlamp stabbing into the blackness. Peering through the glass, she saw glimpses of the underground ribs of the city, etched in stroboscopic blue from the rails. Old wooden support beams, rigged with Y-shaped supports at the top, whirred by. The shiny tracks arched ahead, twin curves of reflected light running into a morass of soot and grime from the heaving, breathing metropolis laboring above.

She leaned up to the glass and cupped her hands around her eyes to take away the reflection. The images became clearer. Piles of trash, an old shopping cart, bashed and mangled, lay off to the side. A stream of falling water splayed with a *whack!* across the glass as the train roared through. Her destination would be coming up soon.

She saw it from the side, quickly there and then gone. A line of tracks veered away and into a dark maw. The tracks were flat black, unused.

Ahead, the headlamp played for a split second off distant walls of grimy white tile. She tried to take it in, absorb everything made visible in that split-second. A subway stop, old, quaint, turn of the last century. Tiled words in Victorian lettering: 130TH STREET – BLAIN PLACE. No graffiti. An old mattress laying on the platform.

Her heart pumped hard and fast. *So, it's there. The map from Professor Tolkien's box must mean something.* She adjusted her backpack. The hard bulk of the flashlight pushed against her shoulder blade. She prepared to get off at 125th Street and walk back along the tracks. She had, of course, done her homework the night before.

Minutes later, she stood at the edge of the 125th Street station's pall of fluorescent light. She looked around the platform. There was just a hint of smoke in the air, but far off, perhaps a cigarette fire smoldering in a trash receptacle on the opposite platform. After a few moments, trains departed in both directions and the platforms were empty. There were security cameras but she trusted them to be permanently "under repair." With a quick left-right glance, she crouched down and lowered herself onto the track bed and skulked into the dark. She kept in mind three lessons from last night's homework— especially from the odd website, subwaytunnelhiking.com. First lesson, avoid the electrified third rail. It is not an urban legend. Second, listen and watch for the next train. Third, have a safe place to get to on the side so you won't be swept away by oncoming trains. Easy. Common sense.

The flashlight did a passable job, but soon it was like a penlight in the Grand Canyon at night. She had a tube of visibility three feet wide and twenty feet long. The darkness that encroached beyond that perimeter was absolute.

Her feet moved ahead, searching with every step, feeling the low vibration of the ground. Her ears became her best sensors. Far away, the sounds of the trains played over the deep, incessant rumble of the metropolis above. On top of those, she could hear, like a metronome, a steady drip of water.

There was a junction in the tracks, and, sure enough, a set of dirty, unused rails led off to the side. She followed them. She stepped over and studied a berm of detritus, most of it covered with soot. A crumpled grocery-store cart lay on its side, black accretions giving it a fantastic countenance as if it once lay at the depths of some unvisited sea. Other piles were so covered as to be unrecognizable. She shuddered at what touched her feet as she shuffled through this debris. The smell of smoke was thicker now, as if the endless whoosh of underground air columns sucked in the essence of some distant garbage dump. Those juju drums throbbed in her nerves.

Now the tracks veered away at an acute angle. Her flashlight's shaft of light caught faint eddies of smoke. She shot the beam front and back. Her nerves, on edge with the suggestion of a fire, jangled toward indecision. She stopped, then decided to quit and go back. Then she stopped again. *Isn't this always when something hideous rises up?*

She stood there, frozen in indecision, casting the light in every direction. She noticed there were many bag-like lumps, probably grimed versions of those kitchen trash bags made of fibrous and flexible material. She moved closer to one, playing the light over a textured surface that seemed to have shrunken around disturbingly familiar bulges and angular lines. She sensed it before she could admit it. They were like cocoons, webbed and closed around desiccated forms. Like adults shrunken to the size of children. She played the light down to the end of one bag, and there protruded a black and silver Air Jordan with the toe bitten off. She thought she could see bony protrusions within the deeper shadows of that toeless sneaker. No matter, she'd seen enough. She turned, almost fell, and stumbled back toward the junction of tracks. She got a few hundred feet, probably within sight of the rail junction if her fading light would only shine that far. She heard a train approaching on the main track. She blew a deep breath of relief, knowing that her bearings were right and the 125th Street station was up ahead.

The train approached with a deep rumble, the ground beginning to vibrate. The whoosh of displaced air came, and with it the acrid taste of approaching combustion. She saw the train's light up ahead, tinged with orange. Then it came barreling into view.

The entire face of the train was engulfed in sweeping wings of flame. It had prowed into a burning shipping crate. Loose metal bands like maimed robot tentacles were flailing about and sparking madly on the tracks. Like some sardonic fire-grinning banshee of the dark underground, it roared toward and then past her, all noise and smoke and fume.

From her point of view it seemed *much* slower. Her mind altered speed and fury to a processional. A thing relentless and somehow grand in its fiery splendor. A thing for which she reserved a special icy ball of hate.

In its wake the train left a firefly frenzy of swirling sparks and these promptly caught the trash berm on fire. It sputtered and flared. As she watched in horrified incredulity, some distant part of her mind recalled the fourth (or was it fifth?) famous lesson of subway hiking: Beware of track fires. She remembered the text: "They are not that unusual, given all the flammable crap that is discarded and accumulates down there. If you are near one, just go the other direction. Fast. They are oxygen hogs."

No argument there, she thought. She could try to jump the fiery berm, but then, of course, she could never, ever do that. No way.

She turned and ran past the shopping cart and the field of ominous trash-bags.

Soon, she was far into the abandoned tunnel. The depth of the debris diminished until she could see the track-bed surface. The track fire smoldered far away and, ironically, she felt safer. She kept going until the first reflection of tiles from the Blain Place station showed in her light.

She walked up to the center of the platform, looking across at the ancient stop with her eyes almost at floor level. But for a grimy mattress, it would have looked enchanted, as if it hadn't been touched in a hundred years. She pulled out the little map and shone the flashlight on it, then to the station walls and back. The door—where was the door? There it was. She smiled in relief.

Click.

Her ears pricked up; every hair on the back of her neck stood out like wires. She wasn't sure where the sound came from. She turned off the light so she wasn't a beacon, and listened. Something was moving, struggling in labored increments, as if it had been still and waiting for a long time. Another sound, as if something were reaching out and then settling down. Then a sound of air—not breathing exactly, but the slow intake of breath not necessarily human. Followed by the faint rattling of things hard and polished as they practiced once again the art of moving together.

It was coming.

It was as yet only a thing surmised out of the blackness from the gooshy scrunch of joints and the low whoosh of baggy body parts. The reptilian complex of her brain, however, knew exactly what it was.

She tried to hoist herself up on the platform, but it was too high. Her feet kicked, her chest wheezed, and she fell back, losing the flashlight.

It clattered away in the darkness somewhere beneath her. She froze with the realization that no nightmare could be this real, this weighted with the realization that she was in imminent and mortal danger. The sounds were getting closer and so distinct she could envision the source: the big, flaccid bag borne toward her by the steady progress of eight legs stepping in an orchestrated pattern. Cadence got down on her hands and knees and searched with the desperate hand-sweeps of the blind. The approaching thing, she knew to a certainty, was now hovering somewhere near, gloating, looking at her in full view. Her hand brushed something . . . a beer can . . . a rock . . . more dirt . . . and . . . there!

She grabbed the light, clicked it again and again until it turned on. It revealed the platform as she took three steps and hurtled herself up. She landed mostly up on the platform, rolled on over and stood up. The flashlight swept out its little halo, and just beyond its reach, she saw eight glints in a pattern.

The thing lurched forward.

Only the bits of image from her shaking, sweeping flashlight could be assembled in her mind into the horrible whole. The immense spider was now moving toward her in purposeful, creepy arachnid strides to match its ten-foot long legs. The details, the spikes and hairs on its legs, the glinting dashboard arrangement of eyes, the uncaring and hungry pincers, the sense and smell of rot and malevolence, all swirled in a chaos of movement and jiggling light. She turned toward the door, described on the map now bunched in her hand. What had it said? Locked? Key? Hidden key? She didn't have *time* for this! She found the door locked with an ancient, unpickable, industrial-strength Slaymaker holding a loop of bulky chains in tight embrace. She pulled at the door handle, jangling the chain and locks. She screamed, "Bastard! Come *on!*" She stopped, gauging the sound behind her and sweeping the light along the floor, around the doorjamb, until it caught something hanging there. The key! Just hanging on a nail! She grabbed it, put the flashlight in her armpit, and began to work the lock and key.

And now the race began. Her frantic hands trying to work the lock, the sound of the thing as it crept closer, the noise made by a talon groping up on the platform. The organic creak of a great bulk being lifted up as the leg took up a full weight, to be followed by another.

Come on, lock!

She heard the plush, velvety sweep of the second leg, the brush of the belly squelching up to the concrete floor of the platform—none of it was as terrifying as the possibility she now faced as she blindly stabbed the key in the lock: was this even the right key? It slipped into the slot, she turned it, pushed against the resistance of years of rust and grime, and then it gave. The hasp opened, the chain fell, and she opened the door.

This time she did look back, stepping backwards through the door into the blackness as she turned and faced the thing. She shone the light—up and up as the spider reared and moved its forelegs with exquisite delicacy toward her. They stopped on the wall above the door as she slammed it shut. The thing seemed far too big to get through, even if it could figure out the door handle.

She turned to see where she was, expecting some new horror.

The light described a room, piled with old rail tools and a few scattered and rusted metal lunchboxes. A pool of water occupied the center, somewhere between an inch and a thousand feet deep. Above, a thin waft of light intertwined with a seep of water flowing down through crevices and storm drains from street level fifty feet above. It was still daylight somewhere far above, and the last autumn rain sought its way down.

Cadence stood motionless for a long time. No sound came from outside the door. Perhaps it was waiting out there. Patiently, oh so patiently, she thought with a trembling inward chuckle. Her eyes adjusted, her heart slowed a little, and the room began to be visible without the flashlight. She shut it off and watched the pool. It almost glowed as the seeping drip sent out oily ripples in overlapping patterns.

She stepped forward and looked down.

At first there was nothing to see but the ripples. But, as she watched, there seemed to be other patterns, movements deeper down. These ebbed and then flowed back with more definition. When she looked directly down into the depths, she thought she could see a light. After a moment it came into better focus, as if the image, in moving closer to the surface, was bringing with it color and clarity.

She stared for what seemed like a long time until she saw, as if through a screen of leaves in a forest, an array of slender plant-like creatures moving as a group. They swept by in graceful and exotic patterns, more purposeful than decorous. This was followed by a fleeting, jarring image of the Head Librarian. He was engaged in a conversation on what appeared to be a videophone. He had a subservient expression; he was being dressed-down by a gray haired man in the video screen who looked like nothing if not a Hollywood producer.

Then the image warped into a graceful waterfall, thin and bright in the sunshine. Through the veil of falling water, Cadence saw a young woman huddled with swaths of hair curled about her unshod and furry feet. She looked, for all her plain and simple beauty, alone and profoundly sad.

Cadence knew at once it was *her.* Ara.

She was looking at Ara through a small cascade of water, someplace where autumn spread a palette of intense colors. As Cadence gazed, Ara turned and stared back, at first startled, but then overtaken with wonder. Their eyes, despite the ripples here and the waterfall there, followed each other as Ara turned and crawled toward the vision that was Cadence. She looked, tilting her head in curiosity, and reached through the waterfall. The pool trembled as the hand stopped just short of breaking the surface. Right there, in that dank room with the distant traffic of Broadway rumbling overhead and the drip-drip of water, the female halfling looked at Cadence and said softly, "I have seen you in your strange clothing. Are you a water-sprite that will cover me with forgetfulness?"

Cadence didn't know what to say. The accent was odd, indefinable. She wondered what she must look like to Ara.

Ara continued, "I believe you are no sprite. You are lost down in there, in a world far away from here. Would you reach out and do as I do, offer to touch my hand?" Her fingers extended up to the very surface of the pool.

"Yes," Cadence said in a hushed breath, and extended her hand. The water should have been an inch deep at most, but her hand continued down disappearing past her wrist. She stayed very still. The water had turned murky, and though she worried that something might take her hand away in one awful bite, she kept it there. Something brushed her skin. Then she felt fingers touch hers. The water calmed and the face, probably much like her own, showed the relief of unexpected, friendly company.

Ara spoke, "I hope we meet again." Then her eyes widened and her hand withdrew suddenly. "Do not stay! Something seeks you, just as it has lured away my Amon from me. Go now. You are in danger!" Her eyes were wide, as if she saw something that Cadence did not. Quickly Cadence looked behind her. When she turned back to the pool, the image was gone and the surface looked again like a muddy pool, its calm punctuated by the hypnotic drip-drip.

Cadence felt a moment of decision teeter crazily before her. She knew Ara was fated. She should do something to communicate with her—reach out, jump in, something. But the moment wobbled away. Hesitation hung in the air like a bitter rebuke.

Cadence now had to take care of herself. She went back to the door. She heard nothing but silence. She waited, breathing slow and deep, until she dared to open it. Her flashlight searched the platform and the train tracks. The dust on the platform was smeared in places, but she couldn't tell her own tracks and clambering marks from anything else. She squinted to see further out, but could only pick up reflections of metal from the support beams around the tracks. Had *that* been what she'd seen? Were those the eight eyes that had stared at her? The hard reckoning of fear told her not to return that way. She went back into the dank room and followed the pool slivers of blue-gray light dancing on the walls. She swept the flashlight beam around until, behind a stack of lumber and an old-fashioned ticket booth, she found another door. It groaned and creaked, but opened just enough to squeeze through. After a few more terrified steps, she was in a stairwell. It led up several flights.

She emerged into the blinding light and blaring sounds of West 130th Street. The door closed and locked behind her, an innocuous rusty thing imbedded in a graffiti-stained brick wall. Cadence's hand flew up to hail a taxi. She couldn't get out of this neighborhood fast enough.

Chapter 58

OCTOBER 24: 9:08 PM

—

By the time she got halfway through her story about the lost subway stop, Osley wouldn't stay still. When she got to the spider part, he got up and paced his hotel room, clasping his hands to his ears in fearful denial.

"I told you to be careful! It's all coming apart at the seams now."

She looked at him, seeing something she never imagined from the many whacko sides of Osley. He was cringing down on the bed, his head lowered, his old-man fists tight as earmuffs to his head. His tears dripped and puddled on the carpet. A sob, like she'd never heard, except from her mother when her dad died, wracked through him. She stood for some moments, and then went over to sit beside him. She put her arm on his shoulder.

Finally he wiped his nose and eyes on his sleeve. "I'm sorry, Cadence. I wish I could . . . could tell you more." He stood up now, fired by some fearful resolution. He drove a fist into his palm and looked at her directly. "You must go home. Now! Forget about finding your grandfather. I'm sure he will write from wherever he is. If he doesn't, then he's gone. Leave it at that."

He looked about, picking up his things and making ready to leave.

"Os, hold on. Look, I'm not going anywhere. Not until I get to the bottom of this. It's all intertwined. These . . . monster things, the Tolkien documents, the Elvish writing. And Ara. We owe her. She won't survive unless we keep on this. Maybe you can't understand that. And most important, my grandfather, he's in here somehow. I can feel it.

Besides, you know what?"

He stiffened further, chin up. "What?"

She smiled. "I need your help. You're the only guide I've got in this. Please."

His demeanor softened. "On one condition, Cadence. Only a few more days. And absolutely no more wandering off on your own."

"Deal," she said, before he could reconsider. "You were going to say something about this spider-thing I thought I saw."

He exhaled and drew in a deep breath, as if re-centering himself. "Well, remember the name I was trying to figure out when you left? It was Errour. The document says she is the oldest and most vile of the Great Spiders of Mirkwood."

"Now you tell me! Anyway, it was all very confusing. Except this, I stink like a garbage fire"

"So then what happened?"

She told him, and when she got to what she saw in the pool, he came out of his funk.

"That's it, don't you see! That's a passage! A place to go through. Maybe it was worth it. You saw her, my God. Ara!"

"Yes, I . . . think so. So let's go through this. I need to read everything you've translated so far."

He got up and gathered an unruly stack of hotel stationary and yellow legal pad sheets crisscrossed with sentences, mark-outs, and lines. It was readable, but barely. She scanned the pages.

"So, is Ara still alive in this story?"

"Yes, for now. I've been tracking her. And so have others. Read this." He clutched a handful of yellow pages.

Cadence read, holding the pages for a long time and seeing a dark trail:

Hafoc became restless and soared away, back to the north, as if scanning for pursuing trouble.

Staying to her southerly bearing, Ara came at last to a frost-stiffened wood. Through it there was but one path, hugging the bank of a fresh stream that led down a wooded defile that grew ever narrower. One other path joined from the side, and by this way entered bloody drag marks, as of a man's body rudely hauled by his feet. These marks were accompanied by the heavy boot prints of a band of men, their feet hastily sidestepping the bloody grooves. Ara slowed. She bent over, her eyes trying to read this tale in the dirt and leaves. She was hesitant to catch up to the track-makers, but the steep gorge offered no other way. Turning back would mean days of lost time, days she already counted as deficit. She smelled the air and surveyed the encroaching forest, then moved on, keeping to the side of the trail.

The path continued into an ever more dismal forest. Trees grew over the widening and now stagnant stream, as if trying to cover it up. The water eddied in dark pools and emptied toward a small mere that she could glimpse through the trees. She heard men's voices, urgent and labored with fear. She left the trail and came upon them, staying hidden but close enough to listen.

Before her were arrayed nine men in heavy battle gear, all facing away and staring down into a rocky cove. They were still gasping for air, swords and bows at the ready. At their feet, where the drag marks went into the water, the pool boiled with bloodshot gore, its dark waters frothing with a red and green infestation of writhing serpents. A black upwelling brought a foul reek of decay and sulphur. Some of the men turned away. Closest to the pool was a large man, evidently the leader, bearing a princely helm hooped with boar-shapes and surmounted with a ridge of shining black bristles. To his right was a smaller man dressed in the cloak of some monkish order. The smaller man spoke loudly to the large man. His voice had surprising articulation and power.

"Is there no true God in this land, that he would allow such blasphemy to exist?"

The leader spoke. "Your new god is for you, scop. I know not who has forsaken whom to beget this corruption. I do know that a man's life is too brief to do more than glimpse such things, and his one true tale is the only creation he can master, if at all." Fastening the leather strap of his helmet and checking his battle gear, he raised his sword and continued. "This abomination, however, shall finally end if I can bring Hruntings's sharp edge to the task full measure."

One of his companions broke in. "Be wary, my lord, the

heat of her blood has melted other great swords."

"Yes, Talis, so I saw long ago in the great hall at Thornland. There, behind the king's own chair, made fast to the wall, is an esteemed relic. A great blade of ents, those mystical giants of long ago. All that's left is a bladeless hilt, its stub of damascened steel diminished to a gory icicle. Her scalding blood may eat all that it touches, but I need but one swift stroke!"

With that, the large man deftly tossed Hrunting into the air. As it twirled and caught flashes of light, he leapt feet first into the pool. So agile was he that in mid-air his hand closed solidly on the hilt even as the water splashed and took him. His companions closed to the bank and watched. The serpents slithered away and his golden helm glistened for a final moment as it sank into the murky depths.

Another man then spoke. "We will wait. That blade has what now seem ill-boding runes. I fear for Beowulf this day."

Then the man looked at the monk and continued. "And you, scop, have you more to show from your relic trade? Will holy nails and wood splinters save us now? Shall I suddenly trust in your fantastic tale of a god that forgives all? Shall I abandon the known gods given to us by our grandfathers, the gods of our sage elders who, unlike you, have wintered into wisdom?"

"Your heart will be your guide, sire."

"For now, our watchfulness will be our guide." The warrior laid aside his shield and stood watching the pool. All of the band gathered beside him and stared into the now still and silent water.

Ara , unsure of the motives of these rough men, quietly moved back and then examined the trail ahead. The way was clear of the drag marks and bore no witness to evil. She hurried on, leaving the band at the mere's edge, their tale for others to tell, if they survived.

Cadence looked up and over at Osley. He was consulting the key less and less now. His eyes and hand danced to the rhythm of his own translation. She thought about the blood that melts swords, and the movie *Alien* and Mel's warning "Don't ever bet your life on a trivia contest." Then her eyes returned to the pages, wanting desperately to catch up with Ara:

The hobbitess moved swiftly all that day, emerging into a plain that left her visible and uneasy. Hafoc returned and stayed close by, nervous and jumpy in his movements, and so aggravating her disquiet. She skylighted the horizon by dawn and dusk, and so spied, far away, what she thought were twin figures following her trail. She changed her path and patterns and often doubled back, but they stayed true to her bearing, as if reading the very marks of stumbling and sliding on rock and branch. They held back, sure and relentless and patient.

She finally lost the sense of their distance and so redoubled her pace. The land rose and became increasingly rocky. It led to a promontory among foothills that were but miniatures of the mountains that loomed ahead in ranks of shade, a range of purple summits remembered from the map she had seen. Everdivide. She reached the small promontory at sunset and climbed and looked back. She scanned the horizon and then looked down. She froze.

Below, no more than a mile away, close enough that her scent was still fresh, loped the pursuers. Two in number and man-like, they stooped low as they ran, like hounds fixed on the spore. The fast-setting sun propelled their shadows far to their sides. They disappeared from her view behind an outcrop, so that only their shadows were visible. These became long penciled creatures, wild and outlandish in their movements, wobbling on exaggerated legs independent of the flesh and blood hunters that now ran full out to secure her fate as their prize.

Their shadows stopped suddenly. They were relieving themselves, like wolves or jackals do before the final chase.

She scrambled on in sheer panic. She stumbled and flushed a covey of wild brautigans that rocketed along with the wind and passed only a foot off the ground through a gap in the rocks before veering up and away. She made for the gap, climbing up uneven tiers that may have been steps for giants with unmatched legs.

At the top she was forced to stop. Before her rose a darkly

veined mountain wall that rose thousands of feet, sheer and void of pathways. Only among the debris field at its base, perhaps a half-mile away, did she spy a darker place, a crevice or, if she was lucky, a cave. Hafoc took wing in a wild flurry and she sprinted toward that spot as fast as she had ever run in her life.

The page ended. *Damn! She has to make it!* thought Cadence. She was finally crashing into exhaustion. She put the pages down and sank into the room's overstuffed chair. She felt the calm helplessness of the lost. The reputation of Elvish was true. It led down strange paths. *She, they, Osley, me, Jess, all of us, utterly lost in Mirkwood. But only my grandfather is missing without a trace. He'll be gone a year on Halloween, and I'm more confused than ever. Well,* her pragmatism chimed in as she keyed her cell phone, *at least I still have an appointment app on this.*

Chapter 59

OCTOBER 26: 8:50 AM

———

Sunday morning. Her appointment at nine o'clock. Cadence arrived early at the office of L'Institut des Inspecteurs, which seemed to be open just for her visit. Per Mel's instructions, she brought an envelope containing three pages, including the original note from Tolkien to her grandfather.

The receptionist noted her name and chirped, "Are you French? *Es-que vous parlez francais?*"

"Uh, *non.*" The best she could do from ninth grade French.

"Wait here, please."

Cadence sat and picked up a glossy brochure from the coffee table. It was bi-lingual, an English version conveniently provided on the opposing pages.

Up till now, she hadn't given L'Institut des Inspecteurs much thought, but flipping through the brochure and reading the qualifications of the experts made her feel a little queasy with apprehension. They were scarily qualified professionals who would go over every centimeter of her grandfather's documents. What frightened her most of all was the idea that maybe the entire thing was a fake. If so, what did that make of Osley and everything she'd experienced since getting here?

The receptionist suddenly asked her if she would like a cup of coffee. Cadence shook her head, and the receptionist smiled back in relief. Cadence watched the institutional wall clock tick off fifteen minutes.

Finally the receptionist stood up and Cadence was whisked into a large office where she was met by a tall, goateed gentleman whose dress and manner struck her as elegant, veering dangerously close to affected. Brian de Bois-Gilbert. He began speaking to her in French, or what her baffled ear assumed was French. Then she caught a stray English word, and another, and it became clear that he was speaking grammatically perfect English in an almost impenetrable accent. Her ear finally straightened it out. "Mademoiselle Cadence, I understand that you have certain lost documents, allegedly part of a secret cache owned by Monsieur Tolkien. May I have the sample documents, please?"

Without waiting for an answer, he deftly plucked the envelope from her clutched hand.

"This is but a preliminary meeting," he told her. "Our team of experts will be examining these today and will give you their findings tomorrow morning."

"They're here? In New York? The people in this brochure?"

He smiled indulgently as she flapped the glossy brochure at him. "But of course. Where did you think they'd be?"

In France, she was about to say, but he didn't wait for her reply. As he went on, itemizing the various aspects of the documents to be examined, she wondered what kind of organization this was that traveled in a pack across the ocean. Who paid for this? And where were the other experts' offices? Surely not here, for the suite of offices was much too small. In retrospect she counted maybe two offices, or this one plus a restroom.

". . . custody, ink, paper, calligraphy, type, and context. These are but some of the elements our panel of experts will examine. These will be the proofs."

Again she got that sick feeling in the pit of her stomach. The reception desk phone rang and Bois-Gilbert answered it smartly. He spoke at length in French before she realized her meeting had ended. When she reached hesitantly for her handbag, he confirmed it by waving an exuberant good-bye.

She found her way back to the reception area, where she was given a different address for the next morning's meeting: 11th Avenue and West 61st Street. Why a different address? It didn't make any sense.

After leaving the Institute, Cadence took a bus toward downtown. She got a window seat and let the blocks and stops roll by. She wanted to see if Ara escaped from the pursuers. She pulled out the last pages

Osley had handed her. She laughed despite herself, thinking of his manic flurries with pen and paper. His translation read:

Ara made it to the rocks. There the hawk, immobile save for the bitter wind rippling through its feathers, rested on a tree that guarded the cleft between two giant boulders. Far above, on the purple flank of the mountain, snow fell and gales moaned to herald the coming winter. The cave was nestled behind a chaos of fallen rocks that gave no encouragement to explore its fissures. Indeed, the entrance twisted between stones so closely spaced that, save for a thin line of shadow, its passage could not be seen from the outside. To enter was an act of faith.

She frantically made her preparations and, with Hafoc unhooded but jessed to one arm, and a crude torch held high before her, Ara slid between the stones.

She soon found a broadening cave, cool and damp at first, which had a single, well-excavated pathway. She followed this for some time, feeling the air grow warmer. She began to hear a distant, subterranean sound, like massive, sonorous breathing. On top of that sound danced the creak of wood and the chip and thud of hammers. At last, she entered a high-roofed cavern, illuminated with an orange glow.

In the center sat some *one* or some *thing*. She approached with caution and looked closely. It was warped in the way of a large beast misshapen, its design errant from the intended stamp of some obscure race of men. Its face, if such could still be said of it, was shadowed by the flickering light of a small fire. Hidden in wreaths of smoke that lifted slowly upward, this being was such as men do not see in a thousand years, and halflings, never. Its face was monstrous. Folds and creases, rather than mouth and nose and ears, were its hallmarks. Ragged, tortured, deeply scarred from upper left to lower right, it was a face tired beyond the endless toil of lifetimes. But a glint shone from an eye socket. All those that rarest chance brought before this creature sensed that here sat a being—not man, not wizard, not named—of knowledge to match those years.

She gazed further into the torch-lit, glowing depths and saw a dozen men sitting before a wall of the cave. The thing before her precariously raised a long, spiraled, goat horn ear trumpet to the nob on the side of its head. Suitably equipped for conversation, it pointed an arthritic finger toward the men and spoke in a strangely heightened voice.

"There sit prisoners unchained save by their ignorance. See how they stare giddily at the wall, entranced by shadows? They came as looters, yet they stay by their own free will. Do you, Aragranessa, do better? Do you know when the unreal is real, and the real is but a shadow? . . . And what of your stewards?"

Stewards? Cadence physically jumped. The drums in her mind thumped in rapid beats. She read on:

Ara replied, "Of stewards I have none, for I carry myself and all that I need. What the mists of things-to-be may bring, I know not. Such is beyond the vision of our kind." She gazed at the "looters," ragged and long-bearded, and saw that much of the light etching the shadows came from a side chamber. From there also protruded a scaled tail. The very breath of some long-sleeping, lesser dragon was the source of the light that shackled these men to a false world. So would they all stay. Men tethered by bonds as solid as clanking iron yet tenuous as untested superstition.

The unbeheld dragon did what unbeheld dragons do best, furnishing unto men false shadows and the spell of its glow until, at some moment, in some tale long hence, it would inexorably awake and visit itself upon the world.

She turned to the figure before her, and their discourse, if such it was, has been lost from this chronicle, save the now-famous wisdom he imparted to her. "Of all beliefs, a vow is the most precious, because it is the giver who must believe."

Aside from the path down which she fled to arrive in this cavern, there was only one way out. The opening which pulsed with the glow that fed the fantastical shadows. As she watched, they expanded and contracted like inky, vaulting phantoms. She left the misshapen creature, ear trumpet still poised, and walked toward the glow. She passed by the prisoners, saw in their glittering eyes and cracked smiles the way of self-delusion and false paths. She hurried ahead, toward the slowly pulsing light of the worm's breathing. An undercurrent smell of something nasty and revolting hung in the air.

In a moment, she stood next to the entrance to a side tunnel, its sides worn smooth by the passage of immense, granite-hard coils. The sounds of picks and hammers and creaky wood wheels and gears came from here. The smell was worse.

She paused, Hafoc still on her arm, then braved a step over the protruding trail to look inside.

It was impossible to comprehend all that she saw, so intense and varied was the activity. Nonetheless, its elements were clear. The dragon was wound on itself. Coil upon coil, edged back into the formless darkness. It lay still, except along one of its side there opened and closed a vent of scales and flesh. From this came light and heat, timed to the cycle of beats of its many hearts. What astounded her was all the activity, oblivious to the danger. Scores of dwarves toiled on and around the worm. They had erected scaffolds, and metal gear wheels, and a massive maul, designed after the engine of a catapult. It pounded the rock with shuddering impact. They were mining at the very foot of the beast, reckless to their peril. The rock they mined was festooned with glistening treasure.

It was not rock such as men knew. The worm had vomited up a foul cement to protect its treasury during its long slumber. Hundreds of dwarves were working the stinking debris with picks and hammers. Jewels and gold, weapons and coins and silver crowns were in piles next to their work.

She thought them as foolish as the prisoners. They would doubtless delve here till they awoke the dragon.

Hafoc fluttered from her arm and sailed in slow wing sweeps into the darkness of the main tunnel ahead. She ran after him, oblivious to peril or time or direction.

A day or days later, Ara emerged from the cave on the south face of Everdivide. She was ravenous. She recovered in a dell of warm sunshine that preserved on the bushes a few berries. Fearful of time, she soon was on a pathway beneath golden-leafed aspens. In those groves the leaves fell lazily, like a gentle, season-changing rain of endless yellow drops. The air was full of flashes of color as the leaves floated like butterflies through the dappled sunlight. The carpeted trail welcomed them. Her feet made a swoosh-swoosh sound to mix with her laughter.

Her thirst grew in this glen, and she came upon a freshet splashing over rocks into a pool. It was smooth and reflected the light and color about her. She bent to drink, watching the water sport bright fans of red and gold.

And she saw in its depths a wonder: a young woman's face peering back at her in amazement.

"That's it! That's me!" Cadence shouted, causing the other passengers to jump up and the bus driver to pump his brakes and regard her sternly in the mirror. Cadence knew that was Ara looking right at her in the pool. Cadence liked Ara, more and more. She felt a courage she could admire. She was confident she could stay to a path and detect a wolf-like presence, man or beast, as well as her halfling counterpart. She felt, finally, that she had embarked on her own journey. It would lead somewhere.

Her stop was coming up.

Chapter 60

OCTOBER 25: 3:44 PM

—

The more Barren thought about it, his training days at Riker's Island had been invaluable. He moved quickly to complete mastery of the guise and mien of residents of this clamorous village. It was all in preparation. He told himself he would, as always, complete his duty without hesitation or mercy.

His base skill set—stealth, lying, assassination—was fully intact. Long practice in the arts of concealment in the service of evil had honed these talents to the acute focus of an exquisitely sharpened blade. And yet, just yesterday, he had stayed his hand. Never before had he done such a thing. He knew that such weakness, once indulged, could infect its host with corrosive sentiment. So while he reprieved Cadence's life for a few days, it was but a temporary stay.

He stood drab and unnoticed in a knit pullover cap, once again outside the West 44th Street entrance to the Algonquin.

Cadence emerged, a plastic shopping bag in hand. Following a mere step behind her, he naturally assessed the quick kill he might execute without a break in his stride. But that was not the instruction for this errand. No.

Bind her, trembling and quick-lipped, to the place of your choosing. There answers may be taken as to the hiding place of these writings.

Cadence, all but oblivious to his presence, rubbed the annoying tingle at the nape of her neck. She walked for another block, finally reaching 5th Avenue. She bounded up the steps to the New York Public Library.

Barren followed, almost at her side, just another patron impatient to enter. He passed the stone lions, bemused by their inert and ineffectual presence. They were hardly the watchful gateway sentinels of the Valley of Shadows.

As he watched her, she checked at the information desk and then struck out, maneuvering hallways and perusing door numbers.

* * *

Cadence scanned the door numbers. There it was: 229. The office of the library's paleographer. As long as she was subjecting herself to Les Inspecteurs, she was going to get more opinions. She knocked politely, heard a voice invite her in, and turned the door handle.

As she entered, a man in his late twenties, tall, lean, and wearing horn-rimmed reading glasses, got up from a desk and came to shake her hand. "Ms. Grande? Bossier Thornton."

"I'm sorry?"

"Boe-sher. Cajun grandparents. With that last name you must have some French in your family?"

That same question, she thought, embarrassed by the answer.

"I don't really know. My pedigree is pretty fuzzy. American, I guess."

"Can't beat that. So."

She took in his watch, smart not flashy, his shined shoes and trimmed hair. "Thank you for seeing me on your day off."

"That's okay. I don't really have any of those."

"You look more like a detective than a forensic paleographer."

He looked at her, surprised.

"The museum website. Your bio?"

"Well, you do your homework. Take your pick. Right now, I'm both. I can't tell which job I'm moonlighting. Neither one pays much." He smiled. "Sit down, please. Now show me the documents."

In her bag was a scroll on a wooden spindle, along with some of Osley's translations. She took the scroll and opened it. There before them, in the middle of an ornate forest of Elvish, lay the great rune that resembled an "A" with eyes and other filigree about it. Ara's sign. Bossier put on rubber gloves and gingerly unrolled the entire scroll on a large plastic examination table. He weighted its corners and sides with beanbags. He flicked a switch and the table surface illuminated, giving a rich, yellow glow to the parchment. She watched his movements, the careful note-taking, the apparent cross-reference to his computer.

After a while he looked up at her. "It's a very old document or a very clever fake. I can give you a pretty clear answer right now, to about seventy per cent certainty." He uncased a small digital device that looked like a hand-held scanner. "Behold the Mancuso Analytics 43. A test model. Wireless, non-invasive, no sample needed. Laser-enabled. Designed for quick analysis in the field and for national security uses. It's a chemical and atomic variance reader. Uses Raman patterns. Instant and accurate enough for on-the-ground decisions. The real brains are in the 429-level server slaved to it."

"Uh-huh." She sounded dubious. "Sounds like Spock's tricorder."

"Raman—no relation to Romulon and not a noodle dish. He was an Indian scientist. He won the Nobel Prize in 1928. In any case, put simply, it's a digital bloodhound." He held it up, his eyebrows lifting in question.

"Okay, let's do it."

He ran the device over the middle of the document. A touch screen menu gave him access to several national databases. After a few moments he looked up at her.

"Unless someone had eight-hundred year-old ink and vellum, this is legit."

Cadence blinked at him. "You're finished? Already? And it's real . . ."

Bossier nodded. "Yeah, you can't fake this."

She held her breath as she looked at him. "I'd been afraid to ask."

"That's just the science, of course. The real truth, the *magic,* I like to call it, may be in what it says."

"Well, you want to read some? Here's a translation of some of this stuff. Knock yourself out. Please."

She handed him several pages and pointed to a spot. "Start here." She sat back in a chair and he began reading in silence.

After a few moments he looked up. "Okay, Ms. Grande, this is pretty . . . out there. I was expecting some royal decrees or land-rent tallies."

"Just keep going, please."

He gave the slightest "oh-well" shift of the eyes and continued to read.

When he finished, he put down the translation and gave a courtesy cough. Cadence stared at him like he was the last sane man on the planet. "What do you think?"

"It's some made-up story from long ago. I wouldn't think it's all that important. The physical document, not its contents, may be the real prize here."

She thought about the pragmatic wisdom in his words. "Only one thing."

"What's that?"

"Someone thought this story was important enough to preserve on this scroll and a bunch of others."

"So what are you going to do with this?"

"That's a really, really good question. Look, I want to thank you." Then she hesitated, "Is there a charge?"

"No, not for using this bloodhound. Here's my card. Call me if you have any other questions."

"Okay, I will."

Cadence left and ran for the stairs, passing a figure in a knit cap studying a 1930s mural of American Industrial Progress: heroic figures, big skies, and big machines. She glanced at the man and the mural but kept going. Before following her, Barren stayed a moment longer, lingering to study the great towers and trains and boats and planes.

He felt resolved now. He would gather his allies and then close on this steward when she had her precious scribblings in hand.

Besides, other of the Dark Lord's emissaries, unknown to Barren but surely already here, would be hunting her now. If her fate was to be in his hands, he must set his traps with speed.

Chapter 61

OCTOBER 27: 10:15 AM

———

Cadence did not anticipate the trap set for her by L'Institut des Inspecteurs.

Clues abounded, but they eluded her. The address was on a steep block on West 61st Street that spilled down to the Hudson River. No tony office buildings here—only warehouses, storage rental buildings and housing projects that must have seemed forlorn when they were built in the early sixties.

The address was a nondescript concrete building with no signage whatsoever. It could have been anything from a wholesale warehouse to an S & M bar. Feeling her confidence sink by the second, Cadence steeled herself and entered the building.

Inside, she passed through a steel door. An elevator beckoned to her. She pressed the button and it whooshed open much too quickly for comfort.

When she arrived at the sixth floor, things were no clearer. Everything was black—the walls, the floors, even the ceilings were painted black. Halogen lights gave their eerie sharp glow. She walked a long corridor until she arrived at another closed steel door.

She didn't like it. She was considering leaving the building when the steel door was flung open.

"Oh, there you are." It was the chatty receptionist from the uptown office. Cadence was whisked away to a room that looked, well, like a television studio. Lights, cables, monitors, blacked-out windows. The chair on which she was instructed to sit was hard-backed and uncomfortable. It was like a set-up for a third-degree. A bank of lights came on.

She faced a panel of four strangers, all sitting and looking at her with clinical smiles. The Inspecteurs, she presumed.

A woman with a Yankees baseball cap scurried around. She brought a wireless mike to Cadence and pinned it on. From the periphery, Cadence saw two people with small, pro-look digital cameras roaming the room. She could feel the close-up focus on her as the side door opened and Bois-Gilbert lurched into the space between Cadence and the panel. He adjusted the conch-shell buttons on his bespoke suit, smoothed his impeccable tie, shot his gold cuff-linked cuffs, and focused a barracuda smile on Cadence.

It fell into place with a thud. This wasn't a scientific exam at all. Feeling ridiculously slow on the uptake, Cadence realized she *was* in a television studio. It *was* a TV show—a pilot, maybe, for a French-produced reality show.

Mel had set her up.

"Are you ready, Miss Grande?" asked Bois-Gilbert in mock-portentous tones.

What could she say? Here she was, pinned like an insect on an examination card. She could make a disagreeable scene or go with the flow. She wanted the three documents back, and going with the flow seemed like the most reasonable path to get to them.

"Sure, what's on the menu today, Brian?"

"The very best thing—the proofs! Are you prepared to receive them?"

Before she could answer, the stage manager called for quiet on the set and the lights went black except for a spot on M.C. Monsieur Bois-Gilbert. As he began reading off the teleprompter, she realized that his natural, over-elegant, slightly oleaginous manner made perfect sense. In front of the camera, his English became as smooth as Jacques Cousteau.

"In the worlds of myth, religion, art, currency, wines, and documentation of all sorts there is a common, immutable, and ancient rule. Where there has been money or passion, there has been deception. Fakery—the practice of flattery by studied imitation or even brazen imagining of what might have been—is indeed an esteemed art. When done at the hand of a maestro, it brings together precise science, extraordinary diligence, and the deft hand of the often unrecognized and unheralded master.

"So too must be the qualities of those who would unmask the imposters. Nothing is so false and so damaging to a culture than the flood of falsehoods that would wash away truth and originality if left unchecked."

He paused for a second, as if the script indicated an insertion point for a pre-taped roll-in. Maybe the show's title sequence, she mused. She felt the sticky, probing, violating fingers of the cameras playing with her features.

"In the fifth century, Greeks routinely faked ancient art for Roman patrons. Much of it sits unquestioned in museums to this day. In more recent times, a rogue's gallery of forgeries has been detected by the forensic sciences. Witness the stream of imposters!"

His voice was like that of a jury foreman, a reader of verdicts. Firm, definitive, pausing after each damning item. Nothing was in sight, but she could sense the montage that would fill the screen.

"The Shroud of Turin."

"The Hitler Diaries."

"The Alamo Diaries showing that, contrary to myth, Davy Crockett did not go down swinging Old Betsy."

"The MJ-12 documents detailing the American President Truman's cover-up of UFOs."

"The lost plays of William Shakespeare."

"Newly discovered masterworks by Vermeer. So good they fooled Herr Göring."

Cadence felt transfixed by the indictment. She could imagine his damning finger itching to point straight at her.

"The Vinland Map."

"The Howard Hughes Autobiography."

"The Jack the Ripper Diaries."

"The fake wines reputedly hidden in a Paris cellar by the American Ambassador to France, Thomas Jefferson."

"And now we come at last to another candidate, adding unexpected chapters to our special mythology. Let us bring the cold eye of science to this most recent candidate. We focus the microscope today on . . . The Tolkien Documents!"

So here it was, the careful turn of the head, the unyielding glare of the Inquisitor. And yes, just as she'd figured, the bony finger unfurling and stretching out to damn her as a member of the League of Frauds. The insta-science of Bossier Thornton's little gizmo suddenly seemed pretty dubious.

The cameraman yelled "*Arêtes!*" and Bois-Gilbert fished a pack of Gauloises from his coat, shot one into his mouth, lit it as smoothly as a finger snap, and walked out the door. A cloud of smoke more foul-smelling than any cigarette she'd ever whiffed lingered in the air after him.

At that point Cadence got up, retrieved her purse, and pulled out her cell phone. Coverage was spotty but she got through. Mel answered.

"Yo."

"Don't yo me, you bastard! Why didn't you tell me it's a TV show."

"Wait! Cadence, slow down. It's just to memorialize things, that's all. Just one more meeting."

"It's not just a meeting, that's what I'm telling you. It's a recorded sideshow at my expense. No more guinea pig stuff, Mel. I want my damn documents back from these jackals."

"Okay, but the results will be in soon. Shouldn't we find out? You want to lose The Mirkwood Forest or save it? Come on, kid, it's your best shot. Now, tell me . . ."

She hung up.

After the aborted phone call with Mel, Cadence waited in a folding chair by a rack of unplugged lights. The crew milled about and she sensed this lull might last a while. She was just getting relaxed.

The receptionist rushed up. "Mademoiselle Grande? Are you ready? *Vitement!* He is coming!"

She was escorted back to her place on the set, the judges re-empaneled, and all eyes went to the stage director. His fingers silently marched down the count. Five. Four. Three. Two. A pointed finger. They were live . . .

. . . and Bois-Gilbert bounded into the room.

"As forgery is an ancient art, so the fineness of its accomplishment must be esteemed, most especially by those whose profession is detection. We judge not on the moral plane, but only on the quality of the product. We are Les Inspecteurs!

"Tonight we bring you the reality of our investigation, our clash between the art and science of fakery and the art and science of detection. We have before us a thorough test of our skills. And in the balance lies authenticity or an unmasking . . ."

Cadence could imagine the images of legendary fakes being somehow blue-screened and rolled in behind the cuts of her sitting alone, accused and friendless. These would be followed by close-ups of her suspiciously darting eyes and tell-tale twitching hands. The background would roll with aerial shots of crop circles, a grainy snip from the lone Sasquatch film, flying lights over desert mountains, the gravel pit excavation site of Piltdown Man, and on and on.

"Cadence, you have met our panel of expert judges. In a moment they will announce their findings. Are you prepared to receive the proofs?"

Now both cameras were facing her. If one missed the incriminating droplet of sweat that now formed on her upper lip, the other would be sure to catch it. But before she could speak, Bois-Gilbert started up again.

"Here, then, are the proofs! And they are stunning. By the classic *methodologie de faux*, the Seven Principles of the Fake, we shall judge now your supposed Tolkien Documents!"

Oh God, she thought, *not air quotes.*

"The Principles are . . . wrong ink . . . wrong type . . . wrong implement . . . wrong paper . . . wrong handwriting . . . wrong time . . . wrong style. Cadence Grande, can you run the gauntlet of our judges?"

What followed was the studied false pause of the reality show. In the strange, complicit seduction of the television camera, she felt an almost irresistible urge to bite her lip.

"Hold, before you answer!" More pause. He raised his right hand, index finger pointing upward, the sign of the Great Idea. "I have, as you Americans say, a deal for you. Let me measure your faith in your documents by the capacity of your purse." *Great,* she thought, *hit me where it hurts.* She thought about her purse, cheap and empty of money, sitting on the chair over against the wall.

"I offer you now *twenty thousand American dollars* to confess the forgery of these pages and call off our verdict. And, before you answer, should you choose to proceed, you shall have the further choice to accept a different, perhaps a lesser but still substantial amount, *if* you confess before the growing weight of the evidence. Thus is the gravity of truth laid on your decision. Wait until the end, and you will receive nothing but the judgment of our experts. Each will, in turn, pronounce his or her verdict, and we will see the results on the screen behind you—a red 'X' for fakery, a green check for possible authenticity, and a yellow question mark for ambiguity."

Glimpsing the monitor closest to her, Cadence saw three large images suddenly illuminated. They were blow ups of the three pages, identified as simply "Tolkien Note," "Manuscript I," and "Manuscript II."

"So it is up to you, Ms. Grande. The money . . . or the proofs?"

She thought about the upcoming auctioneer's cant in Topanga, the "Sold!" exclamation on the steps of The Mirkwood Forest. Three weeks ago, twenty thousand smackers would have bought her soul. Now . . .

"I . . ."

"Yes?"

". . . choose . . ."

The camera zoomed in as the barracuda leered.

". . . the proofs."

Betraying no reaction, Bois-Gilbert turned with a flourish. He raised his hand in the air like a conductor calling a vast orchestra to the opening note.

"Professeur Aranax, you may begin the verdicts."

A breathy female voice-over intoned the first judge's CV as a camera lingered on a grayed, somber-looking man at the judge's table. "Professor Aranax is the Lecard Professeur of Archival Science at l'Université de Cité in Marseilles. He specializes in analysis of the physical characteristics of documents—inks, methods of inscription, papers and the like . . ."

A translator came and sat by Cadence. She intoned in English as Professor Aranax, who used a lighted cigarette held twixt two fingers Euro-style as a sort of signature prop for his pronouncements, rambled on. His speech was interlaced with long, fatigued, smoke-plumed sighs of impatience.

"*Bonjour*, mademoiselle. We have been allowed, thus far, to examine only three of your documents. A pity, and no judgments there, but let's proceed. I speak first to the so-called Tolkien Note."

He consulted his notes.

"The initials JRRT appear accurate as compared to numerous authenticated standards. I have used the Fabian Method to identify the age of the inks. As you can see, the note consists, in its entirety, of three typed sentences preceded by the date of October nineteenth, nineteen seventy, and the letters 'NYC.' It is followed by the hand-scribbled initials 'JRRT.' The ink in the type is from a ribbon manufactured in nineteen sixty seven by Smith-Corona in Litchfield, Connecticut. It was not commercially distributed in Britain. The ink from the initials is from a BIC pen manufactured in Chicago, Illinois in nineteen sixty eight. The paper was manufactured at a mill in Georgia in the same year. Thus, the note is by my measure not provable as inauthentic. Be mindful, however, that my colleagues have other views. I provisionally give you that one, mademoiselle."

Bleep. On the big screen a green check mark went up by the Tolkien Note.

"Now, however, to the other two exhibits. They are puzzling. They are hand-written manuscripts, in what are probably different hands, and purporting to be, by your account, in a language called 'Elvish.' Such matters are of no importance to me for this analysis, as I have concentrated exclusively on the material in and on which they were written. That alone has led to interesting results. The gold standard for authentication of ancient documents is the Pressard-Lyons Gas Chromatograph. These pages have been subjected to analysis by this device. It identified three strange physical characteristics. They are on vellum, made from the washed, stretched, scraped and polished skin of young lambs. The result is a parchment that is quite durable and may be easily dated. The date for these examples is between 1200 and 1210 AD. The margin of error is plus or minus ten years. The lambs were from the variety *Aoriscadea*, found principally in England in that era. They were inscribed with a simple carbon ink made from lampblack of the willow tree mixed with a solution of gum. The soot in both cases is from a species of short heather bush unique to England and Wales and all but exterminated by the clearing of the lands in the period after 1000 AD. Such inks remain black for centuries, and their stability is quite superior to the iron-gall inks, which appeared in the next hundred years. Unsophisticated but effective."

"The age of the inks is consistent with that of the parchments. The inscriptions were made by quill pens, albeit ones with finer points and stylistic capability than is common to the era. But they are not anomalous. Most likely this means that the scribe or scribes   worked in the extensive production of written documents at a place that could afford the finest materials. Thus, I find the documents physically consistent, but obviously at odds with the described provenance of coming from Professor Tolkien. Perhaps he merely had possession of them. Nonetheless, they are simply what they are. Their meaning and import I leave for today to the tender mercies of my most scrupulous comrades. You pass this blow of the gauntlet!"

Bleep. Bleep. Two more green checks went up.

Bois-Gilbert swept to the center of the room. "Well, Cadence Grande, you pass the initial test. But, as you Americans say, 'Not so fast.' For it seems we are left with even more mystery. Few fakes pass the probing intensity of Madame Litton's eyes. She will assess the style and content of the documents. But first Cadence, I am going to make this more interesting for you. In this valise is the sum of *fifty thousand dollars.* A tidy sum. You may release *all* of the Tolkien Documents to us, take the money and walk out now. Or . . . you may stay to learn more of the truth."

With exaggerated ceremony, he placed the black leather bag on the floor before her. Cadence pegged it for what it was: a classic payoff bag from a prop house. Cameras be damned, her mouth was dry and she had to wet her lips. Buyer's remorse was heavy in her heart.

Bois-Gilbert waited. Patiently.

Cadence thought about the black T-shirted Topanga creeker, his warning of gifts-you-most-desire that would tempt her. She began. "I think . . ."

"Do you believe, Cadence?"

"I could . . ."

"Renounce this sham now and take the money!"

"But it's got to be . . ."

"Truth is a rare and flighty bird, often misidentified."

"I wish my grandfather . . ."

"Our wishes dictate much of our perceptions. But money is more constant, Cadence. A small fortune lies before you, within your grasp."

"I'll . . . stay."

"So shall it be!" He swooped away the bag. "Madame Litton, please present your proofs."

Cadence felt the ground go oozy under her straight-backed chair as the lady scientist leaned forward. She looked formidable, like a genius granddaughter of Madame Curie. Madame Litton carefully removed her spectacles and looked directly at Cadence before speaking.

"Cadence, something smells."

She adjusted her bifocals and started to read, but then looked up to deliver her lines right to the camera. She had an intense look that she held for an unnaturally long time.

"*Arêtes! Dix* minutes!"

Madame Litton knew the drill. Camera people relaxed. One camera person, a young black man, hung to the side. He was hoping to steal a guilt-revealing candid shot of Cadence that might secure the pay-bump he wanted when they sold the pilot.

She got up and went out to the lobby. She checked her phone. Mel had called several times. She punched the return button.

He answered. "Hello."

"I'm not signing anything or releasing anything."

"Okay, all right. I've been trying to call you back. Just slow down for a second and tell me what these translations say."

"What? Oh. Well, it's all about a female halfling named Ara. She's been on a helluva journey. I like her. You wouldn't."

"Don't be so testy. I still think I should send someone over to take custody of the originals. Let your friend work with copies."

"There's no way I'm giving the originals to anyone. For now, I trust Osley and no one else. Don't ask me why. I just do."

"These could be priceless."

She decided to deflect his control-freak energy. "Look Mel, I'm not sure these have anything to do with Tolkien's own works. All the pieces—wizards, rings, dragons, and little people—is the same old stuff. She could be Harry Potter's cousin, for all I can tell."

"Well, think of this. At least it's about a 'she.' Look, it's a good story and the documents seem pretty authentic."

"How do you know? Are you getting reports I don't know about, Mel?"

For the moment he seemed to be occupied with an office interruption.

"Look," she went on, "maybe the documents are old, but any physical connection to Tolkien is pretty much based on a scrap of paper found in the attic of a missing person—that and a few notes and translation pages he buried in a box at the Columbia archives. The language may not be anything we'll ever confirm. There's no Oxford

Dictionary of Elvish. And, get this, the supposed translations I'm reading are coming from the head of a fugitive druggie homeless man. He could just as well be inventing all of this as he goes along. And again, he's the *one* guy I trust. I mean, come on, Mel!"

"Yeah, but why take a chance? I'll send someone over to the hotel."

"No! All I want is to find out about my grandfather. Everything follows from that."

There was a pause.

"I can't help you there."

That was it for Cadence. She felt his indifference with the certainty of a door slamming in her face. "Thanks Mel, you've got a way."

"And so do you. Only yours is all tip-toey. I've got ways that make my stomach turn. I grieve over them at night with high-class scotch. They make money for my clients and they pay my bills. Yeah, you're damn right I got ways!"

"Good night. I'll call you if anything real turns up. Better yet, get the news from your spies. I feel like I'm being followed already."

"See what I mean!"

She hung up. Her usual method for ending calls with Mel. Now it was time to meet the dragon lady of document forensics.

* * *

When she went back into the studio the three pages lay on the table, displayed like specimens on squares of black velvet. Behind them, dreaded and venerable, sat Madame Litton. As she began to talk, it seemed she had a binary switch: short and pithy or long and verbose. She was in the second mode:

"As the vast and arcane knowledge of the physical sciences examines documents as nothing but sterile specimens, bereft of the yearnings of the author who presses ink—like the blood of human hope, onto the page in search of meaning and something that may endure—so does the proof thus far lack in the thought and motive of the author.

"I believe this, Ms. Grande, one should respect all writing, for even the forger impresses his work with aspirations, and while deserving of scorn and punishment, is never so loathsome as to go unrecognized in this vein. Thus do I respect my quarry."

Cadence could see Bois-Gilbert fidget. He knew this brand of self-indulgent speechifying was not made for prime time, even for the enlightened viewers in Paris. But the director cast him a winking nod that assured him Madame Gabby's rant would be duly edited in post-production.

"As Professor Aranax has confirmed," she continued, "the documents are what they are. Now, of course, comes the most crucial aspect. Where, if at all, do they fit in the context of Professor Tolkien's works? Are they related to them at all? As he so famously explained, his tales are, in a sense, *discovered*. Could it be that these are part of that same process? The blunt implacable truths are that the documents physically exist and they are very old. But of what import are the unknown words they contain?"

"The study of relationships of context and provenance is no longer a mere art. It is a forensic science guided by empirical principles and relations of handwriting, linguistics and patterns of words and markings. The text you have shown us . . ." she gestured at the three large images on the screen behind her. ". . . is alleged to be samples of a much more extensive collection. That, by the way, is something I would very much like to see." She looked over the top of her bifocals at Cadence.

Cadence didn't move a muscle.

Madame Litton continued, "But now, Mademoiselle Grande, we have a stunning surprise."

Bois-Gilbert perked up. At last some juice!

"As part of our tests, we have employed spectral imaging technology developed originally by your NASA to see through clouds. We use it to probe the minute depths of these historical pages. The different wavelengths reveal high-resolution images that are invisible to the naked eye. In this case, they indeed reveal a story."

Cadence was floored.

Bois-Gilbert broke in. "Mademoiselle Grande, are you aware of this?"

Madame Litton paused, nodding at Bois-Gilbert, and then peered at the camera. "As established by Professor Aranax, it seems probable that the scribes who authored these very documents had ample resources, including available parchment. Nonetheless, these parchments were second-hand. They are palimpsests—parchments that have been scrubbed down with pumice to a smooth unmarked surface, literally erased and overwritten with the indecipherable new text before us."

Bois-Gilbert said, "And what, Madame, lay underneath? What was erased?"

"This is the amazing part. Our examination has revealed an ancient text in Old English. It deals with dark alchemy. Something designed to empower evil. It describes a process whereby an Essence, probably quicksilver—what we know today as the element mercury—could be imbued with fantastic power and so order the affairs of mortal races. As described, it makes The Communist Manifesto and Mein Kampft and the Anarchists' Cookbook all look like Betty Crocker. And it gets more disturbing."

"How so, Madame Litton?"

"I share with you a translation of one section."

"It was written in a hurry, fitting for its tone."

Her eyes checked with Bois-Gilbert, then she re-adjusted her glasses and looked down her nose at the page before her:

"I am Oruntuft, now an old man. I was once a wizard, though none alive believe me. It matters not. I have little time. Here is my account for any that follow.

The Dark Elves have been shunned by their brethren, and in that event lies great danger for the world. Middle-earth is emptying out. Magic and spells may soon crest, but they are only the final wave of an eternally outgoing tide. All will dwindle. The Dark Elves cannot pass over the sea, and thus they devise their own exit."

"Know this adversary as I do, for I was once an enchanter of forest and wild places. These are Elves formidable and sly, of a design beyond mortals' reckoning. They are all but invisible. If they appear at all, it is fleeting, and often as vermin—foxes, badgers, weasels, and the like. Their sounds are as the wind to us, sometimes mimicking the whistle of a zephyr through trees. They cannot act by their own hand, but instead employ others to their service. Their grandiose and errant plot unfolds even now. The Dark Lord, whose power spreads and multiplies before our stunned eyes, was at first their unwitting puppet. By their sly hand, his alchemical skills soared into vast power, and his pride grew to audacity and conceit. He now has the power and ambition to become a fire that will devour the entire world. This struggle, seen by mortals only as a vast war, will rip a seam in this world. Into that will pour the Dark Elves and the residue of magic left to us. We will be left simpler and diminished, but perhaps fortunate. Woe be to the realm which they choose to enter."

"One final warning: their power lies in the Quintessence, distilled and altered from the Source, and hoarded by the Dark Lord. The rings, over which great struggles unfold, are but tokens of its power. It is the acid that will devour the theater stage that is the platform of all mortals. Destroy that, return it back to the Source, and you will save this world and the next. Ara must not fail. Her story must not fail.

They will destroy me soon, along with this account should they discover it."

Bois-Gilbert intervened. "A tale indeed, should anyone believe it. Now, madam, your conclusion."

"This now-hidden text, as originally written, was something to be hunted down and destroyed, or erased."

"My theory, unproven for now, is one of delicious irony: the indecipherable text that is visible may be a history of the victory or defeat of the Dark Elves. Which it is, we may never know."

Bois-Gilbert cut to the chase. "Madame, your verdict?"

"Alas, since on their face they are in what you call 'Elvish,' which we are unable to decipher, we are, I say with regret, stymied. The Old English substratum, of course, admits of a clear scientific judgment."

A long fermata followed.

"I am unable . . . to declare the documents . . . false."

Bleep. A big green check mark flashed on behind her.

Madame Litton now leaned forward, speaking directly to Cadence. "What is more important is where we go from here. There is a mystery waiting to be revealed. I have asked our esteemed host to . . . what's the expression? Ah yes, 'up the ante.' Present us, Mademoiselle Grande, with the full documentation, all the originals, for our scientific review. Let our television viewers get to the bottom of this mystery. We shall increase . . . your prize for their delivery to . . . the amount . . . of . . ." She turned to cue Bois-Gilbert, who once more produced the leather bag and finished her sentence in one practiced, masterful sweep, "*One hundred thousand dollars!*"

The bag plopped to the floor with a louder sound than before. *Bricks, probably,* Cadence mused. She involuntarily stared at it, letting the cameras around her sniff and feed with gluttonous ravening on what they most craved—a real, unalloyed display of the most fundamental human emotions, fear and greed.

She couldn't help thinking about giving in. *Give up the damn papers. The whole pile. Take the money and go home. Leave Ara to her own fate. Save your grandfather's estate, maybe look for other clues, but basically call it a day. He's gone, right?*

Time flowed around her like a river sweeping by a rock. It was getting to be too long. They needed an answer, a reaction. They needed dessert after the pig-out.

Bois-Gilbert had a nose for how to get what he wanted. Just a private little chat off-camera to allow the milking of this situation. He signaled the stage manager to call a break.

"*Suspendez!*"

The crew milled around and the panel of experts all began to smoke. Cadence could feel a second-hand smoke headache coming on.

She got up, swept the three pages into her bag and picked up her coat by the door. Then she walked out—out the studio door, out the steel door, and straight to the elevator.

"Hey!" A production assistant came running up, followed by Bois-Gilbert. "You cannot leave; we are in the middle of shooting!"

"I'm the one getting shot. Save your televised execution, Brian. You can finish the pilot with the footage you got. You know—me sweating, me biting my tongue, me looking guilty. Just finish her speech and edit it all together. Get to Mel for the details."

"But!"

"Oh," she paused as the elevator door opened. "I don't want the money."

She turned and entered the elevator. The doors closed as Brian stood there, his mouth widening into a big silent *Wait!*

She decided not to return directly to the Algonquin. Let Osley do his translating thing for a while. She found her way to a restaurant called Zimbabwe. She expected some Disney-like images of the Great Harare Temple, but found only a long room fronted with battered tables and chairs, and a kitchen in back that smelled like a village. She ordered a porridge-like vegetable soup. This is perfect, she thought, a break from all the over-wrought English-ness and French forensics hocus-pocus that were clinging to her like competing vines of ivy. With this bit of perspective, she pondered the thin dossier of credibility left to this whole affair. What proofs were there? The documents seemed to be related to Tolkien. Two sources, Les Inspecteurs and Mr. Bossier's little machine, said that some of them were indeed old. But what was the meaning of it all? Could she count on a few fragments of readable text and, thinnest of all, the translations of an eccentric homeless man—the only person in the world who knows Elf? What kind of case was that? There were, as she considered it, only two things that kept her indulgence going. Her grandfather, his fate hidden but exquisitely close in this maze, and Ara. Somehow they were connected. One would lead to the other. And wouldn't it be a damn shame if Ara were somehow real and then got erased, just for lack of belief?

She let all the pieces float around like lazy, deflating helium balloons. Today her mind could accept that perhaps the spider was just an illusion down in the dark and confusing subway tunnel. And the feeling of being stalked? Just a case of nerves built upon all this hoodoo pressure.

No matter how hard she tried, the prospect of going home in defeat seemed less like an option and more and more like an inevitable result. A few tantalizing tidbits but basically empty-handed. Her grandfather, Ara, the meaning of the documents, all untethered to any real evidence. Maybe Os was totally right, Mirkwood giveth and taketh away.

She couldn't just hang out here forever. She thought of the practicalities: money, job, getting a life. *Okay, I'll stay four more days. Till the anniversary of his disappearance. Halloween. Then I'll pick up and go home. I'll take the documents and Ara with me.*

She finished with an exotic tea and milk concoction and headed back to the Algonquin, ready to check on The Os.

Chapter 62

OCTOBER 27: 5:10 PM

———

She got to the hotel an hour later. She brought Osley up to speed on Les Inspecteurs—skipping the part about the money bag. She finished with Madame Litton's revelation of the recovered pleas of Oruntuft.

"So what do you think?" she asked.

"It could be important, or just a madman's metaphysical ramblings, erased because it deserved to be."

She looked at him; he was oblivious to the irony of who was a madman.

"For now, it all seems way behind the scenes. If you look at it hard enough, anything, everything becomes a conspiracy. People want to know what makes evil. And they won't hesitate to make something up. Dark Elves, Beelzebub, Cain, Moriarity, Dick Cheney, whatever. Who can tell what fuels the Dark Lord's ravening, or who controls whom? He is a monster, a world killer in his own right. I suspect Ara is going to have to deal with him. Which may tell us why he, someone, is trying to destroy her. In any case, it brings us back to her journey." He held up a sheath of yellow pages. "You see, after Ara left the cave she headed into some very . . . well, here, you read it."

Cadence took his hand-scrawled notes and read:

Within a half day after leaving the cave and finding the enchanted pool, which revealed a young woman's face, Ara came fully into the southern lands. It was a place fitfully wooded and beset by a wind that moaned tuneless, brooding, and fearful.

She came to a merestone, its great rock obelisk pointing upward like a craggy finger. Its exclamation seemed to have been long spent. She looked at its ruin and neglect. It seemed an emblem of some long-departed evil whose peculiar roots and seeds perhaps lay still in the soil.

A hundred yards further, beyond a grove of gnarled oaks of a kind she had never seen, she found greetings more current. Before her, flanking the meager trail, stood a phalanx of pikes. They were stove well into the ground and atop each of their upright lengths was a man's head. There they swayed like a congress of whispering kings contemplating with tragic masks all that passed before them. Whether originally friend or foe to those who so anointed them was a pointless conjecture. The message to followers of this trail was clear enough.

She went past the sentinels, toward a huge oak whose branches hung over the trail. Birds screeched and wheeled into the air. Suddenly she averted her eyes, covering them with both hands. It was too late. The image was already burned into her memory. A hobbit hung by its neck from a rope. It turned slowly in the breeze, the rope and limb creaking in a dirge. The victim was already the sport of carrion-birds. She began to cry, trying to push the image away, when she realized that on his belt, hung by its leather strap, was a green Sibhaet. The cap was just the sort she had given to her Amon! Her heart came to a stop, and before it could summon itself to beat again she opened her eyes and moved forward. She walked right up, nauseous and overwhelmed, and looked.

It wasn't him. This poor hobbit-traveler, his tale ended and never further to be told, was of the Fur-Shoulders clan. His soiled clothing was of another cut and color than would be worn by her love. The face was blackened and well-picked, but she knew.

She began to run, south down the trail, fleeing the images.

The next passage seemed to be Osley's own musings

There exists today, traveled by millions but its secret known to but a few, a multi-laned freeway overlaid on an older asphalt highway, which buries a macadamized road, under which is compressed a foundation of stone. This foundation once bore forth war and rejoicing, commerce and ideas, love and reunion, and the joy of setting forth on destinations unknown. Mad adventures. White line fever. The road that goes on and on.

His text then returned to the pathway of Ara. Leaning back with a sigh of just-let-it-flow, she entered once more into step with the heroine. Ara's journey, life, tale, and existence all seemed threatened by a gathering menace within and without these documents:

On a road once straight and unbroken, laid with stones and mortar so scrupulously correct that only a thousand years of neglect could finally break its order, Ara's path lay uneven and eroded. Each state of being, the perfect and the failed, bespoke the long decline that she knew by the myths served up by tumbled monument and ancient lay that accompanied her to this desperate track.

Hiding in a wild and extravagant thicket of bramble, only feet off the way, she watched through the thorns. Passing before her was the vanguard of an army in irregular array, bearded and braided and dirty, tromping in remnants of footwear. They encased unmatched parts, a left arm shield, perhaps a right shin guard, a breastplate, in dingy and broken cast-offs of metal plundered from the bloody armory of an unburied battlefield. More than a few heads were bandaged, some graced with only one seeing eye.

Slowly they tramped by. Low, ominous vibrations spread from their ponderous steps. Blades of broken swords wrapped at the hilt with uncured hides swung from tattooed arms. Others carried staves and bludgeons. Some bore lances tipped with blades hammered from broken shields, ferrying ribbons of tattered cloth that flared straight back in the cold wind.

This procession was followed by oxcarts drawn by human slaves in harness. Women and children with the mien of captives followed in loose order. The lame and the utterly rejected, unfit even to pull at the traces, drifted behind.

The army of refugees bore no banners. Its cause was survival, its heraldry the leavings of the victorious and the defeated alike, its prey the lost and wayward. It failed any test of allegiance. It had not the memory of any land, and it lacked the protection of any king, wizard, or liege. It tramped on, ill-equipped to resist any side in this great war.

Ara hugged the ground, quiet as the hare that trembled and shivered with her in the thorny nest, and she smelled the soft and pungent earth that remembered still the nameless age that built the road.

The next morning, the horizon showed a land fully at war. Distant plumes of smoke coiled to the skies, each leaning in perfect choreography with the chill wind freshening from the north.

She was a prisoner. She listened to her captor. "Each of those columns of smoke comes from one of our villages," said Thygol, leader of the Cerian Band of the Free. Ara leaned over again to look into the distance from their observation post in a high cluster of rocks. There was an unbroken line of armies and their support in movement on the roads far below. At a crossroads a great encampment sprawled like a black, tentacled fungus reaching across a ravaged landscape.

"They round up our innocents and take them away. Some say into the Black Gate for sport, slavery and . . . food for the man-orcs. Anything to humiliate and destroy us. The goblin camp will pay this night!"

She stared at him, eyeing the swirls of stained scars that festooned his arms, legs, face and hands. "May I make my own way to the south?"

"No. I have some things to tell you, and questions to ask. But first, be still." He watched closely, then whispered, "Since only our sentinel hounds detected you, I know your ability to move with stealth, as unseen as a passing breeze. Do you wish to see my enemy close up?"

Even as she took a deep breath and nodded, he was moving ahead of her down a ravine that cut the road beneath a small bridge. They huddled at the bridge and watched a trudging column approach. It was thick with effort, moving beasts and engines of war. As they waited beneath the timbers, they felt the beams strain and creak as the black army began its passage. All was clank of metal and thud of hard-ridden, lathering horses. Crack of whip at man and beast and orc alike. Complaint and anger moved with the cloud of dust that escorted the column.

With its passing, they crept to the very edge of the enemy camp. The general pall quickly gave way to night. A ceremony began. Dry lightning approached from the distance, the freshening breezes bringing the far-off smells of raindrops on dry soil. Camp bonfires were piled higher. Rising torrents of sparks shifted with the fickle winds. Around the fire, a thousand orcs bearing the sign of a flaming circle, ranks of men, and a hundred great drums pounding in unison. And then came the goblins. A procession of them, each impossibly tall, heads like huge living jack-o-lanterns that grimaced as they moved. They danced, a horrible shuffling remnant of the Days-Before, as six prisoners, bound and greased, were brought forth.

"They are ours," said Thygol. "We must get back and prepare to interrupt their party."

They made their way back along the ravine, through the rocks, and finally to a deep, dry vale. There waited a thousand armed men of mien and marking similar to Thygol. A lonely, blasted tree served as his headquarters. After a moment of dispensing instructions, he sat on a stump and gestured for her to sit likewise. "We will be ready in a few moments. Let's talk while we can. Why do you journey here, alone save for the raptor that circles far above our bowshot? Are you lost in search of Lyfthelm, the gate that cannot be passed?"

"I search for one with whom I began this journey. We were separated. He has since traveled by paths I know not. Sparse clues, some the castaways of a wizard, told me to come this way. I continue on the chance that I may cross his path."

"Wizards once came and went hereabouts, but they have forsaken this land. Or perhaps it was their parting curses that left us to this."

"Tell me, Thygol why don't you submit? Join the forces of the Dark One? That has to be better than resisting and being slaughtered."

"That counsel we have debated many times. Even their company may not be too great a price to pay for life. Or so some say. But I cannot. I know not the right of it. The plain fact is . . . they are, simply and completely, the enemy of my blood. We have fought them since the times of our grandfathers, when we came into these lands as nomads herding the aurochs. And even since the times of our ancestors, a race with armor and bright helms that came to live with us in the smoky world of the Before Time. Now much runs as great storms across the steppes. One approaches even now, and will herald our attack. An omen to our liking."

A plate of simple food was brought to Ara. As she ate, he continued. "At first we doubted you, just for your orc-like size. And even appearances must be twice studied. There are no doubt spells about . . ."

Thygol's sentence was cut short by a bolt of lightning that cracked open the sky, momentarily revealing huge breakers of clouds rolling forth in purple waves. The thunder that followed, hard and swift, pressed them down with its pounding force. The moment is now!" he ordered, "Gather with us the beasts of vengeance so they may feed on our spoils."

At the stern direction of his hand signals, Ara followed Thygol. They were headed toward the goblin camp. The rain swept down on them as thunder rolled overhead in hellish beats. Flashes of light revealed jagged images of men jostling, intent on havoc and destruction.

Ara remembered the final approach only as imagery torn by relentless, windswept rain. She recalled the angled rents of flame and sparks that had been the fires of the camp. The roar of the storm and the peals of thunder masked the clank of metal, creak of leather, and boot treads of a thousand armed men. They lined the wide stone road that ran alongside the camp, waiting for Thygol's signal.

"Young halfling?"

She came close to his side. He bent and said "Hogal, my aide, shall take you now by this western road. Three leagues from here opens the last free lands of this corner of the world.

With the token of my word, you may take respite there. But beware. Prince Thorn and his advisors in that realm survive by audacity and irreverence. They parlay for neutrality with the minions of the Source even as they make jest of him. Dangerous business, this toying. Like dancing in the set jaws of a cave bear trap. Go now, and may luck accompany you on your journey. You may need it more than most."

She thanked him and turned as Hogal beckoned for her to make haste in moving down the line and unto the road. They had just cleared the flank of the Cerian warriors when, from a nearby jumble of boulders, there sprang a great torch. Its light revealed the unforgettable, leering pumpkin face of a fully grown goblin. Two feet wide at the head, twice a man's height at the shoulders, he roared past them. Another six followed as the wish-wash of torch sounds mixed with the storm. A great war cry rose up from the Cerians as they moved on the camp. Ara and Hogal ran into the night.

She never learned which force, each to the other embittered enemies of the blood, prevailed that night.

Dawn two days hence found the storm clearing as they approached the great gates of the castle that rested on the shoulder of the Black Lands and protected young Prince Thorn. The man-size door within one of the gates opened, and Hogal spoke to a guard. The guard gazed past his shoulder, his eyes settling on Ara.

Her escort returned to her, "You may enter and take refuge as the guest of the Prince. I leave you now, lest my entry violate the neutrality of this place. I return to what may survive of my band. Goodspeed!"

"Goodspeed to you and your people." replied Ara, as she thought of the unprotected, silly borders of her own people. No contrivance of politic or force of arms was likely to hold back the enemy that surely approached her village by now.

But my fate and my errand are, for now, here, she thought as she entered the door to Thornland, where intrigue and plots within plots swirled in a cauldron of double meanings.

Cadence reread the last passage. *Plots within plots. Sounds familiar,* she thought. *I'm with you, girl. With you to the end.*

After a moment she looked around the room, the piles of scribbled pages, the strange Elvish documents, the ex-drug king biting his lip as he turned a page with the circular key held upside down. She shook her head ever so slightly and blew out a breath. She spoke out loud to the air, "Professor Tolkien, did you have *any* idea how this would turn out?"

Chapter 63

INKLINGS VII

———

"So Tollers, you're off to America?"

"Sshh, few know of this, save those who plot around me!"

Laughter.

"In fact, no one but my Edith and my travel agent, one of whom apparently is your general informant—and now anyone within earshot."

"Well, it's always a small world, and this business with the inscription on the rock has to be the puzzler—or has the mail got it wrong again?"

"On the condition of privacy, I'll be in New York City for a few days to examine an interesting document that has turned up. An Old English text stuffed, quite out of place, in the Thornberry Collection at King's College or, as they persist in calling it in rude defiance of dear George II, Columbia University. They've offered to help pay my way and insist on the importance of my personal review. So what the . . ."

"Yes, but what about the rock?"

"Well, I suppose 'Elvish runes' on a two-ton rock native only to the island of Britain, found buried in an undisturbed barrow, or 'mound' as they say there in Connecticut, and carbon-dated to 1000 AD is a bit of a strange affair. If they wish to catch up with me in the city, I shall oblige them."

"Aye, and we'll give you ale as wages for your report."

"I'm afraid, on that topic, I don't wish to over-commit. I carry another errand to America, one founded on a deep urge to tidy things up. Un-bear some burdens. This journey is part of that, I suppose, especially the un-bearing part."

"Now what burden could you have?"

Long pause.

"I would rather not speak of that quite yet, or perhaps ever. I am thinking of leaving some papers in America where they may be better off than here."

"Rubbish! Papers? They should be here, at Merton!"

"These papers are, I've decided, best left at a distance. They will not be still."

"What is that? They move around?"

"Worse, Charles, you missed one of our prior discussions about these. As I said then, they are a trove of Elvish texts. Unfortunately they have a kind of voice—almost as if some ... demonic energy was reaching through them."

"I would make light of it Tollers, but you seem genuinely troubled."

"This little I will say. Like my dwarves, I delved too deep. Something stirred. Documents unbidden, and more mysterious than I first imagined, came to me some years ago."

Here there is a longer pause.

"But enough! Wish me well. I hope to return to sit at this very oak table that we have so profoundly educated these many years."

"Tollers, I won't let this go just yet. You are on edge about this."

"More than I can say. But then, we are all haunted as old men. Swirlings of unease hover about our elder years, when there is more in the past than in the future."

"Well, I wish you safe passage, good fortune, and a quick return. We all value your presence. "

"Thank you, Richard. And I feel the same about each of you. Even you, Jack!"

"Hah, you rump!"

A pause. Background sounds. The tape ends.

Chapter 64

OCTOBER 29: 7:15 AM

—

Standing in the lobby in the Algonquin there was a grandfather clock, a staid Edwardian sentinel with a gleaming brass pendulum. It had faithfully kept its watch, ticking and tocking and chiming, since the grand opening of the hotel over a century earlier. If one listened closely, the arc of its pendulum to the right sounded a distinctive clunk. Like Osley, there was a hitch in the old man's gait.

Cadence sat in the lobby across from the embered fireplace and listened. She couldn't help it. The swinging pendulum signaled to her the remaining days of her own watch. Two more days and her stay would end with a long, black train ride back across the fading autumn of America. She had done all she could for a thin skein of hard information and no results on her search for Jess.

She checked on Osley at seven. He was already fully at it, scribbling, hunched over on his desk, uncommunicative and haggard. As she started to slip out the door, she paused and looked back.

There was no doubt about it. The man's circuits were frying. Soon, perhaps before she left this town, he would crash. He wouldn't blow. He would just frizzle out in a fitful spray of sparks and sputters and stinky blue smoke, like that old Emporia mixer her mom once had.

As she poised there, still looking, she saw more. Her inner sketch-artist framed him in charcoal, his hand holding up his head, the desk lamp spilling soft chiaroscuro light on his face and the curious papers spread before him. The imagined sketch was titled. *Too Full of Secrets*.

She would give him another hour and then go up and insist that he take a break. Until then, she would sit down here and commiserate with the clunking grandfather clock.

Across from her, on what she guessed was his own reserved chair, Heraclitus nestled. The hotel mascot regarded her with passing interest, then blinked and turned away, a rude dismissal that seemed to say, "Dog-Person."

She watched him and thought of Graymalkin, the cat named by the strange creeker man in Topanga. That seemed ages ago.

Heraclitus was right, though. Growing up, her household did favor dogs. Nonetheless, the neighborhood felines secretly parlayed with the canines to achieve first an uneasy truce, and then entry into the house.

The terms were direct: dog sovereignty and primacy in all things that matter, food, attention from the humans, first passage down hallways, and guaranteed periodic and unexplained absence of all cats.

Of course, right from the start, the cats breached these terms as often as they honored them. Once they were in, they were in. Like many a sovereign that bought such peace, the dogs rued their bargain and saw their position steadily erode over time. At a notable low point, one really dumb family dog got relegated to sleeping outside on the porch as the cats gloated at him from inside the windows.

One day her father brought home an ocelot kitten acquired through some carnie black-market conniving. It had never seen a South American jungle. It grew to fifteen pounds of amiable human companion and pure dynamite-wild tomcat to others. It took no part of dog-cat treaties. Then one day it disappeared. They never saw it again, but for years there thrived in the canyon obvious crossbreeds whose ferocity, size, feral instincts, and hybrid vigor began a reign of terror over local dogs. These cats were a rare, standup match for squads of coyotes that had grown fat on tabby dining.

The topic of "Cats in History" came to Cadence as a paper in her high school World Civ class. She discovered the Great Cat Disappearance of the Dark Ages. As Christianity evolved, cats were viewed as demonic agents. They were rounded up and dispatched as surely and cruelly as Romans undid Christians. Tortured, eviscerated, burned alive, thrown from towers, cats became all but extinct in the growing towns and feudal kingdoms of Europe. And at just that time, rats and mice found the two requisites of vermin paradise: easy food and, *ssshh*, N-O C-A-T-S.

A plague of rats came, carrying a cargo of fleas, ushering in the Black Death.

So, after experiencing a 40 percent mortality, people lost interest in persecuting cats. They become tolerated, albeit with lingering suspicion, and things got better.

Cadence read these echoes in Shakespeare, who, keen to our basest human superstitions, had cat-loving witches and suspect cats to have fun with. He knew the deep disquiet occasioned when cats go forth lean and high-shouldered, posing as black-paper cutouts arched on picket fences before a full moon. He knew our suspicion that cats slither through cracks in brambled gates to congregate in unholy rituals, there to flow as outlandish shapes malevolent beyond fantasy. Thus do cats conspire with evil where none can bear witness.

As if reading her thoughts and impatient with them, Heraclitus looked at the fire and blinked. The fire erupted in green and purple flames. Cadence looked at him and said with raised eyebrows, "Did you do that?" Heraclitus yawned and licked his paws. But in that blink Cadence thought she saw a multi-hued fire of warning.

Whatever it was, she would heed it. She got up and took the elevator. When she got to Osley's room, she knocked. He let her in. He was holding two pages in front of him, gazing first at one then the other. He looked like a man who had rolled the bones and seen his death sign.

"Os, are you okay?"

He didn't seem to hear her.

"Tell me what you're seeing, or I'm going to bonk you with this lamp!"

He put the papers down solemnly and looked over at her. "We're in trouble, Cadence. More than I thought." Then he again stared at the pages. "I'm going to read you the first one. It's short. It's in beautiful Elvish, by someone that seems to have the power to see at least some of the future. I may stumble a little, but here goes:

The fate of the tale of the hobbitess lies at a time and place distant even to my eyes. The world changes now with breathless speed, and much will be sundered from our influence and concern. But this I have seen: Holder will be the Hunted. Alansis!

"I think," he interrupted, "that last word is a colloquialism, an imprecation like a 'God Be With Them' sort of phrase. So then it finishes with: 'May they sense the monsters that follow.'"

"What is *that* about?"

"It's a warning beacon. Buried right in these texts. Putting the documents back together with the translation key just upped their power to attract these, what did it say, monsters. I think this is real. This isn't shadows in the subway or a fairytale or a video game. There may be no second chance, no restart."

"So what's the other page say?"

"Here, you read it. It's a note, probably from Tolkien, probably never sent. It was paper-clipped to the piece I just read."

She picked up the page. It was undated, but in the familiar scrawl of the Good Professor Tolkien:

Jack,

Your point on the lectures is well taken, though some may not take it well. We shall see. As we discussed last Tuesday at the Bird and Baby, the approach of All Hallows Eve increasingly fills me with a dread that isn't about Hollywood monsters.

It's about something both ancient and unsettling. I have found a translation tool for much of this trove of documents. Use of it has unnerved me, for I fear that some, at least, of this Elvish must be the work of Dark Elves that make merry with caprice and ill-luck to others. It may be far worse; they may seek to forge a portal into our own time, into our very midst. The crux is this. The intensity of this damnable pile increases every fall, peaking on All Hallows, that ancient pre-Christian time, like the rise of some marauding fen-beast from the wastes below the keep.

Let's hope I am just imagining things again. More when next we see each other.

JRRT

As she put down the page, he said out loud, "Don't you see? *We're* the Holder. *We're* the Hunted!" He was losing it. She could almost smell the fried rotors in that old Emporia mixer.

She decided to stop the madness, at least temporarily. "Os, you're at burnout. Put down the paper and pen. Stand up and walk out the door. We're going to sit down and have a nice, civil lunch. As usual. On Mel."

They convened in the Round Table Room. The same waiter fussed agreeably over them. They munched on designer bread and didn't begin to talk until the soup came. She waited until they agreed that the bean and ham soup was quite nice.

"Os, what do you think is going on? You *know* something."

As usual, he deflected. "I can tell you the big picture as I see it, and then the situation we are in right now. And, Cadence . . ."

"What?"

"After I say my piece, will you agree to return home, go somewhere? Leave?"

"I'll think about it. Now tell me."

Chilled forks carried by unobtrusive hands came in from the side, along with icy plates of asparagus spears.

Osley began, "Here it is. All boiled down. Let's indulge the assumption, one held by the majority of people—including Professor Tolkien in his own heart-of-hearts—that all sorts of fantastical things and places do exist, right here in our midst. Indulge, also, the thought that maybe there was once an embodiment of power, a wand or ring or pointy hat or something like that. The name of it—'Bind'—keeps coming up. Maybe it was evil. But for every ounce of malevolence there was an equal measure of magic bound to it. With its loss went much of the magical power of our little corner of the universe. The twinkle went out."

He took a swig of iced tea to bolster his pace. "This left a vacuum. The loss of this object *did* cost the world much. Into that vacuum, evil once again crept—not the evil that bears a capital letter in its name, but evil that is diffuse and cannot be wholly cornered or pegged down. It lives everywhere and compounds the petty and tawdry into horrors that are unnamed and often unnoticed. You can see this everywhere."

"Try right here. Give me a for-example."

He held up both hands to form an oval window the size of a football. "Fume, Narcross, the Great Eye that sees all . . ." then his right hand closed to a smaller circle, ". . . has been replaced by the little eyes. First TVs, then computer screens, now these phones. They are everywhere. They communicate to all. They speak the perfect hidden language of the pedestrian evil that is the lot of the Fourth Age. This manuscript, and all those who consort with it, are in danger. Someone is uncomfortable with it, not merely for the tale it tells, but with its very physical existence!"

"You think this Elvish keeps some of the original twinkle alive?"

"Most certainly, even though the hands that wrote it will never return."

"But Ara, her story and her existence?"

"I'm afraid, whatever we do, her days may be numbered."

"Why?"

"Do you not suspect the answer? You are the steward of this document. Surely you must see something. Speak up!"

"Well, I've thought for a long time . . ."

"Sometimes Cadence, behind everything there is a question. It may be so hidden we never see it. It may be at the edge of our mind. It may be a whisper on the sea sounds floating up through the long spirals of a shell held to our ear. But not this question. This one is clear. Tell me the blunt question."

"Okay. What happened to the women?"

"Precisely! There must have been a process of censorship. Tolkien was discovering a myth. But myths don't stay still. Something wants to erase the story of this once-famous heroine."

"All right, Inspector Os, who is the culprit?"

Osley looked stymied.

Cadence picked up the inquiry, "Okay, let's look at what's evident. This manuscript maybe, just maybe, fills in something from the Middle Ages, or Middle-earth or Middle-somewhere. Take your pick. Or out of the mind of some writer."

"Or some translator. Is that it? You think I'm making this up?"

"No, Os. You're a type, just not that type." Cadence didn't signal her lingering doubt.

Osley kept on rolling. "Look, Ara was a mover and a shaker. She must have played a role far bigger than we have read so far. *That's* the key!"

Cadence thought for a second. "Fine, I'll play. We're here eating. Let's set the rest of the table, a mystery-story dinner to find the culprit. Who are the guests?"

"Well, not the authors of these manuscripts. They could have been participants in the tale, their descendants, or, more likely, historians in later ages. But that's missing the point."

"Ara?"

"Yes, at our own end of the table, at the head, is Aragranessa, the famous halfling, daughter of Achen. And you, my dear Cadence, are the Steward and the Holder. You sit at her right hand. Now who shall be our other guests?"

"Professor Tolkien?"

"Ah, yes. Our special guest. Just to stir things up. Let's seat him in the middle, on Ara's left, so he needn't have to take sides."

"And you, Mr. Osley, where's your seat?"

"Consider me the *maître d'*, standing and attending exclusively to this fine table."

Cadence laughed for a second, then paused. "My grandfather?"

"Yes, Jess. A place set in his honor. Alas, the chair is empty. My dear, you must accept that he probably won't show. I'm sure he is, well, somewhere, with important things to do." Osley briskly moved on, finding a new question. "What of your friend, Mel?"

"Yeah, he should be a guest."

Osley put a finger over his lips in mock concentration. "I think he is . . . the bus boy. An errand runner for forces as yet unseen."

"He doesn't have bosses. He's an independent agent."

"There's no such thing, my dear. Everyone works for the man. Even I, a derelict of the street, serve some masters. Like the gangs that let me come and go unmolested."

"He doesn't act that way. He acts like all his angles are his own."

"Well, for all his façade, he may yet serve as your tool. I know I'm ungrateful. Look at this French dip and julienne fries he's paying for. Anyway, as to his 'bosses,' I know of them, or at least of their kind, and can surmise the rest."

Osley sat back, savoring the last morsels of *roastbif* and *au jus*. "Name a name. Who had long-term access to these writings? Someone that lives a long time."

She thought she was in tune with him. "The Elves."

"No. They left and knew they were leaving. Their writings are but a glowing artifact, priceless and radioactive with their power, but not really *them*."

"Wizards?"

"Close, but no cigar yet. Someone who had a particular dislike for

Ara and her story."

"So we're left with only one other suspect, Sherlock."

"Precisely, Dr. Watson."

They both leaned over and whispered simultaneously, "The Dark Lord!"

Osley gave a grand gesture. "Then seat him at the far end of the table and order his favorite meal."

"Anything that's not on fire. No Baked Alaska!"

He grew solemn. "You know, Cadence your thing with fire. You can't take vengeance on a thing. Fire, wind, day and night. They are just dumb things."

She listened but, deep down, she didn't buy it. Fire was *the* enemy. A monster that stalked her. If she could, if she had the courage, she would one day confront that monster.

Os kept on talking. "Okay, the fun's over. At stake here is nothing less than the fate of each of the guests, good Professor Tolkien excepted, bless his soul. That means you, Cadence. You cannot stay. The more you seek to help Ara, the greater your danger. You must leave tomorrow."

"All right, I'll go. Just as soon as you finish the translations. There aren't many pages left. Don't you want to know what happens to Ara?"

"I've learned to be cautious about seeking our fates. But so be it. And for you, no wandering around alone in the subway. If something bad happens before I finish, you must leave immediately. Agreed?"

"Check."

BOOK VII
THE TREE OF TALES

We lack the word for it, the lost tale that takes us into a deepening place where no steps can be retraced.

~ Timothy Lessons

The human word is but a battered timbale, beating out patterns fit for making bears dance.

~ Mel Chricter, paraphrasing Gustave Flaubert

Words are, of course, the most powerful drug used by mankind.

~ Rudyard Kipling

Chapter 65

DETERIORATION

From Silicon Blog, Timespan:
Loss is the handmaiden of human archives. Ancient documents come and go. In the end, like most things, all are doomed. The culprit isn't a dark overseer or a conspiracy. It's water, the great solvent that allows us to exist, and which dissolves all.

Other natural forces, of course, also intervene to destroy our archives. Fire, earthquake, mold, and insects do their fair share.

Our digital information is eroding from cosmic rays, solar flares, and quantum indeterminacy far faster than stone carvings fade. This is not to mention technical obsolescence and the stranding of vast content in archaic hardware and unlockable digital codes.

Alongside these, human folly is never to be underestimated. Things just *get lost*. Or consider that the greatest library ever assembled, containing originals from the hand of Aristotle and other giants of intellect and art, was at Alexandria in Egypt. It was put to the torch by an overzealous bishop. There you go.

All we have from the past is a declining base of information. The point of the lesson is humility. Never trust a history to be the only story.

Chapter 66

INKLINGS VIII

———

The sounds of greetings and bustling, overcoats thrown aside, and chairs pulled up.

"Tollers! You return looking hale and refreshed. Was it absence from our witticisms that was so good to you?"

"Yes, that and more. Since you ask, I do feel invigorated since my little adventure to America. Relieved and unburdened, I should say. Able to look forward and see farther all at once."

"Well, we missed you. Our topic last week was the de-foresting in the highlands. Another old-growth grove once protected on an estate. All under the axe."

"But first, a toast to your safe return."

Cries of "Hear, hear!" An amiable clanking of beer glasses.

"Alas, to trees, men are infernal. They fulminate and pollute and heat the world. They hack away whole forests. For this, why should trees see men as better than orc-kind?"

"You may think that a tragedy, as one of many you have seen, but is not the loss, once perceived, at least the affirmation that it was? What if it never existed at all?"

"Ansel, your mind is a wind-up toy, all whirrs and wheels but not sure where it's going."

"I'll go with Ansel. Better than knowing and have no whirrs to get there!"

Groans around the table.

"You should listen to Tollers and Jack. They never stop testing the boundaries between the real and what you Victorians call the Realm of Faerie, the mind-state of imagined worlds. They would say there's just one step, onto a road, perhaps through a hidden gate, and you're there. Have I got that right?"

"Pretty much. There are indeed many worlds. This one is ours. But it's all a tale and tales change backwards and forwards. Life is an interweaving of tales lived, thought, told, heard, scoffed, and believed. A summing up. Or a hiving off. Ah, but here's the thing damnable and divine. It's in the seams that the truth lies. That which intricately binds it all together in ways we can't imagine how to imagine. That's the wonder. That someone, something, somehow knows and tells our tales. We hope so, but we can't be sure. So we have to tell them ourselves, all the time. Backward and forward and reassembled. Unravel a tale and much more may be lost and gained than just some quaint fiction. There is no end, and all tales are one, and people should never forget this."

"Unless the worst of fates overtakes a tale."

"And what might that be?"

"Erasure."

A moment of silence.

"I suppose you're right. Life comes and goes. Death is common to all, and our fate is to be stalwart before it. But elimination from the very Tree of Tales?"

"As if you never existed?"

"You're right, that is a terrible fate for a story."

"Tollers, you're quiet for one who prides himself on retrieving stories."

"Yes, well, I've seen forces that would inflict such a cruelty and seek, as you put it, to erase a tale and its heroine."

"I thought you didn't find many true heroines in your discovered mythology?"

"Aye, but there was one, and she may yet survive if my strategy works."

"And what is that?"

"Let her, and her tale, hide for long a while."

"But who will bear witness for her, if not you?"

"That role was denied to me by forces I shall not speak of here. But you are right, nothing exists except by witness. And to a great tale we all bear witness, and the meter of truth is told in our hearts. Who then is the last and the first witness, between which all else bounces?"

"Bounce that extra pint over here."

"So are you going to complete your other writings?"

"I doubt it. My major books are done. Even those would have been fated to oblivion had Stan Unwin, my editor—you've all met him—had not given his ten year old son the first manuscript. Raynor gave it a jolly good review. There's a bit of seams and joinery for you. Anyway, there are other steps to take, perhaps the children for the father. Perhaps for others."

"But what about this mysterious cache of writings?"

"My work on those documents of antiquity, delivered to me in the night long ago, has ceased. I long suspected their most recent history, that they were the very documents buried away by S.I.S. before the war. My doorstep was but one stop in the long, desperate journey of these fragments. Now they have traveled on. I've rid myself of them. They are across the sea, in America. They exist and they have a destiny, but not one in which I play a further role. They are the lost tale we just spoke of, whose heroine some would erase forever. And yet . . . by the valiant hand of some witness as yet unknown, that heroine may still survive. I hope so."

Chapter 67

OCTOBER 30: 7:30 AM

—

The next morning, Cadence was cruising the shelves at Orkney's Grocery on West 55th Street. Her hands moved briskly, selecting edibles for Osley. She planned to keep him fueled up and going strong to avoid any more fried circuits. She had resolved to quietly finish out the string of this trip. Tomorrow she would gather up (she hoped) the last of the translations and pack her bags and go. Nice and simple.

The "dinner party" exercise had been entertaining, and it let Osley blow off some steam, but the only real thing left to do was nurture him along until he tracked Ara's destiny down to the end, if it even existed. The manuscripts might peter out, her story just another path lost in Mirkwood.

As she glided along the store shelves she even began to rationalize the confusing—her mind had already downgraded it from *horrifying*—events in the subway tunnel. A track fire. Okay, scary but natural. The rest? Well, darkness like that *is* like a theater screen. Your mind can throw whatever it wants up there. Her reasoning had only one sticking point: why a spider?

If she were to imagine elemental monsters in the dark, they wouldn't include a spider. Maybe Morlocks or bubble-headed Martian invaders, or the veiny-headed mutant under-people from *Beneath the Planet of the Apes*. She could even conjure up the Mud Men, oozing out of sticky cave walls in *Flash Gordon*.

But the spider? *That* came from somebody else's imagination.

And Ara, the wavering vision in the pool? She should have followed her instincts and done something right there. Now she would have to see where Ara's written trail led. Most likely nowhere. Cadence felt again that need—beyond admiration, beyond role model—to connect with Ara. She felt their crossed destinies were already entwining.

She carried her basket up to the counter. Bacon and egg burritos and double-stuffed Oreos would keep Osley focused this morning, like a bloodhound on Ara's trail. She left the store, turned the corner, and stopped.

In the midst of a flowing crowd, a man stood still and stared at her. His look was not the moon-eyed hunger for recognition typical of the don't-make-eye-contact-with-them cast-offs of the city.

She stood still for maybe three seconds to confirm the gut-raw certainty that this was real. It was a man, but what she really saw was the unwavering focus of a wolf looking out from the eyeholes of a man-mask.

The look was exacting, the binocular stare of the predator that detects distance by the centimeter, that reads bearing, alertness, and fear like beloved poetry.

This particular rendition of a derelict human was different from the wild taxicab driver of her first night in the city. This . . . *thing* was inexplicably fat, almost corpulent. He had hair that looked like moldy hay. He was dressed in a filthy blanket, billowy and bearing witness to hygienic breakdown. But the eyes revealed that it was all a costume. They said here lies a true monster, a thing sent, a creature capable of surprising quickness that was unstoppably coming for her.

She turned and clambered aboard a waiting bus. Anything to get away, anywhere. The door whooshed shut, and the bus rumbled into traffic. She watched the large man dwindle on the street corner, turning to study the colored route map of the city bus system.

Cadence dug in her purse for Bossier Thornton's card.

His phone rolled to voice mail. She paused then said, "Uh, Bossier, this is Cadence Grande. From the other day. Could you please give me a call? It's . . . urgent." She left her number and hung up.

After exiting the bus a dozen blocks from where she saw the strange man, Cadence walked, directionless as a disturbed ant. She finally stopped looking over her shoulder and bumping into people. She sat, exhausted, in a space amidst a long row of lunch-eaters perched on the edge of a fountain. Through a high cleft in skyscrapers, sunshine shot down, creating a narrow hall of bright light. The light and the crowd made her feel safer.

She regulated her breathing and tried to assemble the jigsaw puzzle. The careful reasoning of a few moments ago was out the window now.

Her cell phone rang: 213 area code. L.A. Absolutely the last person she wanted to talk to. She listened until the last ring and took the call.

As usual, no hello.

"Cadence, Mel. Listen. Great news. I've received an offer for the manuscripts. Through another agent. Anonymous client. It's a sale. A hundred grand for all the documents. As is, just the way they are. That's a hell of a deal! Especially when you have nothing, really. They could take all this away with a court order."

"Who said anything was for sale?" Her anger momentarily pushed back the tide of fear.

"Cadence, that's my job. I'm not a potted plant here. What did you expect me to do?"

"I guess be like you are, like everyone else. Bois-Gilbert put a lot of money on the table just for spilling my guts on French TV. Even more for letting them have all the documents."

"And?"

"I knew you'd say that. Just that way. It would help pay off my grandfather's debts. But it would sell out what he left. I said no. I don't trust them."

"You're right. Bois-Gilbert is an idiot. I was just playing there. Here's a real deal. Maybe we should counter. Keep some rights, sure. But how am I gonna help you if—"

"Tell them no."

"Look, if we don't act now, there could be no residuals for anyone."

"Jesus, Mel."

"Come on kid. This—"

Click. Man, that felt good.

The phone rang again. She thought it would be Mel, but it wasn't. She answered.

"Cadence? Bossier Thornton."

"Oh yes, thank you! It's been . . . very hectic . . . since I saw you."

"You sound nervous. You all right?"

"Well, to be honest I've been worried that someone is following me, a stalker type. He's gone now. I just thought I'd call you."

"You did the right thing. Are you in danger now?"

"Oh no, I'm in a public place, corner of 6th Avenue and 52nd Street."

"Okay, good. Just be careful and stay with the crowd in public places. Are you sure you're safe?"

"Yes. I'm all right. Thank you for calling back."

"I can be there if you want . . ."

"No, I'm all right for now."

"Call me if he shows up again. It was nice meeting you the other day. Did you find out anything else about your documents?"

"More that I would have imagined. These seem to be very interesting to a lot of people. I appreciate your help. The library just told me to come on over. I hope I didn't intrude."

"Not at all. I'm only there once a week. Sort of a volunteer thing. NYPD lets me do it so I can practice with their gizmos."

They said good-bye. She felt better, knowing there was a decent, slightly oddball, sane person to turn to. The Algonquin was only a few blocks away. She decided not to trouble Osley with her latest scare. He needed to concentrate.

Unfortunately, waiting for her when she checked on him in his room, was Osley the Wrecked. He looked like he'd slept, if at all, on a rack of nails.

"Osley, what gives?"

"I haven't slept so well. Looking at, working with these documents, after so long. At first they seemed like old, interesting friends. But then I felt their spell. A siren song that is turning into a maddening screech in my head."

She set out the food from Orkney's and made him stop and eat.

After a while he recovered to ragged good spirits. He resumed his work. His eye and hand once again became a relentless team as the pile of translations grew. Pieces of a time and a world emerged, some from the middle and some from the beginning, but none telling of Ara. He gave her a report. "Her fate seems lost. A fate of its own kind." Then he resumed with dogged intensity until, without explanation he just stood up.

She looked up just in time to see him leaving. "Where are you going?"

"Out for a bit. Meet me at two this afternoon at our library table. I found her trail. The name is spelled differently, but the story fits. The pages are on the desk."

"But . . ." The door closed.

Cadence thought about Osley's mercurial tendencies. If he were a playing card, he'd be the One-Eyed Jack. She needed to see the other side of that face. Before she left, she would find the moment to corner him and flip that face card over.

She stacked a foursome of Oreos and picked up the scrawled yellow sheets. As she munched and smiled, she felt as if she sat right next to Ara as they blended into the torch-lit Great Room of Prince Thorn's castle:

"Hwat!" announced the crier, and the banquet began. Threescore gentlemen and ladies, amidst laden tables and bustling servants, spread down the axis of the vaulted room.

Ara, seated at a side table of minor guests—most appearing to be wanderers and emissaries from distant lands—tried to match the nobles with the wild tales and earnest warnings given to her by Lady Bregan. In those few hours since she entered the castle, the Lady had provided a short oral history of the realm. "A place where, by the patronage of my father the king, the arts of verse and tale have grown strong and bold. It is such great irony," she sat at the main feasting table and looked past Ara, "that we huddle here next to the Great Blackness and yet are allowed to idle and make merry. So long as we muster no army, and pretend to neutrality, we are overlooked."

"And where is your king?" Ara asked.

"Gone. Perhaps lost to us." She paused. "We have neither tidings from him nor demand of ransom. In our world, that means ill. Even were he dead by someone's hand, they would seek our treasury as bounty for the return of his bones."

She shook her head and looked to her hands, as if they were little dead birds. "We warned and pleaded, but he said that the arts are vital, even as woe and fear spread through the lands. He was asked to come to the north. Our troupe would perform for a great stipend. We last heard that he was en route, entering a domain at the far end of the Northern Road. Then all has been silence. Each visitor we politely interrogate. Have you heard any news that may help?"

Ara knew a truth here, and decided to reveal it. "My lady, you have been most gracious, and I must tell you that there are no longer any domains north of the few villages that huddle where that road ends to a mere track. I have been there not two months ago, and I know those lands by my own reckoning. If the king journeyed there, he was misled for some ill purpose. But of his specific journey, I know not."

"This confirms the worst. I fear I have no father and we have no king."

Ara realized the sadness she had now given in return for kindness and hospitality.

"I am sorry, my lady. Perhaps he journeys here by paths unplanned, as many are forced in these days. But what of the Prince?"

"Prince Thorn," said the lady, "though he is my brother and is dear to me, has fallen under the influence of a certain dissolute and disreputable knight. They drink and revel and squander the thin coin of safety by which we survive. We are on a precipice, and they jest and pimp the emissaries of the very hand that can destroy us."

Ara, sensing that this hole was getting deeper and that the ear was the best instrument of policy, nodded with empathy. Lady Bregan then revealed more, "I must tell you, that there have been questions, raised at our borders, subtle inquiries, as to whether any of your size and appearance has ever entered our realm. Thus far, we have had the luxury of truth and could say 'None.' Now that you are here, I know not what our policy will be."

Ara was totally alert now. "Were the questioners of fell mien? Wraiths on black horses?"

"I saw them not, but their inquiry was relayed to the prince as one more signal of our failing sovereignty. He no doubt will speak to you."

"When?"

"Perhaps now, as the banquet begins. Do you hear the cry?"

Ara listened as a voice from somewhere on high, echoed through the castle.

"To sup and be merry! To sup!"

The lady whispered, "Be attuned. Much will unfold as the evening grows. We are a nation that lives in theater and, I fear, at times cannot tell our own lives from the tales we spin. Let us go."

The prince, fair and tall, stood and eyed the room while roasted meats and root vegetables on steaming platters were served. His eyes stopped on Ara, as if he knew much of her already, and then moved on.

As of one great voice on cue, the assemblage of actors roared, "Hail to the Prince!"

"Hail, yes!" answered Thorn. Ara watched his careless swagger.

After a further filling of flagons, he stood.

"Our first toast," he said in voice loud and clear, "even before we hear a tale, is to our king, Lady Bregan's and my father, and to his safe return!"

The entire hall duly stood and, to a loud "Here, here!" all drank their flagons to the last drop. Other toasts followed in close order. A noble of dubious lineage but definite girth rose, unsteady as if that were his steady state, and intoned in voice deep, resonant, and intoxicated.

"Now the sun is in her retreat. A fair hot wench, but not of our time. Our mistress is the moon, under whose countenance we do plot. We that live as good neighbors to the Dour Eye should do him a favor. He is too downcast and graceless. 'Cheer up!' I tell him, by his minions' ears. 'Come and drink with us, and let us conspire together to wind a bawdy tale, and much redeeming will be done. What of passion, and lust, and gentle grace, and the good gift of irony at our fate? Or do you, Red Eye, know only of the hunger to complete your darkness and then blow out the torch?' There's no irony there, and perhaps that's the crux. His minions may yet visit us this eve, and we shall once more give it a try. My prince."

At this, the servants all grabbed the torches from the walls and with wet skins extinguished them all at once. Only the flickering light from the huge hearth illuminated the hall, now washed in yellow glow. Four players in outlandish minstrel costumes vaulted into the hall, one from each direction, and landed as one, each upright on a separate table. They spoke in turn, back and forth, full and clear across the hall, the crowd turning to each voice:

Cadence stopped reading for a moment. The day had grown to noon. She would have to go to the Library soon. She settled in the overstuffed chair and picked up where she left off:

"A tale to be told at every feast! And of a good tale none can foretell where it may lead. For each is but a setting out on a road that may reveal a hidden gate."

"Our tale is of our times."

"*A Prospect of This Middling Earth* is our humble title."

"Though its very prospect may deal with its end."

"An end to be commenced on strands far remote, with furious close of butchery!"

"With great losings and findings. As of our noble King, lost in lands beyond our horizon."

"And findings of a token precious, that does awake great strategies and cause this very age to shake and convulse with self-inflicted change!"

"As the lantern doth signify that night has fallen, so this token, despite its scale as but a coin pence in the hand, tells us that a night has come from which this age may not awake."

"A changing, clear as the sudden smell of fall over the northern horizon, now comes to us."

"And for our age, as certainly as we ask the sky each for ourselves, what will be left, and who shall care?"

"Will any tattered pennant, carried forth today with great bravery and purpose, flutter in the world to follow?"

"Will any word, or name of place, or keep of tumbled stone survive to speak of us to the ages to come?"

"This we ask, as your humble entertainers of this night. We who are but students in this land of word-masters the equals of whom do not strive in Middle-earth. Will even our august tales live on?"

"Will some quaint word, like a lost artifact lifted from the farmer's plowed row, give birth to the story from whence it came?"

"Fools, all of us! For with this coming whirlwind there shall survive but tatters."

"*Be silent!*" thundered Prince Thorn as he suddenly appeared standing on another table. A hushed silence settled on the crowd. "My troupe has set well the stage, but they do lament the final fall of a blade that may yet be turned to the side."

The guests were rapt as he continued. "I shall now unclasp a secret book. And with your quick-conceiving discontents I shall share a matter dangerous and deep."

Unveiling it from a robe, and undoing its brass hinge, he held forth a heavy, leather-bound book, its pages thick and warped, and its writing dark on the yellowed vellum as from a heavy hand.

"Minstrels, you despair too quickly. Yes, we are not of warlike powers. Yes, we are surrounded. But we are armed nonetheless. This is our weapon!"

The book he extended and slowly turned so that all could see.

"Its edge is subtle, yet it cuts. It stays both our enemies—the lesser and the greater. The Dark Lord, and Time."

He knelt and placed the book solemnly on the table on which he stood. Rising, he spoke again.

"Now, I know well that among us tonight is some disguised ear, bought by the Great Evil that borders our land. Listen then, ears of friend and foe. I shall address the lesser enemy first. We raise no arms, nor hinder his armies crossing our sovereign; indeed, we tithe our share to the coffers that feed his war machine. Granted, rings have been neither offered nor accepted, and thus the unbreakable Vow of Protection does not exist between our realms. Nonetheless we sleep well, for our treaty among men stands intact. The terms of our contract of peace we honor in full to thee."

There it is again, Cadence thought, *this "vow" that was highlighted in the Wraith-poem.*

Thorn's arms were outspread.

"Champion of the Oppressed, Ringmaker, Spell-Holder over Mighty Kings, Adversary, Familiar of Evil, Eye of Menace, Bastard Spawn of all Witches," he hesitated for a dramatic count. "Master of the Source. Supplicant of . . . Bind."

His arms and his voice dropped.

"And for our contract, we enjoy the security that allows us to mock him and ridicule his many names. But mark this! Our survival is not cowardly groveling. It is not so that we may babble strong language to the wind but not to the face of our enemies. We do not mutter low-breathed in fear.

"Our weapons are the words we speak. Remember this: words are acts. They cut like sand in a windstorm. They break the rocks of untruth like the seepage of water and spread of roots into crevices. Winter and summer they break the rock. Thus did my father, the king, take pilgrimage to spread words of hope against our mighty neighbors. May the king return to us!"

He became silent. The hearth light flickered off wall and ceiling, glowed faces upturned and flashed glints of light in many eyes.

"In a moment, I shall tell you one part of a famous story, a saga crucial to remember in our time. For, of the great kings that fell before the false songs of the rings, this one, this man, this king, defied the overture of the Dark Confuser. A hero he should be, the greatest of men whose glory-song and exploits should be recounted at hearthside a thousand years from now. His should be a tale to rival brigand dragonslayers and trove-thieves. His name should be honored in the Great Lays.

"But without our voice, and the ear and the memory it serves, his tale will pass. Few of these lays, I fear, will survive the unraveling of this age. Perchance some fragment may survive in some vault to be unearthed and seen with fresh eyes. Our greatest enemy, then, lurks not on our borders, but here. There are no curse-names for it. It is simpler. It is time.

"Against this, the greater foe, we yet have some power. For words and tales may float on its great tide. The very commerce of our kingdom is our tales. These, some of them at least, may live on.

"Now note this well. Should they ever be stilled, with their bridle cut so that none may ride them, then will the world turn to ash. That fate is not of our time, for we bequeath both well-cobbled roads and secret gates to all that may walk in the continuing story. We live here by the tales of forebears and the bonds of our stories. So long as the tale is freely told, it and we may live on."

Cadence put the pages away and leaned back.

Her chair might as well have been an open boat with no oars. She couldn't help feeling a rush of waters, with Ara sweeping downriver to some treacherous cataracts.

And to mix metaphors, a clock, complete with tightly coiled springs of fate, was still ticking.

Her phone rang. Damn! It was Mel.

Chapter 68

OCTOBER 30: 4:18 PM

———

"The coincidence of fear is no coincidence."

Osley was talking too loud. She shouldn't have told him about the call with Mel. He paced in front of the usual table at the Columbia Library, ignoring his own warnings of caution.

"First your grandfather. No, first Professor Tolkien. Then you. Then me. Now even him, this Mel guy!"

Cadence was thinking, replaying the call from Mel in her head. He was no longer being the deal guy. His voice had a quiver in it, like a blade rested against his throat.

"Cadence," he had said, "don't hang up this time, please. Just listen. I have received another offer. It's one you . . . we . . . all should take *very seriously*. I have it . . . written down right here. I'll read it slowly so I won't mis-say it. It's like a riddle."

"O-kaay, Mr. Agent Man."

"Don't fool around. I'm not kidding. Here's what it says." He took a breath and began:

> Ara's tale entire
> Scroll, bit, branch, and twig
> Barters Sharpener's return
> And taleholder's life.
> Refusal forfeits all:
> Taleholder, guildtrader, sharpener, fool.

"Is that it?" Cadence asked.

"Yeah."

"Who sent this?"

"I don't know. It's on plain paper, from an agent who got his AGA card only last week. Someone I've never met. It's a swap. The references to forfeiture are clear enough."

She now turned to Osley. "That's all he said. So now even Mel is wigging out. Someone got to him. I told him no. If you're up for it, let's get back to the hotel and get on with the translation. Before I do anything else I want to know what finally happened to Ara."

As they rode together in the subway, standing and jostled like bobble-dolls, Cadence looked at their reflection in the windows. They were moving in tandem, almost identical in posture and reaction.

Suddenly Osley broke into her reverie, speaking over the subway noise, oblivious to those around them. "It is not like elves to record a story of men and halflings. Such petty, low tragedies. Why not turtles and insects? We are but a footnote to their history. But here . . . here they have chronicled, at least from what remnants we have, many pieces of her story. Did the endurance of her tale bear import for them?"

Cadence ignored the other strap-hangers looking and listening to them. "I hope she was important to everyone."

"One other thing has me worried, Cadence. This 'Vow,' the one that keeps cropping up. The Elvish phrasing is deeply laden with meaning— alternatives and nuances and depths I don't understand. It can also mean, roughly, 'Secret Gate.'"

She listened as the train whooshed down the tunnel, as if hurtling them blindly into some hungry maw.

They spent the rest of the day secluded at the Algonquin, blending into the dreamtime of Mirkwood. Osley was parsing the texts, consulting the key, laying pages in different orders. Once "into" a page, it might be seconds or hours before he emerged.

The events in Thornland continued as Osley, in a far distant realm, toiled and scribbled to reveal them, his eyes bleary from exhaustion:

Lamps had been relit and merriment returned to the Great Hall in Thornland. The prince continued his speech.

"If food's to be well served, it must be accompanied by the spice of a tale, that well-munching is married with well-thinking.

Eat fully then, and listen."

Fresh platters, piled high with dripping slabs of meat, came to each table. Knives carved. Hands reached, dodging knives. Mouths chomped and slurped.

"This tale . . . but a remnant in our time, reminds us of the seething and loss that the span of but a few lifetimes, much less a thousand winters, lays upon our lore. Be not unsettled, for this saga is clear enough and fit for telling still in our time.

"Much of it is buried beneath the words to a children's song. You remember, of course:

> Black king from desert hot.
> Journeys to ice where summer's not
> Offered ring of magic and power
> Spurns the lot for life's flower.
> Baladyne! Baladyne!
> Tell him no and go.
> No and go.

"And here is what remains of the greatest tale of our time. To begin, you must see yourself as he did. I will take you to that world through his eyes. You are from the farthest south, a king not unlike the noble lord in whose hall we relax this eve. But his hall is a flowing, great-walled tent, four spans tall. It stands this night erected in a copse of trees, an oasis. Those trees are palms, and they bear the fruit called dates. Sweeter than blossom honey. You, that king, are restless. Once on a ride in the desert, on a clear night when the stars are of such number and brilliance as to drive a man crazy with the most profound of questions, you see on the far northern horizon—a wonder. A vision distant even in legend. Never before seen in living memory. A faraway, swaying curtain of light. It flows like the walls of a great tent in a celestial breeze.

"You resolve on this very night to see this great curtain in the sky. Nay, to strip it from the heavens, and bring it back, and form your royal tent from its glowing folds!

"Your house has ruled well, and your seitch is in order. As did our lord here in Thornland, you leave your realm.

"A thousand regal warriors form your train. Horses and strange horse-headed but back-humped beasts bear northward."

The princess turned to Ara and whispered, "I wish we still had adventures and such heroes. Perhaps some may arise, for dread times have arrived. It is surprising, as you know, who arises in such moments. The meek and small may, if necessary, carry the day beyond men who bluster wildly while they inventory their armory, but do not show so much as a shield on the field of battle."

"Now let us journey with this questing king whose travel has endured for years," the prince continued. "The great curtain returns at times in the northern fringe of the sky, ever uncertain, and now only in the ever-colder winters. Great seas and mountains wild you cross. You yet rule your kingdom by daily sending southward one of your men, each with the day's orders as you see fit. Though you have received back little notice, you send forth your daily orders for your kingdom with confidence. The timing of the future date harvest, the allocation of water from each well, the comings and goings of the tradesmen.

"In time, your letters of governance have outstripped the numbers of your men, and you at last stand with but twenty stalwart warriors on a hill overlooking a deep gorge filled with the sea and there a rough village hove close to a row of long boats. Rivers of ice descend down to the water and the peaks are snow-full even in the fullness of summer. It is by your accounting night, but the sun hovers still above the horizon. You descend to parley and gain passage on to the north.

"As fall's stealthy approach quickens, you are on the sea bearing northward. You and your men are hosted on one of the long boats of that village, piloted by men as foul of smell as they are red of hair. They know the sea through the very soles of their feet, steady on the heaving and slippery deck.

"A fog has engulfed you for weeks. It lifts. Relentless, deep, black swells menace the boat. Spume sprays high and drenches you. It freezes to your beard and face. The sun is cold and sharp. Thrydwulf, your captain, barks and points northward. At the crest of the next wave, you see what no man of your race has seen, a great blink of whiteness on the horizon. A span of ice as far as you can see, off every point of the bow.

"Here at last you have come to find the bounds of a failing world.

"And that very night, amidst the blue glow of floating mountains of ice, and crystalline shimmering on the wave crests, you see the Great Curtain unfurled full overhead and enveloping the world from end to end. A wonder of weaving so full and glorious as only to be made by gods! You covet this tapestry, but no tassel, no thread reaches down by which to grasp it.

"Now! Let us drink to this brave king, for more adventures in store has he for you as his companions in this tale."

And to a person in that hall, they swilled all that was before them, so that servants had to be chastened to replenish their drink. This done, the tale continued.

"The weight of his three years of absence and his failed errand now press full on Baladyne's mind. The boat is turned and haste made back to the village in the sea-gorge. Beasts of the sea hunt them daily. White bears stand on the ice and watch them pass, huge-tusked creatures gape and fall into the waters at their passing. Others run smooth, swift and happy in the waves before their bow. Thrydwulf and his crew are eager to return to their village.

"As you approach the land, the village appears empty. A lone pilgrim, tall and dark, stands on the shore.

"Standing at last on the land, Thrydwulf retires quickly to the village. He finds his people frightened at the appearance, that very morning, of this stranger. The man is humble in clothing, with a black cloak and long black beard. By his left side heels a fearsome dog. He approaches Baladyne as a cold wind seethes along the rocky strand. He speaks, 'Have you enough of this need-fare, great king?'

"Baladyne replies with grace, even as this beggar forthrightly addresses him. 'Tell me, stranger, of your heritage, your state, and your needs, and I may assist you. This at least, before we speak of my business.'

"'I am The Offer,' the pilgrim says. 'The hand that proposes two gifts. To you, a small ring, beautiful and of subtle craft, but less esteemed than those you now wear, to grace some finger of your noble hand. And perhaps of more interest to you, as boon to that ring-gift, a full swath of the great curtain in the sky that you seek. Its colors are changeable and your seitch it would grace through the councils of your descendants, through all of time.'

"'You speak of an offer, but not the offerer,' says Baladyne. 'By whose leave do you speak?'

"'By a king also of the southern realms, yet not so far as your liege lands. A monarch who values his relations with other great leaders, one who seeks to unite in common discourse all the tribes of men. These he favors over the races of elves and the pointless grubbings of dwarves.'

"'Of the elves and dwarves I know not. Of the other tribes of men I have learned much. Their common discourse is a good I would not bet my horses on.'

"'Perhaps if their kings had the kinship of common rings. Each equal in power, prestige, and none beholden to any. Accept and wear this token, great King of the South, and be part of the League of the Fourth Age. Accept also this sample of the celestial cloth.'

"And with that, the stranger unwrapped from an oilskin a bolt of multi-hued cloth. He handed it forth and Baladyne held it. In the fading grey light of this desolate beach, it shone of its own light and promised a wonder of colors.

"He then handed it back. 'Give your lord my thanks. I must say no. If not offered by the sky, which formed it, then the cloth must be reserved for the tents of powers greater than I. This yard is wondrous, but of its provenance I cannot be sure unless I pull its thread from the heavens by my own hand. The ring, likewise, is a token that I must not accept. Nothing in my land is freely given, save hospitality. And you are an itinerant on this desolate shore no less than I, for I see no roof or meal in your wares.'

"The stranger looked angry but hid it behind a smile. 'Perhaps, my lord, I can mitigate your just concerns.'

"Baladyne nodded to the pilgrim. 'I wish your liege well in his quest of fellowship with the many tribes of men.'

"Now," Thorn continued, "the dramatic turn of this tale. I

speak of Baladynes's betrayal, capture, and imprisonment. Of his refusal to wear the ring. Of his mighty words and his escape. These we will tell once again, waiting only one more course of draughts and meaty slabs to be consumed."

A train of torch-bearers entered to further lighten the room for food and merriment. Bustling and talk began, laughter peeled forth, and then a noise and great tumult.

A herald entered the hall, sweaty and stained from travel, and shouted forth, "Lord, the truce is broken! The Black Army spills forth across our borders. A column bent on war approaches not three leagues from here!"

Cadence thought that the abrupt ending of Baladyne's story, including the wonder of a piece of the very fabric of the Aurora Borealis, would probably remain forever untold. She picked up another page Osley had placed next to his own scrawls. It was a companion piece written in English:

The arts of Thornland were not altogether thespian in character, for their absent King had also collected an impressive treasure of crystals and perfumes. These were stored in a vault room deep beneath the castle. In that vault fell the first stroke of the failure of policy that caused this realm to vanish completely.

There was rumor, repeated but unheeded, that the Dark Lord was at displeasure with Prince Thorn.

Even as the feast was at its merriest in the Great Hall above, there came a servant warning of intrusion into the sealed vault. No matter whether the intruder be some lost animal or thieves, the personal guard of Prince Thorn was dispatched in train to oust the invader.

The storeroom was festooned with delicate hangings, exquisite crystalline urns, and vases filled with a thousand carefully collected and preserved scents that were organized in a warren of intricate wooden shelves.

The first guard, girded in armor and advancing into the darkened room, discovered a waiting array of orcs. Lancalan it was that raised his small torch and beheld the fell insignia of the Source.

More guards crowded into the vault, and the flickering light of their torches soon discovered the two bands—men and orcs—nigh a span apart and staring each unto the other. Stillness held sway as the pine smoke from the torches drifted upwards, and they paid each other the quiet regard of mortal enemies. The air played a subtle mixture of scents, some disturbingly clear, the work of many years of the king's collecting.

An orc captain turned to grunt a command and was skewered by a well-thrown pike. The room exploded with a confused and fragrant violence. Men and orcs hacked and cut, shelves tipped like great oaks and came crashing in eruptions of broken vases and strange liquids. Men screamed. Orcs howled in rage.

And around them swirled the many scents of death.

Cadence looked at the centuries-old paper, redolent with mustiness. She put her nose to its surface and inhaled deeply, searching for the exotic, faintly fabulous perfume of ancient truth.

Chapter 69

OCTOBER 30: 10:15 PM

—

As if by the turning of a cogwheel, Halloween ratcheted closer. After retiring all the original documents to the valise in its under-the-bed hiding place in her room, Cadence and Osley went to his room and reviewed his day's output of scribbled translations. She consumed the revelations silently, her mind running as fast as possible to catch up with Ara. Somewhere far ahead, the hobbitess was already ensnared by her fate. The first page confirmed the danger:

> With the approach of the Black Army, the feast at Thornland Keep ended in torch-lit disorder. Stunned guests, at once well-drunk, well-fed, and fearful, upset laden tables and overturned sloshing flagons as they panicked toward the exits.
>
> The prince's leave was neither asked nor given. He stood atop a table, feet astride, in dazed wonder. Had his policies now utterly failed? The jests and mockery lay at the very foot of the Evil One. Had they finally yielded intolerance? Doom was marching with iron tread into his tiny realm. Should he escape with his court? His jocund counselor, besotted with wine and ill-advising, was nowhere to be seen. His thespians alone stood like he on the other table tops, balanced as if walking on the choppy waters of pandemonium, each awaiting direction for their play-acting.
>
> He marked the simultaneous appearance of a halfling and the coming of this fate.

Ara was ushered by the princess to a side door. "Descend here. Stay true to the main steps. Come at length to the outer walls and strike southwest for the steep hills. These found the deep mountains you will see. Trust your skills and luck. To stay or chance other direction is folly. I fear our small sovereignty is now closed on all sides save the black wall of the mountains themselves. Now, flee!"

Within the hour Ara was afoot on the rough night road. It was painted in the dim starlight that silhouetted soaring barriers of black that seemed to her not unlike rotten tooth stumps. One sound only she dared, a high, quick whistle as she exited the keep. The signal summoned the hawk, which had been awaiting her call on the battlement.

By morning a descending swirl of clouds obscured the approaching mountains.

What substituted for Ara's day was a failed sun that never fully dispelled the darkness. A deepening fog shuttered away all sense of time, so that the moving sun, perhaps dancing merrily on the cloud tops far above, was but a guttering candle in the icy drizzle. She felt the water seep through the wool of her cloak and wriggle down her neck. She stumbled on as the road once again fell to disrepair. It labored on, and then cut straight down into a dell.

It led straight into a camp of guards, as surprised as she. They were sodden, disheveled, and reticent, as if no one should be on this sorry road to interrupt the laxness of their vigilance. They were men pressed into service by fear, looking always for a truce before trouble. Their look was unusually troubled, as if they weren't sure who they were guarding for or from. Now they were unsure whether Ara was not an emissary of their command. They stood uneasily, off-balance, without weapons at hand, as uncertain as men standing on thin ice far from shore.

Ara put her hand beneath her cloak as if to the hilt of a weapon, and said, "Forget your swords! Place that food here and retreat to the far side of the stream. Now!'

Without a word the nearest one, straw-haired and jack-o-lantern-toothed, placed a sack on the trail and the three of them backed away. Their swords and bodkins lay haphazard on the rocks.

She grabbed the food sack and a scabbard knife, amenable as a sword, and marched up the bank on the far side.

The hawk flew in short segments, a bellwether for her in the fine mist. Soon a huge black squirrel began to follow her, tree to tree, chiding endlessly. It was the only sound in the saturated stillness.

She wondered if it was in league with her enemies, a scout of some vast, innumerable legion that had spread forth to find her and her kind. Its excitement on such a day as this did not bode well. Any other squirrel would be busy counting nuts and adding to its stores.

The squirrel looked down at her from a high limb, switching and sweeping a proud black tail silvered at the tip. Its eyes were dark pearls of hatred. It chided once more, hurling personal and angry squirrel insults from its impregnable perch.

Suddenly it was gone. Multicolored leaves exploded in the air as a tumult of talons and fur and flapping wings disturbed the treetops. The hawk had seized it and was now swooping low and away, its wings beating full and loud and strong, gaining altitude with each sweep. The obnoxious squirrel was clutched head forward, as raptors will, with its long bushy tail trailing behind.

She continued on the road. With luck the squirrel had not relayed to others a message of this diminutive stranger on this unlikely path.

Through a long night that became a frost-rimmed dawn, Ara fled southwest along an ascending forest road.

For a brief moment the horizon cleared and an almost full moon, its prow cutting waves of glowing cloud, announced that little time remained to find her Amon.

The road degraded to oak brush path, then rocky track, and finally to intertwined, twisting trails of high mountain sheep. Even this tenuous way she abandoned in her fear of pursuit. She trusted her instincts and so left little mark to show her route, and moved all but unseen.

Unaided by magic cloak or spell, Ara possessed facility for stealth that had allowed her in times past to observe undetected the passage of elves and even once to watch their secret council.

From treacherous screes to shady defiles to barren stone expanse, she moved haltingly, so that no sentinel's glance from above would detect her movement. Autumn-dried highbush berries served for food, drip-springs for water.

Three days carried her to a ledge just below the summit. At its top, a hundred steps above, sat the hawk, its wings splayed for balance and its feathers rustling in the cold gusts rushing over the crest.

Looking back and far below, she saw, vibrant in the streaks of new dawn's light, smoke coiling up from the sacked keep of Thornland.

She rested and then clambered to the top.

The hawk faced west, and her eyes, weeping from the ripping cold of the West Wind, followed its gaze to a valley of ghostly ruin. Laid out steeply below her and spreading to the mountain walls bordering dimly in the distance, writhed a land in agony. Fumaroles, smoke holes, fissures of steam, slag heaps, burning pyres, all was pustuled and packed in a miserable expanse bisected by a long road. On that path scurried the ant-like commerce of war. Encampments scattered randomly. Great battle flags of purple and green and sickly yellow undulated slowly in the smoke-thick air. Dead center smoldered a volcanic cone. A road zigzagged up to a black maw that glowed and pulsed like a questing eye. A land of ruin feeding an empire of the enemy on the march.

Whether it be the first step or the last, all journeys are defined by a moment when one can go forward or retreat. Ara studied the land until the thin soup of light failed and she beheld an expanse of black velvet dotted with tiny fires more numerous than the stars she knew she would never see again.

She stepped forward and entered the land of the Dark Lord.

Chapter 70

OCTOBER 31: 12:42 AM

Cadence put down the last yellow sheet and looked at the bed stand clock. It rationed out barely audible tocks, struggling to hold back what now seemed a breakneck, falling-forward stumble of time.

She looked over at Osley, and he nodded back to her. Each knew what day it was. Each could sense in the quiet of early morning a coming change that compressed all the trick or treats, jack-o'-lanterns, and Batman and Sarah Palin costumes into the crude ox-horn funnel of an ancient time. A time that might spill forth shadows capering in silhouette before a roaring night fire high and wild, sparks intermingling with stars, fed by the rich fat of a meat-harvest bone pile. A time when walls dissolved and secret gates swung open, creaking and untouched. A moment of passage and peril.

The tocks slowed and stopped for a full second.

Ka-ching!

They both jumped. *Ching! . . . ka-chi—* Cadence pounced on the room phone and ripped the receiver from its cradle.

"Hello!"

She listened, then spoke. "Yes. That's me . . . what? . . . what! . . . yes! I'll be right there."

Osley stood up, his hands out, palms up. A big "what?" expression on his face.

"Someone broke into my room!"

She stopped mid-stride and they both yelled out loud, "The valise!"

She ran for the door, closing it with a muffled, "Osley, don't go anywhere!"

* * *

Sixty seconds earlier, Barren had stood, deeply frustrated. He regarded with a calm and deadly focus the entirety of an overturned hotel room. *It has to be here!* Pillow feathers still floated in the air. A few graced his shoulders and Mohawked hair. A set of drawers from the dresser lay in a shambled heap. The dresser itself was tipped over on its back. Mattresses were askew on the bed frame. Perhaps he had been too intense in his search, too noisy. *Too careless,* he thought. The insistent knocks on the door continued. "Ms. Grande? Hello, Ms. Grande?" The meddlesome authority of this inn was now present and interference— unwanted, unsought, but here—had to be reckoned with. If he could not find the documents he would take care of them otherwise. As for their troublesome steward, Cadence, well, he had tarried too long. There were other emissaries here he could call on, oh yes.

He took from his pocket a simple little box, the size of a coffee cup. In it was a crumple of paper, well soaked in a foul incendiary brew of Barren's own devising. He put it on the floor of the closet, then put a small candle on it and lit the wick. He walked to the door, released the security latch and waited. The key card lock clicked to green and the door swept open even as he hid behind it.

Framed in the doorway was the officious manager of the Algonquin, his hand poised to knock and his eyes like saucers. To his side hovered his sidekick, the hotel detective. "Ms. Grande?" the manager muttered as his neck craned forward and side to side to better see the destruction.

They stepped into the room, stunned by the disaster, as if an angry tornado had compressed its entire energy into the suite. The manager picked up the phone up off the floor. His eyes wide, cataloging the destruction, he handed the phone to the detective. "Call her other room, 608, and tell her this room has been broken into." They were oblivious to the barely audible swish of Barren departing the room.

The little candle flame flickered, almost down to the crumple of paper.

* * *

It took Cadence one minute to sprint to the elevator and go to the fourteenth floor. As the door started to open, everything happened at once. The doors froze half-open. The elevator gagged to a stop. She piled out of the doors into a smoke-tinged hallway.

A siren klaxoned an idiotic up-and-down warble followed by three whoops, again and again. To her right, alternating red and white strobes flashed above the open stairwell door. The hotel manager and another man were in the stairwell, coughing and yelling for her to follow. A sign above the door suddenly lit up and flashed a sequence of "Emergency Exit" and "Do Not Use the Elevator." On and on. The ceiling sprinkler system was dribbling and coughing, ready to burst, but somehow stalled. Her room door was open, and from it the fire, fresh and hot, was having its way. It receded for a moment, keeping one tongue on the door frame as if inviting her in for a visit. She knew that in there lurked the smoking, apocalyptic man, the one that took her father. Now it wanted her. Ara, the surviving remnants of her existence stashed in the valise, was in there too.

Cadence could see from her angle, as smoke rolled out and flames danced around, that the room had been ransacked. Maybe this Barren had already found the valise. Maybe he had simply left his fiery cohort to cover his tracks and entertain pesky Cadence. But maybe not.

She had never stepped *toward* a big fire in her life. She quailed, adrenaline dumping thousand-volt juice into her raw senses and psyche. The reptilian complex of her brain was screaming over and over. *Run!* was all could she hear.

And she found herself at the threshold to the room.

The fire sucked back and she saw him, black and smoldering, almost grinning, with eyes that showed the flickering red flames behind him. He waited for her in the back of the room on the far side of the bed. He made a polite and almost courtly gesture, bowing with his arm outstretched.

The mockery of it all! She lunged forward, knowing that staying low was her only chance. She lizard-crawled to the bed. She squirmed underneath as far as she could, feeling the temperature that here seemed wretchedly, falsely cool. Her feet, sticking out from under the bed frame, felt like they were on a charcoal grill. She stretched for the area behind the headboard, groping, trying to feel anything. Nothing. Just empty space. The heat was growing exponentially. She felt like a stick figure made of tinder wood. In any second she would burst into flame, pirouetting as she rolled on the floor.

Then her fingers felt a leather corner. She pushed herself, reached further. Her hand was getting a grasp when the bed moved. The fireman was lifting off the mattresses to get her! The bed frame skooched away from the wall and the valise fell into her hands. It was hot and seeped smoke, but it felt intact. She wriggled back, crawdadded out from under the bed, and made for the door.

She looked back and the smoking thing lifted a flaming Hotelier Quality Sleep-Eze King Size Double Coil Top Mattress and flung it across the room like a feather pillow. The thing roared and jumped up and was now astride the bed, standing on the bottom mattress. It was pissed off and coming for her.

Cadence got to her feet and ran blindly. She slammed into the hallway wall and got up and ran for the flashing exit sign. She clutched the valise with both arms, for all the world looking like a somewhat cooked version of the lost Professor Tolkien wandering through Idlewild Airport so many years ago. Behind her, a blast of fire surged out of the room.

She made it three more steps before the ceiling sprinklers came on full force. Then, underneath the sirens, came sounds of elemental struggle, fire and water, heat and cold, vapor and steam, rage and deluge.

Her clothes emitted a smoky steam, her hair felt frizzled, but as she bounded down through the acrid air in the stairwell, she was exultant. She had faced up to her deepest fear, and she was alive. She had beaten the smoldering man! She also had saved Ara, now safely tucked away in the valise under her arm.

Now she was going to get some final answers

She disregarded the evacuation alarms and returned by the stairs to Osley's room, wired with adrenaline and wanting truth. She threw the valise on the bed as he looked at her, smoky and stinky and wet. His mouth and eyes were big Os and he was dumbstruck ... and defenseless. Just what she wanted. She came up close and looked hard at him. Osley, the One-Eyed Jack. It was time to see the other side of that card.

"So, Mr. Osley, now they're trying to kill *me*, but I'm not going to let them. And I've got some serious questions for you."

He tried to move away, but the desk and chair and bed hemmed him in.

"You know my grandfather disappeared a year ago today?"

He nodded yes.

"You know these documents, especially this 'Elf,' have a power to confuse?"

He nodded again, almost in resignation to the coming third-degree.

"You know that something wants to destroy the documents, and Ara, and if necessary, you and me?"

The nod.

"But you're not telling me everything, are you?"

Sideways nod. Head down.

"So what is it, Osley; what's your secret? And don't try to get all Shakespeary on me!"

He started to open his mouth.

"And don't tell me I should pack up and go. I'm not leaving till I find my grandfather, and he's somewhere, somehow hidden in this murk. I can feel it. So, now, damn it! Talk!"

"I am just . . . Osley."

"I know that. That's not all. The truth!"

"I am a fugitive."

"Cut the crap. The real truth."

"I am a wanderer."

"Damn you, fess up. Did you do something to him?"

"I don't know."

She did the unthinkable. She slapped him, hard.

At that instant the fire alarms stopped. The sound of the slap ricocheted through the room.

Osley took the deep breath of the penitent and held it. It sighed out as if, finally in his life, there were no place to go.

"Very well, I will tell you."

At last, she thought, the card is about to be flipped over.

"Okay . . ."

"I am he."

"What?"

"Him . . . Jess . . . your grandfather."

Her face went blank. Wheels and gears tried to mesh, to comprehend what he just said. Then the gears clenched together and there were storm clouds in her narrowed eyes. Lightning flashed.

"This is no joke, Osley. Quit screwing with my head. It's not helpful, especially now."

"It's true. Just that simple."

She tried to pick out his lie. "My grandfather had legs of steel. No limp or hitch in his walk."

"The night I disappeared, a blade thrust into me. It never really healed. I got out through the trap door."

Cadence thought of the iron ring in the floor, the open trapdoor showing the creek side brush, the cloven doorframe.

"You don't look like him."

He looked up. "How would you know? What picture have you seen? Shave off my beard, cut my scraggly hair. I'm him, your dad's dad."

"No one ever mentioned the name Osley."

"No? What's a name, and what can be more easily invented, or discarded? Why did I wander and hide my identity for years? Why did I, Jess, never get a driver's license?"

She felt herself sliding down a slope, struggling between doubting him as an extravagant imposter and wanting to yell, "Why did you leave?" Instead, she heard her uncertain voice saying: "But you were a teacher. Here. All the Tolkien stuff."

"Absolutely true. All of it. He, Tolkien, was here. He entrusted the documents, the ones you hold, to me. To whom else could he? He left and, given my past and what I held, I knew I had to disappear as completely as possible. I had learned the trade of sharpening from one of the last itinerant practitioners in the Bronx. He gave me my sharpening machine. So I left and never really stopped, except for a few years, which is where you come in."

"What do you mean?"

"I met Brigette, your grandmother. We got married. We had a child. His name was Arnold. Arnie."

As she looked at him she almost cocked her head, trying to see her dad. She couldn't resist making a little jump to belief: "*You* left them. *You* were the one who was never there."

"Yes. I failed. Both of them. I failed the very chance in life I took as my own. I only stopped wandering when I thought I could, when my own demons and those in these papers seemed to rest. I finally stopped and hid out in plain sight. In Topanga."

"I think you're a consummate, no . . . psychotic, liar."

"I am totally that. But not just now. Do you want some ironclad proof?"

"Yes."

"First, your keychain, the tooth. It's a talisman. I hope it's still there in the valise. I received it from a shaman's son in Montana. Second, your dad had a purple birthmark on the left cheek of his ass. He . . . he loved fossils. He had a collection of shark's teeth. He said 'crik' instead of 'creek.'"

Her head swirled. She was slipping toward a tentative "maybe this is all true" stage. "You better not be lying."

She told him about the fiery encounter in her room.

"Look, Cadence," he almost said *granddaughter*, but the word was too awkward. "Time is moving against us. This Elvish is too true, too important, but that's not the point. I fled from it. To save you. Now you're here. You're in mortal danger, more than you know. You must go. Now!"

"Cut and run? Leave? After I've found you?" Some part of her wanted to put her arms out, two fragile overtures, but her heart still held them back. He stood there stiff and awkward. Long moments passed.

She couldn't call him "Jess." Maybe she never would. Still, she felt a growing calmness. She rubbed away emerging tears. "Whoever you are, this is all too much."

"Cadence, we don't have much time now. That . . . man could come back. He will try again."

She thought for a second and pointed at the valise. "And what about Ara?"

"Those documents are like a signal fire now. No matter where you go, they will track and find you. They are terrible. Leave the documents here, at least for tonight."

She stared at him.

"Come on, you trusted me an hour ago. I'm still the same. Take a break."

She nodded. "Okay. For a little while. I'm going downstairs. I'm sure the manager is a whistling teakettle. I bet he'll have the concierge hook me up with whatever I need. Clothes, new room—first floor this time. They will want to get the fire inspectors in to confirm the flash fire is out. Get them in and out and keep this whole thing low profile. Not great for business. I don't want to go anywhere else tonight. But hovering around with the documents won't work. We are both hostages to this. There has to be some other way. Think."

"I'm not sure Barren and his types behave by the rules we'd like. He has been sent here, through that pool. He won't stop until he has retrieved all the documents. Maybe there's something that we can use against him, it. I don't know. I've got to think about it."

"Grandpa"—it sounded *so* weird—"I can't think anymore. I gotta try to unwind. Lay down, get some sleep."

"Sure. Police and firemen are all over the building. He won't come again tonight. I'll be out early in the morning to attend to some things. If I decide to leave as well, to go with you, there are people to see, things to do before I depart. Be careful, and let's meet in the lobby. After you get some rest."

"Okay." She looked at him, but her eyes glazed and her mind couldn't find a forward gear. She was exhausted. She left to go downstairs, and he shut the door. Even bone-tired, some heretofore unknown part of her felt lighter.

* * *

Cadence awoke with a start. She was in her new room. God! It was only 5:00 AM She felt Ara's destiny ticking away. Whatever she and her grandfather decided, it only seemed to forestall Ara's destruction. As she lay thinking on the bed, the noise of the sleeping city combined with the hotel's vintage plumbing. Car beeps, sirens, hums, gurgles of something she'd rather not think about flowing through pipes in the walls inches from her head. Something, somewhere, tapped on the pipes. Whose that trip-trapping on my bridge? She let her ears search for sounds. Someone was walking down the hall. Creaking floor joists and carpet shuffles.

The creaking sound stopped outside her room. A shadow lurked at the bottom of the door, followed by that unmistakable quieter-than-quiet sound, when you know that someone is listening.

The shadow moved. She rose and watched in horrified slow motion as an envelope slid under the door. This was not the hotel bill.

She stepped quietly to the door and looked through the peephole. There was only the fisheye view of an empty hallway, and no creaking sound of anyone walking away. Making sure the chain was hooked, she partially opened the door. Looking out as far as she could without opening the door any further, all she could see was the long, empty hall. There was no sound of the elevator bell, no muffled footsteps padding down the fire exit.

She closed and relocked the door and picked up the envelope. Tasteful stationary. Expensive. Vanilla-colored finish. Immaculately sealed. Unmarked except for:

An Invitation for Cadence

She rubbed sleep from her eyes and sat down on the bed and opened the envelope. It held one page, newly folded. On it was written in fine script:

Cadence,
 It is my pleasure to extend to you a request to join our society. We believe we share many interests in common. Our name is the Society of the Rings, but we are so much more. Do you yearn for that luminous, greater truth, and have not found it in family, friends, education, religion, or career? Our search is not based on the demeaning, ritual insistence of "proofs," but on the certainty that there exists a truth to match this inner yearning.
 Visit us, if you please. We await your arrival.
Sincerely,
The Talisman Store
Riverside Drive

There was no street number. On the bottom, written in rough blockish letters, was a last inducement:

"We have the power to save both of you."

Jess . . . Os, she thought. *They will track each of us down if we don't give all this up.*

She was still too tired to think. She forced herself to lie back down. If sleep would not find her again, she would search for it. As it finally crept toward her, she put her fear to the side.

She got up five hours later and called Bossier Thornton. She explained what happened in simple terms. Just the facts. The fire. The note. The new room. As they talked he tried online to find the "Talisman Store" and an address, but came up with nothing.

He put her on hold for a moment, and then came back. "Cadence, I just checked. The Algonquin night clerk is off duty and can't be reached. The staff could've delivered the note. I know you will be talking with the assigned police and fire officers, but I want to sit down with you. I can't get there till early evening. Say six. I could buy you dinner."

"Thanks, you got a date, Officer Thornton."

By one o'clock the fawning concierge had definitely hooked her up—swagged and fed and clothed and spa'd. She had on a brand new Chrome Hearts exercise outfit and Adidas running shoes. More important, she had open accounts, courtesy of the Algonquin. One was waiting at Macy's—another of those purses? Another account waited at—all right! Bergdorf's.

She would get a new purse, some hot shoes and, hell, a complete new wardrobe.

But before that, she had to take a mental break. A short fog-clearing vacation from everything. A freewheeling run might work. Let it take her wherever it might lead. She hadn't jogged since she discovered the stacks of journals in her grandfather's attic, in what now seemed to be another world, long ago.

She recalled sitting there in the attic with the yellow circle of the flashlight, feeling the ebb and flow of a tide of family questions that demanded answers. Now she had the start of some answers. Time might fill in details if they had that luxury. She had to decide her next steps, think about returning to Topanga with her grandfather, think about how to protect Ara's story. More than that, how to keep Ara alive.

Time for practical action, she thought. *I'll take a run and get control of all this.*

An hour later her feet had taken her to West 70th and Broadway. A slight breeze freshened the air that still felt cleansed by overnight rain. It was one of those days when sunlight showed off a bit, splaying broad stripes on buildings and dappling the pavement through leafy tree branches.

She kept jogging. A diner loomed in front of her. Big, steam-fogged windows and patrons posed like an afternoon version of *Night Hawks*.

She turned right, and Broadway opened up, gently curving, lined with buildings leaning toward uptown like a Robert Crumb comic.

Chapter 71

INKLINGS IX

—

This is an excerpt from the last known recorded session of the Inklings, and may have been the last meeting with Professor Tolkien in attendance.

"I have enjoyed this delightful conversation with you, over so many Tuesdays. I regret that my great vice, this occupation with words and stories, may have been inflicted on all of you too heavily."

Protests all 'round.

"Not at all. Don't be daft, man."

"Tell us, Tollers, have we helped you reach any conclusions?"

"Only the happy one, aside from the importance of boon friendships. And that is this: it all goes on."

"But where, isn't that the question?"

"We should always remember, Ian, a tale is like any living thing, it is restless and has a will of its own."

"I applaud your long effort. There are no, or at least should not be, any border police on stories."

"But I think what Tollers is also telling us is that where he toils, on the frontier where making and remaking are as one, is an unruly place. All borders are places of magic. Like your half-mad little character, crossing even the doorstep threshold and setting foot on the road can sweep one away into far lands under strange moons."

"Well, enough of all this. Edith and I are moving to a place on the coast. I shall hear the long clash of waves and rock, and the seabirds repeating sounds like the waking cries of a newborn world."

"And your secret gate?"

"That I have indeed passed through. Many times. Unlike Rhygoal, the Loud-Grating, or Utgard, the Unbreachable, it is a simple quaint, roundish door, decorated with tree branches. It bears no name, but be assured—it is there. It is time for others to find their own gates."

Chapter 72

OCTOBER 31: 1:00 PM

———

Jess returned to his room at the Algonquin, feeling new currents swirling in his life, threatening to jump the banks entire and sweep away four decades of emotional levees and willow thickets. Here, at the vortex of those currents, he had made the single greatest confession of his life. Here he was capable of giving a different answer to his life's riddle: do I stay or do I go? Just like the song. He could stay with Cadence, this family remnant. Or, he could, as always, go. He could flee to the beckoning white line of the road. He felt at peace with the answer. He would stay here and wait for Cadence, and they would set their plans. Together. He shuffled some papers and discovered that before she left last night she had taken something he hadn't wanted her to see. It was a disturbing two-page translation that even he didn't believe. He saw that Cadence had also placed two sketches on his desk. They were two images of the same rounded, ancient gate: one closed, one open.

He sat and resumed translating with a troubled intensity, waiting for Cadence to return. He hoped he could help Ara's story find its conclusion. Perhaps he could even find a safe home for her legacy. Most important, perhaps he could find a safe place for his grandchild.

After a few moments of scribbling, he stopped cold. He could sense that, without warning, the Elvish of Mirkwood was about to reveal the final fate of Ara. He took a deep breath and resumed with a desperate, deliberate run to her final truth:

Ara lay hidden and listening just below the windowsill, her

head pressed close against the outside wall.

"Silence!"

The harsh clicking of orc speech was stopped cold by a single command in the Common Tongue. The voice had a clipped and fast accent. It was deep, accustomed to giving orders. The speaker was southern. His back was to the room as he looked out through the window of the stone building, his scarred hands inches from Ara's hiding place.

"Marshalling an army is like harnessing a river. Confusion everywhere. The order of battle should be precise, but it ends stumbling all over itself. The more security we post, the more disorder and delay we get. Each guard has to be checked by other guards. So on and so on. Wizard hairs! It's not enough that we face an enemy that seeks our extermination, but now we hear they have infiltrated us with 'small spies.' Ball-less demons! One could walk right past us now, and in all the confusion we wouldn't notice. No one can stop this coming battle anyway. But for some weapon of terror planted in our midst, the die is cast and this battle shall unfold within hours. I can feel the victory we deserve and the end of those haughty bastards!"

She was suited in a stolen orc-courier's dress, without armor or weapons. Leather headgear was pulled low over her soot-smeared face. A heavy charcoal streak, black on gray, ran down her face from her forehead to below her chin. Her feet were encased in bearskin leggings. She held a leather case with the simple double-oval mark of the Source inscribed in red dye.

On a crag high above the valley, two sets of eyes watched for Ara. They had been sitting there for three days and nights. The penetrating gaze of each studied, traced movements, saw patterns and clues. Finally they found the small, scurrying form with a gait like no orc. She was moving away from the headquarters of the 'Eye of No Tears' Empi, an elite legion of men. His steed spied first the odd movement, far below. Its tail whipped in impatience; steam flowed from its nostrils. Their eyes locked on the tiny figure three miles away, past heat and fumes. They watched as Ara sneaked along a sidewall, filched some food and water, and then moved toward the slopes of the volcano. Pazal rose and slipped the tough, braided dwarf-skin harness about the creature's neck in preparation for flight.

As she darted among the battle groups, Ara felt unnoticed. She was safe as long as she ran. And that she did, propelled by dire urgency and duty. The pass-sign, a quick cupped hand in the likeness of an eye, she had mastered, although none in charge seemed to notice.

To her left, the slopes of Fume rose, impossibly and neck-craningly high. Its base was less than a mile away. On the plain before it massed an army making ready for battle. A thousand clock drums relentlessly measured the final hours toward battle. Every few minutes there thundered out a single, unified, resounding *Boom*.

She passed through the smells of strange creatures sweating in fear and exertion. Soon she was surrounded by clanks of metal and creaks of leather, cursing, and beneath all, the ceaseless, burdened tramp and thud of feet and hooves.

She entered a crossroads, helpless to take her gaze from the mountain, when a huge hand splayed in front of her. A troll guard directing traffic had signaled her to stop. She watched as one wing of the army passed.

Boom.

It was loosely formed of diverse and malformed troops. Then, moving fast, brandishing outlandish, long-stemmed weapons, boiled a vanguard more like a swarm of giant lethal insects. They were organized by no single commander. They needed no indoctrination, no order save sight and smell of the enemy. Their faces were twisted and tubered with yellow and purple bulges, as if designed to further horrify their foe.

Make way! The Swarm comes! Orcs and men stepped back warily to let the horde pass.

Boom.

Next came shambling ranks of great orcs. Heavy and grunting with complaint, all faced forward, eager to bleed the haughty elves that, outside battle or blade of treachery, knew not death. They jostled on, ready to fall ten to one if only to close with the tormentors of their race.

There came a break in the march's flow. Ara started to move but the guard's hand stayed in her face. She kept her eyes down. The hand reached out and pulled her closer, as if for safekeeping.

Boom.

A legion of men came next. Ara of the village stood in awe bordering on admiration. They were disciplined, clearly seasoned in battle, resolute in the patience that precedes great contests. Mounted captains stood high in their stirrups, exhorting them forward. "Today we meet the Meddlers!" they shouted. "The Great Imposters, the False Kings and Deceivers. Do you wish to see their Horse-flag over your villages? Show them our strength!"

Boom.

And with a single great shout and raising of blades, the sound of thousands roared forth as one, a force and conviction terrible to behold.

Ara saw that this array was not purely one of craven curs whipped from behind, but was of men and orcs ready to mark their enemy, including her own people, for death and defeat. The gravity of implacable, physical opposition, the blunt, grinding purpose of war unleashed, passed her in review. Whatever was about to happen, it seemed destined for a grim field where destiny is unveiled by wager of battle.

Boom.

Soon there was another break in the line. The giant hand guided her forward, as if saying, "On to your errand, little one."

Now only a league from Fume, she continued the steady, jogging shamble that seemed her best disguise.

The unseen eyes that tracked her from above poised until she entered a small defile.

Boom.

As she emerged, Pazal stood before her.

Ara stopped. She heard a displacement of air and the leathery slap and folding of great wings behind her. Worst of all, she now recognized the thing before her. It was the black wraith from the gate. The same that had picked her up like a toy.

It spoke:

"Twice I find you standing before me, small one. Are you so enamored of our power that you have deserted your band and volunteered your lot with us? Or are you but a spy to be drawn on the rack before being fed to my pet? Do you have any idea what it feels like to be eaten alive? To see your insides in its mouth? I think you will . . . cooperate."

Ara knew her life was forfeit. Boldness, even to the point of folly, might still play a role, however. Bad information might help in some way. She spoke loudly, "Hold your boast, Unman. I know of a hidden trifle much desired by your master. Would you destroy the clue that points to the one thing he covets?"

The tail wrapped about her legs as a great talon thudded to the ground by her side, its scaly knuckles level with her eyes.

Boom.

And there, for now, the trail of Ara the Hobbitess swerved into the vastness of unintelligible runes and was lost to Jess as surely as a blind turn in Mirkwood itself.

Chapter 73

OCTOBER 31: 3:15 PM

———

Cadence jogged on, fitful in her direction and pace, until her legs found their stride. She would indulge this time to let her feet and her thoughts seek their own paths. She crossed an intersection with a construction project underway. Slabs of steel, blowtorch cut, flat like lasagna, covered car-sized holes in the street. It was surprising the weight they bore, she thought as she watched cars and trucks kaboom hollowly over them. One of the slabs had been removed, and she stopped and looked down, like an observer of open-heart surgery. In the deep she saw ghastly confirmation of her sense of the unseen anatomy of the city. Looming in the shadows was a beamed and crusted urban skeleton. Relic iron trusses lay tied with bolts the size of sledgehammers. Leaking pipes ran past, each of a size that could transport trash cans, each made of wood held together with wire. Around these were ultra-modern, blue and yellow, gooey rubber cables, intertwined in insane symmetry. This was the bare guts of urban civilization revealed. All of it overlay a deeper shadow land lurking beneath, descending to perhaps untested depths. It struck her as indecent, exposing the quiet, eternally waiting gloom of that long-hidden world to garish daylight.

A piece of older asphalt pavement was exposed. Like dinosaur tracks on ancient sediment, it hosted random fossil remnants of the twentieth century. Pop bottle caps saying Big Chief, Nehi, and RC. Flattened, steel beer cans with tabs church-key cut in double V-shapes. A wondrous bird skeleton, perfectly mistakable for archaeopteryx, even to the back-arching death crane of the neck, with feather remnants and side-looking, traffic-polished skull intact. A rut, as if made by the last iron-wheeled horse wagon. A wood handled screwdriver. A brick peeking out, revealing a stamped date of 1908. A pair of smashed tortoiseshell eyeglasses caught in the black amber.

The late-blooming eighth-grader that still lived inside her had been on these streets before. It was a school trip remembered chiefly for ditching the chaperones and kissing Jimmy Friedlander, while The Police sang in the background.

That fall her dad would die in the Topanga fire, and she would never really graduate to the ninth grade. *I am a fossil*, she thought, *until now*.

As she approached 92nd Street, the sidewalk featured an array of buskers. A black man picked out Louisville-style blues with Dobro and bottleneck. She dropped a dollar in his hat, and he picked her a special lick. A group of rappers, bearing wireless mikes working through tinny little amps, accosted the crowd with earnest sexual lyrics acapella. Then there was a sandwich board sign that had somehow captured and enslaved a shoeless human who looked like the unshaven, older brother of the creeker in Topanga. The front board said:

> Expect as ye see.
> Signs and wonders,
> Ye will finally believe.

And on the back:

> Quoth the Raven,
> Eat Kraft Cheese.

The next few blocks were strangely quiet, almost empty. Cadence glimpsed New Jersey to her left, down a long street corridor. Her sneakers squeaked. She slowed to a sputtering walk and sorted once more through jumbled pieces of this puzzle.

At the top of the pile was her grandfather. Much was left to do—getting to know him, for one.

Don't they say that the trauma of great loss has aftershocks that can come back years later? Unresolved good-byes, I-wishes, and if-onlys are the bread-and-butter regrets that always resurface. They are like errant locomotives sent off full-throttle into the trackless interior of the heart, that somehow find a turntable and now are heading back into town.

So finally, she thought, *we're at the core. I found him. I found the secret gate to answer those questions.*

No discovery is complete unto itself, and she could not turn her back on the final question. *Who was Ara, really?* The tale still glinted from the rune scribbles, as interpreted by a man—who happened to be her grandfather—who last bought a new pair of shoes in the 1980s. The "translations" could be just the musings of his alter ego, Osley the LSD guru. Hell, they could be the invention of some grand pranksters of the past, or Dark Elves, or the fevered dream of a refugee monk gone off the medieval grid, or anything. Seeing Ara in the pool? Perhaps she had. Or maybe it was just fear and light on an oily water surface.

A rational person, like her mom, or Cadence as Cadence used to think she was, would see this clearly. There was not even a high-class mystery here—forget the fairytale dust about trying to save a heroine. This was echoed by a cracked, gravelly voice, as if Burgess Meredith was in her head reprising a corrupt, cigar-chomping manager, telling her, *Throw in the towel and go home, kid, 'cause this fight is fixed anyway.*

She took another step. *Bullshit! It's not about fairy tales and it's not about rationality. The truth is just what it is.* She did a double-skip and upgraded her pace back to a full run. *I'm not leaving Ara lost in Mirkwood! I'm going to get those last answers, and I know where to go.*

At West 100th Street, she passed a shuttered McDonald's that had been an infamous "SmackDonald's" in the 1970s. As Osley, her grandfather had talked about it as if he had been one of the regulars. More dollars were generated in horse than burgers. Dealers were always loitering out front, while a stream of noddies queued to buy. Piss and barf smells clung to the perimeter, and it wasn't much better inside. Supposedly Ronald visited once, all suited up in clown garb. He was a narc.

She kept running.

The extra-sensory perception of being stalked once fell into the camp of old wives' tales and superstition. It has of late been resurrected for study by serious science, and with good reason. Perhaps it results from an aggregation of subtle clues that trips some primitive wire in our brains.

By West 104th Street, the tripwire had been snagged, and Cadence felt the queasy certainty of being followed. Her juju feeling reverberated like a drum circle. She had a good idea of who, or what, it was. She felt for the fine stationary letter folded in her pocket. Her feet had delivered her to the neighborhood where, if ever, she might find the Talisman Store and dare to save both her grandfather and Ara. Her hand also felt the two pages of new translation that she'd picked up off Osley's desk. She felt edgy. She would look for a quiet spot to read them.

* * *

Barren's own favorite among his many talents, aside, of course, from raw adaptability, was to let his preys' own skills work against them. This was how he ensnared the Woodsmen. He let their own sixth sense first detect him, then he let it drive them to his trap.

It saved a lot of work.

Just to test things in this new world (he was constantly trying to update his thinking now), he would direct Cadence west, toward the river. He was two full blocks behind her, indistinguishable in the crowd. His signals, aura, pheromones, vibes—whatever there were—herded her as effectively as a spear to the rump of an aurochs.

Up ahead, Cadence hurried her pace, fidgeted at the light, looked around, and crossed over against the traffic to the west side of Broadway.

* * *

Past 113th Street, the West End Bar hunkered down, looking dreary and idle in the afternoon light. There were more trees after that, creating a slow strobe of light and shadow as she ran. The Columbia University enclave was coming up on the right.

The neck hairs' sensation of being followed came on strong once again. She turned left at 114th, cut down the block, and stopped. She was on Riverside Drive in front of a neighborhood deli with a wooden half-wall gate across the door. Inside, one tough, uniformly auburn-hued dog sat watching. Smart dog. Waiting to chomp on the uninvited. *The neighborhood must be tougher than it looks*, she thought.

She found a brownstone doorstep that had been freshly swept and sat down. She pulled out the clump of translation pages and began to read. At the top, Jess had scrawled a note, probably a reminder for when they next talked: "There are two fragments here. By the tears and folds, each may have been secreted away many times. I don't know if these are reliable. The first is part of a History of Aragranessa."

Ara, the prisoner, stood in a darkened cavern before a large, ornate doorway that was almost closed. Torchlight flickered from inside. A fearful orc guard proddled her with his spear, backed up several steps, and then ran away. She forced one foot forward, then the other. With the certainty of ascending the gallow's steps, Ara knew she walked to her death.

She thought, *I am Aragranessa, daughter of Achen. All he can take is what must be given up in the end anyway. I will not fear, and, though none may ever know, I will sell my life dearly.*

She thought of her Amon, of his sad, desperate determination. She took a deep breath and slid through the crack . . . into the presence of the Dark Lord.

The room was large, long as a spear's flight. Its ceiling dimmed in the waving shadows from torches jutting from each column. The walls rose with tier upon tier of shelves stuffed with codices and scrolls. At the far end, held in a luminous glow of changing colors, was the shape of a man. He turned slowly, as if he awaited her arrival, and began to walk toward her.

Despite the length of that hall, it seemed he had taken but one step and was now before her. His hand held a robe, which he slipped over a chair. He wore a simple tunic and brought his hands together in supplication. He looked at her as one might a much anticipated guest. She was stunned by his gentle demeanor. His eyes spoke at once of need and hope. His gestures were those of a weary man of peace.

"Please, sit and eat." He indicated a chair sized just for her. Before it was a low, broad table laden with food such as Halflings crave—biscuits and butter and fried bacon with roasted grazus. She had eaten naught but roots and brush bark for days. Her nose involuntary flared and tweaked at the smell. But her heart resisted, and she stiffened. He looked unjustly offended. "After all this way? And still not happy? Let us test the ill humor that sets itself against your happiness." He motioned again. "Come, indulge an old man and sit with me."

Something in his voice relaxed her just a bit. She sat gingerly on the edge of the seat. She reached out for a vessel filled with sweet, fresh smelling water, and drank deeply. The food suddenly was irresistible. He sat and watched and waited, passing untried dishes to her as she ate.

His patience was rewarded, for in time, her hunger sated and her thirst slaked, she was ready to talk. After all, he seemed both reasonable and gracious. She would go so far as to be polite. "Thank you for the food and drink."

"As you deserve. May I speak to you? I take your silence as permission, so let me say this. Your well-being *is* important."

She felt herself falling into a pleasant and amiable conversation, relaxing as if this peaceful old man were one of her great-uncles voicing concern for her. It was a kind of glamour, something only trust can provide, and she found herself trusting him.

The Dark Lord asked her to give voice to the anger that smoldered within her. By her answer, he discovered its true root to be righteous, for it was based on the injustice meted out to her people. He then told her that he, too, had been wrongly judged. He spoke of his long learning, and of the rebuilding of his library. How he assembled it from materials secured by stealth from a great library, since burned to the ground that lay in the far lands to the south. Then he spoke of the nature of his art. "I deal with all substances. I find the essential value in all—including the debased, the vile, and the shunned. I take the life of a mere insect, a thing deemed worthless, and elevate it, in its purity and essence to the great stature it deserves. This I can do for you, Ara, who are already a noble and fearless warrioress. You have been deceived by others, even your Amon, who deserted you for his own adventure. Would you now embrace your own purity, your own destiny? She ate and drank further and asked him to explain many things, for he wished her to know all and to make her own decisions. He told her of the elusive nature of the lights in the northern sky, and then showed her a fabric that embodied the very nature of those celestial colors, that *was* those colors. "Thus can I distill your essence, Ara, and together we can discover the high-born and rightful Ruler of the Halflings that you are meant to be." She nodded. There was truth to his words. All she could say was, yes. *Yes.*

Here Jess's notes began again: "This is from an official record of the Canton of the Halflings. It's disturbing."

I am Mercy, humble crier of news for the Realm of the Halflings.

Hear now the Chronicle of Ara's Betrayal, a quick-spoken account of her collaboration and her ambition. Woe to us all, and woe of greatest measure to the race of Halflings who for generations have shunned the hamlet of Frighten. Guilt for this outrage is theirs.

Ara was brought into the presence of the Dark Lord, still dressed as an orc-messenger bearing the insignia of the Source. So was she condemned to death as a spy. Her guilt and her defiance were evident, but by his glamour and her misguided will, she joined his cause.

Now his emissaries come to our lands. They command us to pledge our fealty to the Lord of the Source and agree to live under the Dominion of the Queen of the Halflings, or suffer war!

Cadence looked down at the last page and bit her hand. She couldn't believe it. All this long tale as but testament to the pervasive powers of evil. All this tortured path she had followed. Ara The Betrayer! She could feel the air wheezing out of her soul. She dithered with the pages until a mist of angry tears came. They stung like hot acid. Like the truth.

Well, maybe that's just what real stories, the ones with real truth, are. She deserves to be erased.

She wiped her eyes, put her chin on her hand, and stared at a disciplined column of ants marching toward the wilds beyond the curb. They took their lumps and reorganized, and so could she. Besides, she was a huge winner, wasn't she? She had found her grandfather. But, truth be told, the edge was off. Crazy as it sounded, if you couldn't trust Ara, who could you trust? It ate at her until the tears dried and she resolved to go back to the Algonquin and hold those original documents in her hand. She would challenge Jess and together they would test the veracity of this Elvish scrawl.

She rose to her feet and looked up.

Directly across the street, perhaps exactly where it should be, was a door with a discrete black-and-white sign: "Talisman Store." Below that was a tacky stick-on metal sign in red and fake brass: "No Soliciting."

She walked over and looked at the building.

It was a brownstone that loomed up three stories. A hand-manicured garden patch, bounded by an ornate metal fence, waited out front, along with two healthy oaks for summer shade. She watched as a breeze reaped the last few leaves.

She went through the fence gate and approached the wooden door guarded by an iron doorknocker in the shape of a boar's head. An intricate latch substituted for a door handle. She knew that here was a reckoning. She owed something—to herself, not Ara. She had hesitated at the pool and regretted it. She wouldn't freeze up now. Go with your gut, as her Dad might say.

She raised the knocker, paused, and let it fall.

The resulting sound was a disappointing clunk. She waited, reluctant to disturb the privacy of some family, probably a hard-working doctor or diplomat.

Finally she heard dim sounds from inside. The door latch moved in unexpected ways, as some inner bolt released, then the door opened.

The man before her was tiny, genteel, and hunched, like a retired watchmaker. He studied her through thick glasses, and then stepped aside enthusiastically, as if in sudden recognition.

"Please, come in."

Almost without thinking, she stepped across the threshold. The door closed behind her with a solemn, unnerving breath, as if wood and frame had somehow melded. Just like that, she knew her gut call had been hasty. Here there were two possible outcomes: very good or very bad. She'd left a note for Jess listing this vague address. Other than that, no one knew.

"Welcome to my . . . store."

He showed her down a brief hallway that led to a bright room. Cadence stepped into a rich, cascading flow of soft daylight. She looked up. A resplendent glass skylight, decorated with stained glass, filtered a waterfall of light that fell through large banistered stairwell openings in the upper two stories.

The room was tastefully arranged with illuminated, museum-quality exhibition cases, each treasuring a few objects. Large gold coins, some ancient, some new, and none from the Franklin Mint. Small, brass-capped feet of unknown animals—perhaps ferrets or mink. What was almost certainly a duck-billed platypus foot, fitted with an ivory cap and an attached chain of irregular drilled pearls the size of marbles.

She walked along the last row of cases, their contents adhering to no apparent order, but each containing items capable of transfixing the viewer. Here was a crucifix with a mast of antiqued brass and a crosspiece of a polished wood splinter. No doubt a medieval relic. Next, laid on its side on a field of black velvet, was a World War II era Zippo lighter with "36th Texas" etched on it and a bullet crease along one side. There followed a small demonic face carved in jade. On and on: a scrimshawed ivory tooth, three inches long, depicting a full-sailed whaling ship being Evel-Knieveled by an enormous Leviathan. An incongruous Alpha Tau Omega pledge pin from the Vanderbilt University Chapter, Class of '90.

Finally, she came to a case with a solitary object—an oversized pocket watch, case open, displaying a score of tiny dials, one whirling madly counterclockwise.

"You got our letter." She jumped, the little man was hovering so close.

"Well, uh yes, but how did you fi . . . select me?"

"Our invitations are very . . . exclusive. Don't worry, we're harmless. What do you think of our collection?"

Her neck hair wouldn't go down. "Its . . . interesting."

"Do you have a talisman?"

"Well, I inherited one. I'm not sure if that's a good or bad thing."

"They can be either/or."

She decided to quit talking and get out of there. She casually surveyed the exit. The inside latch on the front door looked complex— wheels and levers and a solid metal bar seated firmly in an iron trestle on the wall. Barred.

"Well, who are you, this . . . group you have?"

"Ah, thank you. We are enthusiasts for the reality that is proven by the very longing of the human heart. Much of that longing is channeled into religion, and that is wondrous. But a fine distillation of that longing, the romantic, the hunger for other worlds, needs other direction. That's why they say myths and legends come about."

"I—uh—see."

"The rarest thing, however, is discovery for oneself that such a world indeed exists. A world more palpable than these objects, more amenable to feeling and to sight than our present world, more real that the drear plains we traverse daily."

He paused to catch his breath. "And so we study here. Our foundation is the art of belief itself."

Cadence noticed a single ring on the man's hand. The stone in it caught the light. Arcs of opal-blue seemed to flow out from the stone, filling the air with sparkly dust motes. She blinked and made a decision.

"Hey, I gotta go. I'll stop by again. Thanks. Nice place."

"It's no trouble. Please sign our guest book, and I'll escort you out. We've had other visitors lately."

The little man gestured toward a bound ledger on a counter. She went to it hurriedly and searched for a pen.

She heard the quick thumb-click of a ball point pen, followed by a different voice. "I have a different guest book for you to sign, Cadence."

She looked up. Across the counter stood the man she knew was Barren. She turned, but the munchkin proprietor had positioned himself in a wrester's stance, set to bar her way.

She bowled him over like a sock 'em balloon.

She reached the door. The main lever handle seemed locked, held down by a cogged gearwheel turned by a polished rotary handle. She thought of a fine millwork for making cake flour, or the innards of a talking doll. She thought a thousand things while she fumbled with it.

A hand slammed flat against the door next to her face.

"First, we have a bit of commerce to complete."

She couldn't really move. She opted, instead, to study the intricacies of the grainy oak inches from her face.

"Will you hear the offer? Or should we kill your grandfather now?"

A thin cloak fell over her head. Cadence felt the world drop out beneath her feet. Wind rustled the cloak as she began to freefall. Images came to her—first still, then moving like pictures in a thumb-operated flicker book. She knew that she was dreaming as she was falling, falling to depths where oblivion was an unknown word, so dense was the darkness.

In the dream, her father faced a blazing man at the edge of a fire. He sought to pass to freedom, but the blazing man, shaped by furious black coils of smoke and the reek of hot diesel oil and burning flesh, barred him. There was talk of commerce which no path could warrant.

Her father said *No, it's not worth that price.*

The blazing man held out a steaming oilcan. *As you please. Here are special things for you to ponder. Sort of little kittens. He gestured a flaming hand. Come take a look.*

Her father nodded.

The smoking eyes, darker in the flameface, narrowed and the indescribable contents of the can were poured on the ground.

* * *

As if at the snap of a hypnotist's fingers, Cadence woke up, clearheaded and sitting in a chair. She was not surprised that her adversary was sitting across from her.

From the smells and style of the room and the furnishings around her, she guessed that she was still somewhere within the little shop of talismanic horror. She had the chance to study him. She realized that he had also been the strange cab driver. He had those same oily, dark eyes, but he was clean-shaven, the Mohawk gone, and his hair was buzz-length and neatly trimmed. He wore a loose-knit, orange polo shirt, nice pants, and a pair of khaki-colored Air Jordans. Almost as if for effect, he held a pair of wire-rimmed glasses in his manicured hands.

She said the first thing that came into her head.

"You learn fast."

"That is my core competence."

She tried to move, but while each of her parts moved and felt fine, the act of getting up from the chair just would not happen. One of the objects from the exhibition case, the backward-running clock face, lay on her lap. Was the wrong-way whirr and sweep somehow keeping her sitting there? She wondered if she could scare this weirdo.

"You and the munchkin are going to be in some kind of trouble when the cops arrive."

"I don't think we need to worry about being interrupted here. He glanced around, gesturing magnanimously with his glasses, saying in effect *Aren't we lucky to be in such a swell place?*

"I have an idea."

"Please, tell me."

"Go fuck yourself."

"Now, now. No reason to be unsociable. At least, not yet. Perhaps we should clear up just who I am so that it doesn't get in the way of us getting to know one another. I am known locally as Mr. Peaches. In my own country, I am called Mr. Barren or, simply, Barren. Before that, my name was Seax. My employer values my skills, which he sees as considerable. He too believes that I learn fast, and thus he chose me to make this trip and straighten this whole thing out. That, and the fact that I can be charming or one mean son of a bitch. I am to use my discretion, as he put it, although not exactly in those terms."

Cadence stalled while she looked around for the door. "And just where is this employer, and who is he?"

"Far away, yet close. Down a road, across a bridge, burned in the words of a book, or behind a secret gate. My employer is powerful and used to getting his way."

"Is he a wizard?"

"If you believe in such things."

"I'm not into believing in things I can't see."

"I'm right here. The other pieces you've already seen, if you allow them to fit together."

She started to get up, but nothing happened. The watch with the backward-running dial stirred in her lap like a purring cat.

"You're a fake!" she spat out.

"You seem to have some issues here beyond me, Cadence. Forget about fire, for which I know you have a weak spot. To get to the point, you seem to be troubled by what's real and what isn't. Are you a doubter? Does your doubt ensure that your world is made up of low hopes and petty requests? That is to say, barren?"

She looked at him.

"Don't think I don't know the meaning of my name. And yet my world is rich beyond your imagining. I not only believe it, I live it! A philosophy you might wish to embrace if you ever get out of this. Now, in any case, I've come to like this place. The perks aren't as good, but there's lots shaking."

"All right, I've heard enough. I want to go."

"Yes, yes. That has already been arranged. Do you want to know where?"

"Yeah, home. Out of here."

"I'm afraid it's not that simple. We, you and I, have some beez-ness to conduct."

"What's that?"

"A simple contract. Very little to negotiate. All it really is, I offer and you accept."

"I know some lawyers."

"Don't threaten, child, it's unbecoming. It's also futile. Let me proceed as I have planned. Now, pay attention! My profession is to humble men much tougher than you, hard men who are used to ranging in the wilds and spying on my employer's interests. I can break you. Now, what I'm offering you is as good as it gets. Far better than Les Inspecteurs." He caricatured the name in phony French. "I implore you, don't go down the path of your grandfather."

"So what's the offer?"

"The offer is that you deliver, at my direction, each and every page of each and every one of the documents given to your grandfather so many years ago. In other words, the entire peach crate stash, everything in that elusive valise. Upon delivery, I shall arrange for your release as well as . . . the survival of your grandfather."

"What do you mean!" she exclaimed.

"I thought that might get your attention. Yes, yes, he is alive. He worries if he'll ever see you again. He seems to have learned a huge lesson. Rather late, but still better than never. He needs your help, Cadence. Will you let him down the way he let down your father?"

"No! Of course not."

"Good. Because that means that you and he, gosh, even Mel, may be allowed to live. Call it a performance bonus."

A fine mist of sweat sprang out upon her forehead. The man was speaking in a mishmash of television dialects, but the gravity of his message was clear. "Okay, I'll play. Deliver my grandfather first."

"I'm afraid those aren't the terms. We have to have some trust if we're going to work together."

"Where do I make the drop?"

"The what?"

"Come on, you were doing so well with your I'm-just-learning-the-language routine. The place of delivery of the documents."

"They have to be delivered in person, as it were. The place you already know. A pool of water in a storage room beneath the city."

"*You* deliver them!"

"I'm afraid, on that score there, has been an adjustment of plans. I'm not in a position to deliver them."

"Why not? You came from there, didn't you?"

"Yes, but plans change."

"If I go, can I get back?"

"I'm afraid not."

She watched his demeanor. He didn't blink. He was confident and focused solely on her. She had no doubt he'd delivered polite but deadly ultimatums many times, in many languages and places. She shook her head. "I don't believe this."

"What's not to believe?"

"If I go, I save my grandfather. Fine, I'll do it." She took a deep breath. "Count me in."

"Yes, well, here's the truth. You can never do what you don't absolutely believe in. You'd better find somebody that does."

"No, I'll give it all I've got."

"Well, it's pointless to test this further. I wanted to see how you'd react. But just to be sure, I've arranged for an alternate."

She said nothing.

"Someone who believes completely. Someone who was always eager to go and, at last, wouldn't hesitate to save his family."

"Grandpa?"

"Precisely. 'I'd go— in a shot,' I believe, were his exact words."

"I couldn't ask that." Her voice was so small that it shamed her.

"You don't need to. I did; he's agreed. He's ready. I just need a sign from you."

"Like what?"

"I think you know. Show it to me."

She hesitated and then realized her hand was involuntarily moving. Like an ant in honey, it slowly pulled her keychain from the pocket of her sweat top. The tooth talisman was attached.

"Not this."

Barren smiled. "What better?"

Despite her resistance, her hands slowly removed the keys and gave the tooth to him.

Barren held it up, squinting and turning it in the light like an admiring scientist. He looked back at her, showing the slightest sign of ... what? Empathy? Admiration? Then he gave her a look which she could read in an instant. *This young woman is a bit of tragedy, a cautionary tale.* He returned his attention to the tooth, "It's got to bring better luck to someone else anyway."

"May I ask another question?"

"We've got lots of time."

"Is Ara real? Or is she only a story?"

"As real as me."

That's not . . . altogether helpful."

"I could tell you she never lived and is no more than bits of doggerel from an older time, misinterpreted by the present. I could tell you she is, at most, a part of what are called 'storybooks.'"

"Yes, you could, and I would accept it."

"Oh, but there's danger there as well. I'm finding that my greatest power is plain old truth, so I'll tell you true. She lives, this very moment, in a place you would recognize. A place that is vibrant with peril and resolve and great purpose . . ."

She interrupted, "and she betrayed everyone? Is that right?"

"You seem to have a desperate need to know, but I could hardly spoil a good ending, now could I?"

"You *are* a bastard."

"You're in no position to be insulting, young lady. Now, as I was saying, she lives in a place that indeed exists."

Cadence paused, thinking his statement over. "How do I know?"

"Because your heart tells you so. If you listen to that voice but a little, belief follows like dawn on the night."

"How do I really know?"

"Because it's not me or what I say that matters. It's only you. I'm sure we agree that it's a shame her story has to be erased. Especially after she did so much work. Blame it on those Dark Elves who cursed her in the woods so long ago."

"I blame you and your, what did you say, *employer*."

"Well, you can't expect him to leave his former enemies around. He might have plans for, how do you say, a *comeback*. Don't ever count this guy out."

She listened, marking his slang but thinking in particular about Tolkien's admonition that evil ever renews, that monsters do not depart.

"Now, young lady, I have a question."

Silence.

"How does this work?"

He held a Nokia cell phone in his hand.

"I'm very glad you have that."

Moving in the allowed slo-mo, she gave him a show-and-tell lesson, he holding it up to his face upside down and backwards, she correcting him, showing him the buttons to push. His eyes opened wide as a voice came through.

"Thornton here."

"Don't mind that, the person on the phone can't hear us."

The line was silent. Cadence watched the green light on the phone showing the call was still live.

"If you would, please let me go. I'll do anything to get out of this place!"

Barren thought for a moment, then put the cell phone aside. The green light stayed on. He had some other questions. This was the best time to milk her for information.

"I've been watching *The Sopranos*. I can't decide if I should be a gangster or a businessman. They're so close. Now, I think the businessman has the edge. He can start up anywhere. All he has to do is be whatever it takes at any given moment. The gangster, though, he's gotta have a gang, otherwise he's just a freelancer. So how does one find a gang? Should I be part of some family, like my prior employer? Should I be a Jet or a Shark or a Crip or a Blood, part of NG Purples or the Stony Hill Gang? Maybe join a club. Like eBay? All I know is I'm tired of working for the man. So I'm gonna freelance, just see what comes up. Not bad for an orphan kid from the other side of a dark and stormy rainbow, huh?"

"You could care less about orphans. You don't have the balls to care."

"Again, I've touched a tender spot. Well, before I go, let's play a game, with a prize."

"What's the prize?"

"Well, normally I'd say we had already bargained for your life, so I can't negotiate over that. But since you've already given me this," he hefted the tooth in his hand, "I feel like I can put it back on the table, your life that is. That's my specialty, after all."

"Liar! Asshole!"

"Now, now."

"Relax. If you do this right you'll come out alive. It's not like fairy gold. You'll be real and walk and talk like the other boys and girls."

She squirmed, knowing he wasn't kidding. Not one bit.

"This isn't going to involve riddles, is it?"

"Oh no, that would put you at, shall we say, a grave disadvantage.

That is an art lost to your times."

"So what is it?"

"Just names. Trivia. You guess the name of the person I'm thinking of, sort of, *becoming*. That's the great thing about your world, Cadence. Aspiration. Ambition. You can be anyone."

"I can't just guess names."

"Oh yes you can. I believe you know them already. And I shall give you a few clues."

"How could I know the names?"

"Because they are in the little box that people and places live in. The television. I've been spending time with it. It's everywhere. People have told me people and places inside it aren't real, but believe me, I know a thing or two about reality. I'm going to become someone different, and you're going to guess who it might be."

"You mean TV and movie stars?"

"That's what you call them. You know something of them, yes? Here's your real chance to use your learning. Only not stars, villains. It's a weakness of mine."

"Do I get a clue?"

"Three. Just to keep with tradition. I just gave you your first one. And . . . I'll throw in a comment when you're wrong."

"How many guesses?"

"I'll let you know. So start."

She thought for a second, Mel's warning about *never . . . ever* betting her life on movie trivia rocketing around inside her head. Then she focused, thinking about weighty bullshit thrown about in a class on cinema history.

"Okay, uh, I'll start with . . . Norman Bates."

"Come on, I may be from another world but I'm not crazy."

Then she took her absolute best, intuitive guess. "The Alien."

He scoffed. "You know I have affinity for blood that melts swords and armor. Like Beowulf's moment facing Grendel's dam. Great talent, but not so good for these times."

Now she was truly at a loss. "Uh . . . the Wolfman."

"Well, I know the night-blooming wolfsbane, but I am most certainly not pure of heart."

"HAL. T-1000."

"Enough of the nonhumans."

"Hannibal Lecter."

"Better. Nice selection. Too gruesome, though. Not my style."

"Say warmer or colder."

"Huh?"

"If I'm close, say 'warmer.'"

"Very well. I'm ready."

"Jack Torrance."

"Uh, warmer. I like his mind, but I'm too pragmatic. Anyway, I never drink . . . wine." He laughed at his own joke.

"Tony Montana."

He laughed. "Scarface? A loser. Also no drugs. You people obsess with such false realities. They are like stinks of fart-clouds. Your fool of a grandfather was one of those druggies."

"Okay, let's see . . ."

"I think we're on our last leg here, Cadence. Think of coin, scratch, silver, and gold. That's your last clue, and you have three guesses left."

"Okay. Hmm. Auric Goldfinger."

"Ah, very warm. But he's too arrogant. He should've killed Mr. Bond and moved on."

"Noah Cross, no . . . no . . . Gordon Gekko!"

"Whatever you may think of me, I don't necessarily think greed is good. It's a fine distinction, I admit. So now, this guess is your last one."

"My last one?" She only then realized how she had wasted her guesses on some of the unlikeliest movie villains.

"Yes, my dear. Alas, we're there."

She took her time, looked at him carefully, thinking about his style. It came to her. Something in his manner suggested it, the same world-weary, dissipated sang-froid. Besides, she remembered the movie *Die Hard* was on TV late earlier in the week. It was worth the gamble. "I've got it."

"I doubt that."

"Hans Gruber!"

He seemed surprised, and then raised his hands to give a soft clap clap clap. "Very well done, my dear! Ordinarily, I would say you have won. But, as you might expect, there's a catch. I must confess."

He paused.

"Come on," she said, "there's no John McClain that could stop *you*."

"No, I'm afraid not. These police detectives are a joke. They could never, as they say, get the drop on me. As for you, there's no way you *could* win. It's like life. You play, but you don't know the rules of the game."

"You are a bastard. Now you do sound like Tony Soprano. You don't have the balls to have rules!"

"Now, now, there you go again. I truly did enjoy our conversation. I will now pay a visit to your meddlesome gramps at ye olde Algonquin. And then all this will be finished."

She looked down and saw the sweep hand on the pocket watch quit moving. It chimed softly, with each note she seemed to stiffen, and the world went an uneasy gray.

Chapter 74

OCTOBER 31: 2:40 PM

—

So in tune had Jess become with the syren melody of the Elvish writings that, when they so desired, they could speak on their own and his translations somehow ended up scrawled across the pages. Almost without effort, the story of the final chapter of Ara's Tale was now creating itself. He awoke to find his scribbled pages spilling onto the floor. He leaned back and stretched.

At that very moment, outside the very room in which Jess sat and stretched, a very real, steel blue Beretta Px4 9mm pistol was pointed dead center at the back of Barren's head. The man pointing the pistol was Bossier Thornton. He cocked the trigger. He had just come out of the elevator to find the man from Riker's Island. The man was now standing stock still, senses alert, assessing every detail of the situation. Bossier had, as they say, most definitely gotten the drop on him. It was a first in Barren's life. He assayed the hallway, the lighting, the footing on the carpet, the distance of the man behind him, his age, his breathing, his fear.

Bossier spoke in quiet tones. "Don't move. Stay still. Hands and palms up and away from your body."

Barren didn't move. And then he moved quicker than any cat ever. Bossier sensed a blur sweep past him and then felt his head being pulled back and a knife-edge rest cool and competent against his neck. The touch of steel on his skin, the presence close behind him, all were exquisitely delicate. They were so effortless, so *silky*. He dropped his gun; it bounced softly on the carpet. The voice next to his ear was soft and familiar. "If you resist in the least, my meddling friend, you won't even feel the cut. So be as still as a spring dawn. How did you come to be here? Quick and quiet your answer."

Bossier swallowed and gulped. His throat twitched, every pore and follicle testing the blade. "The call from your cell phone. You were talking to Cadence. You said you were coming here."

It was meaningless to Barren, but enough to complete his decision. Finish this, he thought. He could complete the task here, but it would be messy. Besides, he had not yet killed in this world. His master was far, far away, and the completion of his single task was within his grasp. His place in all the rest of this world, in all its details and decisions, was his alone to define.

Bossier's heart thudded so heavily that he could hear nothing but the boom and roar from inside. His only feeling was cool metal on the skin of his neck. The knife lifted away. He felt a hand push hard below his ear. No icy line along his throat. He felt almost a relief at being lucky as the hand pushed harder and the world fell into compressing grayness. *I actually may live,* was his last thought as he passed out.

Inside his room, Jess hunched over and translated feverishly. Elvish nuances flowed as if they sensed that time was dear. A familiar figure emerged:

> The Wraith Pazal, standing poised on a precipice, steadied himself. Before him was an open shaft, falling to a deep river of lava that boiled beneath Fume.
>
> He had spent a long day assisting his master's armies as they assembled and departed for battle. Even now, the horns were blowing, summoning him and his brethren.
>
> He had failed as a king. Likewise, he had failed to do his master's bidding, to find the documents in that other world, or to secure the halflings here in this one. The female halfling had escaped once before, only now to be caught, almost by accident, in the very midst of the marshalling armies. Her capture was an exclamation of his failure.
>
> The Dark Lord, his ring-liege, the one who had bestowed this existence upon him, was beyond fury. His very essence

flamed and then brooded in smoky coils. His bellow had perhaps been tinged with fear, "The same halfling that you let slip away, now in the center of my hold?" Days of confusion and fruitless disarray had followed.

This but engraved the Wraith's disgrace deeper in the lore of the Land of the Source—perhaps as deep as the well before him. He had long ago failed as a man governed by his own will. He had abandoned even the nobility of his own mortality.

Across the black land, the horns blew forth, filling every breast with fire and calling the wraiths to war. Criers exhorted the assembled army:

"Come forth and slay the Unbelievers! Wreck and lay havoc to their homes! Burn down their sacred holds! Punish their arrogance! We are the People of the Source!"

Pazal's ring, Greypoint, clasped his finger as it had for long centuries. It could not be removed from his left hand, though it was now well worn from long use.

In his right hand he held forth Arac, ancestral sword of his house, notched deeply but still gleaming and fearfully sharp.

He let it drop.

It twirled in its descent, its mirrored edges reflecting blood-red gleams. Moments later, there was a single flash as it thrust into the boil.

The final lines of the poem he had written long ago came to him:

> No king will leave the sword of his ancestors,
> Nor can he betray his lineage.
> Legends of his falling, preserved in all time, matter not.
> It's his own assay, that of a man of himself,
> That yields strength in the end.

For the first time since the ring had grasped his finger, he smiled a genuine smile, without the puppet's smirk of malice imposed by his master.

He stepped forward into the void, slowly rolling as he fell. Red gleams played out from the ring as it slipped from the finger that hosted it for centuries, and together they passed into the maelstrom of fire.

Jess put down the pen and massaged his cramped hand. He had to keep going. The Elvish tale of Ara's fate boiled and rolled in the cauldron in which he and Cadence had been cast. Peril weighed their lives on the same scale as the Tolkien documents.

This was his state of mind as he sat in the room at the Algonquin and completed the last chapter of the Tale of Ara.

There was a knock on his door.

* * *

Jess Grande cursed Murphy's Natural Law of Flashlights. His flashlight wavered. Bright. Dim . . . dim . . . Shake. Brighter . . . dimmer . . . dim.

The soot-covered tracks to the abandoned 130th Street—Blain Place subway stop were strewn with the debris from a flood of time. They led through a smoky junkyard of incongruous objects: grocery store carts, beams of wood, twisted tree branches, lunch boxes, street signs, railroad tools, clothing, loose strata of ancient glass pop bottles, and beer cans topped with the froth of plastic beverage containers. And gruesome pod-like trash bags.

Nothing would stop him now.

So he progressed, the light dimming with every fateful step, catching still-life images of cracker boxes and a mangled pair of sunglasses staring back with one dark, all-seeing eye.

He and the dimming flashlight were one, for there would be no return journey.

An hour later, when the flashlight was exhausted, Jess shook it and then let it fall from his hand.

He sat on a wooden box in the storeroom. The thin, purpled light was jeweled with intermittent greasy drops falling from the ceiling grates. He listened to far distant rumbles, car sounds like the cawing of crows.

The pool lay before him, fanning with ripples from each drop. It waited, implacable in its own small completeness.

He waited there, dressed once again and now forever as the homeless man in cast-off clothing, holey socks inside heel-less boots with knotted twine for laces.

Hours passed, and the deep breath before the plunge would not come.

The choir of selves that had long peopled his soul came and berated him. The buzz-cut young Osley catching fly balls and overjoyed with the promise of a long summer mocked him. The crew-cut freshman Osley from Los Gatos stood at the Berkeley Gate looking in with disbelief. The white-coated chemistry student Osley glanced up from the lab table, regarded him sadly and shook his head. The drug entrepreneur Osley, riding shotgun in the tractor cab as they barreled through the night, turned to him and said, "How?" The radical assistant professor Osley, sitting impudent and cigared at President Grayson's desk, as Columbia seethed with tear gas and angry shouts. Even the scissor-sharpener Jess, sitting across from Professor Tolkien, who was swearing him to the fealty of preserving these precious writings. They were all there. Along the way, a thousand road signs betokened the long highway of his life as it twisted into a far distant vanishing point. Each sign pointing at him with long fingers of silent accusation.

More images came in stately procession—family, friends, mentors. Their garbled voices began to chime together, "Look at you, living out the end of your wasted life in fear."

Still, the deep breath of true belief would not come.

At last the voices became simply his own as he spoke aloud in the dark room, "How did you *think* this would end?"

The valise with all the original documents, plus the archives materials and the translation key, sat at his side. He fished in its contents for a while, then plucked out a single leather scrap, which he rolled and put in his pocket. Then he sat. He finally picked up a broken yardstick from the debris underfoot. He could just make out the inscription: Holland Hardware 143rd and Broadway. On the back side was etched a calendar for 1948. The year he was born.

He poked the stick in the pool, felt the scratchy rough concrete an inch underneath. Felt it again, confirming the absurdity of the real.

Go away now. Turn your face from Cadence. Find your way to the surface and let the street take you and finish you off in some pee-saturated doorway squalor, furnished with rags and cardboard, the other street people picking through your things like night vultures.

Die, Gutless Wonder.

He realized he hadn't believed in himself, or anything else, for decades.

He had this one last chance, and he couldn't measure up.

The certainty of his failure angered him. He poked the stick hard. It hesitated, and then it *went in*. He stirred and felt the stony firmness give to mush and then thin liquid. He pushed harder, and the yardstick went in two feet.

He stood up, his heart pumping, valise in hand, his stature erect as a novice cliff diver gazing down from a rocky aerie at the wavering dime of blue below, circled by razor-sharp volcanic outcroppings and the relentless pounding surf. Timing the waves.

He took a deep breath and plunged.

Chapter 75

WAKEUP

—

Consciousness came to Cadence in a rush of disoriented fear. All she could think was that she was in the center of a giant stadium, the Klieg lights suddenly flaring into blinding light and the marching bands sounding a thunderous crescendo.

She blinked. The rush passed, followed by the Rip Van Winkle effect. She felt a sense of precious time having passed and momentous events having occurred. All while she slept. It was a sense of being left behind and catching up, with a yawning hole in the middle.

The room where she had conversed with Barren was the same. She was alone. Her keys lay on the coffee table, the talisman removed.

The keys held down a note on folded stationary similar to that slipped under her hotel door. She looked at it in the same way that people regarded a telegram in the 1930s. Bad News. Yellow Death. Don't read it.

She read it. It said:

> The deal is afoot. Pray that it goes smoothly.
> If so you shall never see me again.
> If not, perhaps a glimpse as my swift knife falls.

She knew somehow that the other rooms would be different than when she entered. First was the waiting room, perfectly appointed in Victorian furnishings and décor. The skylight was still there, letting down a cascade of soft afternoon luminescence. An adjustable sky curtain in semblance of the aurora borealis spread overhead at the second floor to filter and direct the light. A single thin rope of the material hung downward. She touched it. It felt light to her touch, almost alive with changing color and organic tension.

The display cases and their odd contents were gone. She toed the corner of a distinctive blue-yellow, antique Persian rug that had not been there before. She saw that the fade marks on the wood perfectly matched the shape of the rug, as if it had lain there unmoved for years.

She went to the front door. It was the same wood but a simpler latch and pull assembly. She pushed down on a bar and the latch released. The door opened. It was afternoon, as if she walked in only minutes ago. But she knew that was not the case. Not at all.

She stepped out and smelled the air. Raw and new. The door snicked shut behind her. She jumped and looked at its unyielding façade.

She pushed and fiddled, but it was locked tight—no budge or latch movement. She felt for Barren's note, but realized she'd left it on the table.

Both outside signs were gone.

The time vacuum that she knew was there scared her, as if its unfilled potential could suck in all sorts of horrendous possibilities. She began to run toward Broadway, looking to catch the first downtown subway train back to the Algonquin.

* * *

As Cadence left the Talisman Store and began to run in sweating desperation, a few translated pages sat alone on Jess's desk. Those pages gave witness to Ara's final destiny unfolding in a far distant realm:

> Just as Pazal unsheathed his sword for the last time and stepped into the abyss, so the halfling Bearer stood a mere pebble's toss from another edge, on the far side of Fume.
>
> Thunder coughed up deep within the earth. A rush of steam, scalding and scorching, shot forth.
>
> The Dark Lord was calm, even as he watched the halfling dither.
>
> Beside His Darkness, Lord of the Eye, loomed a tall contraption studiously assembled from glass and wood, and served by hunched minions of a race unlike any she had ever

seen. Meticulous piping led here and there from an immense clear bowl in which danced a silvery substance. Lesser vials held churning liquids of different colors, jade green, horse hair yellow, autumnal orange. It was the Source. It was the sum of it all, the ultimate mixing of alchemic fluids, decocted from a special chamber deep in the earth's heart.

The Bearer stared down, wavering and almost toppling over the edge. His heart seemed compressed, squashed and unable to perform beneath the weight of his burden. He could not catch his breath. His mind cycled in a whirlpool of indecision. His fingers mirrored this, fluttering in a repeated, futile dance. The Object, now fully alive, jumped and pirouetted on its chain entangled within his fingers.

This is my final role, he thought, and now I've lost all. Because of that, that Wizard. Bind I shall keep. I shall find Ara. I shall . . .

"Halfling?" the Dark Lord said, barely loud enough to be heard. The Bearer turned slowly, his body now rigid. His eyes were glazed with exhaustion, and then he saw clearly who was there.

Ara stood at the Dark Lord's side. She was watching him.

She was dressed in tattered rags, yet wearing a dark crown. A necklace of resplendent black stones encircled her neck, each stone shining forth with a brilliant red spark.

Like spider eyes, thought the Bearer, his mind still defying the plain truth revealed by his senses.

Ara's eyes glittered, drinking in the conflict laid before her. Oh, the possibilities! She could be a princess of supreme power, ruler of all the lands of her kind. How her people in Frighten had been slighted!

Or she could be wife and Amon to this honest and brave halfling before her.

The Dark Lord enjoyed the dumbstruck look on the Bearer's face. He feared no resolve in this halfling. Not with Ara, his prize, dangled before him. The Bearer's servant, his fat companion, hovered at his side. He was a less predictable thing. But the answer there was at hand also.

Behind them arose that slinking gargoyle the Dark Lord had

trained to follow them like a jackal to offal.

The Bearer faltered and then fell before the terrible beauty of the Halfling Queen. There he cried out in the pain of his burden and the loss of his beloved. He saw the clinging one who shadowed him always, creep toward him on all fours like a loathsome spider. The power within the Burden had wrung its destruction.

"How does it come to this?" the halfling cried.

The Dark Lord gloated. He felt no humility in his dependence on the Source, of which he was but an imperfect copy of an unnecessary part. His avarice and arrogance in this moment far outstripped his malice, and in this his focus wavered.

There they stood, frozen in tableau, as the fumes rolled up over the precipice and the earth at its core trembled and rendered up its boiling soup.

Then the Lord of the Source, soon to be once again Wielder of Bind, extended one hand in gracious direction before Ara. She stepped forward. She walked across the rubble to where the Bearer lay. She knelt by him and gently uncoiled his fingers. Bind she took into her own palm, rising and displaying it to her Master in triumph. Its spell swirled about her. It tugged and writhed in anticipation of its return to the Hand of the Source.

The Halfling Queen turned to the defeated halfling who was once her Amon. "Rise," she said, "and let us try to speak the words."

The Bearer looked up, fighting the pain and struggling to see around him. Ara's eyes pronounced the secret of their vows. The words that just might break the invisible chains that yanked them here and there like clumsy puppets in some crude minstrel show. Whether the Dark Lord, or Bind itself, pulled the chains in this macabre dance, she could not tell.

The Bearer coiled tighter in a returning spasm of pain. He uttered, "Down . . . roads . . ."

The Halfling Queen's obsidian eyes softened. She also spoke: "Past . . . borders . . ."

He raised his head and reached his hand to her: "Through . . . gates . . ."

And in unison they groped to speak: "Each . . . together . . .

to spy that . . . sea!"

Tested, the spell would not unclasp its chains. They and the Dark Lord were for a moment rendered still, as a painting might preserve their demeanors for all time. Even then, the air about them swirled with the tumult of contesting wills. Suddenly, as if the chains were but smoke rings created by jesters, their power fell away. The Bearer was himself again. Free to choose.

He stood up, retrieved Bind from Ara's open hand, and held it over the precipice.

"My fate is my own," he said calmly, looking into the dismayed eyes of the Dark Lord.

There he held Bind for a moment. All was still. Tensiles of fate adjusted and rearranged beyond the vision of any of the races of Middle-earth.

The Bearer looked at Ara, then yelled at the Dark Lord to divert his attention, "Red-Eye, your vision and your spells are weak. Like the Source itself. You have no more days."

Many things happened at once: Ara moved quickly to stand beside the device that supported the Source. The minions scurried about, oblivious to her and servile to their tasks of adjustment to valve and stem. The great glass bowl at the top shimmered with its precious contents. She saw that, like the Dark Lord's empire, the contraption was top heavy. She grabbed a wooden strut and pulled. The mechanism wobbled. The Dark One turned around, then looked back at the Bearer, then back to Ara. A ghastly, unbelieving look of dismay crept across his features.

Ara jumped up on the strut and leaned impishly back. The device teetered beyond its center of gravity. Like a great tree, stiff and solemn in its slow fall, it leaned and then fell in a thundering crash of heavy liquid and exploding glass and splintered wood. Ara, nimble as ever, jumped free at the last second. The broken vials burst forth their contents. The essences, loose and hurried, ran with lives of their own, from ledge to floor to precipice. The Dark Lord danced awkwardly as the metallic liquids of the Source slithered and scurried, shimmering and deft as eels, to pour over the edge.

Still standing at the precipice, the Bearer opened his hand

and Bind glinted forlornly as it fell away, following the Source to oblivion.

Barren picked up the pages and tucked them in his coat pocket.

Chapter 76

RUSH

—

Cadence banged her own cell phone with her fist. It was shut down. Dead battery.

After surfacing from the subway stop, she took a wrong turn, walked three needless blocks and finally swept into the lobby of the Algonquin. Heraclitus bolted from his perch. Guests' heads turned, the desk clerk stood up straight. Cadence made it to the elevator. Her head was ringing like an in-use anvil.

First floor. Out of the elevator. The hallway loomed in two opposite and indistinguishable directions. She had to concentrate, holding her plastic key card and remembering the room number. It was fuzzy, like trying to remember the street address where you lived in the fifth grade. She tried several doors and finally one worked.

She burst through the door and shut it behind her. Safe.

The room was empty. The bed was made. The room was clean and arranged in impeccable order. Her shoe crinkled on a note on the floor. She picked it up, opened it cautiously.

M. Lawrence Novell, the manager, was inquiring whether, as her reservation was through Monday only, would she be extending her stay?

Monday was yesterday, according to the newspapers she glimpsed while running to the subway platform. She held the note like it was heavy. A reminder of an incongruous, alternate world. A place of quiet despair and frozen rivers of indecision, where petty errands sailed haphazardly on the air currents from the sea cliff of her inertia. A place that would be a prison where it was always three o'clock in the morning.

She scrunched the note and threw it aside and looked at the room desk. Her cell phone charger cord was there, neatly coiled. She plugged the phone in. She used the hotel phone to call Jess's room. A stranger answered, indignant about her questions. She called the front desk. Sorry, he checked out. No, no note left behind for her, nothing in Lost and Found. A Mr. Thornton called. "Oh yes, has madame had a chance to do her shopping?" She said a deflated "yes" and hung up and flopped on the bed, crushed.

After a moment, she folded over like a collapsing tower of sticks. She took in the world in sideways view. Maybe that would help her think. *Something else is missing!* She sat up. She crawled under the bed, stabbing her arms up to the hiding place. She groped. Nothing. The documents, the valise, all of her grandfather's translations and notes—all gone!

She checked drawers, the closet, inside the shower.

She repeated the entire search, overturned all the trash cans, and ransacked the couch. She grew still and contemplated a return to that perpetual, pre-dawn prison cell that yawed open in her mind.

Just me and my ticket home now.

After a while her room phone rang. "Cadence, Bossier. I've been calling your cell and your rooms. I cornered a man, the one who was stalking you. Outside your other room. He got away. I fainted or something. I just blacked out. You were missing . . ."

"No, I'm okay, more or less. How did you find him?"

"I got a call on Monday from a different cell phone. You were talking with someone . . . like you were in trouble. I heard a man say he was going to the Algonquin. So I went there and saw this guy outside your grandfather's room. Then I woke up in the maid's closet."

"So, are you sure you're all right?"

The second line of the phone rang, the light blinking with idiot insistence. "Uh . . . hold on." She punched the blinking button. It was the desk clerk again. Sorry, he'd forgotten. There was a note for her from Mr. Grande, formerly of Room 608. She punched back to the first line. "Gotta go. Yes. Yes. I'm okay. Bye."

Counting the elevator time, she was downstairs in thirty seconds. She got the envelope, Algonquin stationary, her name on the front in Jess' erratic handwriting. She ripped it open and read the wobbly, trailed writing that spoke of adrenaline and haste:

Cadence only few seconds. I have the
docs. Hope we filled in some blanks.
Like in that old song, I have to go. So
you can stay. I love you. Maybe I'll get
lucky.

Jess

Just like that, everything . . . gone.

She let the note fall, its wish-wash flutter perfect closure to the
yellow telegram flimsy that had ignited this journey. A horde of
emotions jostled in her mind, like sale-mad shoppers bottlenecked at the
opening doorway of Walmart on Black Friday. All her naïve family
questions, Jess, Os, the ancient documents, Elvish, belief, cynicism,
Ara—everything, at least whatever was left, was being trampled in this
mad, mindless roar. She squeezed her eyes shut and jammed her fists
against her mouth to keep in the simultaneous screams of fear and
loathing and grief. For just a moment, it felt as if her head was
pressuring with explosive gas, a mere spark away from blowing
completely apart.

Then it passed. She opened her eyes and let the squeeze-tears fall.
Her hands brushed back her hair as she took a deep breath.

She sank into the big lobby chair and just let the world slowly cave
in around her. Like some Hollywood Spectacular set, it fell ponderously,
pillar by pillar. She accepted the collapse. It would be all right, even the
long noir movie that would be her return trip to Los Angeles. *Last Train
to Mirkwood*, it might be called.

She left New York City the next morning. Just like she imagined,
just like in those old-timey movies, the next four days flickered by in
grainy black and white.

The *things*—the lost documents, the translation notes, the clues—she
let them go with each westbound hour, like confetti loosed into the
wind. The rest was hard. She mourned for Jess because, somehow, she
couldn't be mad at him. She understood now something of the forces
that can sweep people away on journeys that must be taken. Strangely,
she grieved also for Ara—her fate twisted to betrayal and her tale so
forever lost. Jess was gone, but he had left something, a grandchild
named Cadence. Ara, even if deservedly so, was *erased*.

It was only at the other end, as the cab left her off in front of The

Mirkwood Forest, the dust settling in motes of slanting, pure California sunshine, that the world returned to full color and Cadence came alive again.

* * *

As she stood there in the dusty sunshine in front of The Forest, its door plastered with a foreclosure notice and "Entry Prohibited: LACSO" yellow tape, Barren stood, six states away to the east, alone in wind-whipped rain. His boots were soaked through. With his baseball cap pulled down to eye level, the rain cascaded down the bill and onto his soaked denim jacket.

Splatters that felt like liquid quarters pelted him. On the pavement they made *bonk* and *splank* sounds that threatened golf-ball-sized hail.

He stood as still as if he were a hunched tree improbably sprouted from the asphalt shoulder.

He smiled. The elements of rain and lightning and thunder were contesting like petty gods, like the caped and marquee-titled wrestlers he had seen on TV. The display came and went in a moment, and the storm raced on. He stood in the lessening drizzle. He had seen the great storms, the ones that included molten fire and flashing light and soul-breaking thunder.

This world was not ready for the making of a new age. That was part of its quaint charm.

The temperatures dropped, and a fast-gathering fog emerged as the storm barreled off to the east. A car came by, its *slish* of tires advancing almost ahead of its headlights. There was a last note of thunder, and the fog enshrouded all.

Behind him was a field of corn. The fog poured like a gauzy, grey-white liquid into the rows. The stalks stood there, ghastly yellow and abused, like ranks of lean and tested soldiers ordered for one last review. Some were already faltering, leaning on their comrades.

A few smeared points of light hovered up ahead where the road disappeared. He would walk into the town and decide.

Chapter 77

NOVEMBER

—

Time did its thing. The foggy, surreal hangover of New York City and Halloween and the rage and the sorrow, all passed. Cadence puttered and planned and took action. She sold the Jaguar and gave the money to the bank in return for a stay of execution on the foreclosure sale.

She reopened The Mirkwood Forest. She rearranged the merchandise and put ads first in the local paper down in the Valley and then in the *Los Angeles Times*. She built a website, TheMirkwoodForest.com. She applied for real jobs.

Mostly, for the first time in her life, she felt filled-in. There was no more ice pick hole in her mind's family portrait. The details might be sketchy, but the hole was filled in. A fleeting hug and squeeze of hands with her grandfather would have to do as the patch for a lot of uncertainty. He was there—marooned, missed, bizarre, eccentric, deeply flawed, but with the one redeeming quality she hungered for. He was real, and he had loved her enough to sacrifice himself. She had enough history to stop the questions.

Ara was different. For a while, Cadence kept those uncertainties with her like the charm bracelet she had as a little girl. Each precious, glittering doubt jingling with her throughout the day. Was the account of her betrayal, her turn to the dark side, just a piece of misinformation? An odd, easily misinterpreted fragment from the rubble of history? Did she and the Bearer ever go to that Rock by the Sea? Did any fragment of her existence yet survive to be unearthed by some future Tolkien-like mythologist? Would she ever, however imperfectly, be rendered again?

Cadence realized that the answers were all no. Her elusive grandfather and Ara, along with the mystical, Mirkwoodian magic of Elvish, had all finally winked out of this world.

So that left one more tidying up task, from which some slight perverse pleasure might arise. Getting on his calendar was a snap this time, even though she had to wait for him to get back in town. Monday, two weeks from now, she had an appointment with Mel.

On the next day, Saturday morning, Cadence opened The Forest at ten. A clear morning when the canyon's first (perhaps only) true frost of the season promised a crisp, mild day. The ocean below would be sparkly and bright, and its clean smell would waft all the way up to Topanga.

The bell over the door tinkled as a first customer wandered in. She was in the back of the store, but briefly peered out and yelled "Good morning!" A man was by the front window with his back to her, checking out the shop. He whistled a singsong tunelet as he bent over to inspect the Abbott and Costello shakers in a glass case. Buzz cut, gray hair, Hawaiian shirt. Tourist.

She hibernated the computer sitting on the calico tablecloth. As she got to the front counter the tourist had wandered off to inspect the Vintage Vinyl section she had put in.

She fussed at the counter, looking down through the top glass as her hands re-arranged the perfectly boxed Barbies. She saw a man's hand come to rest on the counter.

"Do you still have Riker's Island comic books?"

She froze, sensing the image of Barren, his leering wolfen face gathering up like a conjured demon. With one swoop he would uproot her from this soil and send her off to roll like a tumbleweed in a high breeze. *How?* She thought. *Not here.*

She looked up. Instead of the gloating face of Barren, a never-before seen version of Jess Grande was there. Clean-shaven, but older, more worn, creases and crags etched deeper into a face previously hidden.

She was stunned. Her eyes took it all in before she could react. "Grandpa!" She screamed, flying around the counter to grab him. "What! How?"

"Shush. Shush. All in good time." She stepped back and held his hands, old and new entwined, and looked at him. What she saw, even in that first study by her artist's eye, was a man emptied out. It was as if he had been scraped hard on the inside by some terrible and primitive tool. What was left, she would see.

The first installment of "all in good time" came an hour later. They sat at the kitchen table and he told her what little he could recall, ending with the end.

"So, I had it all along. The document we talked about."

"I don't understand."

"The scruffy piece of leather. It was the Vow. Rings have no power unless the promises that accompany their giving are honored. This was a Vow of Protection and it was a coin that the Dark Lord had given long ago. As the holder, even as I gave up the Tolkien documents, that coin was bound to be honored. I suspect it may have been given originally to Pazal. Or perhaps not. Somewhere in those documents, never found by us, may have been something of that tale. The point is that the Vow was given, a deal was sealed. The rest we'll never know now."

"Like a get out of jail free card. Or the Letters of Transit in *Casablanca*."

"Except this was real."

Cadence relaxed her watchful eye and laughed from a depth of peace that surprised her. "Yeah. Real. I believe . . . for real."

* * *

That night the man once known as Barren ate somewhere at three in the morning sitting on a stool in a diner called The Eat. After that, he walked out and hitched a ride to anywhere.

Anywhere ended up being Texas City, Texas. He stood at night on a bridge over a dredged canal, beneath a drooping yellow sky.

There it was, a vast world clear to the hazy horizon of interweaving pipelines, tanks sized from hills to horses, valves, gauges, flanges, heat exchangers, absorbers, pumps, containment pits, shacks, and metal buildings, all overlaid with soot and black pools of oil and water and crud. Behold a wonder, a hundred, nay a thousand, giant flares whooshing, roaring, lighting anew like a never-ending fireworks display. He stood there, his pupils wide with awe, the flares reflecting in his eyes like a coal sack of troll candles.

The next night he was far away. The sky dark as upon it floated a barnacled moon sculling on a flow-tide of black clouds. He pulled the small leather pouch from within his shirt and opened it as it hung from the cord around his neck. He dug deep with his fingers, as if trying to catch a living thing. Finally he pulled out his hand and opened his fist. There gleamed a simple ring, silver-hued, almost smoky in color. Its only adornment was the restless flow of rich, satiny hues in its surface, like the folds of a wizard's robe.

He had not looked at it until this moment. He had kept it secure in its pouch. He suspected it had an august heritage, perhaps once intended by the Dark Lord for some unsuspecting king, some future wraith. He knew to wear it was perilous so long as he walked within the reach of that power.

But now he felt beyond that realm. His errand he had acquitted well. The meddlesome fragments of Elvish, including much of the Tale of Ara, were now cast out to their destruction. A shame, but unavoidable if he was to, as they say here, be his own man. He knew that the ring was responsible for the quicksilver increase in his ability to learn and speak their language. Perhaps magic would come of it. He took it from his palm and put it on his left index finger.

He breathed deep and focused on his surroundings.

The night was coming. He stood in the middle of a crossroads over which trees leaned, so massed and drooped with kudzu as to be unrecognizable except as the hulking shapes of night ogres. A few late fireflies played in the boughs and made momentary eyes among the leaves.

Here, he thought, *is a place where souls pay an evil tithe or be taken.*

He imagined the crunch of gravel, forewarning a legion of his otherselves trudging the road this sultry night, coming to each take back their piece of him.

He looked about, pondering the itinerant's question: whether some escape, some secret gate lay within these bordering thickets.

He knew that world and those times were gone, and no escape waited in this world.

With that, he chose a direction and began to walk swiftly away. He accelerated to an easy jog, his aspirations high. In his head played the theme from *Shaft,* the sixteen-note Motown high hat, Isaac Hayes funking up the tempo. "*Whoo is the man . . .*"

He had a further errand to attend to. A bit of evening things up. Something he alone had devised.

In a moment he was at a distance from the crossroads, another itinerant disappearing forever into the Great American Night.

Chapter 78

PIECES

—

The Topanga Commune Organic Restaurant had changed the menu—out with the squash and corn, in with the broccoli and spinach. The creek burbled. The overhanging oaks, brown-leaved and asleep, waited for spring.

Cadence had a letter sitting on the table in front of her.

"Go ahead," said Jess, nodding at it.

They often spent lunch hours here. Sometimes talking, sometimes just letting the time pass. These moments wouldn't last, they both knew, but they were important for now.

"Okay," she said, and opened the envelope from the Los Angeles School District. It was an offer for a full-time position teaching fifth grade, beginning in September. Yes, fifth grade. The age when a child's ability to project and believe takes root or begins to wither in a long, weedy path of self-disappointment.

She wanted to work in that garden. She had a week to decide.

She handed the letter to Jess and said, "What do you think?"

He read the letter. "Take it. You should stay here."

These days they talked like the reunited orphans they were, piecing together fragmented bits of a family. They knew that some pieces, a lot really, were missing forever. Others were being fitted together—cracked fragments of an enigmatic picture that was her father. Little details, tears, regrets, laughing. A lot of guilt de-crusted and examined and then put aside, like odd jigsaw pieces that you can worry over forever, or just throw over your shoulder and get on with the rest of the puzzle.

He summed up a lot of the pieces in a few sentences. "I never knew my natural parents. Osley is my adopted name. I made myself up out of whole cloth after that. The name 'Grande'? I got it from a dingy little coffee shop. In Seattle in 1970. A Starbucks, maybe the original one, trying to survive after the folk-music coffee house era They got their name from Melville's first mate to Ahab. I took the name of their drink size. I never knew who to tell. Even Arnie. I never told anyone. So what's a name?"

"That's poor comfort a couple of generations later, Grandpa, but well, I guess we're in good company. Even Tolkien borrowed names."

"Maybe we should change it."

She laughed. "Hardly, I like it. I was born with it. I'm keeping it. So are you. This is all just gonna stick from now on. Okay?"

"Okay."

"After all . . ."

"What?"

"A name *is* a promise that something exists. It's strange, but for the first time in my life I feel that way about myself."

The pony-tailed waiter, John, came and cleared their table. They ordered a shared pot of the tea of the day, specially imported from some Malaysian village.

She looked at Jess. "So what did you decide about The Forest? Are you, we, going to keep it open?"

"I think so. It keeps things interesting. For me it's like, well, traveling without leaving home. The old weirdness of the road sometimes just walks in the front door."

"Grandpa. There are some things we haven't talked about."

"Really? Because we've done a lot of talking."

"I know, but I wanted to wait a bit." She looked at him, studying his eyes. "Did Ara deserve to be erased? Like a traitor?"

His look of astonishment was genuine. "What do you mean? She was a heroine. She saved them all."

"But the record from Frighten, the account of her betrayal?"

"Rubbish. That was a snippet, a passing black cat that can mislead you, a misguided fragment of history. Look, if future historians dug out a Leni Reifenstahl flick, like *Triumph of the Will*, from the rubble of our civilization, they'd think Hitler was a stern but benevolent guy who ruled the world. It's all happenstance." Then he stopped. "You never saw the last chapter that I left on the desk?"

"No, nothing. It was gone."

He recounted the destruction of the Source and the apparent end of the Dark Lord. "I *guess* he ended; at least that's where the story ended.

Cadence let out a slow breath of relief. She felt a quiet, solemn pride in having been a final witness to Ara's journey. Her tale was gone, but it was enough to know that she had been true to herself.

"What else?" Jess asked.

"Oh, well," Cadence recovered, "tell me some more about Professor Tolkien. Do you remember some other things about him?"

"Some. Like a handful of snapshots. I remember his long-winded moments, his mumbling, his excitement about the stories he was discovering."

"But what about the documents, the Elvish?"

"In truth, those memories are fading. I can see him unrolling the scrolls, his hands moving over the symbols, the sense of magical power imbedded there. But now, like the Elvish, it seems to be fading. More like something I read than lived. Maybe that was his point. Once in a while there's no difference."

"So what about Osley and the Scissor Sharpener, Grandpa?'

"It's funny, I know they are, or were, me. But they're the same way. At some point your past life gets to be like an over-read book. They were as real as the sunshine and breeze where we sit, but now they feel like exotic contrivances—lives I manufactured and dwelt in. Then I shed them. When I went away with the documents, I don't remember much. I know I stood, naked and wrinkled. Exposed just as myself. Those people, Osley, the Sharpener, they fell away like old skins. They stayed there. They didn't come back with me. As if all this had scraped me down—to a husk."

She let the silence unroll, looking at the man that was both less and more than the Osley-slash-Jess she had met. His mask, if he still had one, was just himself.

He broke the interlude. "And one more thing."

"What's that?"

"I finally knew the answer. 'Do I stay or do I go?' I finally knew—if I ever got out of there—I would stay. Right here at The Forest with you. As long as you would tolerate me."

"Sometimes I can't help but feel that one, or both, of us dreamed all this up. What've we got to show from it?"

"Everything. The main thing. You and I sitting here talking."

He reached part way across the table, his hands browned and purpled with liver spots. "At that pool, the thing that came home to me, finally, was that I couldn't stand leaving all this unsaid, undone. You can't make up for the past. But you can own up for it. That's what kept me going. The rest was like a blur. Men and these gnarly, runty ass-hole creatures came and talked to me. They took the valise, then came back with an executioner. But I had the ace. The Vow! I shook it in their faces! Then I woke up."

"In Hoboken?"

"I agree it sounds like a dream. A dream that lingers but doesn't make sense."

"Forget it, Grandpa. It's Middle-earth."

"Yes. But it's gone now. All the Tolkien documents. All the originals. All the Elvish. Ara. Gone without a trace."

She hesitated. "Do you think the Dark Elves are gone?" Even as she spoke, the image of weasel eyes and ferret faces in the woods loomed up.

His face darkened, as if a curious, fast-moving thundercloud had swept over a sunny day. She could see him drifting into that long-seeing gaze again as he mused out loud, "They are resourceful, and they want out of Middle-earth. In fact, they covet our world. They are subtle, and they definitely don't work for the Keebler Cookie Company. But . . . time will tell. Let's not speak of them."

The shadow passed, and she asked, "You know what?"

"What?"

"You're the original, Grandpa. You're the prize. That's what I went searching for. However we got here, we got here."

He laughed. "Like you said, don't ask. It's Mirkwood."

The lunch was over. Birds wheeled above the trees toward a blue sky and puffy white clouds.

"And what about the bills, the foreclosure?"

"It's all on hold. Thanks to you, I'm not an 'estate' anymore. So they had to start over. Everett said to wait for a notice in the mail. Something will work out."

She looked over at the tiny Topanga Post Office, nestled a block away. "Well, stay here, and I'll get today's mail." She hopped up and jogged over to the Post Office. She returned with an armload.

"There's a lot today." She pulled up a stack piled high with the usual postal debris of unsolicited catalogs, flyers, penny ad papers, mortgage offers.

They set to the stack like trash-pickers. Hiding at the bottom was a rumpled brown envelope. It was twine-tied, no return address. The stamps upside down and misplaced. It had forklift tracks down one side. The address for The Mirkwood Forest was printed as if by a nervous hostage working in charcoal.

They both stared at it. "You open it, Cadence."

She undid the twine and pulled at the flap. She didn't want to put her hand in there. She held it up, open at the bottom, and the contents spilled out: a pile of yellow legal sheets and Algonquin Hotel stationary with intense, familiar scribbles all over them.

And, at the end, out plopped the tooth. Jess stared in disbelief. "Be careful! It could be another trick, maybe from that Barren thing!"

She reached over and picked up the talisman. "I don't think it's a trick. I think it's his way of evening some things up with his former . . . employer. Barren's little diss to the Dark Lord by sending all this to us. And the tooth," she held it up firmly in her hand, "it's still searching for someone to believe in it, to receive its luck."

"Well, maybe that's both of us. And even more important?" He looked at her.

She held up the piles of papers, clutched like a victory trophy. "Ara's back!"

"And you've got something to talk to Mel about."

Chapter 79

DUCK SALAD

———

"So, aside from thanking you again for picking up the tab at the Algonquin, that's pretty much the story."

Mel listened. His iPhone was silent, resting ceremoniously to his right. It was untouched by his hand, which held one of the Peninsula's embossed salad forks in mid-air. He finally took a bite.

"Cadence, it's a sad turn of events, tragic. If I hadn't experienced one piece of it firsthand, I'd say you made it up (chomp), that it's all bullshit. But since I can't dismiss it all, I'll go along."

He took another bite of the lunchroom's signature duck salad, then continued, "Shame. I (chew) had imagined a great meeting." His other hand swept in the air. "A big, top-floor, teak-lined conference room high above Century City. The publisher, maybe Alrop or Freidken, would be there (gulp), flanked by his VP of Sales. Two or three lawyers. One from an outside firm, maybe Brunson and Cayhill. The others, 'his people,' as he might say. Go ahead and eat."

She started on the salade Niçoise, glad to let him talk.

"We would be there—you, me, some lawyer. Maybe Everett. We would have the upper hand. They'd say, 'Where'd you get the documents?' We would tell them, pointing out that they were a gift. They would politely ask questions, testing the edges for ownership. Everett would politely set them straight, then we'd get into some blah-blah about copyright. 'What copyright?' Everett would say, 'It's fair use in any case, allegory, dogs and cats, all that.'"

He snuck in another bite.

"Then (chew) I would take over. Look the publisher in the eyes, point my index finger down on the table like so . . . and I'd say, 'Buy this now and I can keep it off the storyboard circuit. Let us walk out of here, and we'll have ten competing bids by tomorrow. You'll never get this back!'"

She put her fork down and let him continue.

"They'd pause for a moment. See, they'd already prepared for this. Their outside attorney would lean in, fold his hands, and say, 'To resolve this matter, we are willing to put X'—call it whatever you want for purposes of this conversation—'on the table. Total residual rights. We publish it or bury it at our discretion. You and your clients walk away.'"

"And right then and there we have them. Now, as they say, we know what they are, and the only question is the price. Plus a few other terms, of course, like them paying my outrageous fee separately."

Cadence put down her fork.

"Mel, you really do live inside your own movie. Do you write the script dailies up every night?"

"No, butterfly, I make it all up as I go."

"Well, the bad news is that the original documents are gone, I'm sure of that. Want the good news?"

"There is some?"

"We got a package. No return address."

"Wait. I got it. From your Mr. Osley. The Figment. Another magically there and gone again character."

"Figment? He was real as you are, Mel. But no, not from Osley. Listen, you called me, scared as a puppy. Peeing all over yourself about the mysterious offer. I still don't buy all you've been telling me."

"It wasn't very magical. Just a nasty squeeze. Dressed up as business but the menace and the message came through, all right. I'd say it was the Mafia but they don't care about books and they don't play with riddles. Your lives were threatened, which I was considering, and then mine, whereupon I immediately took action."

"And one more time, who was saying this to you?"

"It was all by phone, and the message by courier. The voice, he knew the industry well enough to pull off some lines. Clunky and borrowed, like he watched *The Directors* a few times and was a quick study."

"Any accent, odd figure of speech?"

"The speech was, oh, imagine a Bulgarian that learned English from watching American TV. It wasn't just a crank. Like I said to myself, when it's your ass, you gotta believe. So anyway, what was in it? The package?"

"Ah, that's what's interesting. Not the Tolkien documents. Not the originals. But all of the translations."

"So, the original stash of documents, the invaluable for-sure-Tolkien-owned-it stuff, the ones pretty much verified by Mr. Bois-Gilbert and his Inspecteurs, the ones I saw here at this table? Gone?"

"Yes."

Mel sighed and put his chin on his fist, dejected.

"What's so wrong? There's still the story. If that's the thing, and all stories continue, who cares who wrote it? She, Ara, was really real."

"What, you're believing your own soup now, Cadence? What's missing is the proof. The Good Housekeeping Seal of Approval that makes it all sellable. Let me boil it down for you: It's not the story, it's the sales."

"I disagree. In fact, that, right there, is where I learned we are very different. I don't give a damn about money except to fix something broken in my life. But you, you do."

He waited.

"So that's why I'm going to give you one last chance. I want you to set up that meeting with the publisher."

"There's nothing to go on. No one will take the meeting."

"I don't believe you for a second, Mel. You know deep down that this is a real thing. Like you said, people want to know. And the most important part, the story that's just as magical, is the bigger part about how it came together. Me. My grandfather. Osley. Even you. See, Mel, when this gets written, you'll be in it. You're an aspiring author yourself. Come on. You'll love it."

She pulled her keys from her purse, signaling an end to the lunch. A large tooth was attached to the keychain.

"That's some tooth. You grow that yourself?"

"I found it, lost it in a way, and then re-found it. It's a good-luck charm, but only if you believe. Otherwise it's bad luck. I carry it, because, in a way, you taught me something."

"What's that?"

"About stepping up and betting your life on things. Take your cynicism, Mel, your greatest asset. I would hedge your bets before relying on that."

Before he could speak, she stood and offered her hand. He rose and they shook hands.

"Good-bye Mel."

She turned and walked down the hallway toward the foyer, thick with an exuberance of orchids in Sevres vases.

Mel's iPhone buzzed angrily. He let it ring.

Chapter 80

SUITS

—

The view from the floor-to-ceiling windows in the thirtieth floor conference room looked south, across Century City. It was hazing quickly in the L.A. smog, suggesting the low, boxy outlines of the Twentieth Century Fox studios.

The conference table was massive in breadth and length, done in some obscure, threatened rainforest wood. It boasted seating for twenty in chairs finished in some obscure, threatened animal hide.

Like many expressions of opulence, this combination of window, light, rare wood, and rare leather was hardly intended for meetings. It was an instrument of intimidation.

Cadence and her grandfather had been ushered into the room alone and left waiting. To stew. To take in the power.

The door opened, and in came the suits, two men and one woman. First came the legendary publishing executive, tall, immaculate, with a full head of gray hair coifed to slightly long, Hollywood-irreverent length. Flanking him was the grim senior law partner. Next came the shark-like associate, the ace, the lady attorney with Ivy League training and acid for blood. Behind them, looking rumpled despite his fifteen hundred dollar Armani suit, came Mel. In this crowd, he looked like a used car sales associate hovering around for his commission.

The suits worked the introductions, graciousness overplayed because they held the cards. They all sat down, each side arrayed across from the other.

"Ms. . . . Grande." The delay was calculated as the senior partner glanced down at their clothes, their status, then continued, "I want to thank you for coming here. My clients have reviewed Mr. Chricter's query regarding certain . . . uh . . . supposedly lost documents owned by Professor Tolkien."

A long pause as he studied them.

"We suggested this meeting to avoid any . . . misunderstanding."

More pause.

Here the executive calmly put his hand on his trusty counsel's arm, and leaned over. "Paul, let me step in here." He looked engagingly across the table and folded his hands, pre-announcing the finality of what he was about to say.

"Ms. Grande, Mr. Grande, our position, to be frank, is that we will not allow publication of these materials. Nor will we allow you to keep any of the originals, wherever they are. As our attorneys can no doubt explain fully to you or your counsel, we will do all within our power to prevent their publication."

To Cadence, despite his lack of pointy hat and a wand, his look could not have been more wizard-like. She knew, deep down, just what he was. "Sir, you may think you can secret away the truth. And in part your people," she left a long, deliberate pause here, "have already stolen back much of this. But not all. I can't prove the authenticity of the words anymore. But you can't disprove them either."

The executive's hands unfolded and sat palms-down on the table. His attorney stiffened.

"And in any case, they're part of what happened to my grandfather and me. And that we own."

Like a confused puppy sensing things are not going well, Mel interrupted. "Cadence, look, I'm sure there's a modest but still meaningful price you'll accept to turn all this over, all the copies, everything. Perhaps an amount that would save your grandfather's property."

Cadence turned to face him. "Mel, I know you got something out of this already. I checked the Les Inspecteurs website. They got a one-season deal on French TV off of the pilot made about me. The money was probably a bluff. Like reality TV. Like you. Anyway, I know your motto. You're opposed to any deal you're not part of. But there's just not a deal here. We don't want to relinquish this. I think someone, maybe, might care about what happened to us." She gestured to her grandfather and herself. "And I'm damn sure a lot of people *will* care about what happened to Ara. The heroine that you . . . people . . . are trying to erase. You can't handle her. But she'll survive. In many names, many guises, but always her. Look, she is her own tale. She belongs to all that would find her first steps," Cadence hesitated and then finished by looking straight at the publisher, "beside a secret gate."

The words sounded odd in this conference room, but they were exactly right. The executive's eyes opened like an imposter revealed.

Cadence slid a page across the table. "Part of her story may be lost, but not all. She lives."

The lady attorney was fidgeting, getting ready to do her thing. "I'm afraid, Ms. Grande . . ."

Cadence cut her off. "Excuse me. We're leaving. We withdraw our . . . Mel's query. Thank you and good day."

She rose. Jess looked at her and followed.

The suits didn't have a chance to stand. As Cadence and Jess left the room, the gauzy, yellow morning light of L.A. dressed them, still-sitting in silhouette as they gazed down at the single page left by Cadence. On it was sketched a large inscription of Ara's Rune.

"Who were those guys?" Cadence asked in the elevator.

"Depends on your point of view. Some people see suits. You and I might see an evil wizard and his entourage. In this town, who knows who's right?"

"So what should we do? How are we going to make sure Ara survives?"

Just as the elevator doors began to close, Mel ran up. He put his chubby hand out and the doors backed open. "Cadence, isn't there some way to get this done?"

She looked at him, remembering his frustrated inner-writer, the fragile bit of Luke Skywalker hoping to have a chance. "You know, Mel, you've given me an idea. A really good idea. I'll call you."

He backed off, and the doors came together and sealed the elevator for its passage down to the real world.

Chapter 81

1973

—

The man who walked the beach that morning was still the adored Professor. Even with his retirement, he had more than enough to do. His step was light, and his cheeks were ruddy with the complexion of a brisk walk in the wind.

Later he sat at his desk, the little electric fireplace once again settled near his feet. He was finishing a letter.

> Jack,
>
> Though you are gone these years, I still find it comforting to address an undeliverable missive to you, old friend. I find that for all my labours I have collected only a few leaves, many of them now torn or decayed.
>
> But then I look upon this northern sea, and I know these same waters have borne to long voyages many of those that I have imagined. The world continues much as you and I have discussed. New leaves will come from those that seek that Tree of Tales.
>
> And with that I am happy.
>
> Ah, but that we could rejoin the sluggards at the Bird and Baby!
>
> Your friend,
> J.R.R.T

Chapter 82

HOME

——

In a small town in Wales there is a one-room museum. In it are various archives, including a clipping from a local weekly newspaper dated May, 1880:

There is a view from the town center to the west, where a long gentle valley meanders from the uplands down to the sea. At the top stands a rock the size of a modest manor house. The rock is unique, a stone from an outcropping over twenty miles distant. Whether brought to that resting place by the ancients on an errand of folly or great purpose, or dropped by some giant on his way elsewhere, the facts are unknown. It has always been a resting place for those bound to the sea to take a journey.

The rock is roughly pointed at the top. On its sides are carved uneven steps that wind about and stop just below the crest. At that spot is fashioned in the stone a small seat that espies the view to the sea.

And what a view it is. Like a framed painting, one can see the forested cleft of the hills descending to the vivid green expanse of an estuary, and the sea with crashing waves breaking on scattered rocks offshore. Beyond lie white capped rollers and the deep blue of the boundless ocean.

Behind the seat, on a spot plainly visible but precarious to reach, was long ago carved an inscription followed by two name-runes. One of the names has been partially obliterated where a fragment fell. The other remains clear and distinct. It is a unique letter A, whose owner's tale has been lost in time.

The spot to this day is a favorite for lovers as well as those that gaze at the sea, think of tales and legends, and wonder "Are they true?"

* * *

From the *Topanga Times*
May 24, 2009

The rite of passage from spring to summer in Topanga Canyon is nominally the Memorial Day Parade. It winds from near the canyon crest, down the two-lane road, to the little town center where San's Grocery and The Mirkwood Forest huddle between road and creek. In it flow goofy cars, every form of person-powered cycle, baby buggies, middle school and elementary school bands, and arrays of clowns and mimes, enemies of the blood eyeing each other warily. Crowds, basically everyone in the canyon and a lot from neighboring communities, line the road.

"Nominally" is the apt word, because the real rite of passage is the Great Water Balloon War. Since inception in the hazy days of the 1980s, with a few prank balloons lobbed at friends, it escalated faster than most third world arms programs. There were, of course, unwritten rules of engagement. Only certain paraders and certain watchers were legitimate targets. No moms with babies, no one with a disability. Common sense rules. Unless, of course, they attacked first.

That's the way it progressed, mostly the paraders enduring the assault, until the unveiling of a tarp-hidden water cannon rigged on a truck of quasi-nudists who had gotten tired of just throwing back their own, limited supply of jiggly water bombs.

The water cannon sprayed the crowds with the shocking efficiency of a new technological weapon. And that changed the complexion of the engagements. The next year, scores of water hoses showered down on the paraders from strategic bluffs. In good *guerillista* fashion, the watchers broke and reformed and got their own roadside cannons. The paraders upped the ante with assaults from an antique LAFD fire truck.

In short, everyone got wet. Pity the poor Valley tourist, sporting along top-down in his new convertible, who gets caught unawares in the parade flow.

* * *

Cadence burst through the door of The Forest. She was drenched. She sat down at the kitchen table, dripping water from her limp hair and soaked sweatshirt into the red and white gingham tablecloth.

Jess leaned back and smiled. "I just got in, too. The tourists will start to come in, once the parade dispenses. Oh yeah, you got a message on that new machine. That Mr. Thornton fella."

She knocked the phone over as she punched up the replay.

"Cadence, Bossier. Look, I'm going to be in L.A. this week. I'd like to see you. No official stuff. Call me if that works. If you have a favorite place for dinner, that would be great."

Jess was shuffling papers and envelopes on the table.

"Grandpa, what's the name of the new place down at the corner, the turn up the canyon?"

"Easy. It's called The Eat."

"Great. Let's finish up and go celebrate."

She smiled and came over to the table.

"Cadence! Don't get your drips on this. Here's the final copy of Mel's manuscript. All of our edits are in. He did—we all did—a great job. It's ready. Here's the envelope, here's the letter. Let's each sign and send it off."

"You know I could do this easier on the computer."

"It wouldn't be the same. I like the old-fashioned way. You know, the sepia-toned image of the veteran publisher. The one that responded enthusiastically to our letter. I can see him, fussing around. Pipe smoke. Messy desk. Piles of manuscripts. He's still a hard copy man. His best-seller products are lined proudly on a bookshelf. He opens the envelope, nodding as he adjusts his bifocals. He leafs through the manuscript, smiling, puts it in his briefcase to savor at home. Picks up his tweed sport jacket. He—"

"Grandpa!"

"Huh."

"No one publishes on paper any more, it's all going digital. More important, the publisher is a lady—a very successful lady, like more than half the industry. It's increasingly strong, competent women."

"Okay, I got lost. Change the scene."

"Well, let's seal it with good luck." She licked the flap and pressed it with the edge of the tooth on her key chain. "I'll walk it over to the post office."

"Get a return receipt."

"It's great to get this done, Grandpa."

"Done? We haven't even started. You should see the other stuff up there in the attic."

"Hey, one story at a time."

"One thing's for sure . . ."

"What's that?"

"We're home."

EPILOGUE

—

The wind blew Ara's hair. The grey sea swelled and lifted the bow until she could see a line of land on the western horizon. Sunlight streamed through breaks of cloud, and she and her Amon next to her felt what all the wounded of the world desire—the freshening breeze of a new life. Here they would dwell until all memory fades.

THE END

DREAM OF ANOTHER'S WEAVING

(MiRKWOOD CODEX, VOLUME II)

———

The dark magic that wormed itself into the world that summer came as quietly as a cool zephyr ruffling the tablecloth of a long and lazy picnic. No portents, no zombie armies, no lights in the sky. Just the cat-pawed entry of ancient relics, superstition, and evil. Evil, that is, with malevolent ambition and unflattering names. The so-called "Tolkien Documents," that brazen trove of unproven writings, were only the tip of an iceberg. The entire Library of the Source now lay hidden in a red-brick warehouse in a decaying section of Los Angeles. All because the Fourth Age was emptying out. After all, where do unemployed wizards go?

And of what profit be their endeavors in this world?

Chapter 1

At two thirty on a quiet Wednesday afternoon, the flesh and blood man once called Barren stood before her in the empty one-counter, six-stool establishment called The Eat. It was new, jammed into the corner of the mini-mall in Topanga. She looked up, blinking as her eyes morphed from saucers to steaming slits.

He spoke quietly. "You needn't be scared, Cadence. Not of me anyway. Here is what it all boils down to. An epic war for knowledge, learning of a kind you cannot fully understand, has erupted. Many now seek to escape. To here. A diaspora of wizards and Dark Elves is upon us."

She was standing now, the chair grating as she moved it between them, her other hand clutching a puny dinner knife. "I finished that chapter with you. You can't hurt me now. I'm my own person. I've got my own life."

He laughed as if that were the most futile and ridiculous thing he'd ever heard.

"Whether you wish it or not, my dear, we are never free of another's conjuring. You can flee from me now and fear such as you have never known will still seep about you. They are coming. Mark my words. They are coming for you!"

About the Authors

Stephen Hillard grew up in Bossier City, Louisiana, and Grand Junction, Colorado. He graduated from Colorado State University and also earned a degree in philosophy at Columbia University and a Juris Doctorate from the University of Colorado. Before settling into his current career as a private equity entrepreneur, Steve was a teacher at Rikers Island Prison, a welder, a carpenter, and a practicing litigation attorney. He is the founder of Council Tree Investors, a private equity fund involved in the entertainment and telecom industries.

Steve has also been an active philanthropist, focusing primarily on higher education as well as at-risk Latino and indigenous youth, at the Escuela Tlatelolco in Denver, Colorado. In 2011, Steve published *Mirkwood: A Novel* about J.R.R. Tolkien, which sparked international controversy, became an Amazon best seller, received a national prize, and was subsequently published worldwide in Spanish by Grupo Planeta.

In addition to collaborative efforts with his partner, Joel Eisenberg, on *The Chronicles of Ara*, Steve is developing other projects. These include *The Lost Chronicles of Ara, Farway Canyon*, a retro-horror graphic novel about radiation, blobs, and (of course) Cold War zombies, and *KNOLL*, a novel about JFK, Carlos Marcello, Elvis, the NSA, and Edward Snowden. He resides with his wife, Sharmaine, in Grand Junction, Colorado.

Joel Eisenberg has been interested in the mechanics behind artistic creation, an ongoing theme of *The Chronicles of Ara* series, since he penned the nonfiction *How to Survive a Day Job* in 2004. Interviewing seventy-plus professional creatives, including celebrities from several artistic industries, he credits his "mentor in a box" tome with hastening the realization of his dad's inspiring words from forty years ago. Writing a novel with similar objectives, much less a series, has been on his bucket list since.

Professionally, Joel has worked primarily in the movie and

television industries as a writer and producer. The film he is most proud of, *April Showers*, which he executive produced, was based on the Columbine school shooting tragedy. He is a former special education teacher and supports school safety causes.

Joel lives with the only woman in the world who could put up with him, his wife, Lorie, and their rescue dog, Koko, in Los Angeles, California.

Joel and Steve can be contacted directly through their author page:

www.eisenbergandhillard.com

or their "Ara" series page:

www.chroniclesofara.com.

Credits

This book is a work of art produced by Topos Books,
an imprint of Incorgnito Publishing Press.

Deborah Jackson
Managing Editor

Allyson Schnabel
Copy Editor

Celine Boivin
Artist

Star Foos
Designer

Janice Bini
Chief Reader

Michael Conant
Publisher

January 2016
Incorgnito Publishing Press